DICK FOR HIRE

DICK
FOR
HIRE

FEATURING HYMIE GOLDMAN,
THE DEFECTIVE DETECTIVE

THE PENNY BROTHERS

Matador
Unit E2 Airfield Business Park,
Harrison Road, Market Harborough,
Leicestershire. LE16 7UL
Tel: 0116 2792299
Email: books@troubador.co.uk
Web: www.troubador.co.uk/matador
Twitter: @matadorbooks

Paperback ISBN: 978 1803136 318
Hardback ISBN: 978 1805140 603

British Library Cataloguing in Publication Data.
A catalogue record for this book is available from the British Library.

Printed and bound by CPI Group (UK) Ltd, Croydon, CR0 4YY
Typeset in 11pt Minion Pro by Troubador Publishing Ltd, Leicester, UK

Matador is an imprint of Troubador Publishing Ltd

Foreword

This book brings together, for the first time, the four stories about Hymie Goldman, the defective detective, first published as The Golden Pig (2009), Revenge of the Red Square (2012), Diamonds from Outer Space (2013) and Goldman's Getaway (2014). We have amended the title of the first novel to The Golden Hamster and revised a few scenes to restore the stories to our original conception. They were never written to be taken remotely seriously, only to entertain readers with a taste for the absurd and we commend the restored versions to them.

THE
GOLDEN
HAMSTER

(Formerly The Golden Pig)

FEATURING HYMIE GOLDMAN,
THE DEFECTIVE DETECTIVE

Part One

Hymie Goldman was a detective of no fixed abode, hairstyle, or opinions; they all came and went with the North wind. He wasn't Jewish; the closest he'd ever come to Judaism was getting off the tube in Golders Green. His real name was Artie Shaw, after the once-famous, now-deceased Jazz clarinettist, but he'd changed it with a view to keeping one step ahead of his creditors.

Hymie had never felt like a real detective, probably because he'd trained as an electrician, having inherited the firm when his father died. Sadly, the business existed from hand to mouth; if he ever succeeded in getting money out of clients he soon spent it on takeaways. He'd even tried to sell it, but it was more a concept than a business and nobody wanted two rooms of brown furniture and a pile of unpaid bills. The office, aka 792A Finchley Road, doubled as his home as he existed in a near perpetual state of eviction.

The door opened and in walked Janis, the office junior, carrying two coffees from the Black Kat café downstairs. She'd joined the firm when the government launched its hire-an-apprentice scheme a couple of years earlier and already had a better idea of how to run the place than he did.

"Anything in the diary today, Janis?"

"Just one in your handwriting at ten…BB?"

He looked puzzled momentarily until it dawned.

"Barnet Bailiffs. Tom and Jerry. I must remember to hide my laptop."

Sometimes running a small business felt like being under siege.

He swigged the black coffee Janis had proffered and winced.

"Didn't they have any toast?"

"No, it was only doing cremations today so I left it."

"A pity." His blood-sugar level was getting dangerously low.

The office phone rang and he made the mistake of answering it.

"Goldman"

"Twenty four, thirty six, forty two, don't be late!"

"Eh?"

What on earth were they on about? Was it the vital statistics of the girl in the "before" photo at the slimming club or just a series of menu items from the local Chinese takeaway? Special fried rice, sweet and sour pork balls or egg and chips in a black bean sauce perhaps? That was the price you paid for advertising in Catering World. Still, it was cheaper than Yellow Pages.

"New client?"

"I doubt it, probably a cold call."

Janis smirked. It wasn't his fault, he was just an idiot.

"Hadn't you better catch up with the filing?"

His last resort was always to the absurd; since they hadn't had a client in weeks, there *was* no filing. Perhaps he meant her nails.

"It's all up to date."

"Well, go and play with the paperclips."

She shrugged and retreated to the outer office with *The Hendon and Finchley Times* and a small collection of junk mail.

The phone on Goldman's desk rang again. Twice in one day? What were the odds? He answered it.

"Hello, can I help you?"

"Someone gave me your name." A woman's voice.

This wasn't usually a good way to start a conversation.

"In what context, madam?"

"They said you were a private detective."

"They were right. My name's Goldman, Hymie Goldman."

"Are you Jewish?"

"Is the pope a Catholic? Look, I'm a busy man, do you need a private detective?"

"Perhaps."

"Well, how can I help?" He wasn't psychic.

"I don't trust phones, they can be bugged. Meet me tonight and I'll tell you what's involved."

"Sure. As long as it's…" He was going to say "legal" but thought better of it. He couldn't afford ethics.

"As long as it's what?"

"It will keep till we meet, lady. When and where did you have in mind?"

"Tonight at eleven, outside Ritzy's nightclub. By the entrance to the Glitter Lounge, if you can find that.".

"Of course, but how will I know you? Will you be wearing a red tulip in your buttonhole?"

"Don't be so melodramatic. I know what you look like, I'll find you."

She rang off.

He didn't like it one bit, he had the distinct feeling he was being set up. Besides, it was past his bedtime; he was usually tucked up in his sleeping bag with Mister Snuggles and a mug of warm cocoa by ten, but he needed the money dammit.

Janis reappeared before him like a genie from a bottle.

"Your nine-thirty is here."

"Who or what is a nine-thirty? I thought there was nothing before ten?"

"It's an appointment."

"Are you sure? An *appointment*? Who's it with?"

"A lady called Sarah Chandar."

"Sorry, the name means nothing to me. Have I ever met her?"

"She seemed to know you. She said she'd seen the website and was most impressed. She said she could help us grow the business, so I thought as your diary was fairly free, you might as well see her."

He looked slightly irked.

"Thank you, Janis, I know you mean well, but next time, please discuss it with me first. I may have had an important meeting planned."

"Yeah, right," she thought, and only said, "Yes, of course."

6

She remained the consummate professional, even working for a rank amateur.

Janis pressed the door release button, and invited their visitor to join them.

A smartly-dressed woman in a business-suit entered.

"Hello, you must be Mr Goldman. I'm Sarah Chandar from Ceefer Capital. It's good of you to see me."

She was Indian, maybe thirty years old, pretty but with a professional demeanour, like the younger daughter of a millionaire industrialist.

"Not at all, Sarah, I'm glad I could fit you into my busy schedule. Please, have a seat. Can I offer you a drink?" He was determined to maintain the illusion that this was a real business.

"Oh, just some water, please."

There goes my lunchtime drink, thought Janis, as she twisted off the cap of her water bottle, poured it into the office glass and passed it to their guest. She left as quietly as she'd arrived.

"I expect you're wondering what I'm doing here, Mr Goldman?"

"Not at all," he said, unconvincingly. "It's always a pleasure to network with the wider business community. You never know, one day you may come to see me as a client, right?"

"Exactly, Mr Goldman, you're clearly a shrewd businessman. I knew you would be."

"Thank you." She seemed harmless enough, but he couldn't help wondering what she wanted. Surely not money?

"Which is why I won't beat about the bush any longer."

"I'm afraid I make it a habit not to contribute to…"

"I'd like to buy a stake in your business."

"Ahem," choked Hymie.

He was amazed. Just when you thought it was all over; when there was nothing left to play for, life's wheel of fortune was at its most unpredictable. Who would have thought it? People wanted to give him money. It was priceless. It was plainly ludicrous.

"How much?…I mean, what is it that attracts you about the business?" he said, correcting himself.

"Its potential, Mr Goldman."

"Oh yes, we have plenty of that," he conceded. Potential was the flipside of what he generally called problems; if something was in a mess, it could only get better.

"I've examined your website in some detail, and have to say it's one of the best I've ever seen. Your case histories are almost too good to be true, you have a bold vision of the future and you appear to have a strong brand. With a backer like Ceefer Capital you could turn "Goldman Confidential, no case too large or small" into a world-class business."

"How much of the business do you want then, ten percent? Twenty?"

She smiled a winning smile.

"All of it, Mr Goldman. Don't worry though, we'll incentivize you to stay on."

There was always a catch.

"So how much are you offering, Sarah?"

He was either dreaming or she was about to pull the rug out from under him, but he was hooked anyway.

"It depends on your trading performance, business plan and cash-flow projections, but perhaps as much as half a million."

He had begun to glaze over, when the "m" word revived him with a start.

"Pounds sterling?" he asked deliriously.

Even as his conscious mind descended into euphoria, some nagging doubt at the back of it wouldn't quite let him be. Outside his flimsy office walls, the real world was clamouring to get in.

The heavy tread of size-twelve boots on the stairs heralded the arrival of two burly six-footers in ill-fitting suits. Tom and Jerry. They pushed past Janis and peered through his office window, clearly surprised to see him with a visitor.

It was all the opportunity he needed.

"I was afraid of this, Sarah. Some business rivals have got wind."

"Wind?"

"Of your interest in the firm. So I suggest we adjourn for now. I'm very flattered by your proposal and promise I won't do anything rash until I've given it my full consideration. You have my office number, but please take my card," he said, passing it to her.

Ms Chandar found herself whisked out of her chair and politely but firmly shown out.

"I'll be in touch" he added, closing the door behind her.

The bailiffs, two world-weary forty-somethings who'd heard every bullshit excuse ever invented, stopped looking around the office for assets to repossess and walked into Goldman's inner sanctum with Janis trailing in their wake.

"I did ask them to wait, Mr Goldman." She only called him that when faced with officialdom.

"It's okay, Jan, it's only a social call; there's nothing left for them to take. How can we help you gentlemen?"

"You know the procedure, Goldman; we hand you the warrant, you make a big song and dance about it, and then we walk off into the sunset with whatever we can find. Usually zippo. Can't we just cut to the chase? I have a lunch date," said Tom, the one with the mono-brow.

"It may interest you to know I've had an offer for the business. I'll soon be in a position to settle all my debts and then, sadly, there'll be no more of these jolly tête-à-têtes we've all grown to love so much."

"He has me in stitches. What kind of wally would buy *your* business? Do we look like we've just come down with the last shower?" asked the second bailiff, Jerry; the one with the squint.

"Well, now you come to mention it..."

"Button it, Goldman," they snapped, in unison.

"Stretching credibility too far at this time of day? Alright, but I do have *something* of value."

"On the level?" they enquired reluctantly.

"Certainly."

"Go on then, we'll buy it," said Tom. The sooner they humoured him, the sooner they could leave.

"Take my advice and put your shirt on Devil May Care in the 12.10 at Uttoxeter.

It can't lose."

Jerry ignored him and reached into his jacket pocket for his wad of paperwork.

"There you are, Goldman, now what have you got to cover £5,000 in unpaid rent?"

"Will you take a cheque?"

"Do we have to? You know we'll only have to come back when it bounces" said Tom.

"Which it will" added Jerry. That was something he *would* bet on.

"Look, gents, the only things we have which aren't on hire purchase are the collection of stress-relief toys, the fake marble ashtray, and Janis."

"We'll take the cheque," said Jerry.

"And when Devil May Care romps home at twenty to one…"

"Or hobbles in at half-past four," quipped Tom.

"Don't forget to put us at the bottom of your visiting list."

Tom and Jerry exchanged disapproving looks. They knew he was conning them, but couldn't see anything in the decrepit office worth the money they were after.

Hymie signed one of the cheques in his dog-eared chequebook then passed it to Janis.

"My colleague will sort you out. Regrettably I have a business meeting elsewhere. Don't forget, Devil May Care. If you hurry, you may just catch it."

"You'll catch it one of these days, Goldman!" called Jerry, after Hymie's retreating back.

Part Two

It was midday by the time he arrived at the park. He'd had to walk, owing to the increasing unreliability of his car. It had never been the same since he'd spilled hot coffee into the CD player, while overtaking on a hairpin bend. Fortunately, he'd managed to borrow the money to retrieve it from the local garage, but it hardly ever started now.

"Here ducks! Here ducky ducky! Here ducks!"

He threw a low-carb, high-fibre Atkins bagel into the centre of a small gang of ducks, rendering one or two unconscious. He often visited the park, finding it cheap, therapeutic and a good way of killing time between cases. By now he knew every blade of grass in the place.

Eventually he managed to find a bench that was both dry and free from obscene graffiti; no small task in London. He sat and gazed across the vast expanse of mud and dog turds that aspired to be a football pitch. The posts had been used for spare fuel last Bonfire Night and no-one had played there since the *Barnet Bulldogs* were decimated by a drug-dealer's dobermanns.

Hours passed as he paced the footpath, trying to

come up with a foolproof plan for selling the business to Ceefer Capital. If only *one* of the cases he had made up on the website had been true, he'd be home and dry. As it was, he'd probably have to actually *solve* an investigation before they would take him seriously. No-one went around giving out half a million quid for a nice website, surely? This wasn't the Nineties. He would also need to get some *accounts* from somewhere; whatever *they* were. What had she asked him for? Cash flow forecasts? His cash had been flowing out for years and he could hardly bring himself to read anything from the bank any longer. Clearly, he would have to be economical with the truth for a while longer.

"Ritzy's" was the kind of nightclub that used to stand on the corner of every main street in every decent-sized town in the 1970's; grotty and crying out for demolition on the outside, tacky and full of kitsch on the inside. The local council left it standing to avoid having to erect slums or whatever social housing project their planning department was championing that month. Even slums cost money.

Hanging around outside in the pouring dark, he felt purple: marooned in the urban jungle; too scruffy, disillusioned and old to either fit in or care less. He pulled up the collar of his coat, unfolded the "Evening Standard" which he'd retrieved from the bin in the park and settled down to wait. He turned to the horoscopes page and looked up his stars; March 31st, Aries, "Beware blonde bombshells bearing gifts, they are not all they seem. Sunny spells later." It must be that new astro-meteorologist.

Flipping through the remaining pages, he caught sight of something in the racing results. "Well, of all the...*Devil May Care* won by a head; those jammy b...ailiffs!"

A taxi pulled up at the kerb beside him and a vision of loveliness emerged, paid off the driver, and sashayed across the pavement towards him. To call her stunning would have been to cheapen the word; tall, blonde and drop-dead gorgeous with an hourglass figure and a smile that would stop a man dead in his tracks at a hundred paces. She didn't even have to begin to try to impress Goldman.

"You must be the detective." she said, her voice as smooth as velvet.

"Ye...ye...yes, Gymie Holdman" he yammered. He had never been a success with women, but like most men never gave up hope.

"Follow me."

To the ends of the earth if you like, but he was dreaming, surely? She led him around the corner to a parking lot, opened up an immaculate black Porsche and they sped off into the encroaching night.

"I didn't catch your name," he said, fidgeting nervously with his seat belt.

"I didn't throw it at you, but it's Lucretia, or rather, Lucy...Lucy Scarlatti."

A strange name; probably an alias, but he was mezmerised and along for the ride.

Her manner was brusque and business-like. Nothing more was said as they screeched through a myriad of ghastly backstreets, finally arriving at journey's end; a newly refurbished warehouse conversion. Once ensconced inside she became more communicative.

"Take a seat. Would you like a drink?"

"I'd rather hear about the job first."

"So sit down."

He sat.

"It's a family matter really. It all began with the death of my father a month ago…"

"I'm sorry to hear…" It seemed the only thing to say.

"Don't be, he was a terrible man. When he died there was nothing left…nothing but debts…and the statuette. You might almost call it a family heirloom; a golden statuette of a hamster."

"Is it worth much?"

"It's mainly of sentimental value."

That much! he thought.

"In his youth my father travelled the world with the Merchant Navy. I think he bought the figurine in the Far East; China or Japan."

"Where do I come in?"

Hymie was getting the distinct impression that this was another case for his "Unsolvables" file. The file couldn't have been much thicker if he'd been investigating the Marie Celeste, the Abominable Snowman and life on Mars.

"Under the will he left me everything. My sister, Steffie doesn't even get a mention."

"And your sister has the hamster, right?"

"Yes, the bitch! She's always been jealous of my success in lingerie modelling, so she persuaded one of her lovers to steal it. Can you get it back for me?"

"Why not call the police?" he asked.

"As I said, it's a family matter."

"It could get messy," he said. He didn't like the sound of it, but still needed the money.

She looked at his ill-fitting clothes and dishevelled appearance and took the measure of him in a glance. "A hundred pounds a day, plus expenses?"

"When do I start?" asked Hymie, resisting the urge to add "How about last Tuesday!"

Lucy left the room briefly, returning with a thousand pounds in used notes. "I'll expect a phone call every few days and a full progress report each week," she said. Hopefully, you should have something concrete within the week."

'As long as it's not an overcoat', he thought.

She passed him a page from a notebook with a handwritten address scribbled on it and her business card.

"Those are her last known address and my contact numbers. There's a photo of the hamster attached. Call me."

"Certainly, now about that drink?"

"Maybe some other time. Find my hamster, Mr Goldman."

It was a long walk back to 792A Finchley Road, but time flies when you've got a grand burning a hole in your pocket. His only regret was not having had the presence of mind to ask for a larger advance, but he had simply been struck dumb at the sight of so much hard cash. It would have been churlish or foolhardy to quibble with a woman so clearly used to getting her own way.

Back at the office everything had gone AWOL except the telephone and the hot-oil stress-relief lamp. How a lamp could relieve stress had never been adequately explained to him, but he'd always liked day-glo orange, and since he'd bought it with the proceeds from his first case he couldn't bring himself to part with it. The bailiffs had dismissed it as worthless junk, which it was.

He rang for a pizza; the biggest, with extra everything. Only when his stomach was full could he think at all clearly.

Leaning against the window sill he gazed out into the empty street below. "Benny's Unbeatable Bakery" flashed in neon lights from the opposite side of Finchley Road. Benny had been baking the best pizzas in North London for longer than Hymie could remember, maybe even a year.

The phone rang from its new home on the floor of his office. It was partially illuminated by the garish orange glimmer of the lamp and cast a distorted shadow on the wall. He wondered who could be calling at this time of night. Some desperate, friendless character, that was for sure. He lifted the receiver.

"Hello, Mr Goldman, it's Sarah Chandar calling."

"Oh, yes, of course. How are you Sarah? I was sorry you had to leave so suddenly."

"Fine thanks…but you *asked* me to leave, don't you remember?"

"Yes, it was essential. I couldn't risk your safety with those two thugs on the loose."

"Who were they?" Sarah asked.

"Just a couple of longstanding business rivals: hardened, cynical men operating beyond the outer fringes of the law; men who would stop at nothing to get my business. After you left, they tried to make me an offer I couldn't refuse."

"So, what happened?" she asked, in a breathless whisper.

"I refused, of course. Call me crazy, but I have integrity. I'd just given you first refusal."

"Yes, but I thought you were just bluffing to drive up the price."

He fell silent, as though he had been mortally offended and could no longer find the strength to continue with the conversation. It worked a treat.

"I'm sorry, Mr Goldman. Can we meet to talk over my ideas for the business?"

"We can meet, but with a business *this* good, you can't afford to hang around. I'm not going to change anything until we've reached a deal on the price.

I believe you said Goldman Confidential was worth around a million pounds and that's my price," bluffed Hymie, the tough-negotiator.

"I said half a million," Sarah corrected him, "and even that depends on the satisfactory completion of due diligence."

She might just as well have been speaking Greek.

"You can do all the diligence you like, but it's a million quid. Take it or leave it."

She left it.

"Sarah? Sarah? Let's not be hasty. How about nine fifty?" He was talking to himself.

She'd be back, of course; businesses like Goldman Confidential didn't grow on trees.

Part Three

Sixty-four Rotten Park Road looked like any other Fifties semi. The district was fairly affluent, indeed it had been tipped as "up and coming" by the local firm of estate agents, Johnson, Blair and Von Munchausen, if you could believe a word they said.

Unbeknown to many, Sixty-four was the home of a premier-league sleuth, that detective giant of the Metropolitan Constabulary, Inspector Ray Decca. The fact that he rarely set foot in the place was more a reflection of his dedication to duty than to any disaffection with the neighbourhood, although having a wife who could have nagged for Britain may have tilted the scales in favour of the police station.

Promotion had come quickly and easily to him; easier still after he'd joined the secret Mah Jong society. So what if he'd had to swear allegiance to the Mighty Jong while wearing a traffic cone on his head with his left trouser leg rolled up to the knee? It was all part of the rich tapestry of police life.

That night he and his wife sat up reading in bed. Decca was reading a detective novel by Georges Simenon. In fact it was lying open in his hands on page 53, where it had stubbornly remained since last Thursday. It wasn't so much that page 53 was particularly brilliant or exciting; simply that Decca's mind was elsewhere. Sometimes he was on the verge of solving a major case and being congratulated by the Chief Constable, at other times, such as after a particularly bad day, he was spending his early retirement on a sun-kissed beach in the South Pacific, surrounded by dusky maidens in little grass skirts with large coconuts.

Mrs Decca, or Sheila as she was known among her friends at the Women's Institute, was gently nagging in the background as Decca's mind raced across the globe to Paradise.

"Did you pay my car insurance like you promised, Ray?"

"Hmmmmmm…"

"Is that Hmmm yes or Hmmm no?"

"Hmmmmmm?"

"You're not paying attention to me, Raymond!"

She always called him Raymond when she was working up to a really big nag.

"Sorry dear…?"

"My car insurance?"

"Yes dear, it's all sorted."

"Did you remember to book a table at "La Bistro"? You haven't forgotten it's our anniversary next week, now have you?"

"Hmmmmm…"

"Don't bother! There's something I've been meaning to tell you for some time…"

"Hmmmm, yes dear."

"I'm leaving you. I've found someone else; someone who appreciates me!"

"Hmmmm, that's nice dear."

"You're not listening to a word are you?"

"Hmmm, yes dear…I mean, no dear. What did you say?"

"Why don't you just get the hell back to the office?!"

"Hmmmm?"

A few short minutes later the sounds of raised voices and breaking furniture could be heard from number Sixty-four. A dishevelled man in a Crombie overcoat appeared at the front door. Closing it behind him he climbed into the driver's seat of the blue Ford Mondeo in the driveway, revved the engine in a belated gesture of defiance, and drove away. Net curtains were twitching all along the road. The Neighbourhood Watch committee would have something to say about this.

Part Four

A shaft of light illuminated the cracked lino. The noise from the street below was deafening. Janis had phoned, to confirm what he already knew, that the bailiffs had taken his remaining furniture. Hymie told her to take the day off. He could be generous to a fault, when it didn't matter.

He sat on the floor of his office, wondering whether there was any point in buying more furniture for the bailiffs to repossess. He tried to lift the loose floorboard to see if he still had a laptop, but his screwdriver had been in the drawer of the desk the bailiffs had taken and his fingernails were too chewed to get any grip. The best detective website in the virtual universe and he couldn't get onto a computer to see if he had any enquiries! What kind of a tin-pot firm was he running? He shrugged and stood up; it didn't do to dwell on things he couldn't change.

"Up and at 'em H, there's work to be done!"

He often talked to himself. It had become a bad habit; a legacy from childhood days when imaginary friends had brought him some kind of comfort. These days he didn't even know he was doing it.

He enjoyed being his own boss and loved working as a detective, but he had a talent for failure and knew deep down that he would never be rich. Even the prospect of an Indian venture capitalist, with an open cheque-book, couldn't dispel the fear that whatever happened, he would lose.

Despite this he was a survivor. He fleeced the occasional punter for as much as his conscience would allow and wrote frequent grovelling letters to his bank manager; Tony Turbot from the bank that liked to say yes, to everyone except him.

In his rented lock-up at the back of the alley he climbed into the driver's seat of his Zebaguchi 650; a red five-litre gas-guzzling fuel-injected monstrosity that belonged in a prehistoric automobile museum and had long since eaten him out of house and home. It looked like an early prototype of a De Lorean and drove like a Chieftain tank.

He switched on the VDU. Lights flickered in the console. Encouraged, he typed in the ignition code and presto! music drifted from the left hand speaker.

"Nessun flippin' Dorma!"

He flicked the transmission switch and turned over the engine. At the third splutter an explosion erupted from the twin chrome exhausts and the car lurched forward belching smoke and flames. Now *that* was something like a car.

After a cursory glance at the scrap of paper provided by his client, he put his foot to the floor. Four bald tyres spun on wet tarmac and the rust-riddled dream-machine careened down the street in a cloud of purple smoke.

An hour later Hymie Goldman, private investigator, pulled up outside a quaint olde worlde cottage in South Mimms. It seemed quiet enough, but you never knew. Parking around the corner, he returned on foot, then rang the front door-bell.

Nothing. Nada. Zippo.

His plan was to avoid climbing through any windows. He would fill in the details as he went along, but first he would have to get inside using some plausible cover story. His name was John; a gas-meter reader from Enfield. He rang the bell a second time and a third, beginning to imagine himself in the part; he was married with two kids, who attended the local comprehensive school. No reply. He rang the bell continuously until it stuck in the "on" position, then legged it round the back of the house. John croaked on the way to the back door and he became Hymie again. That didn't help much, but at least he knew who he was. He tried the door handle nervously. It was open; not necessarily a good sign.

With the bravado of an invited but clueless guest, he breezed through the kitchen and made his way into the lounge.

Trivial Pursuit lay face down on the shag pile, a TV dinner slid tortuously down the flock wallpaper and a man's decapitated body sat bolt upright in the comfy chair, blood oozing from the severed neck.

The wallpaper was liberally spattered with blood and the stench of death hung in the air. Hymie froze in stunned silence. Then he caught sight of the dead man's head, sitting grotesquely in a plant pot on the mantelpiece. It was the final straw.

"Blllaaaaaaaaa...yeeuuuuuurrrk!"

He vomited last night's pizza everywhere. He'd been a detective for eight years without once seeing a dead body. He'd heard about such things, of course. He'd even seen the odd dead pet; Mrs Timmins' cat Tiddles, which had jumped out of a beech tree and broken its neck as he was shinning along the branch to save it. Yet nothing had prepared him for *this*.

He suddenly realised that he had company.

"Banzaiiiiiieeeee!!"

Hymie found himself staring into the wild-eyed face of his would-be executioner; a diminutive oriental dressed entirely in black, the finely honed blade of his ancient samurai sword poised to cut him in two.

Shit! he thought, with panic-stricken understatement, then fell to the floor and grovelled pitifully.

"I've seen nothing; I'll say nothing...to no-one, never. Look, I have money...take it; take my car, my life insurance... anything you like. I only came to read the meter" he gibbered, vainly trying to resurrect John the gas-man.

His attacker seemed unmoved. Lifting the sword until it was stretched at arm's length above his head he began its murderous descent on the southernmost slopes of Goldman's neck.

Hymie closed his eyes and began to think of his schooldays.

"Boy, what a shit life!"

BLAM! BLAM! BLAM!

Three gunshots rang out and the room was bathed in cordite fumes. Hymie opened his eyes. The smoke cleared to reveal his attacker, prostrate on the floor and wearing three rather large holes. Most of his anatomy was now vacationing in different parts of the room.

Standing behind the corpse and racking the slide of an outsized handgun stood the remarkable Miss Turner.

"J.J.J.Janis."

"Hello Mr Goldman, I thought you might need some help."

"But how, why, when? What I mean to say is…I thought..?"

"You thought that after those guys had taken the last of the office furniture you'd never see me again. You told me to take the day off, because you couldn't face telling me I was out of a job, but you're wrong; it's not over yet."

"How did you know where to find me?"

"After I thought it over I went into the office just in time to see you driving off in your car, so I followed you."

"And the gun?"

"Oh, I always carry that. Well, you have to when you live in Finsbury Park."

From the corner of his eye he caught sight of a glittering golden figurine at the end of the mantelpiece. He pocketed it hastily. It might be a hamster and it might not. Either way, it would pay for some new office furniture.

"Let's get the hell out of here."

"There may be more of them; we'll have to be careful."

"That's not what I wanted to hear, Janis." He started to hyperventilate.

"Where did you park your car?"

"Just around the corner, on Coleridge Way."

"Right, climb through the window and get your car while I provide covering fire."

He looked at her as though she'd gone mad.

"I don't *do* windows Jan. Not since I was nearly killed, leaning out of one as a kid."

"There's no time to waste. We all have to face our demons sometime. I'll make sure we're not being followed. See you outside in five minutes."

He looked at her dubiously, then at the gun in her hand and finally at the vomit-strewn carpet.

"We don't want to be here when the owner gets home," he said.

He pushed open the window, climbed out onto the crazy paving and ran as though his life depended on it. Gunshots rang out in the cottage. Once back in his car he put his head in his hands. He hoped Janis was okay, because he was about as much use as a chocolate teapot. The next five minutes dragged on like a party political broadcast until Janis arrived and climbed in beside him. He drove off as unobtrusively as possible, allowing for the fact that his car sounded like an explosion in a fireworks factory.

"What happened?"

"There were two more of them upstairs," she said. He seemed willing to believe almost anything.

"You *killed* them?"

"It was self-defence."

He drove in no particular direction, ending up at a motorway service station, where they sat in the café, talking in hushed tones.

To the casual observer he looked just like any other deadbeat; pale complexion, staring eyes and with the indefinable aroma of regurgitated pizza. To the trained eye, Hymie Goldman was a man in shock, a man who had come too close for comfort to the Grim Reaper.

He sat motionless in the hard plastic chair, staring into the cold black depths of his neglected coffee. It seemed to mirror the bottomless void within him.

Janis by contrast was perfectly relaxed, or as relaxed as one can be in a motorway service area. She leant back, drawing steadily on her Havana cigar and released perfectly formed smoke rings above her employer's bowed head.

"Come on, pull yourself together. You must have seen a corpse before now."

"Never. Look Jan, I'm just not *that* sort of detective. If I've given you that impression then I'm sorry. I'm allergic to guns, bullets, knives, swords and anything else whose sole purpose is to kill. I'm a pacifist. I've got to go to the police. Will you join me?"

"Are you crazy? After your last court appearance they're just looking for an excuse to throw the book at you. Given half a chance they'd lock you up and throw away the key! You have to solve the case. *Then* go and see the police if you must, but only when you have hard evidence."

She was so cool, so level-headed, so worldly to be someone's assistant, let alone his.

"I could be dead by then!"

"So? End of story. Do you want to be a missing pet-investigator all your life? Live a little!"

He didn't look exactly convinced.

"I'd better make that phone call then."

"To the police?"

"My client."

"Now you're thinking straight. Better still, let's go and see her together."

"What makes you think my client is a woman? This is a new case after all."

He was sharper than he looked, although it would have been hard not to be.

"Just call it feminine intuition. You could certainly use some."

They made an unlikely couple heading for the service station car park; the short, overweight scruff-bag and the elegant young woman smoking a cigar.

Hymie revved up the Zebaguchi's six cylinder engine until all eyes were fixed on the source of the apocalyptic noise. Having neither any environmental awareness nor conscience, Goldman remained in ignorance about the state of the ozone layer and thought that "CFC" was a Welsh football team.

Having lost his client's business card, he drove around the district aimlessly, in the hope of recognizing some landmark that would lead him to Lucy Scarlatti. On the whole he would have made a better vacuum-cleaner salesman than a detective.

Much later he spotted the tell-tale black Porsche and pulled over. Taking Janis with him for protection, he rang the bell.

"Who is it?" asked Lucy Scarlatti, on the other side of a security chain.

"The man from Del Monte, who do you flamin' think!"

His nerves were beginning to unravel.

"Goldman! About time, where the hell have you been?"

"To a funeral, lady, and it was nearly mine. Now let me in, I need answers!"

Lucy Scarlatti led him into the lounge of her furnished apartment. Outside, Janis slipped a loaded revolver into her handbag and walked into the flat behind him.

Goldman sprawled across an enormous scarlet satin bean-bag, while Lucy Scarlatti mixed two extra-dry Martinis, blithely unaware of the approaching danger.

"Did you bring the statuette?"

"Sure, but things weren't exactly straight-forward."

She handed him a Martini, waiting to hear the additional cost of the complications.

He took it carefully, but his hand was shaking so much that most of it spilt down his trousers before it ever reached his mouth.

"I'd be pushing up daisies if it wasn't for…"

She'd stopped listening to him and stood with her eyes fixed on the shadowy figure emerging through the doorway.

Framed against the skylight stood Janis, a gun in her hand and with a ruthless glint in her cold blue eyes.

"Steffanie!"

It was Lucy Scarlatti's last word.

Part Five

.

A sadder but no wiser man, he rose the morrow morn. His eyes flickered open. He had a terrible headache and he couldn't see properly out of his left eye, but he was alive. Then he realised he was in a hospital ward and started desperately trying to recall what had happened.

Something was seriously wrong. Someone was dead. His client! He'd lost his client! Yet nothing seemed to fall into place, there was only the terrible pain in his head and odd snatches of a dreadful series of events.

"Nurse! Help me!"

"Calm down, Mr Goldman, you've lost a lot of blood."

"How do you know my name?" he snapped, paranoia flooding his brain.

"It says it on your tag."

"Of course. How long have I been here?"

"Two days. Now you really must rest, Mr Goldman."

"Two days!! But anything could have happened in two days!"

"If you don't calm down I'll have to sedate you."

Hymie closed his eyes. Slowly the memories began to return.

That ridiculous schoolgirl Janis, the one I thought looked twenty-five...she was twenty-five! What a bitch! She must have shot my client and left me for dead. Whoa, hang on, it all sounds totally absurd...why would she do that? No one would ever believe it, even if it were true.

A man in a white coat approached the end of his bed, picked up his chart and frowned at the graph.

"Will I live doctor?" asked Hymie.

"According to this chart, you're already dead, Mr..."

"Goldman," added Hymie, hesitantly. It took a while to adjust to being dead.

"But there's very probably a perfectly logical explanation," he said, trying to be reassuring.

"Sorry, doctor, they forgot to remove the chart after the last patient checked out," said the nurse, sheepishly.

"Checked out? You mean, the poor soul died in this bed?!" cried Hymie.

"Inevitably, with the best will in the world, patients do die, Mr Goldman and we can't throw them out of their beds *before* it happens, to spare the feelings of those who replace them, now can we?" said the doctor.

"No, I suppose not. Can you tell me what happened to *me*, doctor? I don't seem to be able to remember the last two days."

"Ah, amnesia, it's often a factor in cases of this sort."

"Cases of what sort?"

"Eh?"

"You mentioned amnesia, doctor."

"Well, is it any wonder, man? Working around the clock without proper support, I've been twenty hours on

32

the ward without a toilet break, I'm bursting for a…"

"Tea, Mr Goldman?" asked the nurse.

"Yes please, nurse."

"You're a lucky man, Goldberg," resumed the eccentric medic. You seem to have received a glancing blow from a bullet. Half an inch lower and you wouldn't be here now. I'm afraid it's doubtful whether you'll ever play professional darts again, but otherwise you should be able to scrape along in your usual pathetic way," he said, stifling a yawn.

Hymie gave him a bewildered stare.

"Thank you, doctor, but I'm working to a deadline."

"You will be, Goldstein, if you don't get some sleep right now. Lack of sleep can cause all kinds of mental health problems. I expect the police will want to interview you in the morning about all the shootings."

"Shootings!"

"Take no notice, Mr Goldman. Doctor Abernethy has been on duty for almost twenty four hours straight, poor man. You can't expect him to be firing on all cylinders," said the nurse.

Hymie closed his eyes and waited for them all to bugger off. Gradually the ward became quiet while the light outside faded first into dusk, then fell beneath the sable mantle of night's darkest bower. In his mind's eye he could see nothing but corpses, mutilated rotten cadavers, stretching out in all directions. Ugh! A shiver ran down his spine. The only people Hymie had ever known go into hospital had left it in a box.

He surveyed the ward around him. The next bed seemed to be surrounded by curtains. He couldn't be sure who, or if anyone, was in there. The sign at the foot of the bed said simply "MRS A". Whoever she was, she was a deep sleeper.

He tried to sit up, but every movement caused him pain. He felt like Mrs Timmins' cat must have done on first hitting the pavement, except that *he* was still very much alive. The desire for revenge would surely keep him that way.

Bandages covered most of his head and shoulders. He knew he must look a proper sight, like some refugee from *The Rocky Horror Show*. Yet perhaps the bandages would also help to conceal his identity. If only he could get out of the ward. His clothes were gone; all he had was the regulation issue nightgown with the defective ties at the back and a draft around his nether regions.

Pushing the screens aside he walked down the central aisle. It was an experiment in mind over matter; if they didn't mind and he didn't matter, perhaps he could just walk straight out of there. Unfortunately, he'd bargained without the ever watchful Inspector Ray Decca and his dedicated sergeant, Barry Terse. They weren't about to lose the only witness they had to a murder, even if that witness was as unreliable as Hymie Goldman.

"Is that *'im,* guv? the nutter with the bandaged head?" asked Terse.

"Who else would it be?"

"Oi, Goldman! This is Finchley Memorial Hospital, not a fashion parade," cried Terse, trying to recover his change from the coffee machine with his number ten boot.

Hymie walked on unheeding. They were just illusions, if you ignored them, they would disappear. Some chance.

"Hold it right there, Goldman." said Inspector Decca.

Part Six

On the following morning, Hymie sat up in his hospital bed and prepared to give his statement to the police. He didn't expect it to take long, as he couldn't remember anything. It hadn't been a good day for him; he'd survived a trip to South Mimms, only to be shot in the Docklands. All very painful and humiliating, both personally and professionally.

"My name is Decca, Goldman...D.E.C.C.A, that's *Inspector* Decca to you. Before you ask, no, I don't own a record company and my first name isn't Desmond. Some of the lads call me "Chief" or "Guv," rivals call me "Big Ears" because I often hear about things before they happen, and the criminal fraternity calls me "Cluedo", because..."

"You assume it was always Colonel Mustard in the library with a candlestick?"

"...I solve all my cases by a process of deductive reasoning. I shall put your last remark down to the blow to the head you received recently," concluded Decca.

He was about to remark that it would probably be the first of several Goldman would receive, if he didn't co-operate with the police enquiry, but thought better of it.

Times were changing and he couldn't face the additional paperwork.

"Thank you, Inspector," said Hymie.

"Don't mention it. Now then, about a week ago I received a summons…"

"Speeding ticket?"

"From my boss. He handed me your file and told me to look into it. I'd heard you were the sort of low-life scum that gave private investigators a bad name and a quick perusal of your file did nothing to change my mind. It came as no surprise that you were wanted for eighty-six road traffic violations."

"Thirty-five!"

"That's just *this* week's. A joker like you shouldn't be left in charge of a bicycle, let alone anything with a turbo-charged engine, but this was a matter my sergeant could have sorted in his sleep. As you can probably guess, I'm here about a far more serious matter; about a murder, and you are my chief suspect."

"Murder? Me? Look at me. I'm the victim here; covered in bandages and lucky to be alive. Hardly a dangerous killer am I? You're barking…"

"Watch it, Goldman!"

"…up the wrong tree, Inspector."

"Look, don't take me for a mug. We were there when the ambulance took you away. We know all about the girl. We have you at the scene of the crime; you had the opportunity and the motive. We even have the murder weapon with your prints on."

"Not a candlestick, I suppose?"

"When you're in a hole, sunshine, stop digging! Unless you fancy a long prison stretch!"

"None of these things add up. The victim was my client."

"What was her name?"

"Lucy Scarlatti. She hired me to recover a family heirloom from her sister. I was getting nowhere; I couldn't even find her sister," he lied.

"So you killed her?"

"That makes no sense. Why would I?"

"You found the heirloom, went to her flat, and offered to sell it to her for more money than she was willing to pay. She refused and you shot her dead."

"I repeat, why? I had no motive. Besides, I was attacked and injured myself. Whoever shot me killed my client and stole her property."

"So, who *was* with you?"

"No-one, I went to see Lucy Scarlatti alone, to tell her the case was proving too difficult for me and that I'd reluctantly have to repay a part of the retainer. The next thing I remember is waking up here, with a terrible pain in my head, being told that I'd been shot and my client was dead. Now you're trying to fit me up for a murder I didn't commit. I've had better days."

"Your client is dead and you were the last person to see her alive. So if you didn't kill her, who did?"

"Her sister, Steffanie. According to my client they hated each other and her sister had stolen this heirloom from her. Perhaps it was easier to kill her than to give it back."

"What was the heirloom?"

"A golden statuette of a hamster."

"You're having a laugh. A golden *hamster*? Are you sure it wasn't a platinum gerbil or a diamond-encrusted guinea-pig?"

"Now you're just being ridiculous."

"Believe me, *you're* the one looking ridiculous," snapped Decca. "Tell me again, when did you last see your client alive?"

"Two nights ago, at her flat."

"Thirty-five Riverside Drive?"

"If you say so. I had it on a piece of paper but I lost the address."

"You expect me to believe that?"

"It's the truth."

"This is a *murder* investigation. Even these days, that means several years in prison with some real scum. When you get out you'll find your licence as a private investigator has been revoked and your pathetic career will be over. "

"That's why I'm telling you the truth."

"So where did the gun come from?"

"I dunno. It wasn't mine, I've never carried a gun. People who play with matches get burned."

"But you know whose gun it was; this mysterious sister who wanted to keep the golden guinea-pig?"

"Hamster."

"And you saw her at the flat?"

"Not exactly, someone hit me from behind. One minute I was talking to Lucy Scarlatti, trying to get out of the assignment, the next I was unconscious on the floor.

I heard a gunshot from behind me, but I didn't see who fired the gun."

"And you expect me to believe this, Goldman?"

"Yes."

Decca looked at his watch. "Let's leave it there for now. Sergeant Terse will be posted outside till you can leave the ward, then we'll take you down the station for a proper interview. I suggest you get your story straight. One last question, what were you *really* trying to recover for Lucy Scarlatti?"

Hymie paused. "Her father's diary," he said. "It had some clue in it about where he buried a treasure." He sensed that Decca didn't believe in the golden hamster and that a more plausible story may get him off the hook.

The Inspector stared intently at him for a moment.

"OK, Goldman, don't try going anywhere," he said, leaving.

Part Seven

Hymie lay in the hospital bed, planning his escape. He wasn't exactly Harry Houdini, but then this wasn't exactly maximum security. Surely he could get past that dozy police sergeant? He just needed a convincing disguise.

Terse meanwhile was busy trying to chat up the nurse on night duty down the corridor.

"Can I have a look at your truncheon, Sergeant?" asked the nurse.

"Any time, Love."

"Ooh, isn't it *hard*."

"Yeah, like the rest of me. It's made of real wood."

'Dead wood more like', she thought, walking off.

The ward was dark and silent as the grave. Well, apart from a few intermittent coughs and the beeping of a clapped-out NHS heart monitor.

Hymie had settled into a light slumber. Fluffy white sheep were trampolining all over the bouncy castle of his brain. From somewhere far off he heard a familiar voice.

"Wake up you layabout! Sleeping on the job again!"

"Wassermarrer?" he spluttered.

"Look son, cases don't solve *themselves* you know!"

"You can't tell me what to do…you're dead!"

Hymie sat up and opened his eyes. A short grizzled little man with white hair and side whiskers was standing at the foot of his bed.

"*Dad*?! What are *you* doing here? You're dead."

"Oh, *dead* is it! I've got more energy than you, you quitter! At least I'm not farting about in hospital with my investigation falling apart. You're a disgrace to the name of Shaw."

"Ah, yes well…I was going to tell you about that."

"About what?" asked his ghostly father, suspiciously.

"Oh, it'll keep. Look, Dad, it's very kind of you to drop by like this, but…"

What was he talking about? The man was dead. He had to pull himself together. Sadly, the apparition was having none of it.

"Dad nothing. I didn't say anything when you threw in your apprenticeship as an electrician, I tried to teach you the tricks of the investigations business…and failed, and I planned to sell the business and leave you with a nest egg…"

"Only you died first. You never kept an opinion to yourself when you were alive and now you're just as bad after death… and *I'm* the one with the problem."

"Hear me out! You were never suited to the business, it's true, but I finally realised that you needed to learn from your own mistakes. Now I'm sure as hell not going to float idly by and watch you throw the family business down the drain.

Get out of bed and solve this case, like I taught you."
So saying, the grumpy apparition dematerialized through
the wall.

Dammit, the old illusion was right! Gathering his
nightgown together with a flourish, Hymie adjusted his
bandages and raced down the corridor.

He tiptoed cautiously past the somnolent copper on
watch, PC Reidy, Terse's relief; a former civil servant who'd
been dismissed for showing excessive initiative. Pulling
open the latticed doors of the first service lift he came to,
he stepped inside.

WHOOSH!

He felt a sudden rush of blood to the head and a
sensation of cold air whistling through what was left of his
hair as he plummeted to almost certain death.

WHUMPH!

He came to rest in a pile of dirty laundry with nothing
worse than mild concussion. Not nice of course; dirty
underpants in the face, but much better than certain death.

"Yeuch!!"

"You can't kip in 'ere mate. Try the park down the
road." cried the night porter.

Hymie stumbled through the emergency exit, setting
off the alarm, then headed for the concealing darkness
of the park. Half-naked, bandaged and bloody, he kept
to the shadows for fear of arrest or identification as a
young Conservative on his way home from a fancy dress
party. He scowled at passers-by and they gave him a
wide berth.

North Finchley's first private detective to be listed in

Catering World shivered in the park for ten minutes before deciding that hypothermia wasn't a good career move and what he really needed was pizza, preferably from Benny Baker's. Benny was the next best thing to a really good friend; a really old creditor.

For once the lack of bus fare didn't seem to matter. The driver assumed he was an escaped mental patient and public-spiritedly let him travel for nothing. He left the bus at Finchley Central bus depot and headed straight for Benny's. A bulb had fused in the neon sign outside, rendering the "unbeatable" pizzas "uneatable". The shop had long since closed for the day, but Hymie rang the bell and a light came on in the upstairs flat. A window opened and Benny poked his head out cautiously.

"Who is it?"

"Benny, it's me, Hymie Goldman. I've got the money I owe you."

"Goldman? Is that really you? You look like some old tramp."

"Benny, I need help."

"I never doubted it. Come here, stand under the light."

Hymie walked under the streetlamp.

"Jeez, you're in a right mess, Goldman. What's with the bandages? You haven't joined the young Conservatives, surely?"

"Benny, I hate to ask, but it's urgent. You couldn't rustle up some old clothes and a pizza could you?"

"Well, just this once. I'll come down and let you in."

"You're the best, Benny."

Moments later he appeared at the door, led Hymie through the restaurant and up the backstairs into his flat. From the look of his furnishings, Benny's business was clearly booming. The Pizza-King of North London draped a couple of black garbage sacks across his sofa and invited his old acquaintance to sit down.

"What are you calling yourself these days?" asked Benny.

"Still Hymie. If you change your name too often you can lose track of who you are."

"I never understood what was wrong with Artie. Still, you don't change much otherwise."

Ben left him to settle in, returning a few minutes later with a microwaved pizza.

"You're a lifesaver!"

"Sure, but I'm not soft in the head. It's one night only, Hymie. I'll put some old clothes outside the door for when you get up. Make sure you're out by 9am, I don't want you upsetting the staff with your appearance. And if the police call, I haven't seen you."

"Will do, Ben, and thanks."

He was back on track now; he only had to beat the murder rap, find the golden hamster, stay alive and sell the business to Ceefer Capital and everything would be hunky dory. Easy.

Part Eight

Back in his office at the police station, Inspector Ray Decca was dozing at his desk. He'd spent a long hard night piecing together the few strands of evidence available. It didn't amount to a hill of baked beans. He was a frustrated perfectionist and hated having loose ends on his investigation. The biggest loose end was Hymie Goldman.

Three corpses in close proximity: one decapitated in some ritualistic gangland execution and two ventilated at close range by what looked like the same gun. Someone had seen a short fat guy walking away from the crime scene, and although not a betting man, he'd have put his Bermuda shorts on it being Goldman. Still, he couldn't see Goldman killing anyone; he wouldn't know one end of a gun from another.

Terse and Reidy had cocked-up and he was still at large, but Goldman hardly represented a threat to society; less of one than Terse anyway.

Decca began to snore. His chair, which had been tilted back against the office wall, started to slide down it. Just as he began to overbalance there was a knock on the door that sounded like an air raid on Iraq and Sergeant Terse entered.

Decca sprang up in his chair and knocked the contents of his half empty coffee cup all over the files on his desk.

"Terse, you're a flaming idiot!"

"Yes, Chief."

"What are you doing here?"

"You asked me to let you know if I discovered any leads, sir."

"The mind boggles, Terse…tell me all."

"We've had a positive ID on the dead Chinaman, sir. A guy named Chiu Mann. Nasty piece of work: a hit man for the Triads."

"You don't say, Terse, I never would have guessed it."

Sarcasm was wasted on him.

"Thank you, sir," said Terse, beaming.

"Just leave me the file. Oh, and Terse…"

"Sir?"

"Make sure you're on surveillance duty at Goldman's office bright and early, eh? We don't want a repeat performance of the hospital fiasco, do we?!"

"No, sir."

So saying, the sergeant headed off to arrange the mother of all surveillances. He'd show that smartass Inspector and that toe-rag Goldman. No-one messed with him.

Decca examined the files again. The three deaths had to be connected, but how?

Body number one had belonged to a guy called Tony Martino; a small-time drug-pusher with rumoured links to the Triad. He must have crossed his Chinese paymasters and been eliminated by the professional hitman, Chiu Mann.

Body number two was the hit man himself. Mann had been a ruthless killer, Red Pole for the Second Lodge, so whoever had shot him must have taken him by surprise. The *gun* was mightier than the sword, not the pen. Just imagine trying to fend off a mad Samurai warrior with a biro! No chance.

Body number three was the mystery woman, Lucy Scarlatti; young, beautiful, and affluent, yet she had been tragically misinformed. She had hired Goldman as a private investigator. Even if he was telling the truth, which he doubted, why would anyone hire that idiot to recover a diary from her sister? The Girl Guides could have handled that. So why had Goldman claimed the case was too difficult? There must have been more to it. If Goldman had been there when Martino died, and was still walking around, which he clearly was, then either Goldman must be the greatest actor this side of Stratford; a level-headed hard man masquerading as an idiot; or he was just lucky and the real killer was still walking the streets.

On balance he favoured the latter theory, which meant that Goldman was their only direct link with the real killer. There was still no motive for the second and third murders. Was it really all about drugs? If so, he'd have to turn it over to the Drug Squad and he'd miss the best chance of promotion he'd had in ages. Nah, it couldn't be just about drugs, when you came to think of it. Goldman had said something about looking for a diary and even if that was bullshit, it was a good pretext for extending the investigation.

One thing was for sure; Goldman was mixing in lethal company and if they didn't pull him in sooner rather than later, he'd be found floating in the Thames or propping up some motorway bridge. So Terse and the lads would have to stake out his office and interview all his known associates. Decca groaned at the thought of all the overtime he would have to sign off, and what his commanding officer would have to say at the next budget review meeting. Ruddy bean-counters!

Part Nine

Benny had found some groovy clothes for Hymie at the back of his wardrobe; collectors items which probably hadn't seen the light of day since 1969. Hymie, who couldn't afford to be choosy and had never understood fashion, put them on gratefully.

The ensemble was nothing if not bold; a bright orange pullover, some bell-bottomed trousers in turquoise, an old pair of trainers and a flat cap, all topped off with a promotional padded jacket, bearing the slogan "You can't beat Benny's" in gold transfer lettering across the back. A pair of sunglasses helped conceal his injured eye.

"What are your plans Hymie?"

"Oh, you know…keeping a low profile."

"You'll be fine…" Benny assured him.

"Yeah, as long as I don't go out in daylight in these clothes."

"Are you going to the police?"

"No. They have it in for me. Inspector Decca practically told me he thought I was some mass-murdering loony."

"Well, what about the case?"

"Technically I don't have one. My client's dead so I won't get paid. It's just that I can't let them get away with it. There's such a thing as professional pride, you know."

"Leave it to the police, mate. You're out of your depth."

"Oh, not you too. Look, there's a valuable objêt d'art out there with my name on it."

"How much is it worth?"

"Fifty, maybe a hundred…"

"What, quid?"

"No, grand!"

"That's a lot of mozzarella."

"No, really."

"The only catch is, people get killed for that kind of money."

"It had crossed my mind. I'm just not cut out for dodging bullets. Finding lost cats on a good day, yes, getting shot at, no. Look at me; nerves in shreds, bandages all over my head and I haven't got the faintest idea what to do next."

"Just keep a low profile. Or maybe even go abroad."

"I always keep a low profile. The trouble is, everyone's got it in for me and I can't even afford the tube fare to Golders Green, so emigration is a non-starter."

Benny laughed.

"It's all very well you laughing, mate, I'm in it up to my neck and there's another delivery of shit expected any minute. I should have stuck to investigating lost pets, at least they don't try to kill you!"

"Well, good luck anyway. Here's a few quid for tube fares."

"Thanks Benny, you've been great. If anyone asks about me, just tell them you haven't seen me in weeks. When I sort everything out I'll pay you back big time."

Benny stepped over to the window and peered through a chink in the blinds.

"It looks like someone's watching your office."

Hymie took a look for himself. Aftab Hamid was opening up his newsagents, a few long-distance lorry drivers were filing into the *Black Kat* for the *Cardiac Special* fry up, and a green Renault was parked at the kerb outside 792A Finchley Road.

"Whichever way you look at it, it isn't good news."

"Just leave through the back entrance."

"I will. Thanks again."

The side alley leading to *Benny's* rear entrance offered an excellent, if restricted, view of the pavement outside his own office, so Hymie spent a few minutes standing in the shadows keeping lookout. The green Renault seemed to be an unmarked police car. There was a hefty guy with a crew cut in the back who looked a lot like the cop from the hospital. Times must be tough in the Met.; the car was pock-marked with corrosion spots and someone had sprayed "Frog Shit!" in fluorescent pink along the driver's door. It was probably Terse's idea of a joke.

Suddenly a blue Transit van appeared from around the corner and pulled up behind the Renault. Two uniformed policemen jumped out and headed along the pavement towards the *Black Kat*.

Hymie frowned. If they were searching door to door they needed him and it was probably only a matter of time before they found him. Still, he wasn't going to hand himself in; as much as he feared being on the loose with a killer at large, at least he wasn't a sitting duck in a police cell. He walked down the road away from his office. Passing Aftab's shop he saw the dozy shopkeeper engrossed in something on the counter. Probably one of those Swedish imports.

There were two public phone boxes, back-to-back on the pavement, just past the newsagents. He paused, then entered one. Lifting the receiver he placed a washer in the coin slot and held an imaginary conversation with someone on the other end. It gave him the chance to keep his office under surveillance from a safer distance.

'I must be stark staring mad to leave a nice warm hospital bed for this,' he thought.

'What good am I doing here anyway? Watching a bunch of coppers trying to find me won't solve anything.' He was on the point of leaving when he saw Janis emerging from the small car park behind *Hamid's*. She clocked the unmarked police car and started walking away; directly towards Hymie. Behind the sunglasses he closed his good eye and raised his hands to his face in a despairing gesture.

'Why me, God?'

He'd tried to work it out, he really had. He 'd given it his best shot, but the harder he tried, the more confusing it all became. The case was like his life; a huge shattered looking glass, whose splintered shards had become an increasingly distorted series of images. There was no pattern in the chaos. Janis, who'd been his strong right arm, now seemed to be working against him. She'd shot his client in cold blood and set him up for it. All for some piece of jewellery. He could only assume she had the golden hamster now, because he certainly didn't.

With his good eye open he peeped between his fingers. Janis was opening the door to the other phone box and appeared not to have noticed him. She was now close enough to hear, but he was terrified of being recognized. Keeping his back turned he pulled up the padded jacket's flimsy collar and continued his own one-sided conversation in case she began to think he was listening to her.

Why was he afraid of her? On the one hand, she was a killer; reason enough, but on the other, she'd saved his life. Had she only spared him to become the patsy for the murder of Lucy Scarlatti? He'd have to have words with her at her next performance appraisal. Ah, no, those days were over.

Janis was deadly and unpredictable and she unsettled him, but he didn't know for certain that she had killed Lucy Scarlatti. He hoped against hope that she was still on his side. He'd even lied to the police to protect her, yet he hadn't the faintest idea why he'd done it.

He tried to make sense of the dribs and drabs of conversation he overheard.

"You cowardly turd…mumble, mumble."

"This is the last time…mumble, mumble."

"…so you say, mumble. Look, I want those numbers, mumble, mumble. Twenty four, thirty six, mumble, mumble. Tonight…right."

She slammed down the receiver, scribbled something on a piece of paper, and then walked back down the road.

After Hymie had recovered from the shock, he hastened to examine the vacated phone booth. Those numbers had sounded strangely familiar…his overdraft limit? No…it was that random phone call at the office with those pairs of numbers! The call must have been for Janis, but what were they for?

There was nothing obvious in the booth; no box of matches bearing the name and address of the secret dope den, no map references, nothing. Yet she'd written down those numbers. Using an old technique from *The Investigator's Handbook,* he took a pencil rubbing from the phone book she'd rested her paper on and discovered that the message read 'Rainbow Rooms 11pm, 24, 36, 42, 60.'

She'd clearly said *tonight.* This was one appointment with destiny he intended to keep. He didn't know what he would do when he got there yet, but somehow he had to be there.

Part Ten

Hymie stood on the southbound platform of a Northern line station and watched the world go by. A young couple were kissing next to him and seemed to be in a world of their own. He found it hard to remember the enthusiasms of youth. He'd been in love and even married once, but it didn't last. Things changed, people too, and all the good intentions in the world couldn't prevent your world from falling apart.

"Duz deez wan go to Lundun sur?"

He was about to tell the curious stranger that they *all* went to London, because it was a *big* place, but allowed himself to be seduced by the latter's use of the "s" word in relation to himself. He rarely received even so slight or unintended a courtesy.

"No mate, this one's for postal deliveries only. Try the other platform."

Soon his Tube arrived, the doors hissed open and he was swallowed up into its monstrous mechanical belly. He studiously avoided eye-contact with his fellow passengers in the age-old ritual of public transport in London.

"SHTOOM!" The train disappeared into the shadowy world of subterranean tunnels in pursuit of timetable compliance while Hymie worked out his strategy for getting into the nightclub. Looking as he did, the options were strictly limited; the eccentric millionaire or the escaped mental patient in search of tea and sympathy.

Above ground and outside the club, a tall, statuesque brunette with opalescent eyes approached the doors of *The Rainbow Rooms* with a winning smile on her beautiful face. No-one had ever refused her entrance to a night club and they weren't about to start now. Though dressed to kill, she hadn't come to dance. Her name was Janis Turner and she had an assignation at the roulette wheel.

"Is Tony in tonight?"

"Tony who?" queried the doorman.

"Lee."

"Oh, the croupier…I think he'll be in later."

She smiled graciously. If he'd been wearing glasses they would have steamed up.

"Which is the nearest bar?"

"Over there, lady," he said, pointing.

Back on the Underground, the short fat guy in the flat cap and charity shop gear was catching up on his beauty sleep. Five or ten years would have been in order with a face like his. The serpentine sound of doors opening roused him just in time to disembark at London Bridge. Outside the station he hailed a taxi. The first driver put his foot down on spotting his potential fare and sped past the shady-looking P.I. in search of American tourists. The second one pulled up for long enough to catch his destination and then took a chance. Perhaps he'd pick up a fare back from the club.

It had been years since Hymie had ventured into anywhere which could be described as a nightclub. With his planned big entrance as an incognito oil-billionaire, the possibility that he might get turned away at the door in Benny's garish clobber, simply hadn't occurred to him. Apparently it *had* occurred to the doorman; a man-mountain in a ridiculously small tuxedo.

"Can I help you, mate?"

"Waahl, hah there, Buddy. Ahhm a visiting yor liddle ol' country from Hoostun, Texas an' ah thought ah'd lahk ter see wan o' yore casino boars."

"Sorry, members only, mate."

Close up, Hymie began to appreciate just how vast and imposing the bouncer actually was. He seemed to completely blot out the light. His chances of getting into *The Rainbow Rooms* were beginning to resemble the prospects of a one-legged man in an ass-kicking contest.

"Aahl mek it wurth yore wahl, Buddy," he said, reluctantly proffering one of his chronically few fivers.

The bouncer looked down disdainfully at the meagre bribe.

"Bugger off, Hank!"

Clearly the exaggerated American accent hadn't stacked up with Hymie's apparent deficiency of moolah and he'd been dismissed as a fake; an impecunious phoney. The denizens of Texas hadn't previously been noted for their reluctance to part with their greenbacks on a big night out. Deflated, Hymie turned and began to walk back down the street. He stopped abruptly.

Something about the way the bouncer held himself and the matching pair of cauliflower ears rang a distant bell. He turned back to examine the massive road-block more closely.

"Hadn't you used to be Mad Mike Murphy?" he asked, from a safe distance.

"What's it to you, mate? Coming here with your dodgy yank-accent and your cheap bribes. I ought to punch your face in."

"I used to be Artie Shaw."

Blank look. Dawning recognition. Sunrise over the industrial park of his face.

"Artie Shaw! I remember. Are you still the same loser you used to be?"

"Well, I never aspired to the giddy heights of being a professional chucker-out like yourself, but I do have my own business."

"No kiddin'?"

"Yeah, it's the old family business… private investigations."

"So you're under cover then?"

"No, but I will be if you let me into the club."

"Look, I'm off duty in ten minutes so if you can keep a low profile in the bar till then, you can buy me a beer for old times' sake if you like."

"Sounds like a plan. Which way is it?"

"Just follow the lights and the din."

Hymie passed through the double doors and followed the noise. It made a change from following his nose. Standing at the bar was Janis Turner; a vision in Versace, and Cuban heels, with a cigar to match. Fidel would have been proud. Hymie couldn't tell if she was surprised to see him or not, but she hid it well.

"It's good to see you on your feet again. I've been trying to get in touch with you, Hymie. The hospital didn't know where you'd gone so I thought I'd have to find you myself. You had a call from the Total Disaster Insurance Corporation. Apparently they want to retain your services in recovering a golden statuette…"

"Of a hamster?"

"Exactly."

It seemed unlikely that she didn't know where the hamster was, but he played along.

"So someone had it insured."

"I guess so."

"Yes, but I thought someone shot the owner, so who's claiming on the insurance? Look, Jan, you never did tell me what happened on the night Lucy Scarlatti died. You were there too, remember?"

"I feel terrible about it Hymie, I really do. I just popped down the road to the off-licence for some cigars and when I came back it was all over. The door was open and everything was in complete chaos. I phoned for an ambulance and the police and then drove home in your car. There wasn't really anything I could do by then and I didn't want to get involved with the police."

He nodded dumbly, not believing a word. He'd seen

her gun down a hired killer and although she'd saved his life in the process, these things left an indelible impression.

She seemed to be getting agitated and then he noticed it was almost 11pm by the clock behind the bar.

"I have to go," she said. "They're sending a claims investigator to see you tomorrow."

"What time?"

"11am sharp."

"Is it safe to go back to the office then?"

"I said you'd meet them at *Benny's*."

"Are the police still infesting my office?"

"No, they left today. They told me to let them know if you came back."

"Thanks, Jan."

"Don't mention it."

She turned and walked over to the Casino.

"No sign of Tony Lee tonight, Mike?"

"He hasn't been in tonight, Steffie. Maybe he's doing a double shift at the Take-away."

"Good night, Murphy."

"See you, gorgeous."

Hymie had followed at a discreet distance and overheard all that was said.

Why would Mike be calling Janis Turner "Steffie"? And why did the name sound so familiar? He felt sure his old friend would be able to explain and if it was over a few beers for old time's sake, then so much the better. Murphy appeared a few minutes later and led Hymie around the corner to a pub for the promised drink.

Part Eleven

In the words of the late, great Irving Berlin, "There may be trouble ahead, but while there's moonlight and music and love and romance…" yowza, yowza, yowza!! Love and romance may be on the ropes but giving oneself up to wild uninhibited pleasure was as fashionable as ever and high on the agenda for Janis Turner aka "Steffie".

First, however, she had to get rid of Hymie Goldman. He'd always been disposable, like a soiled nappy, but it had suited her to leave him bumbling around in his ineffectual manner. He was becoming a bore and that would never do.

She pressed the keypad on her mobile and dialled the ex-directory number of a certain Master Lau. He was poor value as an entertaining after-dinner speaker, but he knew how to eradicate vermin.

In his tenth floor apartment the phone began to ring. The King of Evil was at home. "Lau."

"Just listen. I understand you're in the market for a golden hamster. My partner will meet you at *Benny's Unbeatable Bakery* on Finchley Road at 11am tomorrow."

"Who is this?"

"Be there."

Where was that useless waster Tony Lee? He'd better keep out of her way for a long, *long* time unless he wanted to look like a portrait by Picasso. The deal was, he'd meet her at the roulette wheel at 11pm, arrange for the little ball to stop on four pre-arranged numbers and they would split the proceeds. Even as she cursed him, Tony Lee lay face down in a nameless alley with his throat slit.

She took a cab to her favourite dance club.

"Leptospirosis!"

"Never heard of it, love. Sounds like a bacterial infection in rabbits."

"You're not as dumb as you look, are you?"

"Thanks, I think, but what a stupid name for a nightclub. Whatever happened to *The Palais* or *The Tower Ballroom*? Things never get better anymore, they just get weirder!"

"Do you want the fare or not, dog-breath?"

"Yes, God help me, I want the fare. So where are we going?" he enquired, cagily.

"Just off Finchley Road. I'll show you when we get there."

The yellow cab trundled off down the road. Twenty minutes passed in brooding silence, before Steffie spoke again.

"This will do."

The cab pulled up in front of a neon-lit sweatbox. She climbed out and passed the driver a banknote.

"Don't go spending it all at once, honey."

"Take it easy, lady." He felt like he'd just released a leopard from his taxi.

"I always do," she purred.

She climbed the cast-iron spiral staircase at the front of the building in a few athletic leaps, pushed through the swing doors at the top and bounded into the club like a coiled spring eager to unwind. Passing through the doors she was quickly devoured by the bright lights, body heat and pulsating high-energy dance music.

On the dance floor she became another person; a lithe and powerful force of nature, which neither beat nor rhythm could control. She knew exactly what she wanted and exactly how to get it.

Steffie gyrated across the floor in ever wider circles around her handbag, while the butt of her favourite handgun began to rub against her inner thigh, sending her all too soon into paroxysms of pleasure.

"Ooooooooooooooh! aaaaaaaaaaaaaah!!"

"Who said dancing wasn't as good as sex?" she murmured.

A guy in his twenties stood before her, drooling at the sight of her aroused body.

"Not me, goddess."

"Are you talking to me, pretty boy?" She was laughing at him.

"If the cap fits, wear it, I always say."

"Do you always come on so strong, honey?"

"Only when I like what I see."

"Good, then follow me."

She winked at him then led him by his bootlace tie into the Ladies toilet, pulled him into a cubicle after her then slammed and locked the door behind him.

"Show me what you can do, honey."

They kissed, a long slow passionate kiss that left him gasping for air, and caressed, gently at first but with mounting pleasure, until his senses were engulfed in the tidal wave of her desire. He ceased to be a person and became an object of self-gratification, rising and falling in the age-old choreography of sex. He became exhausted, she, momentarily at least, fulfilled.

"Wow! What's your name?" he asked, dazzled.

"I don't use names, lover," she smiled.

"If I give you my number will you call me?"

"Of course not."

There was no pleasing some people.

"Come on, lover."

She led him out of the cubicle and back into the club by the remains of his shirt collar. His clothes bore their dishevelled state like a badge of male pride; he had conquered this lioness of lust, although he knew in his heart she had conquered him.

"Hang on, babe."

"I'll have a double brandy, with some crushed nuts…I mean ice," she smiled. He was a *nice* boy really, the kind you could take home to meet mother; fifty years or so ago. It wouldn't do, of course; just one complication too many.

He walked dutifully to the bar to get her drink, while she walked back to the top of the spiral staircase. She looked up at the stars wistfully for a moment. We were never really free, not like shooting stars in the great infinity of space; just so many birds in a gilded cage, hoping for the chance to spread our wings. Freedom came at a price;

a price she would pay come what may. It was time to dispense with her alter-ego; Janis Turner, and anyone who had ever known her.

Part Twelve

The Pink Parrot was *the* definitive example of late 80's bar room décor. You took a perfectly respectable pub, ripped its insides out and festooned it with fifty-year-old gardening implements. The pièce de resistance was a mock-up of the bonnet and bumper of a 1950's Caddy which some public-spirited soul appeared to have driven clean through the wall above the bar. Clearly it didn't pay to drink and drive.

As if the décor wasn't sufficiently challenging, the piped music was loud enough to wake the dead, as a quick glance at the clientèle readily confirmed. The drinks were so expensive that cocktails were de rigueur and the landlord had felt obliged to give them all pretentious names, fit to adorn the children of A List celebrities.

Mike and Hymie sat on their chromium-plated bar stools and looked down the drinks list for a laugh.

"What's it to be, Mike, a Brooklyn Sunrise or a Madison Marvel? No, wait, what's this? How about a Yachtsman's Willy?"

"No thanks mate, this place is already giving me the

willies. I thought we came in here for a drink. Do you serve beer, sunshine?" he enquired.

The barman looked at him as though he were a visitor from another planet, or something unpleasant he had found attached to the sole of his shoe.

"*Beer,* sir? This is a cocktail bar. All we have is on the list."

"Let me see then…we'll have a couple of Dental Drills and have a Big Greeny on me."

"A *Big Greeny,* sir?"

"Just my little joke. We'll be sitting at that corner table over there" he said, pointing.

"So, you've got your own firm of private investigators, Artie. Any money in it?"

"Do I look like there is? Incidentally, I've changed my name to Hymie."

"Why? Have you done a runner with the VAT?"

Hymie appeared to be considering it momentarily as a new source of income, before coming clean. "I don't *earn* enough to charge VAT…although the clients won't know that I suppose."

"Are you any good?"

"I get by. How about yourself? What have you been up to for the last twenty years?"

"A bit of this, a bit of that and a bit of the other…you know how it is."

He knew exactly how it was. You did what you could and lived on dreams of a bright tomorrow.

"I'm working on a big case right now. It could set me up for life."

"Sounds good. I could use some extra cash if you need an extra pair of hands."

"I can't pay you until the case is solved, but I'm meeting a representative from the Total Disaster Insurance Corporation tomorrow. Perhaps you could join me?"

"You're kidding me, what kind of insurance company would call itself that? Still, I'm free tomorrow, I'll be happy to come along if there's a few quid in it. I mostly work nights. Where are they from, the Total Disaster guys?"

"America apparently."

"That figures."

"We'll find out more tomorrow."

"When and where shall I meet you?"

"You know Benny Baker's place on Finchley Road?"

Mike nodded.

"There at 11am."

"You're kidding. So you run a detective agency from a fast food restaurant?"

"No, of course not, it's just a place to meet."

"Don't you have an office then?"

"Of course, but I've had a bit of trouble at the office lately so I thought I'd steer clear for a few days. How about you, Mike, have you been doing *security* work for long?"

"I was in the Army for twelve years; the Gunners."

"Do you still support Arsenal?"

"Naturally. You can't be in the Royal Artillery, grow up in North London and support *Chelsea*, can you?" he grimaced. "Anyway, as I was saying, I was with the old '*Ubique quo fas et Gloria ducunt*' boys…"

"There's no need for bad language."

"Save it, there's nothing funny about being in the Army. After twelve years service I got fed up taking orders from cocky young upstarts who didn't know their epaulettes from their elbow and decided not to re-enlist. Since then I've been throwing people out of a succession of nightclubs. It ain't a bad crack really, or at least it wasn't until the Triads moved in and used the clubs to front their drug pushing. That doesn't sit too well with me. I've seen what drugs can do to kids and it ain't pretty."

"How do you know about the drugs?"

"I'm not blind. They have couriers going back and forth all the time. They do the job and don't ask questions and they stick around, otherwise they don't last long."

"I meant to ask you, that girl you were talking to at the club earlier..."

"Steffie?"

"That's the one."

"Have you taken a good look at yourself in a mirror lately? You'd have no chance."

"Very funny. No, I wondered if you knew her surname? She looks familiar."

"Part of the case you're working on?"

"Could be."

"Sorry, I don't know her last name, I just know her as Steffie. She's as smart as paint though...lovely girl."

"Do you know who she was after at the club?"

"A guy named Tony Lee, a croupier. I haven't seen him lately though."

"Thanks, Mike."

"No worries. Does it help?"

"Too early to tell." Hymie paused to reflect. Were the cocktails beginning to take their toll, or was it the cumulative effect of sleep deprivation and poor diet?

So Janis or Steffie Scarlatti, as she probably was, had been in league with this guy Tony Lee; one of the croupiers at the club. Something had happened to him as he hadn't shown up. People rarely failed to show up for Steffie.

"Tell me about this case you're working on." Mike seemed interested.

"I'd be happy to tell you, but first you'll have to sign the Official Secrets Act in triplicate…oh, go on then, buy me another drink and we'll call it quits. I'll have a U-Bend… easy on the mara..chino sherries."

The booze, credit and bullshit flowed freely as the two old cronies caught up.

"You never could hold your drink," said Mike at the end of the session, bundling the inebriated investigator into a taxi.

"What kind of detective are you anyway?"

"The old fasshioned kind that never sholves cases and shpends mosht of his shpare time in hoshpital."

"You'd better kip on my sofa tonight then or you'll never make it to Benny's," said Mike, getting into the cab beside him.

Part Thirteen

The following morning the papers were full of the suspicious death of the croupier, Tony Lee; found, by an unfortunate dustman, with his throat slit; the croupier, not the dustman. It only managed to make page seven of "The Times", but was all over the front page of the "Hendon and Finchley Times", with photos, and an editorial on the decline into gangland violence of large parts of North London. Sensationalism sold papers, especially in Hendon and Finchley, where it made a welcome change from missing pets.

In her luxurious first floor apartment Steffie Scarlatti cut out the column inches devoted to the murder of Tony Lee and pasted them into her scrapbook. She hadn't *actually* wielded the knife this time, but he was dead because of her. She kept a grisly record of all her killings like an actor collecting performance reviews.

Goldman meanwhile sat in the grottiest flat he'd ever seen, and he was something of an authority, drinking black coffee and reading the "Finchley News". Lee's death would have made more of an impression had he been less hung over.

"You sure you didn't know Tony Lee?"

"Poor slob, no I never met the guy. Got any orange juice, Mike?"

"Never use the stuff."

"What time is it?" Hymie's watch had been broken for months, but he still wore it to suggest punctuality.

"Nearly ten."

"We'd better be making tracks if we're going to keep that appointment."

"I'll ring for a cab," said Mike, doing so.

"'Ramjam Taxis here, weir jawanago?"

"My name's Murphy and I want a taxi from 62 Swanswell Road to *Benny's Bakery* on Finchley Road, pronto."

"Fifteen minutes man."

There was only one thing worse than taking a cab in London; public transport. If it wasn't the strikes, there were any number of other random service disruptions which could screw up your plans. Hymie was beginning to regret parting with the Zebaguchi 650. It hadn't been from choice. He should have asked Janis for the keys back at their last meeting. Now he didn't even know where it was.

Half an hour later the cab arrived. They heard it first; the sound of a large and well-attended reggae concert featuring the legendary Bob Marley. The volume grew exponentially from a few blocks away until it sounded like Bob was in the room with them. The black "R" reg. BMW 3 series had clearly been a quality car in its day, but its day was long gone. Its owner, Elroy Moses Zachariah Smith

III, lived by three golden rules: keep no written records, always arrive fifteen minutes late, and above all, "be cool".

"Hey mon, getta move on, you're wastin' ma gas!" said Smith, uninhibited by any notion of customer service.

Mike toyed briefly with the idea of taking issue with him, but then remembered that this would mean using public transport and thought better of it. One of the cab's electric windows seemed to be moving up and down at random.

"Ehh man, is your name Murty?"

"No, Murphy."

"Murty, Murphy, whaddever…dats close enuff!"

They climbed into the back of the cab. The cabbie put his foot down and they sped off to join the nearest traffic jam. Every time the car stood idling in traffic for a few minutes the faulty electric window seemed to suck in every noxious exhaust fume for miles around so that they were glad to bail out by the end.

They paid him and he passed them a dog-eared business card.

"See you agin man."

"Not if I see you first, sunshine!" said Mike.

They arrived at Benny Baker's place with five minutes to spare so sat in the restaurant within sight of the entrance.

"Morning boys, what can I get you today?"

"Hi Ben, this is my old mate, Mike."

"Pleased to meet you."

"Likewise."

"Two teas and two of your breakfast specials please."

"Coming right up."

While the waitress made up their order Benny took off his apron and crossed to the other side of the counter for a chat.

"How's the case going? Any progress?"

"Fair to middlin'. Did you get a visit from the Fuzz?"

"Yeah, some vicious-looking sergeant called Terse. He wanted to know if I knew you and where you were."

"What did you say?"

"Just that I knew you by sight, but that I hadn't seen you recently."

"And that was it? He left?"

"Pretty much, although I'm sure I've seen a few more plain-clothes detectives around than usual."

Suddenly it seemed like the end of the world. Years later, those present remembered every last detail of where they'd been and what they'd been doing. Those that survived.

As the clock struck eleven there was an almighty explosion.

BOOM CRACKA THOOM!! KABABOOM!!!

The front of the restaurant imploded into a gigantic fireball. The plate glass windows shattered into a million splinters, flying in all directions, the frames melted and warped. Mike hit the deck first, pulling his friend and their host to the ground with instinctive urgency. No sooner had the glass fallen than the front of the *Bakery* was raked with wave upon wave of machine-gun fire. The noise was apocalyptic. Everywhere tables, chairs and catering equipment were torn asunder and scattered far and wide.

Hymie noticed that his mobile phone was ringing. He must have accidentally switched it on when he hit the floor.

"Hello, Mr Goldman, it's Sarah Chandar. I wondered if you'd had time to consider my proposal for your business?"

"Sorry, Sarah, I'm a little busy right now," he said, switching it off.

Alarms rang throughout the building and in the neighbouring premises. The police, fire brigade and ambulances started to arrive. The army of hell-raisers responsible seemed to have just melted away.

"I don't think they were from the Total Disaster Insurance Corporation," said Hymie.

"If they were, they certainly lived up to their name," said Mike.

Benny was in too much pain to comment, having taken a deflected bullet to the shoulder. He was escorted away to Edgware General in an ambulance with a couple of his staff. Mercifully, there was only one fatality; a regular customer in his eighties, whose arteries were too hardened to allow for fast evasive action.

The restaurant looked like it had lost a fight with Lennox Lewis. Restaurants rarely faced such tough opposition.

"Is there something you haven't been telling me?" asked Mike. "Some heavy duty villains really don't like you. Who have you upset?"

"Where do I begin? Old Mrs Timmins, Inspector Decca and Sergeant Terse, Janis Turner, Tiddles the cat, my ex-wife…"

"The Triads?"

"Well, I'm not exactly on their Christmas list, but this is a bit much."

"Goldman! I was wondering when we'd be seeing you again."

"Hello Inspector. Good of you to drop by. This is my friend, Mike Murphy. Mike, this is Inspector Ray Decca, known to his friends as Clueless...sorry, *Cluedo*."

"It's lucky for you we were passing, or you'd be pushing up daisies by now."

"Most thoughtful."

"No trouble. Now, I'm sure you'll both be only too happy to join me down at the station for a chat, because things have been getting a bit out of hand lately and you wouldn't want to be accused of obstructing the course of justice."

They were escorted into the back of an unmarked police car and driven to Finchley Road police station. Hymie stared into space, trying to collect his thoughts, while Mike wondered what the hell he'd got involved in.

Time alone would tell.

Part Fourteen

Police Interview Room One, Finchley Road nick, later that day. Goldman was still staring into space. A telescope would have helped. On the other side of the desk, Inspector Decca was trying hard not to lose his patience.

"Stop the tape, Reidy. When I want to listen to Book at Bedtime, I switch on Radio Four. You *have* heard, I suppose, of wasting Police time, Goldman?"

Hymie smiled the kind of smile that implied it was one of his hobbies.

PC Reidy, who'd almost mastered the ancient art of sleeping through a witness interview, sat bolt upright in his chair, reached over to the Taiwanese cassette recorder and pressed the pause button.

"I've a good mind to charge you for it, failing first degree murder, of course. Incidentally, we've noticed that the incidence of motoring offences has dropped significantly of late, have you sold your car?"

"I haven't seen my car for a few days. My assistant, Janis had it last, but as for the murder, give me a break! You ought to be out there trying to catch the scum that destroyed Benny's Bakery, not hauling me over the coals for something I didn't do. I nearly got *killed*…or do you think that was just an elaborate suicide attempt?!"

"Reidy, switch the ruddy tape *on*!"

"I want to see my solicitor," said Hymie.

"So do we, he jumped bail on a fraud charge six months ago."

"I wondered who that postcard from Alicante was from."

"Are you ready to tell us what you know, or would you like to spend a few more hours in the cells?" asked Decca.

"I'll tell you what I know. It isn't much. The way my life's going at the moment, police protection is better than nothing. Is there any news about Benny Baker?"

"He's stable. He'll be fine in a few weeks."

"Good. Right, where shall I begin?"

"At the *beginning*.

Down the corridor in Interview Room Two, Sergeant Barry Terse was applying all his ingenuity to the task of interviewing Mike Murphy.

"You did it, didn't you?"

"I don't understand the question. Was it a question?"

"You know damn well what I'm talking about. You killed Lee and destroyed Benny's Bakery to make it look like a gangland killing."

"Yes, that's right, you're too smart for me. I should have known I was no match for your *clever* interview techniques."

"Dammit! Switch on the recorder *now,* Potter!"

Mike's tongue had talked him into as many scrapes as his fists had fought him out of. Usually he was big enough and ugly enough to get out on the side of the Angels, but Barry Terse was built along the same lines. His response to heavy sarcasm was a smack in the mouth and he administered it before Mike had time to reflect that winding up coppers in a police station was a mug's game. Murphy reeled back in his seat, bounced off the wall and leapt to his feet brandishing what was left of the interview room chair.

"Switch *off* the tape, Potter!"

In the Mexican stand-off that ensued, Terse and Potter prepared to overpower their desperate witness, while the latter came belatedly to his senses.

"Happy Birthday, Sergeant" he said, handing the chair fragments across the desk to Terse with a broad grin.

He wasn't going to give them the pleasure.

Down the corridor Hymie was warming to the task of spilling the beans. He was chucking them around in all directions.

"…and that's all I know about Lucy Scarlatti," he said, a few minutes later. "She was my client for three wonderful days before she died in a hail of bullets. As I said, she hired me to recover a memento of mainly sentimental value which her sister had stolen from their dead father."

"A hamster?"

"I don't like to speak ill of the dead, but he wasn't very popular, apparently."

"Who, the hamster?"

"No, her father."

"The memento was a hamster, right?" persisted Decca, "not a diary?"

"No, different things entirely…hamsters; small fat and hairy with a leg at each corner, diaries; small but rectangular, made of pulped wood."

"The last time we met you told me she was trying to recover her father's diary, as it contained a treasure map."

Hymie smiled sheepishly.

"Ah, yes…sorry, I wasn't feeling well at the time."

"So let's get this story straight, you went to visit your client on the night she died?"

"Yes."

"Alone? or with someone else?"

"With my assistant, Janis Turner."

"Again, that's not what you told me earlier. You said you were alone."

"Well, she stayed in the car so in a sense, I was alone; she wasn't really there."

"It's you who's not all there, Goldman."

"I have reason to believe that Janis Turner and Steffie Scarlatti are one and the same person and that she murdered her sister; my client, Lucy Scarlatti," said Hymie.

"Over a statuette of a hamster?" queried Decca.

"Yes."

"Not over a diary with a treasure map in it?"

"No."

"You're sure? You don't want to change your story just one more time?"

"Yes…I mean no,…I mean yes and no." Hymie was confused.

"Okay, tell me again; what happened on the night of the murder?" Decca felt he was making progress at last.

"Janis Turner, aka Steffanie Scarlatti, and I drove over to Lucy Scarlatti's apartment."

"In *your* car?"

"Yes. The Zebaguchi 650."

"Never heard of it. What's the registration number?"

"R256 HOG."

"Colour?"

"Red."

"So, what address did you drive to?"

"Riverside Drive…over in Docklands, but I can't remember the number offhand."

"You've previously identified it as number thirty-five. When you got there, what happened?"

"Like I said before, I went into the flat to tell my client I hadn't made any progress with the case and that she was wasting her money."

"It's a pity you didn't tell her that the first time you met; she may still be alive."

"Then later I heard she was dead and that I'd been shot; as if I needed telling. I couldn't recall what happened at the time. They told me when I came round in hospital."

"So you have no idea who killed Lucy Scarlatti?"

"All I remember is my client's last word; 'Steffanie!'"

"Just that?"

"Just that."

"And what happened to Janis Turner aka Steffie Scarlatti?"

"She told me she drove away, but I don't have any evidence for that and if she did, I don't know when she left or where she went."

"Do you think she killed Lucy Scarlatti?"

"Yes. She had the motive, the opportunity and the inclination. She gunned down a Triad hitman the day before."

"You saw her kill Chiu Mann?"

"*Chiu Mann*? Was that his name? He was barely human; a vicious killing machine. I didn't catch his name as he was trying to cut me into little pieces with a ruddy great sword at the time."

"Did you ever meet Tony Martino?" continued Decca.

"What is this, twenty questions? No, I never met him, should I have?"

"He was murdered by Chiu Mann shortly before you arrived at the scene."

"Then I did meet the poor slob, although he was already dead when I met him."

"What were you doing there?"

"I've always wanted to visit South Mimms."

"Goldman! Just get on with it."

"My client gave me the address as the last address she had for her sister Steffanie."

"Did you ever find the hamster statuette?"

"No."

"Stop the tape, Reidy. If you'd told me all this earlier, Goldman you might not be looking at a charge of obstructing a Police murder investigation."

Decca stood up and left the room. Back in his office he rang through to Interview Room Two for the sergeant to join him.

"So, what have you got for me, Terse?"

"Got 'im bang to rights, Chief…with a little judicious editing of course."

"You disappoint me."

"He practically confessed to killing Tony Lee."

"*Practically*? How practically?"

"Well 'e took a little reminding, Sir."

"I thought as much. How are you at finding things, Terse?"

"Chief?"

"See if you can locate a car. It's a red Zebaguchi 650, registration R256 HOG."

"You havin' me on, Chief?"

"No, get out there and find it man!"

Cross-examining witnesses may not be his forte, but surely even Terse could find something as outlandish as Goldman's car. The Inspector walked along the corridor to Interview Room Two.

"Hello Mr Murphy, I'd like to ask you a few questions."

"Ask all you like, but I doubt if I'll know the answers. I hadn't seen Goldman for twenty years until we bumped into each other last night."

"So, your luck's taken a turn for the worse, then."

"You could say that. I see my share of trouble as a doorman at *The Rainbow Rooms*, but no-one ever tried to blow me up until this morning."

"Well, that's the price of associating with Hymie Goldman."

Mike's eyebrows knitted into a frown.

"Working at The Rainbow Rooms you must have known Tony Lee?"

"Not to talk to, no. He was a croupier and they don't tend to mix with the doormen."

"When did you last see him alive?"

"Weeks ago…I dunno exactly."

"Can you think of anyone who may have wanted to kill him?"

"No, but like I said, I didn't know him *that* well."

"Where were you last night?"

"Down the Club till about eleven, then I went for a drink with Hymie Goldman."

"And where was that?"

"The Pink Parrot."

"Did anyone try to get in touch with Lee over the last few days?"

"Only Steffie."

"Steffie?"

"A friend of his," explained Mike. "I think they used to work together."

"What was her surname?"

"I couldn't tell you."

"Describe her for me, then."

"Tall, maybe 5'10". A looker; brunette with long legs and a killer smile."

"Thank you, Mr Murphy. Sign your statement and you're free to go."

"What about Hymie?"

"He should be out shortly if you'd care to wait."

Decca returned to his prime suspect with a heavy heart. It looked like Goldman had been telling him the truth. Still, he could have him for obstruction.

"OK Reidy, start the tape. Interview with Hymie Goldman resumed at 4.50pm. Just a few more questions. Can you think of any reason why Janis Turner, aka Steffie Scarlatti, would want to murder Tony Lee?"

"They were working a numbers racket at the casino in The Rainbow Rooms, only Lee failed to show up," said Hymie, wondering how long the questions would last. "Janis seemed surprised when he failed to keep their appointment, so I assume someone else killed him. Besides, the papers said he was found with his throat slit and that's not her m.o.; she prefers guns."

"What do you know about the numbers racket?"

"Not a lot. Someone rang my office a couple of times, shouted out four pairs of numbers, which, before you ask, I can't remember, and hung up. In hindsight it looks like the call was for my assistant, Janis Turner, aka Steffie, who seems to have known the croupier Tony Lee. She went to see him at the casino on the night I ran into Mike Murphy at The Rainbow Rooms."

"Thank you. That will do for now, you're free to go as soon as you've signed your statement. Oh, and Goldman…"

"Inspector?"

"Don't leave London unless I give you permission first, *right*?"

"Of course not." Were they really letting him go? Since it hadn't occurred to him that they might release him, he didn't have the first idea of what to do next.

At the desk he was reunited with Mike.

"You okay?"

"Yes thanks, Mike. I feel as though a great weight has been lifted off my shoulders and I have a sudden craving for pizza."

"Me too, but Benny's is out of action."

A pained look flitted across Hymie's face. "Now we have another score to settle," he said.

Part Fifteen

The Prince of Darkness was just settling down in his favourite pink velour armchair to watch his favourite game show, "The Price Is Too High", with a nice hot cup of cocoa when his phone started ringing.

He toyed with the idea of ignoring it, but he simply *couldn't*. For an ex-directory number it seemed to get far too many calls. He had gone ex-directory many years earlier on discovering that his name "P. Lau" was an open invitation to small-minded pranksters to call him up and ask if he had prawn balls. What was the matter with people in this country? Pilau rice was Indian, not Chinese. They were not only rude, but stupid. It was some consolation to know that those who crossed him generally found themselves on the wrong side of the Great Divide.

"Lau."

"Hello Mr Lau, Mrs Timmins here. I've got a bone to pick with you. You promised me faithfully you'd get rid of that awful man Goldman and I have it on reliable authority that he was released from Finchley Road Police Station not ten minutes ago."

"But my dear Mrs Timmins..."

"Don't give me the old soft soap Lau, when I pay good money I expect the best service available. You gave me your word they'd be scraping him off the pavement within twenty-four hours. What kind of hit-service are you running?"

"I'll look into it, Mrs T. Rest assured no effort will be spared to put things straight at the earliest opp..."

"I hope you're right. When I think of the way that dreadful man killed my prize pussy Tiddles, my blood runs cold. I want results, Lau, not blether. Do I make myself clear?"

She hung up, leaving the P. of D. feeling both a little foolish and somewhat incensed at the nerve of the woman, and more alarmingly at the ineptitude of his hit squad. They only had to eliminate a complete idiot, a job he could have done himself with his eyes closed. You just couldn't get good help these days, he reflected sadly.

He descended in the lift to his office on the first floor and dug out the "Contracts Pending" file. There it was, in black and white, contract 207;

"Termination of one H. Goldman of 792A Finchley Road, £10,000 plus travel expenses, 48 hour priority service."

Everything seemed to be in order, except that the party of the third part was still walking the streets of North London.

There was a file note stating that a woman had called to notify him that Goldman was in possession of the golden hamster. It seemed unlikely. Perhaps that was why they hadn't finished the job.

The hamster was still missing, so it was possible. He would need to have a little chat with Goldman before they completed the contract. He dialled a familiar number.

Hymie, walking around with a spring in his step and a smile on his face, remained in blissful ignorance. Nevertheless, it was with a heavy heart that he headed back to Edgware General to pay his respects to Benny Baker. After all, he'd been interrogated by the Fuzz, fallen down a laundry chute and nearly poisoned there after eating the canteen food.

"How is he, nurse?"

"Suffering from severe shock I'm afraid. A delayed reaction is quite common in trauma cases like his. Someone destroyed his restaurant, you know. He may not recognize you…are you family?"

"Yes, er, I'm his brother Sydney from Australia." When called upon for a spontaneous response, all originality deserted him.

"Mr Baker, your brother Sydney has come to visit you."

"I don't have a brother Sydney."

"Poor man…don't expect too much of him, Sydney."

"Thank you, nurse."

She walked off down the ward leaving the two *brothers* to talk.

"How are you Syd? How's the family?" asked Benny. He seemed not to recognise Goldman at all.

"It's me Ben…Hymie, I've brought you some grapes and a Get Well card."

"Sorry I didn't recognize you Ben-Hymie, it's this condition I've got, I'm not even sure who *I* am half the time."

"Ben, watch my lips, it's *me*...Hymie Goldman, your mate."

"Are you the one with his own business?"

"Yes, we were only talking about it a few days ago."

"I expect there's a terrible recession in Melbourne...it must be affecting you."

"Not so you'd notice...my office is in Finchley."

"It's okay Syd, don't worry. I know things haven't been exactly rosy between you and Joyce. She's at that *funny* age when all you can do is grit your teeth and hope for the best."

Benny seemed to be out of his gourd. There was a homicidal maniac roaming the streets and the Pizza-King of North London didn't even know what continent he was on. 'I should be so lucky', thought Hymie.

He collected Mike from the waiting room and they took the lift down to the hospital's main entrance.

"They may have allowed us to walk out of that nick, but I'm not daft enough to think that we're out of the woods yet, Mike."

"Its been nice catching up, Hymie, but there is no 'we'. I may not own my own business, but at least I've got the flat, three square meals a day, a job I can do standing on my head and footie on a Saturday." Mike held out a hand like a bunch of bananas to shake goodbye.

In just a few short hours Hymie had come to rely on his old friend, the man-mountain, and the thought of trying to solve the case without him seemed overwhelming.

"Well, that *is* a shame, Mike," he said. "I was so impressed with the way you handled things at Benny's that I was thinking of inviting you to join the business."

"Thanks for the offer, but if the last forty-eight hours is anything to go by then I'd need some serious danger money to get involved in *your* business. What were you going to offer me? Equal partnership and a bullet-proof vest?"

Hymie, who'd had no such thought, struggled to find words.

"Well, I was, er...thinking more of... a *junior* partnership. After all, there are people interested in buying this business."

"Oh, well, I'd *definitely* need to be a partner then. Otherwise, what job security would I have?"

Caught between a rock and a hard place, Hymie could neither face running the business single-handed, nor giving any of it away while there was a chance of cashing in for megabucks. He wondered if the sight of his office might dampen Mike's enthusiasm for partnership.

"Let's go back to the office and discuss it further," he said.

"Fair enough. Then you can tell me how you're going to solve this case."

Hymie nodded. It didn't do to give too much away, especially when you didn't have a clue.

Part Sixteen

It was late; one or two a.m., when they arrived at Goldman's prestigious office. The plaque on the wall outside said simply "792A", as if it didn't wish to commit to anything further. If you worked there, it *didn't* pay to advertise.

Leading the way, Hymie crept up the staircase, signalling to Mike to be as quiet as possible. His caution was born of the fear that whatever *could* go wrong almost certainly *would*. The list of things which could go wrong began with eviction from his office-cum-flat and ended with another attempt on his life. He had no illusions that he'd been anything more than lucky thus far.

He searched his pockets for the office key with a growing sense of frustration. A small pile of litter accumulated on the floor before him as he extracted fuse wire, paper handkerchiefs, a part-sucked boiled sweet, paperclips and an old Swiss Army knife, but nothing vaguely resembling a key from his voluminous pockets. He was a past master at losing things. In a long and illustrious career he had lost keys, cars, car keys, money and clients. He'd even lost a wife once and that wasn't easy.

"Oh, sod this!" cried Mike, running at the door and hitting it at shoulder height with his full body weight.

There was a dreadful crunching sound.

"Mike!"

"Oh, don't tell me you've found the key!"

"No."

"So?"

"That's not *my* office."

The big man looked crestfallen.

"Mine's next door, that one belongs to the opera singer."

"She doesn't *live* here I take it?" queried Mike.

"No, she just uses it as a rehearsal room."

Mike poked his head around the door, now hanging forlornly by a solitary hinge.

"Do you think we should leave her a note or something?"

"Or something, definitely."

Mike shrugged. "She's *your* neighbour. So this one's yours," he added, turning the handle of the adjoining office door. It was open.

"That's odd. It's not usually left open. Unless, there's someone in there…"

"Don't be so paranoid. No-one would try stealing anything from a dump like this."

"Thanks. At least I'm self-employed, not like you… someone's hired help."

"Well at least I get paid regularly," said Mike.

As they stood there bickering, the lights came on.

"Good evening gentlemen. Good of you to join us." It was the crime boss, Lau.

They stared at him in disbelief. Behind him and on all sides, dressed in martial arts gear and with red headbands, stood his personal army.

"You must excuse our unorthodox method of entry, Mr Goldman, but I was so keen to meet you I could scarcely contain my enthusiasm. My name is Lau, Master Lau."

"Pleased to meet you" said Hymie, who was clearly anything but.

"Whadda you want?" asked Mike, more abruptly. He could see that they were up against it and didn't see the point in playing games.

"I hope we can conduct matters in a civilised manner. I detest violence." He was toying with them. Who took their martial arts class on a social visit at two a.m.?

"I couldn't agree more," said Hymie.

"Perhaps you'd like to leave us, Mr Murphy? It's no concern of yours."

"How do you know my name?"

"I know many things about you. As owner of *The Rainbow Rooms* I also employ you."

Hymie looked at him resignedly, but Mike was neither a coward nor a deserter.

"I'm not going anywhere."

"What's with the *army* then?" asked Hymie.

"They are merely some of my associates."

"But what are they doing in my office?"

"Well, if Mr Murphy is sure he won't be running along…I've come for the hamster."

"I'm not running a pet shop here."

"You disappoint me. Perhaps it has only been luck that's kept you alive for so long. But I'm sure I'm doing you a disservice and you were about to tell me that you know where it is and are prepared to get it for me. It really is very important that the statuette is returned to its rightful owner; myself."

"I was told it belonged to someone else."

"They were lying."

"Do you have evidence of ownership?"

"Naturally, but I expect you'll take my word for it," said Lau. People always did.

"It's kind of academic anyway, as I don't have it."

Lau's gaze fell on the empty office. "I wondered where you could have hidden it."

Mike lifted the last remaining piece of office equipment not removed by the bailiffs; a green plastic phone, and threw it at Lau's head. "Run for it!"

Lau ducked instinctively, but one of his henchmen received the phone in the face. "Ah so!" he cried, or something similar.

Mike lashed out desperately with his fists as he followed Hymie's retreating form down the stairs. When they reached the bottom it became clear that Lau was taking no chances, as a second band of martial arts enthusiasts filed in from the street, blocking their way. Lau descended the staircase and struck Mike across the face.

"Resistance is futile. Take them away."

Mike was manhandled back upstairs into the office, where he was tied up and blindfolded. Hymie, who was clearly no threat, followed under his own steam."

"What makes you think I have the hamster, Lau?"

"You were seen leaving a cottage in South Mimms on the day Chiu Mann died. He'd gone to collect the statuette from the petty thief who'd stolen it."

"But I wasn't the only one there that day. There was a girl too; Steffanie Scarlatti. She shot Chiu Mann. She nearly killed me. If anyone has it, it's her," insisted Hymie.

"A convenient story, Goldman, but I know Scarlatti; the only reason she's allowed a bungling pet-investigator like you to live so long is because she thinks you either have it or know how to obtain the statuette on her behalf."

Why did it feel like everyone was a better detective than he was? Hymie didn't for the life of him know what had happened to the hamster. Oh, he'd picked it up, but he hadn't seen it since South Mimms so assumed that Steffanie Scarlatti had taken it.

"Well, if I find it, I'll let you know. Now, can we go please?"

Lau smiled.

"Do you know what this statuette is worth? Do you really think I would stop at anything to get it?

"I dunno," said Hymie. With no prospect of its recovery, he'd begun to lose interest.

"It's a priceless religious artefact, removed from the Temple of Wei Wei in the early Sixth Century. Since then it's been sought, fought over and coveted by some of the most powerful and ruthless men in the world. Your life would be snuffed out like a candle if they even suspected it was in your possession."

"Nice to know."

"Unless you help me recover it, it's curtains for you, Goldman."

"Look, I really don't have it. You must have searched my office, right?"

"It didn't take long," said Lau, dismissively.

"A misunderstanding with the bailiffs."

"So we'll have to resume our talks at my premises."

"Well, I do have plans of my own…"

"I insist."

"How can we refuse?" said Mike.

"You can't," confirmed Lau, who insisted on having the last word.

A Six O'Clock News reporter was interviewing Inspector Ray Decca of the Metropolitan Police Force. His wife, Sheila was impressed for once.

"Is there any truth in the rumours of gang wars on the streets of Finchley?"

"No. We're currently investigating three suspicious deaths in the area, but there's no evidence to support that particular conclusion. We live in troubled times and only the efforts of our professional and dedicated Police force prevent them from becoming more troubled."

"Tell me, Inspector, has anyone been arrested in connection with these murders?"

"Several people are helping us with our enquiries, although no-one has been charged yet. If any of your viewers has any information which may have a bearing on the case, please contact us."

"So you are treating the murders as one related case?"

"We believe so, yes."

"Thank you, Inspector. Anyone watching who thinks they may have information which will assist the Police should call 0845…"

Steffanie Scarlatti switched off the TV set and lit up a Havana cigar.

Police…what did they know? What did *anyone* know? She was invincible.

Sitting in her luxury West End apartment with a golden statuette of a hamster in pride of place on the mantelpiece, having gunned down two people in as many weeks, no-one could touch her. She pulled out her pistol from the holster between her thighs and polished the barrel. It was a beauty, like herself, but she wasn't about to spoil her curves by wearing it in a shoulder holster. Men were so *crass*.

For months she'd masqueraded as that gauche seventeen year old school-leaver, Janis Turner, to get revenge on her sister Lucretia, and no-one had suspected a thing. She could simply have shot her or stolen the statuette, but it would have been so *obvious*. Now there was nothing to connect her with the crime. She simply left her clothes on the beach, or in the wretched girl's digs, with a suicide note and she was free of her alter-ego forever. Everything had gone to plan; Lucretia was dead and she had the statuette. Frankly, it bored her. She only valued what she *didn't* have; her dead father's love, her next lover, the next kill, the next million dollars.

How tiresome the Triad was becoming. They had the local drugs racket all sewn up, but that pompous old fool, Lau was still acting like everything depended on him.

How sweet and fitting it would be for her to bring about his demise. He knew too much about her and that would never do.

Part Seventeen

Master Lau was worried, *very* worried. He may have
scaled the heights of the Triad, but no-one was
indispensable and he was getting old. Not *too* old, of
course, but definitely more mature. He'd become a little
forgetful of late. He still got a mild thrill from inflicting
death and destruction on the nameless masses, but to be
honest, he'd rather be watching "The Price Is Too High", or
any of those other high quality quiz shows on daytime TV.

As for that fiend in figure-hugging jeans, Steffanie
Scarlatti, she'd outstayed her welcome. Unlike Goldman
and Murphy, you couldn't just send her on her way with
a salutary beating, safe in the knowledge that she'd keep
her head below the parapet forever after; she needed to be
exterminated. That irked him. It wasn't that he objected
to killing anyone per se, he just hated the increased police
surveillance and reduced business takings that went with
it.

Lau prided himself on the scrupulousness of his
record keeping. *Some people* thought that keeping records
was a dangerous self-indulgence, but you had to have a
hobby. Besides, he still planned to write his autobiography

at the end of his career and achieve a kind of posthumous notoriety. There was no index-linked pension and retirement home in the Cotswolds to look forward to in his organisation, just the flash of silver and the taste of blood.

Business always came first with Lau. Drug Baron Chang had insisted that the price for the forthcoming year's opium contract was the golden hamster and it had been non-negotiable. Since Scarlatti seemed to have the hamster, she'd have to be eliminated to recover it. She wasn't the type to just hand it over. For some strange reason she wanted Goldman, possibly for target practice, so the easiest route to her was through him. The merit of silencing Goldman was that it also got that old bat Timmins off his back. It was hard to imagine what it was about the inconsequential detective that provoked such hostility, but that was *his* problem.

It would be easy enough to find Scarlatti; anyone whose calling card was a 45 calibre shell wasn't exactly the shy retiring type, but he wanted her to come to him. So he'd left a trail for her to follow, leading to Beachy Head, where he planned to dispense with the services of Goldman and Murphy. His only concern was the reliability of his own team. Their work of late left much to be desired, resulting in an increased burden on the local Casualty department rather than the local crematorium. If only he had a few more assassins like Scarlatti instead of a bunch of amateurs, the Triad would command the fear that was its due.

Dawn broke over Beachy Head. On the shoreline below the cliffs, waves crashed with a wild thunderous roar, swirling and spraying their white foam skywards. Three white vans came to a halt on the cliff top and their passengers disembarked. Master Lau stood quite still, gazing out to sea, as though in a trance, then turned back to give his instructions.

Two of the assassins unloaded their human cargo from the back of the second van; a battered and dishevelled looking Goldman and a heavily sedated Murphy.

All of Lau's men were meticulously dressed in black with red headbands and ceremonial swords hanging from their waists.

Not for the first time, Hymie wished he'd stuck at it and become an electrician. He'd probably be rich and content by now, with a fat wife and two-point-two children, instead of staring down the barrel of a point-four-five handgun. Still, you couldn't have everything.

The ground cover on top of the cliff wasn't best suited to hiding spectators, even those as lithe and slender as Scarlatti. She'd camouflaged herself and taken refuge behind one of those wind-blasted trees that seem to lean at an angle of forty-five degrees to the horizon for years with no ill effects.

Goldman's car, the ill-fated Zebaguchi 650, lay concealed under two tonnes of camouflage. It had proved nigh on impossible to make it blend in with the landscape, so she'd gone for the iron-age burial-mound effect.

'Why should Lau have all the fun?' she thought, as she shouldered her newly acquired anti-tank gun, flicked up the sights at the end of the barrel and took a final look in her rear view mirror. Party time! She lined up the third of the white vans in her sights and teased the trigger with her finger tip.

Lau had a distinct and persistent feeling of unease. He hadn't lived to be sixty three without a talent for survival. He'd sent out his scouts, but as yet received no reported sightings of Scarlatti, nor of anything suspicious. Yet his instincts were never wrong.

"Well gentlemen, any last requests? A cigarette? Some new office furniture?" Levity had never suited him.

"How about some prawn balls with pilau rice?" quipped Hymie, strangely liberated by having nothing left to lose but his life.

Lau scowled. He was on the point of signalling for the headsman when he checked himself and an evil leer spread across his normally inscrutable face.

"You're simply the bait for the Diva of Death."

"You want Steffanie Scarlatti? Is that it? I can tell you where she lives."

"I fear it's too late."

His prophetic words died on his lips as, looking up, he caught sight of a glint of light in the tree cover on the horizon.

"VAVAVOOM!!!!"

Lau stood pointing at the trees with his mouth open, but all anyone could hear was the roar of a high speed projectile as it blasted across the sky, locked on its target. The third van burst into flames as its petrol tank exploded, sending black smoke up into the ozone layer. Within a few minutes all that remained was a charred remnant.

"Try selling *that* on ebay!" snarled Scarlatti.

Hymie gazed across the clifftop. Funny, he didn't recall seeing a burial mound there before. Well, it was burning away nicely now.

"It's that woman again, let's get outta here fast, Mike!"

Lau focused his binoculars on what looked like a dancing shrub. Scarlatti was desperately hopping around trying to avoid the flames created by the blowback from the AT gun. Their eyes met across the field of battle.

She discarded the cumbersome metal pipe and unstrapped her beloved handgun; a modified Colt 1911, from its holster. "Come and get it while it's *hot* boys!"

The Lau pro-celebrity synchronised hit-team was nothing if not ambitious. From all directions they broke cover and ran at the crazy bitch. Sadly for them she had a weapon and knew how to use it. Gunfire rang out.

"BLAM, BLAM-BLAM, BLAM-BLAM, BLAM, BLAM-BLAM-BLAM-BLAM!!"

The cliff-top was beginning to resemble Boot Hill.

The man who said 'he who lives by the sword shall die by the sword' has been dead for many years, killed by a runaway horse. No-one uses swords these days, except as ornamental letter-openers, apart from psychotic Triad hit-men with a hankering for the glory days of the Samurai. So it came as no surprise that the outcome of the first innings was Swords nil, Guns and Rockets, eight. There was no second innings.

While Mike and Hymie were contemplating the merits of lying face down in a pile of rabbit droppings the Seventh Cavalry rode over the hill in the shape of D.I. Decca and a Police Armed-Response unit. The cavalcade of cop cars paraded along the cliff-top and police marksmen were deployed to cover their entrance.

The area was soon cordoned off and most of the survivors apprehended for questioning. Master Lau was not among those detained.

As the sun climbed over the wreckage of his Zebaguchi 650, Hymie gazed forlornly out to sea, tears of regret welling in his eyes. He approached the colossal wreck with an aching void in his heart. It was foolish to love a car, and yet, why not? In this veil of tears called life, what made more sense; to put one's trust in man, with all his fickleness and deceit or in a machine that gave long and lasting service?

He stood and surveyed the ruins of his car with a feeling of total desolation. What was left for him now?

"Don't get too close, Goldman! It's only a *car*." shouted Decca.

"*Only a car*?! Do you understand nothing, you crass commercial oaf?! It was the last of its kind. The last Zebaguchi 650 anywhere. What would *you* know anyway, you…you *Mondeo driver!*"

Sometimes there were just no words.

"That's enough bullshit for one day, Goldman. You're under arrest for causing an affray." Decca smiled. Some days you couldn't help liking this job.

Part Eighteen

"**I** don't know. How many times do I have to tell you?" pleaded Hymie.

"As many as it takes, Goldman."

He was in a police cell late at night. Deep night.

"Oof! Uurgh! Aaargh!"

He was spitting out blood and teeth, but Terse continued to hit him. This couldn't be right, this couldn't be happening, it was an outrage.

"You can't do this! This is England, we have the rule of law, we have rights."

"If everyone has rights then no-one does!" cried Terse, punching him.

"You did it, didn't you? You're scum. I know your sort and you did it alright."

Hymie's mouth opened in an involuntary shriek, seeming to last forever. He was looking through the eyes of Edvard Munch, down by a fjord in Oslo, being sucked into an apocalyptic orange sky. This *couldn't* be real, he was from Finchley.

He woke up, sweat pouring down his face.

'What the hell am I mixed up in? It's getting so

bad that I can't sleep without Class B drugs or Class A nightmares.'

He was back at 792A Finchley Road, lying on the floor. He sat up and lit a cigarette. He hated himself for his weaknesses, but they were a part of him; he might just as well have loathed himself for breathing. Even his solicitor had been surprised when they let him out on bail.

Benny had advanced him the bail money against the insurance proceeds from the Zebaguchi 650, although he wasn't entirely sure he'd paid the premiums, or even that it was registered in his name. Possession was nine tenths of the law.

Finally, as the icing on the cake, he'd persuaded the judge to let him pay off his long list of parking fines at the heady rate of £2 a week. Judges didn't live in the real world, so Mr Justice Williamson probably thought he was driving a hard bargain. Mike had been released with a caution; not to associate with Hymie Goldman, and been bound over to keep the peace for twelve months.

Hymie picked up the newspaper he'd been using as a blanket and re-read it. Under the headline "Beachy Head Horror" it gave a somewhat skewed account of events, focusing on the stunningly attractive chief suspect, Steffanie Scarlatti. There were pictures of her in a state of semi-undress, looking like Miss Whiplash with a black basque and riding crop. Heaven knows where they got the photos from.

It wasn't that she didn't have the figure for it, just that she didn't seem to need the money. As usual he was wrong; she loved power and money and was only too happy to provide risque pictures of herself, at a price. Now languishing in HMP Holloway awaiting trial, Steffie Scarlatti had become something of a media celeb. Master Lau, by contrast, had gone to ground and no-one seemed to know anything about him.

Sergeant Terse had been transferred to traffic duties. The view from the top was that the casualties would have been significantly lower without his involvement and that a spell in Traffic would calm him down. This, at least, was the view before Monday 23rd August or "Black Monday" as it was afterwards known in Traffic circles.

The day commenced as dismally as most Monday mornings, with hordes of Vectra-bound reps and MPV-mums on school runs tooting and fist-waving at each other in the age-old ritual of the rush-hour traffic-jam. Fate, however, was about to play a hand in events.

At 08:05, Sergeant Terse and PC Reidy were proceeding along The Broadway, Hendon, in a westerly direction. At 08:06 their attention was caught by the "Plink! Plink!!" sound of a computerised traffic-signalling system going kaput.

As later recorded in his notebook, Terse turned to his junior colleague and said "Oh dear, Reidy, how unfortunate. We'd better conduct the traffic until the engineer gets here." To which PC Reidy replied "Yes Sarge. I'll go and call for assistance at once."

With the air of an experienced conductor assuming charge of a forty-piece orchestra, Terse strode out into the path of the oncoming vehicles, narrowly avoiding death and serious injury. He raised his baton and miraculously the traffic all around him stood still. He smirked.

At this point he appeared to drastically overestimate his own skill and began waving the baton around with wild and enthusiastic abandon as though about to launch into a high-speed rendition of the William Tell Overture. The traffic lurched forwards in all directions simultaneously and pandemonium ensued; screeching brakes, colliding cars and, on all sides, the sound of breaking glass, metal and plastic.

BANG! CRUNCH!! TINKLE TINKLE!!! KERRUNCH!!!!

Row upon row of assorted vehicles now cluttered up the street like some giant discarded metal concertina. Terse became more introspective.

"Oi, PC Plod!" cried a distressed motorist.

"*Sergeant,* thank you!"

"Sorry…*Sergeant* Plod! What are you going to do about my bloody car? It's completely knackered!"

"Get that pile of junk out of here lady, before I arrest you for kerb-crawling!"

He looked around for signs of Reidy and reinforcements, but finding none, quickly removed his helmet and started to walk off down the street.

"Oi, where do you think you're going?" asked a passing yobbo.

Terse was about to claim to be going off duty when he caught sight of the huge biker blocking his path and thought better of it.

"You're nicked, Scumball!" he snapped.

The Dudley Road Chapter of the Walsall Sixty-Niners had spent weeks cleaning and polishing the chrome on their choppers and tuning their engines to the peak of perfection. They had planned to spend a jolly weekend of mayhem and carnage in Brighton before returning home after tea on Sunday. Being stuck in a pile-up in Hendon had never been part of their plans and their feelings towards the man responsible bordered on the homicidal. Terse neither knew, nor cared.

Mitch Maguire, their leader, weighed in at 22 stones in his stockinged feet, not that he ever wore stockings. At six feet six inches he towered over Terse and glowered at the poor specimen of a policeman as though disappointed that his country had come so low. He needn't have worried.

Terse pulled back his right fist and plunged it into the man-mountain's massive gut. Maguire doubled up, as much with surprise as pain, then landed a blow on Terse's left ear. They traded punches for a few minutes until the sergeant realised that without back up he was on a hiding to nothing and the biker realised that spending the rest of the week in a police cell wouldn't go down too well with the missus.

Maguire climbed back onto his chopper and revved-up the engine.

VVRRRoooommmm, vrroom!!

Terse caught sight of Reidy, ambling along the pavement in his general direction, whistling a happy tune. He hoped that meant that help was on its way, otherwise it was just him and Reidy, and Reidy was about as much use as a fart in a spacesuit.

Terse presented his open palm to the approaching biker.

"Come off it Fatso, even you couldn't be *that* daft. You so much as scuff my shoes and you'll be on the wrong end of a charge sheet as long as your arm."

Maguire, displaying a complete lack of concern, revved-up his bike again, then released the hand brake. The chopper lunged forward, threatening to flatten Terse where he stood, but the bloody-minded copper maintained his steely composure. Like some bizarre suburban matador he spun on his right heel, lurching out of the path of the chromium-plated killing machine.

Terse looked on in smug satisfaction as the hairy biker flew hell-for-leather through the air, maintained his trajectory with sylph-like grace for several seconds and then ploughed headlong into an approaching articulator. The crunch of breaking bones and mangled motorbike parts could be heard streets away.

"Call an ambulance!"

Reidy arrived just in time to see the denouement and promptly radioed for medical assistance.

"They'll never get through the traffic, Reidy, we'd better *carry* him to the hospital!"

"You're never going to move him in that state, Sarge?"

"No, but he doesn't know that."

At this juncture, the rest of the Sixty-Niners decided that they'd never live it down if they sat idly by and let a copper get the better of their leader.

"Oi, Plod. Like to try that again with the six of us?"

They dismounted and marched as one towards Terse, swinging their bike chains about with gleeful abandon.

"We're gonna rearrange your face, copper!"

This was something Terse could understand. The Road Traffic Acts failed to hold his attention. The Highway Code was apt to pall over the long haul, but give him a bunch of plug-uglies with chains and he was on home ground. He unfastened his truncheon.

"Boys, boys, give me a break."

"Where do you want it, copper? Arm, leg or head?"

"I've got my quota of dumb-ass thugs for this month. Do you really wanna join Giant Haystacks over there on C Ward? Just put the chains down while you can still walk!"

By pure chance, Inspector Ray Decca was on duty and passing along the Broadway at the time. Once he knew why he'd been sitting in his car for the past hour; while a sergeant in the Traffic Division had a punch up with a gang of bikers, he reflected that it could only really have been Terse and that the man's innate aggression would out.

Terse belonged in Homicide; but whether as a statistic or a detective he wasn't sure.

"Hold it there, gents!" said D.I. Decca.

It was difficult to say who was more surprised: Terse, at the sudden reappearance of his former boss, or the bikers at being referred to as gents.

"Keep your nose out, mate, or we'll re-arrange your face too!"

"It's okay, Chief, everything's under control."

"That's *one* way of looking at it."

"I've called for backup, sir."

"Thanks, Reidy," said Decca.

The penny dropped with the bikers. "Hey! He's just another copper!"

Their difficulty seemed to lie in knowing which policeman to hit first. Terse was in his element; unwinding a bike chain from around his neck with his left hand while executing a perfect polo swing with his truncheon hand.

"OOOF!"

One of the bikers lay indisposed on the pavement, clutching his leather-clad balls in obvious agony.

"Enough! Put the chains down now!" cried Decca. He was holding a revolver in his hand and aimed it at the chest of the nearest biker, who stood very still and appeared to be struggling with deep emotions.

"'Ere, Chief, you can't go pulling guns on people. Low-life scum they may be, but this isn't the answer."

"Thank you for those words of support, Sergeant. Now, read these men their rights and cuff them to the car."

Terse and Reidy soon had the bikers handcuffed at all points around the Inspector's car. Only then did the sergeant return to his grievance.

"I'm sorry, Chief, but you're under arrest for the unlawful use of a firearm."

Decca's face assumed a look of total bemusement.

"And they told me you didn't have a sense of humour, Terse!"

"This isn't a laughing matter, Sir."

"Sergeant, do you realise the seriousness of the allegation? Do you really want this on your record?"

Reidy looked at the ground and shuffled his feet, clearly wishing he could be elsewhere. The bikers were beginning to warm to Sergeant Terse.

"The rulebook is my Bible Sir, and you're in clear breach of Section 4.2 of the Firearms Code."

"That'll do Sergeant. Here…this was the weapon in question; it's a kid's toy gun. A replica made in Taiwan. I took it off a juvenile delinquent earlier this morning."

"'Have you been drinking, Chief?"

"What's that got to do with anything? I had a drink a few hours ago, it was old Jack Harrison's leaving do. Do you think I'd be *that* stupid?" Secretly the doubts were beginning to creep in.

"I'm afraid I'll have to ask you to blow into the bag, Chief. We can't have Joe Public thinking we think we're above the Law, can we? The job's hard enough as it is."

One blow in a bag later and Inspector Ray Decca was looking distinctly embarrassed.

"Look Sergeant…Barry, it could happen to anyone. I need hardly tell you as a highly esteemed colleague, Barry er…"

"That's not what you thought when you had me transferred to Traffic."

"A misunderstanding Barry, nothing more. Stick with me and you'll be an Inspector before you know it."

"Not in *Traffic*?"

"Of course not. I knew it the moment I saw you handle those bikers. You belong in Homicide, Terse. I'm only sorry I didn't realise it sooner."

"So am I, Chief. You're nicked for being drunk in charge of a motor vehicle."

"Look, I barely turned the crystals pink. By the time we get down to the station for a blood test I'll be in the clear. Besides, I'm late for my appointment at the Marriage Guidance."

"Are you going to RELATE, Chief?"

The sergeant's hard-bitten exterior became noticeably less hard-bitten.

"Do yourself a favour, Chief, get a divorce."

Decca looked at him for some clarification, but none was forthcoming.

"And if I don't get the transfer back to Homicide by next week I might just have second thoughts about booking you."

Well, thought Terse as he walked to the Tube Station, principles were one thing, but you didn't have to be stupid about them.

Part Nineteen

The RELATE offices were in a converted semi-detached house formerly occupied by the Citizens Advice Bureau. Marriage guidance had become more of a pressing social need than advising the local population on what to do when their furniture was repossessed. Marriage itself seemed to be in terminal decline in the modern live-for-today era; when responsibility and commitment had become dirty words.

Rita O'Nions had been a counsellor for many years. She'd seen and heard everything from the sublime to the ridiculous and thought she knew it all. She had resuscitated a few marriages along the way, by metaphorically clumping together heads that should have known better, but she was inclined to be prejudiced against men.

"Hello Mrs Decca, take a seat. No, not *that* one, that's mine. Is your husband with you today?"

"No, not yet. He said he had a few things to sort out at the station first."

"Oh, righty-ho. I didn't realise he worked on the railways. *He's* the one is he, ho, ho."

"No, the Police station, he's a Police Inspector."

"Oh, ah, yes."

"He shouldn't be too long, it's just difficult getting time off when you're in the Police."

"Perhaps we should start the ball rolling in his absence?"

"If you think it would help."

"Of course. Tell me, Mrs Decca, what seems to be the problem with your marriage? Has your husband been violent or unfaithful?"

"No, nothing like that."

"Does he drink or take drugs?"

"No, nothing out of the ordinary."

"Well, that's an encouraging start, don't you think?"

"If you say so."

"So what's causing the trouble between you?"

"It's his job. He's hardly ever at home and when he is, it's as if I'm not there."

"I see, well nobody likes to be undervalued, but have you tried to improve things between the two of you? Do you ever have sexual relations?"

"Not with each other. Not for a long while."

"So you have sexual relations with someone else?"

"No, but I've thought about it."

"I'm sure you have. It's important to feel satisfied and sex can be a very positive force in a relationship."

"He was never what you'd call a great lover. It was all finished in about five minutes."

"You poor dear. But don't get too hung up on sex. Many perfectly normal couples don't have relations as often as they used to." She looked wistfully out of the window.

"He sounds like a good provider anyway. Inspectors in the Police must be reasonably well paid, I would have thought."

"Yes, but we don't live in a hunter-gatherer society any more, do we?"

"No. Besides, gone are the days when a husband could be relied upon to provide a decent standard of living for his family. These days they're all a bunch of sponging loafers who run off with next door's au-pair when you're not paying attention."

"You poor thing," said Sheila Decca, "and you're a marriage guidance counsellor too. It just shows you."

"Oh no dear, I wasn't speaking of myself, no. Just a *friend* you understand."

Out in Reception Ray Decca leant down to the sliding glass window and asked to see Mrs Onions.

"Don't for Heaven's sake call her *that* will you? It's *O'Nions*. She gets ever so narked. Especially recently. You'd think her husband was having it off with the au-pair or something."

He smirked at the girl's indiscretion.

"She's in Interview Room Two. Just go right in, she'll be expecting you."

He knocked, there was a muffled sound from the other side of the door and he entered.

"Sorry I'm late, there was a terrible traffic jam in Hendon."

"Please sit down, Mr Decca. Excuse us for starting without you, but I'm a bit busy today so Sheila has been filling me in on the background."

"Fine," he said, resignedly.

"Good, then let's make a start. The objective is for you both to do the talking, work out what's going wrong in your marriage and agree on how you can fix it and for me to act as an impartial adviser. There are no right or wrong answers here, it's all about what works for you. Successful relationships depend upon good communications. So Sheila, would you start by telling Ray what's going wrong from your point of view?"

"Yes. Well, you can't have communications when one person in a relationship is never there...and when he is, he ignores you. I get more attention from the postman."

"What does that mean? What has the postman got to do with anything? You know I have a difficult job, Sheila. I can't just leave at five o'clock when I'm on a case, it's just not that kind of job. When I do get home, I'm drained. I just want to relax in front of the television and forget about the day I've had. I can't make polite chit-chat about Mrs Doodah from the women's knitting circle."

"So why don't you give up the job?" asked Sheila.

"I can't. At my age, what else could I do?"

"I don't know, but at least we'd be *together*."

"Besides, I love the job, I always have," he admitted.

Rita reflected that the incidence of divorce among marriage guidance counsellors was one of the worst of any profession. They didn't tell you that when you started.

"As you can see, Rita, there's just no romance left in our marriage. He's married to the Police force, not to me," complained Sheila.

"Can't you try to meet Sheila halfway, Ray?"

"Halfway? Where do you mean? Enfield?"

"Buy her the occasional bunch of flowers, take her out for a meal."

"For Heaven's sake, we've been married twenty-three years. How many married couples do *you* know that even preserve the romance more than a few months after the honeymoon?"

"Sheila, I sympathise. Ray, if you want to get the best out of your marriage, you need to try to find ways of building bridges with your wife. Can't you suggest anything?"

He raised his eyes to the ceiling and stood up.

"I'm sorry, Sheila, I have to go. I've got a departmental meeting at two o'clock."

"Ray, we need to sort this out."

"I'm afraid it'll have to keep."

He crossed the room, opened the door and passed down the corridor back to the street. He could imagine what they were saying about him, but he had no choice, couldn't they see that?

Part Twenty

In her tastefully but fussily furnished apartment in the West End, Mrs Edna Timmins was holding court. She looked like everyone's favourite grandma; the archetypal sweet natured, white-haired, little old lady. You could imagine her serving tea and scones at a village tea-party or singing feebly in the congregation of a rural parish church.

Looks could be deceptive. In reality she was a hard-bitten multi-millionairess and ruthless bitch, running every kind of racket from drug-pushing to gun-running. She controlled all the wild flower pressing from Golders Green to Dagenham and was just moving in on the W.I.'s jam-making monopoly west of Croydon. She enjoyed the disparity between her public and private personas and sustained her public image by the convenient fiction of telling her gangland acquaintances that she worked for a schizoid drug dealer called Baron Chang. The picture she painted of him was so appalling that they were all delighted to be dealing with her instead.

"Queen's Bishop to King's Knight Five. Checkmate I believe, Lau. I win again."

"You are a remarkable player, Mrs T." said Lau, patronisingly.

He studied her wrinkled face, looking for the slightest glimmer of weakness or frailty, but found none. Her face was as blank as a saggy ceremonial mask.

"You on the other hand are not, although I sometimes have my suspicions that you are not playing to the best of your ability."

"My dear lady, whatever gives you such an impression?"

"Anyone with your talent for saving his own skin, must surely know all about chess. Although it's the game of kings, not gangland killers."

"If I'm honest, dear lady, my own interests are more in the field of TV game-shows."

"You surprise me yet again, Lau. However, getting back to the hamster, it's a pity your unfailing instinct for self-preservation didn't extend to the Baron's hamster."

"Mrs Timmins, I can assure you that the Baron's interests are of paramount importance to me.

Scarcely a day passes without my offering up prayers to Heaven that the Baron should receive his just deserts in this life and the next. If I could have retrieved the golden hamster for him already, I would have done so. Unfortunately, I have my suspicions as to its whereabouts but no hard evidence."

"So, what about Goldman? I paid you to kill him, yet he wanders around freely. Is this your idea of a joke? If so, it's in extremely poor taste. Will you finish the job or shall I tell the Baron that you were unequal to the task?"

"I understand and share your frustration, I really do.

I was on the point of disposing of him when the Police arrived. Goldman is a surprisingly resilient man."

"Surprising is right!"

"Nevertheless, he won't last long with me on his trail."

"You have a plan, Lau?"

"I am never without one, I assure you, Mrs T."

"So tell me how you plan to pay the Baron his two million dollars?"

"Two million dollars? But the hamster isn't worth as much as that, surely?"

"It's worth whatever someone is prepared to pay for it, Lau. To the Baron it's worth two million dollars."

"It's uncanny how you know his mind so well, dear lady. You must be *very* close."

"We are. So, about this plan of yours."

"Lucretia Scarlatti has it. So *if* I can retrieve it, I'll let the Baron know in due course. As for raising the two million dollars, I have a betting scheme in mind."

"What, rigging a few races?"

"Not just any races, *the* race; the Cheltenham Gold Cup. I know of your sporting interests and thought it would appeal to your sense of occasion. I have a number of contacts in stables around the country and plan to call in a few favours."

"And you're confident of success?"

"I can be very persuasive."

"Two million dollars confident?"

"Yes. I just need a small advance to defray expenses. Say £30,000, dear lady?"

"*Dear* is right, Lau. I may be able to raise £20,000, but

I'm not independently wealthy and it would be out of the question to ask the Baron for the money."

"So be it, madam."

"And Goldman?"

"That's the beauty of my scheme; we use the Gold Cup as a pretext for his disappearance. This year's favourite is a horse called…"

"Summer Lightning."

"Precisely. We fabricate a kidnapping plot and persuade the owner to employ Goldman to protect the animal. My associates can then easily dope him."

"Goldman?"

"The horse."

"And Goldman?"

"We can either kill him, or so discredit his pathetic little business that no-one will hire him to protect so much as a child's bag of sweets."

"Or both."

"Exactly."

"I like it Lau, I like it. But make no mistake. This is your last chance. The Baron doesn't suffer fools gladly."

"Who does, madam? I will call you to confirm the arrangements in the usual way."

The sound of a bird's wings flapping could be heard outside. Mrs Timmins turned to see what it was, but all she saw was a cloud of blue smoke.

Did he really imagine he could impress her with his Ali Bongo magic tricks?

Part Twenty-One

The telephone trilled intrusively like a budgie on heat. Otherwise all was quiet, if anywhere in North London could be said to be quiet. The intrepid Goldman lumbered across his empty office and snatched up the receiver. He didn't want to be Hymie Goldman any more, it just meant trouble.

"Spear and Jackman!"

"Sorry, I thought this was the number for Goldman Confidential."

"It is, lady, but we have to be careful."

"Do you? Why?"

"No names, no pack drill, I'm sure you understand. What can we do for you?"

She sounded well-to-do, if you could sound affluent and well-educated on the phone.

"I gather you have experience with horses, Mr Goldman."

He resisted the urge to say 'nothing was ever proven' and started trawling through what passed for his mind to see if he either knew anything about horses or could pretend. He drew a blank.

"Yes, I adore them," he said, unfazed.

"Oh, splendid. My name is Hunting-Baddeley; Lucinda Hunting-Baddeley, one of the Suffolk Hunting-Baddeleys. You were recommended by an old friend of the family as a good man to have around in a tight spot."

How did she know; he'd been in a tight spot for years.

"Of course, but could you be a little more specific?"

"I thought I was being as clear as crystal; I want you to come over and babysit Summer Lightning in the run up to Chelters, as we've had kidnapping threats."

"Chelters?" he queried.

"The Gold Cup."

"Oh yes, of course."

She wasn't on acid, she was just la-di-da.

"Well, perhaps I can drop in and see you to agree terms?" she suggested.

"Spiffing. Or shall I come to see you? It's no trouble."

"Thank you, but I'm often down in the old Metrop., so it's no bother and I rather like to see who I'm dealing with on their home turf. I always think you can tell a great deal about someone by their taste in furnishings."

He wanted to laugh hysterically. She wouldn't be able to tell much about him from *his* furnishings; he didn't have any. What did that signify except bankruptcy?

"Did you say who recommended me? I'd like to thank them personally."

"Why, it was Edna Timmins, such a nice little old lady and so knowledgeable about equestrian matters. She did ask me not to mention her by name, but I can't see what harm it could do. Of course you'd want to know you had a satisfied client, but do keep it to yourself please, as I wouldn't want to upset the old dear."

Mrs Timmins? Was the world going mad? Why would *she* be recommending *him*?

Something didn't add up.

"Of course, Mrs Hunting Badly."

"Hunting-Baddeley."

"Quite so. How about next Thursday at 4pm?"

"Shall we say next Tuesday at 3pm? You're at 792A Finchley Road I believe?"

He groaned inwardly. "Yes. Yes, of course. I look forward to it."

It was inconceivable that Mrs Timmins should have recommended him. The last time they'd spoken she'd threatened him with bodily injury, and she had meant it. Perhaps she had something against this Hunting-Baddeley woman and thought she was doing her a bad turn. Perhaps she disliked horses and thought he would make a hash of the job. It didn't really matter; he didn't intend to ask her and there was no other way he could find out. He still seemed to have come out on top…as long as he could acquire some office furniture by Tuesday.

He lifted the receiver again and dialled Murphy's number. He hadn't seen Mike since just after their last Police interrogation, but felt sure he must be missing him. The phone number was unobtainable.

As he sat there wondering how on earth he could find his old pal, the clumping of heavy boots on the stair outside heralded the arrival of the man-mountain himself. He wasn't looking too chipper.

"You may not believe it, but I've just been trying to call you. Your phone's been disconnected. Anything I can do?" asked Hymie.

"I think you've done enough already, you great spawny-eyed wazzock! A few weeks ago I was an honest, hard-working doorman with a secure job. Now look at me!"

Tact and the desire not to have his face rearranged kept the irrepressible one's mouth tightly buttoned, but he couldn't help noticing what a state his old friend was in; he hadn't shaved, his clothes were badly creased and his shoelaces were undone.

"I can't get a job as a bouncer *anywhere*. I've lost my flat and I feel like I'm constantly being watched."

"Try not to be so paranoid."

"I'm trying, but it's not so easy when everyone's out to get you!"

"Don't worry, be happy," sang Hymie, tunelessly. "I have a new case and I want you to be in on it with me. We'll be laughing all the way to the bank, believe me, it's money for old rope…"

"Do me a favour."

"Sure."

"*Don't* do me any more favours! Or I might just forget we go way back and beat nine kinds of crap out of you!"

Hymie hadn't realized there *were* nine kinds of crap, but could see this wasn't a good time to broach the subject.

"All we have to do is baby-sit one measly racehorse."

"Oh, pardon me, I was forgetting you're a qualified vet, known throughout North London as the horse-man of Finchley…what could be simpler?"

"Come on, what can it take to look after a racehorse? We just have to make sure no-one nicks it before the Gold Cup."

"Where's the catch?" asked Mike, like a man covered in bee-stings being asked to collect some honey.

"I don't know what you mean."

"If this is one of your cases, there *must* be a catch somewhere, it stands to reason."

"Well, I wouldn't put it quite like that, but we do have to find some office furniture for a meeting with the client next Tuesday. But other than that…"

"Other than that? Where are you going to find some office furniture that quick?

"I thought maybe you had some contacts?"

"You thought wrong. I'm broke and my credit rating is only just on the right side of criminal. A blind beggar wouldn't lend me a brass farthing to please his dying mother. Don't look at me like that either; it's not my fault."

"Look, Mike, this could be our best chance ever of making some easy money. Trust me. We're not gonna throw it all away just because we can't get our hands on a few sticks of furniture, surely?"

"Why do I know I'm gonna live to regret this?"

"You *do* know someone then?"

"Hold it, no promises, but I think that perhaps, maybe, possibly I might know someone who could help."

"Great!"

"Wait a minute, what's in it for me?"

"The satisfaction of a job well done?"

"How much?"

"You get the furniture and I'll cut you in for a third of whatever I make."

"A half!"

"Forty percent?"

"A half!"

"You're a hard man to do business with," protested Hymie.

"Do we have a deal?"

"Alright…half it is." What was there to lose? Half of nothing was nothing.

"Oh, and there's one other thing," added Mike.

"What's that?"

"You couldn't lend me a fiver for breakfast could you, I'm starving?"

Hymie reached into his shirt pocket and retrieved one of the chronically few surviving specimens from Lucy Scarlatti's thousand pound advance. In trying to advertise his own commercial acumen to a would-be business partner he could hardly admit he couldn't spare a fiver.

Mike headed off to the Black Kat to re-fuel, leaving Hymie to mull over how they were going to raise enough capital to get the horse baby-sitting business off the drawing board.

He discounted Ceefer Capital. Somehow he expected them to try and tie him up in airtight legal agreements, even if they were willing to cough up. Besides, he was saving them for a rainy day. Since every day was a rainy day, he was probably thinking of a torrential downpour.

'I'm due for another pop at the bank that likes to say *yes*' he thought. 'Surely they will take the long view and realise that by supporting my fledgling business now, they will reap the benefits tomorrow.' It was an interesting theory.

He thought of his bank manager, Tony someone-or-other. Turbot, wasn't it? and his confidence began to ebb away, like a dinghy with a slow puncture. Turbot was your archetypal bank manager; lacking in imagination, emasculated to the point of needing a chit from Head Office to wipe his nose, and having an absurd obsession with collateral. He reflected on the gross unfairness of life; on how this two-dimensional turd should command public respect, while he, a hard working professional man, should be censured and derided, and then he wrote a letter, never intending to send it.

"Dear Mr Turbot, no, Dear Tony, yes that sounds better.

Thank you for your letter of the 14th inst., whatever an "inst." is, explaining that you had charged me fifty seven pounds and eighty three pence in administration fees. Presumably this was for those charming letters, telling me I was overdrawn. Nice though it was to receive them, I already knew, thank you. In fact I was sitting in my office wondering how I was going to pay your original charges when the letters rolled in to notify me I had struck the bank charges jackpot.

You are an excrescence, not to mention a carbuncle on the bloated rear end of capitalism. Call yourself a bank manager? Why, you couldn't manage your way out of a paper bag. As for *nurturing new business*, as your advertisement claims, you wouldn't recognize an up and coming business if it ran over you in a bus.

Long may you rot,

Kind regards,

H.Goldman (Mr)"

He wondered if he hadn't been a little gratuitous in his insults, albeit fulsome in his praise early on. Nevertheless, he did feel much better for venting his spleen and went through the process of enveloping and addressing the letter just to get some kind of closure. He had done it before; he never posted them, it was just a kind of therapy.

Next he wrote the letter he was intending to send; the one which explained that he needed some office furniture to clinch a lucrative contract with a well-heeled lady from Suffolk. He was sure that this was just the sort of thing the bank would like.

Later that day when a kindly old lady found a dog-eared brown envelope in the Finchley Road, she attached a dog-eared old stamp and posted it. She returned home with the sense of contentment that comes from having done a good deed in a selfish world.

Part Twenty-Two

The night was starless and bible black. A chill wind blew in from the East and anyone who had a home to go to was in it.

In the small wooden hut at the back of Pinner Parish Church strange things were happening. Arcane things, things honest respectable men and women would do well to avoid.

A tall man in a Crombie overcoat passed through the bushes alongside the hut and disappeared into its dark interior.

"Pungghhh! Puuuunnnnghhhhh!!"

The unholy congregation of the Brothers of Pung sat in a circle, cross-legged on the floor. Their garish robes and puerile addiction to saying "pung" at the slightest provocation marked them out both as complete idiots and as dedicated members of the order. They "punged" reverently in the ancient ritual of summoning the Mighty Jong. Brother Decca hastily joined the circle with seconds to spare before the latter made his grand entrance from behind the black moth-eaten stage curtains at the back of the hall.

Only two of The Brethren knew the true identity of the Mighty Jong, and they were sworn to secrecy on pain of the ritual of The Boot. All members feared this dark ritual, as well they might.

It was widely believed that the MJ, as he was referred to, was a senior ranking Police officer; or why else would the rest of them be there?

The MJ stood before them in his blue-grey pinstriped suit, covered with bits of garden cane, symbolic of Holy Bamboo. His face was hidden behind an enormous mask; the ancient Helm of Hendor, which bore a startling resemblance to an outsized policeman's helmet with two eye holes cut out.

He assumed his place of honour at the plinth in the centre of the gathering and commenced the meeting with the usual announcements.

"Are all the Tiles of our Holy Order safely gathered in?"

"Yes, oh Mighty Jong!"

"Are the Four Winds assembled in the eaves?" These were the lookouts posted at the four corners of the hut.

"We are, oh Mighty Jong!" The words were accompanied by a ceremonial breaking of wind.

"Good, then I'll begin. Join with me in our oath of allegiance.

By the Helm of Hendor,

By the truncheon and toecap,

By the Sword of Justice,

And the Might of the Right,

We will strive 'gainst the heathen,

'Gainst the spirits of evil,

'Till our armies have conquered the

Things of the Night."

"Punggghhh!"

"Is the First Bamboo Tile present?"

"Yes, oh Mighty Jong!"

"Louder, the Mighty Jong can't hear you," he cried, like a refugee from a pantomime.

"YES! Oh Mighty Jong!"

"You don't have to shout, I'm not deaf. Pray read from the Register of Righteousness!"

"Brethren let us salute Brother Deccus. He has excelled in the pursuit of our craft."

"Punggghhh!"

"He shall be awarded the order of the Green Dragon, second class, in recognition of his achievements in the pursuit of the one true craft."

"Punggghhh!"

'God this is tedious,' thought Inspector Ray Decca. He'd much rather be down the pub or at the pictures or curled up at home with a good murder mystery. Unfortunately, once you'd joined, you were stuck with it; your career would go into a terminal nosedive if you left. He'd become the prisoner of his own ambition.

At the conclusion of the ceremonies they stuck what looked like a scout's badge on him, passed around the holy scotch and soda and got totally plastered. The MJ's private minibus took them all home at midnight.

Part Twenty-Three

Mike had drawn a blank on the office furniture. It didn't help that they couldn't raise even the meagre few quid it would have taken to hire the stuff. Perhaps the aura of doom was hanging over Goldman Confidential and people could smell their desperation. No-one seemed willing to throw good money after bad any longer.

"Mike, you know as well as I do that we've *got* to get hold of that office furniture and maybe a few horsey prints..."

"You mean pictures?"

"What else would I mean? By tomorrow, or we can kiss the job goodbye. Isn't there anyone else we can try?"

"It's a long shot, a real long shot, but maybe, just maybe, Artful Arnie could lend us some for a few hours."

"Why do they call him artful?"

"I dunno."

"Well, is he reliable?"

"Yeah, you can rely on him to rip you off, but you're no slouch in that department yourself and besides, beggars can't be choosers."

"Right. Pull this off and I'll make you a full partner in the firm."

Mike smiled. "Isn't that a bit like making me Captain on the Titanic, just before her maiden voyage?"

Hymie feigned deaf.

"Let's find this guy Arnie then, there's no time to lose."

Arnold Shoebridge, aka Artful Arnie, was a con-merchant with more fingers in more pies than little Jack Horner. People only dealt with him if they were desperate or stupid. Being both it was inevitable that Hymie Goldman should go to him for some office furniture.

After a few false leads from men in pubs they finally tracked him down to a mobile hovel on the outskirts of Elstree. He seemed to be living the life of a nomad, perched on the edge of civilization. For the last half mile they just followed their noses as the stench of his impromptu sanitary arrangements wafted down the lane. The place had all the ambience of a Brazilian shanty-town.

Arnie was obviously distrustful of his fellow men as he kept two lurchers tethered on long chains outside his caravan. Their barking drew him from his pit, brandishing a double-barrelled shotgun.

"Sling yer 'ook or I shoot" shouted the debonair wheeler-dealer.

"You can't half pick 'em." muttered Hymie.

"Arnie! It's me, Mike Murphy. I've come about some furniture."

"Buying or selling?"

"More of a short term rental," said Hymie.

"Well, you'd better come in."

"The situation is this…" said Mike.

Dusk was descending by the time they found themselves on home turf. They had a deal on some furniture and a great weight had thus been lifted from Hymie's mind.

Benny's Unbeatable Bakery had miraculously been restored to its former glory, although the same couldn't be said of its proprietor. Benny had spent weeks convalescing, first in Edgware General, and later, when he had been discharged to make room for an urgent ingrowing toenail case, in a private rest home. He still had no comprehension of who or where he was and was convinced he was being pursued by leprechauns.

Mike and Hymie entered the restaurant.

"Hi Ben, good to see you on your feet again," said Hymie, brightly.

"Thanks. A waitress will be with you shortly."

"Ben, it's *me*: Hymie."

"I'm sorry, do I know you?"

"We've been friends for years; Hymie Goldman. Don't you know me, Ben?"

"Sorry, no. You're not working for the Little People are you? They're everywhere."

"Who? Are you winding me up?"

"You are, aren't you? They've sent you to spy on me."

"Have you been on the funny fags again? They used to give me a persecution complex like that too."

"Who, the Little People?"

"There's no such people you daft nurk!"

"That'll do. Don't upset him, he's had a tough time of it lately."

It was Susie Parker, one of the waitresses.

"Oh, pardon me for breathing."

"If I must," she sighed.

"I only came to see how he was, I wasn't looking for trouble."

"You never are. Trouble just seems to find you and stick with you. Benny needs complete rest, not World War Three."

"OK, we'll go. Tell him we were asking after him."

"Cunning you see; the Little People," continued Benny. "Never underestimate them; they have eyes and ears everywhere..."

"Ugly little buggers then," said Mike.

"...but I'll outsmart them. I'm gonna sell up and move to Australia with Susie."

She smiled.

"Ben, you can't be serious?"

She frowned.

"You stand alone. No-one makes pizzas like you." Now it was Hymie's turn to be disconsolate. The room did a shimmy as his world rocked on its very foundations.

"I promised my brother Syd I'd go and visit him in Australia. It's a land of opportunity you know."

"You haven't got a brother Syd."

"Well, who else would I go to Australia to visit?"

It seemed impossible to get through to him. Susie may have won the first round, but Hymie wasn't about to lose Benny, or his remarkable pizza, without a fight.

Part Twenty-Four

The sight of the ancient oriental fixer, Lau, sitting in front of her at visiting time in a blue pinstriped suit and with a grey, greasy pigtail hanging down his neck came as something of a surprise to Steffanie Scarlatti. Was there no peace, even in prison? But then what had *she* done to deserve peace?

"Gloat? No, my dear. I simply wondered how you were finding it here and whether you would be interested in a small business proposition?"

"Are you in your right mind?"

"More so than you, I imagine. Obviously there's a serious question mark over your integrity, but then you have more to lose than I." He was just so smarmy.

"You seem to forget I'm on remand at Her Majesty's pleasure and can't just walk out of here whenever it suits me," she said.

"I can help you."

"Okay, let's suppose for the sake of argument you can, what's your price?"

"You insult me. Has everyone become so greedy and self-seeking that they can no longer recognize an act of altruism?" he asked.

"That's rich coming from you, Lau."

"Our time is nearly up. Do you want to be free or not?"

"Free? No-one is ever truly free."

"Don't go all existential on me," he complained.

"And don't you start preaching at me!" she snapped. She'd momentarily forgotten where she was and raised her voice just that little too loudly.

"Quiet Scarlatti! Visiting time is a privilege and privileges can be withdrawn." The warder was watching her closely now.

Lau remained composed and businesslike.

"The price is removing a couple of obstacles."

"Names?"

"Does it matter?"

"Not really."

"Timmins and Goldman."

"Hymie Goldman?" Why was he still free, while she was a prisoner?

"The same."

"Like taking candy from a baby," she said.

"You agree?" He couldn't see how she could refuse.

"A small enough price."

"Is that a yes?"

"Yes."

She would have agreed to anything. She had no scruples about lying, cheating, stealing or killing. They were means to an end, nothing more. Goldman meant nothing to her. She'd enjoyed working for him as Janis Turner because he was so laid back, but that scarcely justified any kind of loyalty.

"We'll be in touch," said Lau, getting up from his chair.

"Good, I look forward to it."

The bell rang to signify the end of visiting time.

Master Lau bowed to his new assassin and left, presumably to return the hire suit to Moss Bros.

Part Twenty-Five

'**W**hy me?' thought Tony Turbot, bank manager, family man and all round good egg, as he re-read the letter on his desk. He couldn't have told you who Hymie Goldman was; he was just a blip on his monthly credit risk report. Now it was personal. The man had gone out of his way to make his life unpleasant and he would squash him like a bug in his salad. He'd never thought of himself as vindictive, mean-spirited or petty, but there was something about the tone of the letter which made him feel justified in a response which ticked any or all of these boxes.

Where did this guy Goldman get off? It was always the bums and deadbeats who complained about bank charges. In fact it was nothing of the kind, but you couldn't get nasty with the better sort of client. He wouldn't have minded, but he hadn't even had anything to do with it; there was a ruddy great computer in Peterborough that invented the charges, they didn't leave things like that to bank managers.

He lifted the red phone on his desk. He had two phones; a green one for nice conversations and a red one for unpleasant ones. They were the twin pillars of his world. Carbuncle on the bloated rear end of capitalism? What did that even *mean*? The man was surely under the influence of hard liquor or drugs. Perhaps both.

He'd show Goldman, that buffoon among small businessmen. He'd call in his overdraft and charge him for the letter informing him. Let him laugh that one off.

"Miss Jervis, send a letter to Mr H. Goldman, pulling the plug on his overdraft. Standard wording. Thank him for his letter of the 16th inst. and charge him for the termination letter." His social conscience had ceased to trouble him years ago.

"Very good, Mr Turbot."

That was what he liked most about the bank; in its rigid hierarchical structure and slavish devotion to the rulebook it resembled nothing so much as the British Army.

He took his blood pressure tablets with a glass of water from the dispenser and lifted the red phone on his desk. Dialling the exclusive London premises of Goldman Confidential he was surprised to find the line still connected.

Hymie was in high spirits. He had a new client, some office furniture was on its way and perhaps this call was another new client in search of his unique services.

"Goldman Confidential, how can I help you?"

"Turbot, from the Argyll and Edinburgh Bank, Mr Goldman."

Hymie's face registered concern.

"Ah, Mr Tur…Tur…Turbot…I'm glad you called."

"Glad? I've just received your letter."

"My letter?" Surely he couldn't have sent *that* letter.

"The one where you refer to me as "an excrescence and a carbuncle on the bloated rear end of capitalism," quoted Turbot, incensed.

"Are you sure it was from me? You see, I have a number of business rivals who would do anything to ruin my business."

"The letter's in your handwriting and you've signed it."

This seemed to stump the resilient sleuth.

"Ah, I see. Well, apologies Mr Turbot, I hope you realised I was only joking."

"No, I didn't, Mr Goldman. I was deeply offended by your attitude and comments."

"So, you don't think you'd be in a position to extend my overdraft just now?"

A hollow laugh escaped the bank manager's lips.

"We take our clients very seriously here at the A & E. Clearly you're dissatisfied with our service and wish to change bankers. I was merely ringing to let you know we won't stand in your way."

"Well, er, it was a mistake and I wasn't planning any such thing. I'm sure we'll all have a good laugh about this in years to come."

"You may, Mr Goldman, but as far as I'm concerned that's out of the question. I'm sending you a written request for the repayment of your overdraft in full in today's post. Good luck with your business."

"But, Mr Tur…"

Click! Silence.

On the verge of bankruptcy and with no credit, how long could he last? He was drinking in the last chance saloon again and putting his shirt on a horse called Summer Lightning.

He reached for the reefer he'd been saving for just such an emergency and lit up. Now wasn't the time to rearrange deckchairs on the Titanic, it was time to get stoned.

A few lungfulls later he stood gazing out of the window of his office with unseeing eyes. The sun shimmered across a desert of traffic. The horizon blurred into a fusion of heat haze and morning mist. He felt like he was floating above his body, looking down on this scene of disaster with complete disinterest. What we shall laughingly refer to as his mind was racing through worlds as yet unknown.

Part Twenty-Six

Who can describe the terrors that lie within even a normal man's mind? The landscape of Hymie's was wild indeed; sheer cliffs of doubt, descending into the slough of despond, surrounded by a quagmire of despair. Not an ideal holiday location, to be sure, unless you fancied a change from Ibiza.

Take a trip with Hymie. Float into the void of his brain. Thoughts like distant echoes collide in the vacuous wilderness of eternity. Electric storms of fear and loathing batter his consciousness, tearing away the mundane, the real, the sane, leaving only the vision of a man; eight feet tall, with long white hair, a grizzled beard and holding a palmer's walking staff the size of a small tree. Wait, it *is* a small tree.

"Zeus? Odin? Buddha?...Big Daddy?"

"Just call me God", said God.

"But how did I get here? Am I dead? You're not here about the parking tickets, surely?"

"No. Just thought I'd drop by. You're having an hallucogenic episode, but that doesn't make me any less real. Consider yourself lucky, I don't usually make personal appearances these days. It's no fun opening supermarkets when there's one on every street corner."

"I'm glad to see you, God. Do you really know everything?"

"Yes, although most of it's not really worth knowing."

"About my life?"

"Yes, and all the others. People blame me for not taking charge of their lives for them, but they should get a grip. Life's no picnic you know."

"You're telling me."

"It's an opportunity…for good or ill, nothing more nor less. Those that rise to the challenge, take responsibility and don't just look out for themselves have a rewarding and fulfilling time."

"And the rest?"

"End up shovelling shit in the basement."

"You mean hell?"

"Yes, it's all part of the contract I signed with Satan. I get the nice people, he gets the scum; lawyers, criminals, high court judges, traffic wardens, politicians, estate agents…he's seriously overcrowded."

"Do you know what's happening next?"

"No. Should I?"

"I don't know."

"You set a train of events in motion and have to wait and see what the outcome will be…nothing's predetermined. Some things are more likely than others, but anything's possible."

"Like me solving a big case?"

"Everyone wants miracles." God smiled and the room was bathed in sunlight.

"I need help, God."

"*You* need help, that's a good one! You think *you've* got problems? You don't know you're born. I have to keep records on everyone. It was easy when it was just Adam and Eve, but you wouldn't believe the state my systems are in now. Personally I blame those temps I've been using since the thirteenth century…bloody hopeless! Most of them don't know the difference between a PC and a microwave."

Hymie sat there gaping. It had never occurred to him that the Almighty might have problems too. When you thought about it, it made sense. Here He was; running the largest organisation of all, with no-one to help Him and no-one even thinking He might need a hand from time to time.

Of course, God, being God, knew how to put the petty problems of even his most forlorn and forsaken sheep before his own headaches.

"Let me tell you a story, Hymie. It is Hymie, isn't it?"

"That's right."

"A couple of weeks ago I was sitting in my office in the Celestial Palace, or "CP", catching up on my paperwork. There was a knock at the door and a cherub poked his head around it to say there was someone at the Pearly Gates."

"He called me "Oh Great One", which usually means they're either after something or extracting the Michael. So I harrumphed a good deal and said couldn't the Archangel

Gabriel deal with it, and they said no, he flaming well couldn't deal with it, because he was out playing golf and besides, it was Lucifer himself.

So after a bit more "um"ing and "ah"ing and generally complaining that no-one else around the place was of any use I flew over to "QA"; that's the Quarantine Area we keep for undesirables, to sort it out.

A couple of seraphim were hovering around outside the ante-room, polishing their halo's and exchanging tittle-tattle about the Devil's latest incarnation as I arrived.

"Go on, tell me…what's he come as today?" I asked.

"Apollo; the Greek god, not the Spacecraft. Golden curls everywhere…must have spent half the morning under a hairdryer," they said, bitchily.

"Well he does like to blend in on his visits here. Trying to pretend he was never really banished after all."

"The nerve!" they said, and I agreed.

"I suppose I'd better get this over with."

So I strolled into QA with my usual effusive charm, whistling the latest Lloyd Webber;"Don't cry for me somewhere or other", possibly Bognor Regis, and tried to get him to leave without further ado.

"Lucie Baby! Good of you to drop by, but you know you shouldn't have."

"I've missed you, Big G."

"Thanks, but you know you're not allowed in here you old goat, its members only."

"I know, but if I have to torture another bloody lawyer I'll go mad."

"Fancy a beer?"

"Sure, what have you got?" he asked.

"Anything you can think of and a few new real ales that I'm working on."

"I'll have a pint of Grunge's Old Dirigible," he said.

The Devil clicked his fingers and a Chippendale chair appeared beneath him. Antique furniture's a passion of his when he's not tormenting lost souls.

"Business must be bad," I told him, trying to wind him up.

"Are you kidding? Mankind's going down the toilet faster than I can handle. I need to rent some more space."

"Not from me, matey," I assured him.

"Look, God, I'm tired of all the recriminations and the backbiting. Tired, tired, TIRED!!!"

"I see…you're *tired*. Ready to quit huh, Lucie Baby? Come to throw in the towel and admit you've been wrong all along? Ready to turn over a new leaf?"

"No."

"Not even just a bit?"

"Well, maybe, but look at it this way: we're neither of us getting any younger are we? So where's the sense in slugging it out for all eternity?" he asked.

"What else is there? Mankind has its life, death, sex and taxes, not necessarily in that order, and we have *this*… this virtual chess game. If you're getting tired, then you can always resign. Put it another way, if you can't stand the heat, get outta the kitchen!"

"Not what I had in mind. Cards on the table…I've had a few setbacks, I admit; that St.Peter doesn't fight fair. But I'm big enough to take it, so I don't complain."

"Much!"

"If you'll just let me finish!" said Lucifer.

"Go for it!" I said.

"I got to thinking…"

"A new departure for you then."

"The whole thing would make a lot more sense if we settled our differences in one championship bout; my champion against your champion."

"Winner takes all?"

"Exactly," agreed Satan.

"So, when I win you'll release all the tormented souls, dismantle the Kingdom of Hades and take up residence in the North Pole?"

"If there's still a polar icecap, yeah," he said. "And if I win?" asked the Devil.

"In that case, as unlikely as it may be, you'll get the CP, the Host of Angels, the gold-plated Jacuzzi, and the fully expensed company cloud."

"It's a deal," he said. "Any rules?"

"*You* want rules? You'd only break them."

"I'd pretend to be offended, but I can't be bothered. I know you like rules so I thought I'd ask before you mentioned it," said the Devil.

"Well, rules are fine and dandy if we stick to them. What did you have in mind?"

"Nothing, nada, nichts; a championship bout to the death between two mortals."

"A bit mediaeval isn't it? Don't you ever move on?"

"There's nothing to compare with a good old fashioned punch up."

"True, true. I take it we're not actually talking about a contest in the ring?"

"No, somewhat passé. The world's their stage, their ingenuity is their weapon."

Hymie, who'd been nodding off to this celestial shaggy-dog story, suddenly sat up.

"So what happened, God? Did you agree to the contest?"

"I'm afraid so, Hymie. I never could resist a challenge. It's always been a weakness of mine. They said I couldn't create the world in a week so I had to do it in six days. Heck of a job that was, my back's not been the same since."

"So who's your champion? Hercules? Albert Einstein? Not Arnold Schwarzenegger?"

"That's what I wanted to talk to you about."

Hymie was beginning to fear the worst, but he couldn't quite bring himself to believe that God, the omnipotent, omniscient being, could make such a dud decision.

"It's me, isn't it?" he asked.

"Yes. You're my champion," said God.

"How did that happen? I'm a complete no-hoper. Surely everyone knows that?!"

"No-one's a no-hoper who believes in Me."

The white-haired giant had spun him a good yarn and he wasn't about to let him off the hook now. Hymie Goldman needed to believe in Him and so he would.

"So, who am I fighting? Hercules? Albert Einstein? Not Arnold Schwarzenegger?"

He wondered what would happen if he tried to edge out of it.

"You'll find out when the time is right."

"Was I your first choice?"

"You selected yourself, Hymie. Now, I must be off. Miracles to perform and all that, you know how it is. Good luck."

He had a million unanswered questions, but never got the chance to ask one. A dazzling light illuminated the entire office. He clutched his eyes to protect them from the searing brightness of the supreme-being. In half a nanosecond God had gone.

A voice like thunder disappearing into a long tunnel echoed after him through space.

"Give up the drugs. Don't fail me."

The words would stay with him. He knew then that he had no choice, that he was irretrievably committed to this contest against some unspeakable emissary of evil and that he wasn't to be allowed even his old psychological crutch.

He sat there for hours. The shadow patterns on the office floor swirled around him like a bizarre kaleidoscope as night turned into day. His mind was locked in torment. Wild imaginings overtook him and transported him to another place. He was sitting in a tram as it rattled through gaudy neon-lit streets in some distant Chinatown.

He saw flashes of glass-columns, chromium-plated superstructures, light displays flashing in Mexican waves across the front of mountainous tower-blocks.

He flew past advertising hoardings too numerous to count, fast food restaurants, shops and bars and everywhere were teeming, milling throngs of Chinese, like a million ants swarming through his honeycombed brain.

Another tram rattled into view. As it pulled alongside he noticed a girl facing him. She was staring with her mouth open as if to speak, but her words were drowned out by the clamour of the passing throng and the clatter of the tram on the tracks. With some consternation he realised that he knew her.

He leant forward to speak to her, but she slumped forward into his arms and he noticed with a creeping horror that she'd been shot. He tried to staunch the blood, but she was already dead; a lifeless thing of flesh, bleeding all over him.

Hymie lunged at the bell and the tram lurched to a halt. People were shouting and screaming at him. Some of the passengers prodded the girl's lifeless body and recoiled in fright. All he could do was point helplessly at the retreating tram. He could have sworn he'd seen a white-haired old lady moving out of sight on the lower deck. He was sure that the dart had been intended for him.

The crowd was turning nasty. He forced his way to the front of the tram and threw himself out onto the street; clear of the doors, of the menacing crowd, of his own descending panic. As he did so the driver called after him.

"Don't fail me! You mustn't fail me!"

When he hit the pavement he remembered where he'd seen the dead girl; long ago in an apartment at Thirty-five Riverside Drive.

Part Twenty-Seven

"**H**ymie! Hymie!!" Mike was gently shaking him and slapping him around the head. Since 'gently' had never been in Mike's repertoire, he was lucky not to be adding concussion to his list of problems.

"Do this to me again, mate, and you're dead, capish? We've got a client to see in a couple of hours!"

Mike had never expected to see the day when he'd be in business with Goldman, and now that he was, it bugged him that *he* was the one taking it seriously.

"Oi! You wanna get stoned on your time, that's up to you, but don't do it on mine!"

Sadly, the crumpled P.I. was in no fit state to heed even Mike's bellowed warning. It took a faceful of lukewarm coffee and ten minutes of being frog-marched around the office before the first hesitant signs of consciousness emerged. He felt like he'd been walking in slow motion down the up-escalator to nowhere.

"Where am I?"

"Boy, you're sharp. Get with it Goldman, you've got to convince this horsey dame you're an ace investigator. Some chance!"

Hymie winced.

"What day is this?"

A low groan escaped Mike. "To think I gave up my position in the dole queue for this!"

"I'm a P.I., right? Do I have any cases?" asked Hymie.

"Not if you don't pull yourself together fast. Does the name Hunting-Baddeley ring any bells?"

"Pleased to meet you, Mr Hunting-Baddeley, what can I do for you?"

"For me? Nothing. For yourself, try being a detective before I'm forced to throw you through the nearest window. Remember me? Your partner, Mike Murphy; the idiot who went into business with you against his better judgement?"

"Mike! Where's the effin' furniture?!"

"Aha, better late than never, welcome to the party. You said *you'd* raise the dosh."

"I drew a blank. The bank turned me down flat. Some mix up with a letter they thought I'd sent. You haven't been writing to Captain Haddock at the A&E?"

"What are you on about?" asked Mike.

"It had something to do with fish anyway."

"Fish? You're babbling man! Snap out of it."

"The name of the bank manager!"

"Clear as mud."

"I'm the world's greatest detective."

"Good to see you're still full of it."

"Confidence?"

"Bullshit!"

"Amounts to the same thing, Mike. Where's the furniture?"

"On its way. Good job one of us gets results. It should be here soon so you'd better get a shave and brush up. You can't see Lady Muck looking like something the horse left in its stall."

"Detectives are meant to look rugged and unkempt. You know, borderline disreputable."

"I know, but you're way over the border, mate. I wouldn't hire you to clean my bog, let alone babysit my prize racehorse!"

"Thanks for the testimonial. That bad, huh?"

"Believe it, Dipstick."

"Okay, I'll get a shave. I still have an old Remington Fuzz-Away somewhere."

While Hymie was performing his ablutions a furniture van pulled up at the kerb outside. Artful Arnie had arrived.

"Oi, Murphy! Do you want this gear or not?"

Mike ambled to the window, opened it and bawled out something which might have been 'alright' and might not, and ended in 'off!' When Hymie looked outside a moment later the two bruisers were deep in conversation.

"Need a hand Mike?" he cried, without enthusiasm.

"You're in no state for lifting furniture, just get yourself ready for the client."

Never the most enthusiastic devotee of hard labour, Hymie declined to argue the point. Mike returned and the two wanna-be detectives adjourned to the Black Kat for some warm grease and caffeine while Arnie and his mate unloaded the van.

Returning half an hour later, basking in the warm glow

of a disaster averted, they stood on the threshold of their business premises ready to be wowed by the last word in office chic. They needn't have bothered.

"What the hell!" said Hymie, struggling to express what they were both thinking.

The filing carousels and personal computer were nowhere to be seen, the workstations and swivel chairs were AWOL and the architect of the chaos that remained was noticeable by his absence.

"I'll kill that toe-rag, Arnie!" cried Mike.

The office seemed to have been transported back in time to ancient Rome. Papier maché columns and colonnades jostled with plaster busts of minor deities and obscure emperors with large noses. Ornate alabaster vases cluttered the surfaces and a linoleum mosaic of a hunting scene adorned the floor.

"We're done for!"

"The client will be here any minute. I've got to think of *something*. Something big. Something so crazy, so unbelievable that no-one would bother to think it up!"

"Oh, yes, how silly of me not to have thought of it myself," said Mike, "…we took this scenery in payment for a debt owed by a travelling theatre? No, too obvious. We've got a new way-out marketing strategy? Or you think you're Julius Caesar! they're sure to believe that one!"

"You're not helping. A lesser man would say it was all your fault."

"Shut it, Goldman. Face it, we're scuppered. We may as well stick a sign on the door, "Gone Away" and head down the Job Centre."

"No way, Murphy. I've been in tighter scrapes than this. I can't immediately think of them, but I must have been. Keep the faith, we'll laugh about this one day."

"Yeah, the kind of hysterical laughter that overcomes you just before the men in white coats wheel you away." Mike wasn't used to putting a positive spin on disaster.

The bickering would have degenerated into a punch-up had it not been for the sound of a woman's heels clicking down the passage outside.

"Leave it to me" hissed Hymie.

"Good afternoon, Mr…"

It took a great deal to stymie Lucinda Hunting-Baddeley, but they'd managed it within the first minute of their first meeting. Walking off the Finchley Road into ancient Rome was liable to do that to a person.

"Goldman, Hymie Goldman. I know what you're thinking," he said.

"You do?" she replied.

"Yes, why the Roman stage scenery?"

"Exactly."

"Well, pull up a divan and I'll tell you. The answer is quite simple. A friend of mine runs an amateur theatre company nearby, The Strolling Players, putting on shows to raise money for charity, and one of his storage warehouses caught fire a few days ago. This was all they could salvage."

"But why store it here?" asked Lucinda H-B.

"Well, as luck would have it we were upgrading our furniture at the time and it was for a good cause and I didn't think my clients would mind for a few days; a bit of a novelty really."

She goggled at him momentarily and then simply caved-in.

"Well, as long as there's an explanation, I suppose," she said, pulling up a divan.

"Naturally, madam. You don't think we make a habit of decorating the office like this surely?" he said, gaining in confidence as every minute passed without the loss of his new client.

"Well, as we've never met before, I can hardly say, but I'm willing to give you the benefit of the doubt, although surely your friend could have found some alternative storage space?"

"Unfortunately he was uninsured, so he won't even be able to replace the costumes and scenery he's lost. I just couldn't bring myself to turn him down when he asked for my help."

"Good one," whispered Mike.

"And you would be?"

"I beg your pardon, Mrs Hunting-Badly, this is my junior partner and security consultant, Michael Murphy. He's currently working undercover, as am I; hence our appearance. We need to be able to move freely through some of the rougher districts of North London."

"Oh I see. I *was* wondering. A high price indeed, Mr Goldman; being seen out in public like that. You will, of course, change your attire when you move into the stables, won't you? I won't have Lightning being put off his food by smelly clothes."

Mike looked alarmed. He wasn't going to ask too many questions of the client on first acquaintance, but it seemed that Hymie was already displaying a serious disregard for the principle of keeping him informed.

"Stables?" queried Hymie.

"Well where else do you expect to stay?" asked Lucinda Hunting-Baddeley. "You can't protect Lightning from kidnapping if you're staying in a hotel now can you?"

"No, I suppose not," agreed Hymie, reluctantly.

"Sorry, Mrs Thing, who or what is Lightning?" asked Mike, who'd been following some way behind the general drift of the conversation.

"Good Heavens, Mr Murphy, I assumed you'd been briefed on the assignment. I refer, of course, to Summer Lightning, my championship racehorse. He's running in the Gold Cup. I've received several threats through the post, telling me that if I don't scratch him from the runners-list something will happen to him."

"How dreadful," remarked Hymie.

"Precisely," agreed Mrs Hunting-Baddeley.

"Have you informed the police?" asked Mike.

"Well, yes, but they didn't seem to think they could do much about it until something had happened; by which time it would be too late. So I asked around to see if anyone knew of a good security firm and someone mentioned you."

Mike and Hymie eyeballed each other in silent disbelief.

"They said you were good with horses."

"You're sure it wasn't hamsters?" asked Mike.

"Why would it be with hamsters? Aren't you good with horses?"

"Just Mr Murphy's idea of a joke," said Hymie. "I assure you we *are* good with horses. Very good in fact."

"Yes, Mr Goldman grew up on a farm and learned to ride at three…" said Mike.

"Oh, where was that Mr Goldman?"

"Out Hendon way."

"I didn't realise they had farms out there."

"Yes indeed, but we mustn't let Mr Murphy hide his own light under a bushel, he used to work in stables as a boy; mucking in and mucking out, over the summer holidays. Mike the Mucker they used to call him. The horses loved him."

Mike glowered.

"Oh that *is* good to hear, Mr Goldman. I do so hope Lightning takes to you both. There'll be a nice bonus in it for you if he wins the Gold Cup."

"Ah that reminds me," said Hymie, hurriedly. "We need to discuss our scale of fees."

She sized him up and took the measure of him in a glance. "A hundred pounds a day plus expenses?" she suggested.

"Each?" queried Mike.

"You drive a hard bargain," said Lucinda Hunting-Baddeley. She was kidding. Stuck in stables in the middle of nowhere there wouldn't be any expenses. "It's a deal," said Mike. He couldn't face living in ancient Rome for long and his own flat had been repossessed.

"Good. Report for duty at two o'clock the day after tomorrow. Here's the address," she said, handing Hymie a card. She turned briskly and clicked off down the corridor.

"Let's get one thing straight, Mike," said Hymie, "*I* decide on how much we charge. We could have held out for another fifty quid a week each!"

"So you say, mate. I just thought we needed a break."

Part Twenty-Eight

The convoy passed at a snail's pace. The traffic in North London had been getting worse daily for years to the point where it was almost quicker to walk. Quicker, but not safer. More accustomed to the soft leather upholstery of her Mercedes-Benz, Steffanie Scarlatti was going quietly nuts in the back of the police van.

"Got a ciggie, Sweetie?"

PC Reidy gazed at her in dumbstruck awe. He couldn't accept that this vision of loveliness was the murdering bitch everyone believed her to be.

"Go on, officer, I'm gasping."

He was the one who was gasping, or rather, drooling. He drew out a packet of cigarettes from his tunic pocket and offered her one. She smiled a devastating smile and took the packet.

"Got a light, constable?"

He lit her and she started to smoulder. As much as he fancied her he was aware of the irreconcilable gulf between them. Criminals were one species, law enforcement officers another. Except in the line of duty, never the twain should meet. It didn't make him feel any better though.

The clock crept on. Reidy's mind drifted to his plans for later that evening. He thought of the barmaid in the *Rose and Crown*, a buxom blonde called Jenny. He'd been seeing her for a couple of weeks now. Maybe tonight would be his lucky night.

It wasn't to be. The great conductor in the sky was on his tea-break.

Outside the van flares exploded, shrouding the convoy in a red mist and spreading a crimson haze across the grey sky. The visibility outside ebbed away to nothing.

Inside the van Steffanie Scarlatti lunged forward from her bench and stubbed out her smouldering cigarette in Reidy's face.

He doubled up in agony, screaming with pain, before being battered unconscious against the side of the van. He slumped to the floor, was swiftly dispossessed of his handcuff keys and took no further part in proceedings. Lau's associates cut open the back door of the van and Scarlatti made a quick getaway down the street. The escape made the TV and radio news within the hour.

"The public are warned to be on their guard against escaped prisoner Steffanie Scarlatti...

Scarlatti, aged twenty five, height 6 feet, was last seen in Camden Town this afternoon when a police van escorting her to Holloway prison was hijacked. The public are advised not to approach her as she is armed and highly dangerous. Police have issued the following photo of the woman. Anyone with information as to her whereabouts should contact the Metropolitan Police on 0845...."

Click!

Lau pressed a button on his remote and Scarlatti was gone. If only life was that simple.

"You've become something of a celebrity, Ms Scarlatti. Let me be the first to congratulate you."

"Save it, Lau. Celebrity has no value to me. It never pays to advertise *my* activities."

"As you wish. I didn't bring you here to discuss your personal popularity, or lack of it. Before we begin, a word of warning: if you have the slightest idea of betraying my trust or murdering me in my bed, get rid of it now. Until you have completed our bargain you will be under constant surveillance. Should that prove insufficient incentive, I need only remind you that I have a file on you so comprehensive it would guarantee your removal from society for decades. When you did get out you would be old, wrinkled and ugly and your future would be bleak." He knew exactly which buttons to press.

"Don't try to threaten me, you withered old wreck!"

"Threaten is an ugly word, and not one I care to use," continued Lau. "Nevertheless, the file is safely lodged with my lawyers in case I should meet with any unforeseen accident. My death or disappearance would certainly trigger its release to the authorities."

"Fine. What do you want?"

"You know what I want."

"Goldman and Timmins?"

"Just so. Goldman is about to start an assignment protecting a racehorse entered in the Cheltenham Gold Cup."

"You're kidding me." She smirked at the thought of

Goldman protecting anything, when he could scarcely look after himself.

"No, I arranged it myself, through a contact."

"What's the horse called?"

"Summer Lightning."

"So, who is Edna Timmins?"

"One thing at a time. First, Goldman, then we will talk of Timmins."

"Can you provide me with weapons and support?"

He passed her a business card. "This man will be your contact. He'll provide you with guns, ammunition, anything you may need. I have arranged a meeting for Friday at 11am. Be there."

"Is there anything else?"

"You don't need me to tell you your flat has police forensics crawling all over it."

"No."

"There's a room available for you on the first floor of this building, until you make other arrangements. Don't forget, you will be under surveillance until the assignment is complete."

She nodded. She couldn't trust herself to speak to Lau. She would bide her time.

Part Twenty-Nine

The sun blazed down on the house and grounds of Baddeley Manor. Hymie and Mike had told the taxi driver to set them down at the entrance to the drive and were now regretting it. The drive seemed to stretch out forever.

"How long does a drive need to be?" queried Hymie.

"Well, it's to keep the riff-raff out."

"But we're here anyway," smirked Hymie.

"Or maybe it's to deter burglars?"

"Only poor burglars who can't afford cars. They couldn't get away very fast down *this* drive, could they? The police would be there to meet them at the gate."

"So maybe having a long drive is a good idea after all," said Mike.

"Tell that to my legs, they're almost dropping off with tiredness. I could swing for that Scarlatti woman. Destroyed my car, tried to kill me…and now leaves us to the mercy of public transport to get to the middle of nowhere." Hymie was nothing if not bitter and resentful. "Three trains, four buses, two taxis and now Shanks's pony."

"There goes today's wages!" said Mike, wishing he'd left the negotiations to Hymie so that at least he'd have someone else to blame.

"It's about time we got some new wheels," said Hymie.

"That's about all you can afford, mate, the wheels."

"Ho, ho. Look, I know I'll never replace the Zebaguchi, but all this exercise is killing me. What's worse is that Scarlatti's on the loose again. Did you hear it on the radio?"

"I was with you when you heard about it, you plonker," said Mike. "Someone hijacked the van they were taking her to prison in. Makes you glad you're out of London, eh?"

"If you say so. Personally, all this fresh air's getting on my nerves."

They finally reached journey's end and passing through an elaborate wooden porch, Mike pulled on an antique metal door-ringer, in the shape of the devil's head.

For what seemed like an eternity nothing happened and then, when they'd almost given up hope, the door creaked open and an even creakier exhibit in butlers clothing greeted them. Jervis had been there so long he was listed in the house inventory; butler, one, clapped-out. He displayed all the usual attributes of his anachronistic class; rotundity, sleekness, discretion and dignity, but in his case all of these things were overshadowed by a forgetfulness bordering on the extreme.

"Good afternoon, deliveries are round the back of the house," said Jervis, in the voice he reserved for tradesmen.

"We're Goldman and Murphy. We have an appointment with the lady of the house."

He looked dubiously at them in a way suggesting that they fell some way short of the guests he was used to and then left to obtain further information.

"I'll be back shortly," he said, closing the door behind him.

After another interminable wait Hymie looked at his watch.

"Maybe he's died on us," quipped Mike.

"Don't make jokes like that, you may be right."

Mike rang the bell again.

Nothing happened.

He rang it again, repeatedly and after a while the doddery old butler re-appeared, like some decrepit genie being summoned from his lamp.

"Yes, can I help you?" asked Jervis, as though meeting them for the first time.

"We're here to see Lady Hunting-Baddeley. You were going to check whether we were expected," said Hymie.

"I was?"

"You were," Mike assured him.

"And your names are?" asked Jervis, scarcely crediting what they were saying.

"Goldman and Murphy!" they cried, simultaneously.

"Perhaps we could wait *inside* this time, in case you forget us again." added Mike.

"Well, I'm sure I would have remembered you two," said Jervis, implying that they were somehow sub-human. He reluctantly let them in.

"Just a moment please." He shuffled off into the house again, leaving the two of them to wait indoors for a change.

They sat on two carved-backed wooden chairs and gazed around the reception hall, drinking in the ambience from centuries of occupation. On every side hung ancient oil paintings in heavy gilt frames. Here an eighteenth-century long-case clock, there an assemblage of antique porcelain. Mike started to pace up and down, stopping in front of a family portrait to stare intently at the signature in the corner.

"It's a Bugrot," he declared, after much deliberation.

"I thought Bugrot did racing cars, not paintings."

"That was Bugatti, you wally!" said Mike, "don't you know anything?"

"Well, I've never heard of an artist called Bugrot anyway. Bugrot's what you get on your roses."

"You're having me on. When were you ever in a garden, except by accident?"

"Okay, have it your way, Mike, I'm no Alan Titmarsh."

"Too true, and the painting's by Bugrot just the same. Come and have a look for yourself." They walked up to examine the heavy gilt frame.

"Must be Dutch school," speculated Hymie.

"With a name like Bugrot? Danish, surely."

"Hello, Mr Goldman, Mr Murphy." It was Lucinda Hunting-Baddeley.

"I'm sorry to have kept you. Jervis came into the drawing room ten minutes ago, but it took him that long to remember what he came to tell me. Poor old chap. He's getting too old for the job really, but they don't make butlers like him any more. It would break his heart if I suggested he retired."

"Think nothing of it madam, we were just admiring your Bugrot," said Mike, determined to get to the bottom of the artist's signature.

"Oh, the *Burgôt*? Yes, it's not a bad daub, don't you think? He's rather a promising French portraitist. It's a particular favourite of mine as it's the only one I have of the entire family." She passed over Mike's embarrassment effortlessly.

"I expect you'll want to see your charge now, won't you?" she asked.

"Charge? I thought you were paying us," said Mike.

"Summer Lightning, Mr Murphy."

"Of course," said Hymie, gesturing for Mike to shut up.

They crossed the courtyard, entered the stable-block and were soon gazing intently into the large brown eyes of the most impressive racehorse either of them had ever set eyes on. It was also the *only* racehorse either of them had ever set eyes on, at least close up.

The horse looked distinctly unimpressed, as though he were being asked to shake hands with the village idiot and his less intelligent brother.

"Lightning, these are Mr Goldman and Mr Murphy. They've come to look after you for a few days," said the lady of the manor.

If he could have put his head in his hands, Lightning would have done so. He settled for shaking his head and showing his teeth.

"Well, I'll leave you to get acquainted. I'll send the head stable boy over to explain what's what." So saying, their hostess headed back to the house, leaving the pair wondering what they'd let themselves in for.

Hymie reached out to pat the horse's head and received a playful nip for his trouble.

"There, there boy!" he said.

"I think he likes you," said Mike.

"I'd hate to see what he does to you if he doesn't like you."

"Hello guys, I'm Jack the head stable-boy. I see you're getting to know Lightning. He's a great horse. He's all heart. Strong and fast too. We're expecting great things of him. Which one of you is Goldman, and which one's Murphy?"

"I'm Hymie Goldman," said Hymie, holding out his hand in greeting.

"And I'm Mike Murphy."

"Welcome to the Hunting-Baddeley Yard, guys. I gather you're with us until the Gold Cup. In charge of security, so I hear."

"Yes, that's right, Jack." said Hymie.

"Mrs H-B tells me you know all about horses," he added.

"Sure, I used to ride on the farm at home," said Hymie, looking daggers at Mike.

"Oh, right, you're from farming stock too. So am I; my family own estates in Berkshire, how about yours?"

"Oh, just a caravan at Bognor."

He'd have to tell bigger lies, thought Hymie, as the words left his mouth. That was where real success lay. As it was, he just looked like a complete plonker.

"Well, you won't need me to tell you much I don't suppose. All the grooming, feeding and exercising will be taken care of by the regular team. You guys just get to move into the stables for round the clock surveillance at other times, right?"

"Right," they said. 'Shit,' they thought.

"Oh I was forgetting, we're a man down. Ted Farrell broke his foot the other day, and we need a driver to get Lightning over to his training camp for 7 am tomorrow. Think you can handle it? We'll help you load him into his box, of course. It's just over there at the back of the stables. I presume you're licensed to drive a truck?" asked Jack.

"Oh, ah, yes" said Hymie. 'Bigger lies' he thought.

Mike looked a little doubtful.

"Great. Here's a map to the training ground. Don't forget, 40 mph max. Got it?"

"Of course, Jack, what do you take us for?" said Hymie.

"Sure, I was forgetting. See you later, guys."

The rest of the day passed slowly and uneventfully. As they were on duty they had their meals delivered on a tray; bacon, egg, beans and chips, which suited them admirably. Lightning soon got used to them and settled down for his shut-eye at around 9pm. At 11pm he started snoring and continued through much of the night.

Hymie and Mike kept watch in shifts until the early hours.

Mike seemed to be afflicted by hayfever, which kept him awake sneezing for much of the night, while Hymie spent his waking moments in trying to develop a Business Plan for Goldman Confidential. The pile of waste-paper accumulating on the stable floor grew to impressive proportions as he discarded one draft after another. Nevertheless, he stuck at it, feeling sure that Ceefer Capital wouldn't be too impressed if he couldn't even tell them where he thought the business was going.

He thought about calling Sarah Chandar, but wasn't sure what to say and assumed she'd take his call as a sign of weakness in any negotiations.

Morning broke over the stable-yard. It was cold with a scattered frost on the fields. The two horse-detectives awoke to their alarm clock at 6am, grumbling.

The ghostly form of Jervis the butler appeared before them bearing a tray.

"Can I offer you breakfast, gentlemen?"

"Nothing could be better, Jervis. Thank you," said Hymie.

He laid the tray on the floor and seemed to be waiting for something.

"Care to join us, Jervis?" asked Mike.

"Oh no, sir, I've already eaten. I was wondering if I could assist you. Perhaps I could load Lightning into his box for you?"

"Well, it's very kind of you, but Jack the lad said he'd come and give us a hand."

"Ah, I thought so, sir."

"Sorry Jervis? What do you mean?"

"Well, he has a habit of playing practical jokes. Far be it from me to criticise, but if I were you I'd make alternative arrangements. I myself know all there is to know about horseboxes and would be delighted to assist you."

"Thanks for the tip off, Jervis. We'd be only too happy to take you up on your offer."

The butler shuffled off with Lightning in tow, heading to the end of the stable block. Once outside he loaded a different horse with similar markings into the horsebox, attached the box to the tow-bar at the back of the truck and, lifting the truck's bonnet, cut through the brake cable. He then loaded Lightning into the back of a transporter and quietly drove off in it.

Mike and Hymie demolished their breakfast, oblivious to it all and then went over to the far end of the stable block to join their benefactor.

"He's gone," said Mike, surprised.

"Strange," said Hymie, uneasily.

"Well, the horse is in the box and the keys are in the ignition," said Mike. "We've got the map from yesterday, so it looks like it's over to us now. You're driving I expect?"

"No, I thought you'd like to," said Hymie. "It's the junior partner's privilege."

"I don't have a truck licence," said Mike.

"Neither do I," admitted Hymie.

"So when you said…"

"I lied, but how hard can it be? We can't go above 40 mph anyway."

"On your head be it."

"You'll be fine. I have faith in you."

Mike drove. He crunched through the gears all down the driveway until they got out onto the open road and then he gradually adjusted to this new motoring experience. The roads were mainly empty and the weather was glorious.

"Don't forget, keep to forty."

"This pile of junk won't do above thirty."

Hymie switched on the radio. Pavarotti was just reaching high C. "Nessun Dorma, would you credit it?!" cried Hymie, turning it off.

"Rain's forecast for later," said Mike. "You wouldn't think it, to look at that sunshine."

"It's always the same; sunshine one minute, rain the next. It's a bit like life; one minute you have a gorgeous blonde client and a thousand quid in your pocket, the next everyone's dropping like flies and the police think you're responsible. I wonder what happened to the golden hamster?"

"I thought you'd dropped the case after Lucy Scarlatti died."

"Well, yes…and no. I mean, it just seems completely wrong that her sister can get away with murder and theft. I'm sure she's got it."

"I'd steer clear if I were you. There's no percentage in it. If you find the thing, it won't bring your client back and Steffie's hardly gonna give it back."

"Did I tell you about the insurance reward, Mike?"

"What makes you think there is one?"

"Stands to reason. Someone owns the statuette and you wouldn't own something that valuable without either insuring it for megabucks or offering a substantial reward for its return." He could be remarkably sensible when he tried.

"You may be right," agreed Mike.

"I'm sure of it. If we can find Steffie Scarlatti, the hamster won't be far behind."

"Just be careful though, she leaves a trail of death in her wake, that one."

"Oh, I'll be careful alright. Now then, according to these directions it's left just here."

Mike turned left. The road was a steep one. It seemed to fall away on an incline of one in ten. At first it was fun to be plunging downhill at forty miles per hour, but when they hit fifty, sixty and seventy and Mike's foot hammered the brake pedal to no avail, they changed their tune.

"Aaaaaaaahhhhh! Try the handbrake!" cried Hymie.

"What do you think this is?!" said Mike, handing him a piece of rusty metal.

The countryside sped past in a blur of green fields, blue skies and brown trousers. Time momentarily stood still, before speeding up exponentially.

"KERRRASSHHH!"

After the dust had settled, they found themselves leaning to starboard at an angle of 45 degrees. Their mangled horse transporter was wedged firmly in a ditch. Hymie was troubled by a persistent ringing in his ears.

"Can you hear that noise, Mike?"

"It's your mobile, you wally!"

"Hi there, Jim Diamond of The Investigator magazine here. Is that Hymie Goldman?"

"Hi Jim, it's a bad time, I'm afraid, I've just been involved in an accident."

"I can't hear Lightning! It's all gone quiet," said Mike anxiously.

"Sorry to hear that, Hymie. I just wanted to tell you

you've been nominated for an award in The Investigator's Annual Awards ceremony."

"An award? Thanks, but what's it for?" queried Hymie, somewhat distractedly.

"Best use of technology, for your website, of course."

"Hold on a minute, Jim, have you been speaking to a lady called Sarah Chandar?"

"Yes, she nominated you. But I did have a look myself, it's a great site. The interactive clue identification game is a real winner."

Mike passed his finger in melodramatic fashion across his neck as though cutting his own throat, to get Hymie to end the call. Miraculously he took the hint.

"Thanks again, Jim. No offence but I have to dash, I've got a missing racehorse to find. I don't have access to the web just now anyway." He pressed the cancel button on his mobile and left Diamond wondering how a nominee for best use of technology couldn't access his *own* website.

"You're right, Mike, we need to stick to the job in hand. We're lucky to be alive after that crash. Why did it happen?"

"I put my foot to the floor and there weren't any brakes, you plonker! Did you think I forgot to try them?"

"No, but why weren't there any brakes?"

"No idea. Look, let's get out of here before the petrol tank goes up. While we're at it, let's see if we still have a champion racehorse in the back of the transporter."

They struggled to free themselves from their seatbelts. Hanging in mid air didn't help. Mike managed to turn himself around to face the door, then kicked out the battered panel until it finally burst open. He forced himself through the gap, jumped down and staggered around to the front of the vehicle to help free Hymie through the broken windscreen. They both looked the worse for wear, but mercifully their injuries were only superficial.

"Have a look in the horsebox," said Hymie.

"Couldn't you? You're the senior partner after all. I seem to get all the shitty jobs."

"I don't like to. I'm a bit squeamish," confessed Hymie.

"Oh and I love looking at squished racehorses, I suppose?"

"I'll do it next time."

"If Lightning's dead or missing, there won't *be* a next time," said Mike.

"All the more reason to go now," said Hymie, gutless but persistent.

He should have known he wouldn't get any sense out of Goldman. The big man walked over to the horse-box and peered inside. It was empty. "No sign of a horse."

"You're kidding," said Hymie.

"Take a look for yourself. There's a pile of manure though."

"You're sure?"

"Positive," confirmed Mike.

"So, let's get this straight. We've *lost* the horse. We've *wrecked* the transporter and we're stranded in the middle of nowhere. I can feel a new identity coming on!"

"Ok, so we lost the horse, but it was hardly our fault. That horse-transporter was a complete deathtrap. Someone must have cut the brakes."

"Yes, but they hired us to prevent all this, Mike. If someone cut the brakes we should have seen it coming and stopped it. We just have to face it, we've failed!"

"No-one said this job was going to be a walk in the park. Some serious villains are planning to stop Lightning from racing, but we're not beaten yet. Let's show them we mean business. First, we've got to find Lightning before someone else does."

"You never said a truer word," agreed Hymie, the light of battle gradually returning to his eyes. "So, what's your plan?"

"Plan? That's your department, mate. We could walk around calling out his name?"

"A bit lame, isn't it?"

"Or we could see if anyone had returned a racehorse to lost property?"

"Lamer still," added Hymie. "Ok, maybe calling out his name's not so bad after all."

"Or we could call the police?" said Mike.

"The trouble is, we don't own the horse so we'd have a job to explain what we were doing looking for it, and if we told them, the first thing they'd do would be to call Lady Hunting-Baddeley, and then we'd be sunk; we could wave goodbye to our fee for starters. If we can find Lightning we may be able to retrieve the situation. Besides, how would you describe the horse? Big, with brown eyes?"

"Does he have brown eyes?" asked Mike.

"Call yourself a detective?"

"Not often," he conceded.

"I'm not surprised, but the fact remains that it's a rotten idea. Got any other winners?"

"We could hire some real detectives to find him?"

"*Real* detectives?! *We're* real detectives! Can you imagine explaining to them why we need their help? We'd be a laughing stock. We have to find the horse ourselves."

"Lightning, Lightning! Here boy!" shouted Mike.

"I admire your willingness to make a complete fool of yourself in a crisis," said Hymie, "but this is a racehorse, he could be halfway across the country by now. We'll never find him on foot."

"That's where you're wrong mate," said Mike. "Don't you know anything about horse psychology? Given the choice between running half way across the country and having a good nosh-up, he'll take the nosh-up every time."

"Thank you, James Herriot. That's your expert opinion is it?"

"Gotta be worth a try."

They ambled along the lane, Mike checking the left-hand side of the road and Hymie the right. "Lightning! Lightning!" they chorused, like a couple of drunks looking for their car keys. They wandered the length and breadth of the area until they arrived at the nearby village of Southam, where they accosted a succession of passers-by with one recurrent question:

"Excuse me sir/madam/sonny, have you seen my racehorse?"

"No, what's he look like?" was the usual response.

They passed pretty stone cottages, a pub; which took some doing, and a small ruined-castle, before finally arriving at an old red phone-box outside the church of St. Swithin's. They'd all but given up hope when a large chestnut gelding materialised, as if by magic, in the front garden of a nearby cottage.

"Lightning. Here, boy!" said Mike.

A little girl with pigtails appeared from the far side of the horse as it stooped down to nibble on a geranium. "Do you like my horse, mister?"

"He's a very fine horse, young lady, how clever of you to find him," said Hymie.

"You're sure it's him?" queried Mike.

"Of course," hissed Hymie.

They led the racehorse back down the lane with the little girl calling after them, "Come back Sugar-lump, you're a bad horsey, leaving me on my own. Come back!"

The relief was incredible. They could hold their heads up high again. Yes, they may have lost a horse-transporter, but they had foiled the horse-nappers and saved Summer Lightning from a terrible fate. He would race at Cheltenham after all.

Part Thirty

All great detectives had to brief their staff, and Inspector Ray Decca was no exception. "I'll keep it short ladies and gents..."

It would certainly be that; he had practically nothing new to say.

"As the Bard said, an honest tale speeds best, being plainly told."

A chorus of disapproval swept through the briefing room.

"Have you noticed, he always quotes Shakespeare when he's got nothing to go on," observed Sergeant Shorthouse. "It's a diversionary tactic."

"That'll do. Cast your minds back to last Tuesday, March 3rd at four fifteen in the afternoon. A prison van containing Steffanie Scarlatti was on its way to Holloway. En route it was hijacked. It was a professional job, smoke grenades, metal-cutters; the works. They didn't know what hit them. Ask Reidy. She escaped from the van and disappeared in this area, here on the map in quadrangle A."

He pointed with an old PT drill stick at an enlarged street map he'd blu-tacked to the wall, to emphasise the point.

"We've divided the area into six zones, denoted by letters Alpha through Foxtrot."

"Any particular reason, Chief?"

"I'm coming to that, Terse. We had forensics all over the crime scene, we conducted a thorough door to door search of the area, we brought in every grass and petty thief for miles around and gave them the third degree, but no-one was talking. They were all scared. We have about as much to go on as a holidaymaker on a French campsite."

"Nicely put, Chief. Except, where's Moffat Road?"

"Moffat Road? Why this strange babbling about Moffat Road, Terse?"

"It's on your map, as bold as brass, but I've never seen it and I grew up around there."

The great man screwed up his eyes and scratched his head. Where *was* Moffat Road? It wasn't anywhere he knew. Suddenly the explanation dawned on him.

"Ahem, well spotted, Terse. I was waiting to see who'd spot it first. This, of course, is a street plan of Dumfries, left over from that strategic policing lecture Jock McTavish gave last week. The moral is…always expect the unexpected," said Decca.

Okay, we haven't found Steffanie Scarlatti yet," he resumed, "but we're going to. She's not the type to leave her home territory in a hurry so we're going to keep on doing what we've been doing and wait for her to make a mistake. Does anybody have any suggestions? Henderson?"

"We could follow-up the nightclub connection, sir. Scarlatti is an active clubber."

"Good. Of course, we've checked out the club where she used to gamble; the Rainbow Rooms, but as you say, she was a keen club-goer and there must be hundreds… maybe thousands of private members clubs around. Terse, you and Henderson get on to the cab firms in the area; see if any of them remember dropping off a woman of her description at a club in the last week or two. Circulate the photo-fit. She's an attractive woman, surely someone must remember her."

"Are you an admirer, Chief?" asked Terse with a grin.

"Certainly not, Terse."

"We also know the Rainbow Rooms are a front for the Triads, sir, perhaps she has links with them?"

"Yes, Jervis, good point. We don't know too much about her involvement with the Triads, but it's certainly an area to explore. Perhaps she knew something they wanted to keep under wraps and they kidnapped her. She may even be working for them. There are numerous possibilities."

"If you're right, Chief, I don't envy them!" said PC Jervis.

"Too true. Reidy's still in intensive care. Don't be fooled by her glamour-model looks, she's poisonous. If you do come up against her, don't take any chances; let her have it with your truncheon."

"You do fancy her, Chief!"

"Shut up, Terse!"

"What about Interpol?"

"Not now, Jackson."

"I mean, wouldn't they have a file on her, sir?"

"Good thinking, but I doubt she's known outside the UK. Follow it up anyway."

"Will there be another press conference today?" asked Jervis.

"Jack Daniels is handling it folks, but heaven knows what he's going to say."

"Sir, Chief Superintendent Morrison wants to see you in his office."

"Thanks, Suzy. Sergeant Terse will conclude this briefing. The real street plans must be in my office, Terse. Give me an update later, alright?"

"Certainly, Chief."

"Ah Ray, come in, sit down. I've been meaning to have a word with you. I'm concerned at the lack of progress in the Scarlatti case. It's bad for morale having a murderer loose on the streets. Where in God's name is she? It's not as if she's invisible and yet she seems to have disappeared off the face of the planet. Do you think she's left the country or is someone harbouring her? More to the point, what are you *doing* about it?"

"Everything possible, sir. I've just given a team briefing on it. We've tried door to door searches, forensics and every grass and petty crook for miles around. No-one knows anything. We're still pursuing a few leads though."

"What leads?" asked Chief Superintendent Morrison, irritably. If his golf handicap began to slide it would take months to recover and he held Inspector Decca personally responsible.

"We know she's a keen clubber," said Decca.

"Yes, she's very violent," agreed Morrison.

"So we're checking out all the clubs and taxi firms in the area."

"Ah, yes."

"We're also exploring possible links with the Triads, sir." He wondered if Morrison even knew what a Triad was.

"That's all very well, Decca, but we need results man, *results*, not leads. Have you spoken to Scotland Yard and the Drug Squad lately? Or Interpol, come to that?"

"We're working on it, sir." He knew it sounded lame, but it was the best he could do.

"What were you saying about the Triads?" asked Morrison.

"Scarlatti used to work at the Rainbow Rooms casino, a well known haunt of the Chinese gambling fraternity. The croupier, Tony Lee was found dead not half a mile from there and the victim of that other gangland killing, Tony Martino, had rumoured links with the Triads."

"Sounds like they've got it in for people called Tony. Glad your name's Ray, eh?"

How could an idiot be a chief superintendent? wondered Decca.

"Lee was also a known associate of Scarlatti's," added the inspector.

"I see. Murky waters eh, Ray?"

"Word on the street is that the Rainbow Rooms is a front for all kinds of illegal activity; drug pushing, pornography and illegal firearms."

"Then why the blazes haven't you shut it down? You could have suspended their gaming licence or kept raiding the place until no-one went near it. Hit them where it hurts and they'll soon move on."

"Insufficient evidence, sir. It's the old, old story; the Drug Squad's after Mr Big, but all they can do is collar the couriers, so they drag a few of them into court and nothing changes. They keep trying to get a man on the inside, but can't pull it off.

Martino or Lee could've been undercover for all we know, they just don't keep us properly informed," said Decca.

"Which Triad are we dealing with, do we know?" asked Morrison.

"Not for sure, sir. We think there are at least a dozen operating in the UK. They stick to their own territories. There are three in Liverpool and Greater Manchester, two in Glasgow and maybe six in London."

"That's only eleven."

"There's one in Gloucestershire, centred on Cheltenham, sir."

"Is nothing sacred!" cried Morrison, who had family there.

"Seemingly not, sir."

"How much information do we have on their activities?"

"Not enough. So far there's been a real lack of the political will to do something about it. We need to set up the kind of organised crime task forces they have in Hong Kong and the States."

"Have you made any approaches in the right quarter, Ray?"

"I've spoken to the Director of Operations of the OCTB in Hong Kong, a guy called Eddie Hu."

"Who?"

"Yes Sir, Eddie Hu."

"You're kidding, right?"

"No Sir, I'm Decca, Wright transferred to Traffic last month."

"Get out of here, Decca, and for heaven's sake, we need results, not excuses."

Part Thirty-One

They made a pathetic sight; two lumbering, rain-sodden deadbeats, being led down the drive of Baddeley Manor by a horse.

Jervis smirked from an upstairs window, and awaited their arrival with anticipatory glee. The front doorbell rang in the distance, but he carried on adjusting the sights on his rifle, which was disguised as a telescopic umbrella. He wasn't about to answer any more doors for those two low comedians. He unscrewed the silencer unit and slid it back into its casing in the handle. It was almost time for the dénouement of this sorry little saga and then his mission would be complete.

He put the umbrella under his arm and headed for the back staircase, which led to the stable block.

Lucinda Hunting-Baddeley had been planning the weekend menus with Cook when the doorbell rang for the first time, but having now finished and with no sign of Jervis, she reluctantly opened the front door herself.

"Mr Goldman! Mr Murphy! What are you doing with this horse?"

They were too demoralised to notice what she was saying.

"The truck broke down on the way to the training camp!" moaned Hymie.

"But where's Lightning?"

"Someone cut the brakes! We were nearly killed!" cried Mike.

"What have you done with my racehorse?!"

"This is it. Don't you even recognize your own horse?"

"Lightning has a white flash on his left fetlock, this animal has one on his right fetlock. Surely you must have noticed?"

"This is the horse your butler loaded into the box. I don't know what the world's coming to if you can't trust your own butler," said Hymie.

"Whether he did or not is neither here nor there. This creature isn't Lightning. Where's Lightning?!" She was becoming hysterical.

Hymie gaped at her. "When did you last see him?"

"Yesterday. What have you done with my racehorse, you blithering idiot?!"

"You said that already. Have you tried the stables? Maybe he never left this morning? Maybe he's a homing racehorse?" suggested Hymie. Mike stayed silent, exercising his right not to incriminate himself.

"I'll ignore your impertinence, but you'd better be right. If he isn't in the stables it will be a dark day for you, I assure you. Let's go and see, shall we." It was neither a suggestion, nor a request, but a command. You had to admire her in full flow, thought Hymie, wishing it was with someone else. They filed out to the stable block.

"Jack! Jack!" she cried.

"Yes ma'am?"

"Is Lightning in his stall?"

"No ma'am, I haven't seen him since last night. I assumed he was at his training camp. These gents were taking him."

"That's all I wanted to know. Phone the police, Lightning has been kidnapped!"

"Kidnapped? But…" He seemed genuinely shocked, while Hymie was beginning to suspect everyone.

"Let's just hope it's nothing worse than that," concluded her ladyship.

"Hey, what about my fee?" asked Hymie, trying to keep a grip on what *really* mattered.

"*Our* fee!" cried Mike.

"Jack, show these two prize idiots to the dining room until the police get here. As for your fee, you can whistle for it! I hope you have a good insurance policy, gentlemen, because you're going to need it."

Hymie had had enough.

"Sue me! I'm sure we have an equally strong case against you, Mrs Snotty. That truck was a deathtrap. You could find yourself on a charge of attempted murder, or at least manslaughter."

"I'll give you manslaughter, you pathetic little man!" snapped Lucinda Hunting-Baddeley.

"Quick, Mike, run for it!"

They turned tail and fled. It wasn't so much the thought of their aggrieved client as the prospect of being questioned by the police again that worried them. Nothing seemed to make any sense out in the wilderness of the countryside, they needed to get back to North London.

Part Thirty-Two

Nowhere on earth looks more out of sorts or more sorry for itself than a second rate nightclub during the day. This was particularly true of Leptospirosis. What passed for street credibility in the dark was revealed as squalor by the sun's merciless rays.

Sergeant Terse didn't register the exterior décor; he was no arty-farty decorator, he had a proper job to do. No-one could accuse him of beating about the bush, he just swaggered up to the front door and pummelled it with a ham-like fist.

His junior colleague, Potter, on the other hand, saw himself as a frustrated thespian in policeman's clothing. He preferred to stand a little downstage of the action, particularly when it became violent. In Terse's book he was about as much use as a chocolate teapot. To Terse the assignment was one of a) getting into the club and b) finding out if the scum who ran the place knew where that slapper, Scarlatti was. Modern policing had passed him by. In fact, it had given him a wide berth, not wishing to get its head kicked in.

"Come on, Pansy, let's get this show on the road."

"After you, Sarge. How shall we play it?"

"That's your trouble, Potter, you're always playing at something. This is police work, not the Old Vic."

"But, what's my motivation?"

"What, the paycheck isn't enough for you? Okay, have it your way. I'm sure you've seen the repeats of *Starsky and Hutch* and all those other old American buddy-buddy shows, well this week we're playing 'good cop, bad cop'."

"One of us is a mean son-of-a-bitch and the other one's as nice as pie?"

"Yeah, that's the general idea, Potter."

"Which is which, Sarge?"

"Well, I know you like a challenge, so you can be the bad cop. Ok with that?"

Potter looked hesitant.

"Got it, Sarge. I'm the bad guy, you're the good guy."

"Exactly."

Potter paused to collect his thoughts, then charged at the door to resume the battering Terse had already started to inflict.

"Open up, scum! Open up!" cried Potter.

The door opened slowly and a massive bouncer poked his head around it. He combined the appearance of King Kong with all the charm of Attila the Hun.

"What kept you, you great spawny-eyed wazzock?! Get the manager, and be quick about it!" added Potter.

He flashed his police badge at the human roadblock, lest the bouncer should think he was just looking for a fight. He was showing a game streak Terse wouldn't have given him credit for. Then it was Terse's turn.

"Excuse my colleague, sir; he's of an excitable

disposition. Could we just have a quiet word with the manager please? Tell him Sergeant Terse and PC Potter of the Metropolitan Constabulary would be grateful for his co-operation."

"Get lost, Filth!" said the bouncer.

"I don't think you heard the Sergeant properly, Fatso. Get the manager immediately or I'll kick you from here to Timbuktu!"

"Just try it, copper!"

"Please, gents, please. We're all reasonable men here. There's no need for any trouble. I'm sure we can sort this out without resorting to abusive language and violence," said Terse. Inspector Decca would have been proud of him.

"Which part of 'Get lost, Filth' didn't you understand?"

"Now, now sir, there's no need for that language." Terse was enjoying himself.

The bouncer looked at him as though he'd arrived from another planet. They were just two coppers; no iron bars, no baseball bats, no knives, he could take them any time he liked. Now for instance. He took a swipe at Potter.

Potter saw a hefty fist approaching at around twenty miles per hour and started to duck. His instincts were good, but his response time wasn't fast enough and he caught the tail end of it on the side of his head. He spun around and fell to the ground, groaning.

Terse had had enough of play acting. He stomped on the partly open door and it crunched onto the bouncer's knee, bringing him down to Terse's level. Then he followed through with an uppercut to the chin.

Normally that would have been enough, but Fat Larry

was made of sterner stuff. Grimacing through the pain he managed to land a couple of retaliatory blows.

OOF! OOF!!

"I think you may regret that, sir" said Terse, through clenched teeth.

He pulled back his truncheon and smacked the bouncer smartly twice across the head.

THWACK! THWACK!!

The sound reverberated like an ancient tree being felled in the primaeval forest and the lumbering doorman went down like a detonated chimney stack.

Terse stepped over him and walked into the club, past reception, past the cloakrooms, across the dance floor and up to the door marked 'Strictly Private'. He opened the door and walked in.

"Is the manager in?" he asked the little old lady behind the desk.

Mrs Timmins considered him briefly for a minute.

"No, he's out," she said. She stood up and emptied the wastepaper basket into a black bag. "I'm the cleaning lady. There's no-one else here, but didn't the doorman tell you that?"

"He had other things on his mind," he said.

"Can I take a message?"

"Just tell him Sergeant Terse was looking for him."

"Was there anything else?"

"If he doesn't call me back today I may have to pay him another visit when the club's open. Oh and you'd better phone for an ambulance, there's an injured policeman outside. These young coppers are very accident prone."

She lifted the phone and called for an ambulance. There was more to him than she'd thought. He may be predictable, but he wasn't stupid. Anyone who could get the better of Fat Larry was no mug. She was going to need to up the stakes from now on.

Part Thirty-Three

Ray Decca was always in a bad mood after talking to Terse. He was simultaneously an incorrigible idiot and the best man he had on his team, and he could never decide which of the two had the upper hand.

Give him a routine enquiry and there would be bodies piled up everywhere in no time. The episode at Leptospirosis was just the latest in a long list. Yet give him something difficult to do and he would sail through it like a small child programming a DVD recorder. This eternal contrariness drove Decca mad.

The phone on his desk rang.

"Decca."

"Morrison here. Can you spare me a minute? I have Charlie Chow of the Organised Crime and Triad Bureau in my office. I want you to hear his briefing first hand."

"Ordinarily, sir, I'd be delighted, but I've an important domestic matter to sort out first."

"Domestic matter? Poppycock! This is vital."

It wasn't going to be easy. "To be frank, sir, it's Sheila."

"Sheila?"

"My wife, Sir," explained Decca.

"Ah, yes."

"We've been going through a rough patch lately, what with all the overtime on the Scarlatti case. We've got an appointment at the Marriage Guidance Council this afternoon and Sheila is counting on me being there."

"I sympathise, Decca, but this is a unique opportunity to hear from a specialist in Triad operations. I'll take a pretty dim view if you can't make it. I'm sure you can rearrange your appointment."

"I'll speak to Sheila, sir." As he said it he knew he wouldn't; that he couldn't face her. Whatever it said on his marriage certificate, he was married to the job.

Chow was a slightly built Hong Kong Chinese who smoked something that smelt like weed, but couldn't be. Perhaps it was some herbal remedy. No-one liked to ask.

Decca held out his hand. "Ray Decca, Inspector CID."

"Pleased to meet you, Inspector Cid, I'm Chow of the Ho Cee Tee Bee."

It sounded like gibberish until he realised that Chow was referring to the 'OCTB' or Organised Crime and Triad Bureau.

"It's Decca, not Cid, but you can call me Ray."

"Charlie was just telling me about the Ho Wop Do, Decca," said Morrison.

It sounded like a doo-wop number from the 1970's and reminded him of the last time he and Sheila had been dancing together.

"Ho Wop Do, sir?"

"That's the name of the Triad operating in the Cheltenham area."

"So our sources were correct," said Decca.

"Sauces inspector?" queried Chow, thinking of lunch.

"Oh, just some local reports, Charlie."

"Eddie Hu asked me to give you a bliefing Chief Sluperhintendent Mollison," said Chow.

"A bliefing?" queried Morrison.

"Solly Sir, I must get these dentures flixed," explained Charlie Chow.

"It seems that Cheltenham is in the control of the Ho Wop Do, Decca. They moved in and took over all the illegal rackets going, and started a few that weren't," said Morrison, gravely.

The diminutive Mr Chow fixed a piece of blu-tac to the back of his dental plate, re-inserted it and continued:

"That's better. The Ho Wop Do or 'Hodo' was set up in Hong Kong by a mysterious figure called Leslie Chang, commonly known as 'the Baron'. No-one knows what he looks like, although his code name in Hodo is King Prawn as he's very partial to seafood. When Hong Kong reverted to China in 1997 many of the Triads relocated to the USA; San Francisco, Los Angeles, even San Diego. The Baron went to Cheltenham."

"So why did this guy, Prawn Cracker, choose Cheltenham?" asked Morrison.

"He's a racing fanatic and big-time gambler. The other rackets; the drugs, the pornography and the rest were all run to secure funds for his gambling obsession.

He lives to gamble and his favourite race is the Cheltenham Gold Cup, so he set himself up there in a luxury Regency apartment."

"Tell us about their rackets. What are they up to?" asked Decca.

"What aren't they up to would be nearer the mark. I wouldn't put it past them to try to fix the Gold Cup itself."

"What, nobble the favourite?" said Morrison, aghast.

"Certainly. Then there are the betting scams, kidnapping, horse napping, catnapping and washing dirty money."

"You mean laundering?" asked Decca.

"Yes, that too. Not to mention dentures," continued Chow.

"Good God, man! They haven't infiltrated the British Dental Association! Is nothing sacred?" Chief Superintendent Morrison was shocked.

"Dentures is the codename for drugs, sir," explained Decca.

"Of course. I knew that, Ray, what do you take me for?"

"So this King Prawn character, what front is he using in Cheltenham? Presumably they also run legitimate businesses?" asked Decca.

"Oh, the usual stuff, Chinese restaurants, Chinese laundries, a hotel or two and the casino."

"And in Prestbury Park itself?" queried Morrison.

"You can be sure he has a team on the inside, especially on race days."

"Do you have any names?" asked Decca, who'd already forgotten his appointment with Sheila.

"No. It could be anyone; the bookies, the jellied-eel sellers, the catering franchise holders, the bar staff, any or all of them."

"Can you give us the names of any Ho Wop Do members operating in the area?"

"I'll gladly share my files on those suspected of being in the UK," said Charlie Chow.

"Thanks, Charlie. The immediate concern is the stable yards in the run up to this year's Gold Cup. Do the Triads run their own?"

"Yes, but the bigger challenge is what they get up to in other people's yards."

"So they bribe trainers and stable-hands?" asked Decca.

"They own them," said Chow.

It looks like my overtime costs will be going through the roof again this month, thought Decca.

Part Thirty-Four

"I'd like sausage, eggs, bacon, toms, mushies, beans and fried bread," said Mike.

"And to drink?" asked the waitress.

"Tea with four sugars."

"And you…?" She'd been about to call him 'sir' before she caught sight of Hymie and decided you could only stretch a point, or a word, so far.

"The same, but with black coffee."

The waitress turned back to the serving hatch.

"Two cardiac specials, Harry!"

They sat in the Black Kat after what felt like days of travel on public transport.

"It's good to be home," said Hymie. "I thought we'd better get some grub before returning to the office. I can't face ancient Rome on an empty stomach."

"Know whatcha mean, mate. Things haven't been too rosy lately. I don't half miss being a bouncer. I'd wake up around noon, have a full English breakfast and do nothing for the rest of the day, until it was time to check in at the club. Then I'd get a bit of exercise chucking people out and before you'd know it, it was time to go home.

Even the traffic was lighter on the graveyard shift."

A wistful look flitted across his granite features.

"Don't you start! People are forever prattling on about the good old days. Take the Sixties. They reckon if you can remember them, you weren't there, as if that sounds impressive. What a load of bollocks!"

"Oh I dunno, the music was better then."

"Are you kidding? It's collective brainwashing. Cliff Richard? The Stones? Absolute tosh. As for the Beach Boys, I'd rather have a heap of manure dumped on my swivel chair than listen to another track from 'Pet Sounds'. It's all dreadfully overrated and I really object to still having to listen to the geriatric perishers just because the only people who can afford to go to concerts are middle aged," said Hymie, incensed.

"Like yourself you mean? only with cash, obviously," said Mike, smiling.

"I was forgetting you're such a style guru, but I don't think any of the Sixties legends you've got it in for will lose sleep over it; they're laughing all the way to the bank."

"Even the food was worse then," said Hymie. "There was no choice of takeaways; it was chips or nothing, no Kentucky Fried Chicken, no McDonalds, and if you'd asked for a pizza, they'd have said 'piece of what, mate?' No, the Sixties should be sealed in a lead canister and buried with instructions not to be re-opened until after I'm dead."

"Well, I don't care what you say, I quite liked that Livin' Doll."

Hymie looked at him in disbelief.

"Yeah and people were friendlier and there weren't so many foreigners in London," continued Mike, getting into his stride.

"You're kidding, right? London's *always* been full of foreigners," said Hymie. "Who else do you think would be daft enough to live here? You're a foreigner yourself; I expect your granddad came over from Ireland to avoid the potato blight."

"What, in 1953? Just put a sock in it, mate, this is my hometown and I won't have you or anyone else badmouthing it."

"It's mine too, but it doesn't mean I have to like it. Maybe if we were rich we'd enjoy living here, but as it is, it's just a relentless battle against insurmountable odds. I'm gonna make my pile and get out. Somewhere warm and sunny with lots of scantily-clad women in skimpy grass skirts."

"Dream on."

The cardiac specials arrived and the conversation dried up while they replenished their cholesterol and carbohydrates.

"You can't beat a good fry up," said Hymie, tucking-in.

When they arrived back at 792A Finchley Road they were greeted by an eviction notice nailed to the door, while inside on the mat lay several days worth of final reminders, free newspapers and a postcard from Australia.

"He's only gone and flown out to Australia!" said Hymie.

"Who?"

"Benny Baker."

"Well, what's wrong with that? It looks like a great place on all the holiday programmes," said Mike. "Have you seen this card? 'Greetings from Bondi Beach'. Just look at that lady lifeguard; she can save me any day."

"What's wrong is, I gave him the idea."

"What, with all that pony about being his long lost brother, Sydney? I don't buy it. He was just looking for an excuse to take his favourite waitress on a long-haul jolly."

"Who's that then?"

"Susie Parker, of course; the blonde with the forty-inch bust."

"I can't say I've noticed," said Hymie.

"Really? There's more to life than pizza, you know."

"So what does he say on his card?"

"That he's having a marvellous time with Susie and that he may not come back."

Hymie sighed. There may be more to life than pizza, but nothing compared to one of Benny's pizzas.

Mike opened the front door and removed the eviction notice. "What are we going to do about this? We have seven days to find £10,000 plus interest. In fact, it's dated two days ago, so we actually only have five days."

"Seven days? Five days? They're both virtually impossible. We may as well just leave now," said Hymie. "I'll take the stress-relief lamp for old time's sake, but it's unlikely to be worth anything."

There was a knock at the door.

"Parcel for Mr Goldman. Sign here please." The courier seemed to be in a hurry.

Hymie took the box and signed for it.

"How would anyone know I was going to be here at this precise moment?" he wondered.

"What's wrong with a parcel once in a while…as long as it's not ticking."

"Funny you should mention it, but I *can* hear a faint ticking sound."

"Well, we don't have a clock," said Mike.

"And my watch is broken," added Hymie.

"Run!! Chuck it out of the window now!!"

Hymie ran to the nearest window, undid the catch and dropped the box. Before it hit the pavement it exploded.

"KABOOOOOM!!!"

The walls of the office shook. All the windows of 792A, 792B and 792C Finchley Road shattered in a tidal wave of glittering destruction.

Goldman and Murphy, who'd instinctively leapt face-down onto the cracked lino of their office, received only superficial injuries.

They shook off the glass fragments and made a hasty retreat down what was left of the fire escape ladder. Past experience had taught them that the only thing worse than a near death experience was talking about it to the police. Mike scanned the street for would-be attackers, but seeing only an old man walking away in the opposite direction, assumed they were probably safe.

"You seem to have a talent for upsetting the wrong people," said Mike.

"*Wrong* people?"

"People with guns, bombs and high explosives."

"Ah yes, those wrong people. Well, wrong they may be,

but how I could have upset them, I have no idea."

"Maybe just by being yourself. Perhaps you should try acting like someone else?"

They headed for the park to clear their heads and become less of a sitting target.

"I think I'm beginning to see the light at the end of the tunnel," said Hymie. "What links everything that's been happening is Steffanie Scarlatti. Bad things happen to people involved with her. She sent me out looking for the golden hamster and I nearly got killed, then we ran into that madman from the Triad, who was also looking for the hamster, and he nearly killed us and then we nearly got blown up in the office. Normal people don't try to kill me, so I can only assume that she's the root cause of it all."

"That's all very well, but where do we go from here? I was better off as a bouncer and you'd have been happier as an electrician, but I can't help feeling that they're not going to leave us in peace."

"There's only one place left to go," said Hymie.

"Where?"

"To Cheltenham for the Gold Cup. That's the only way we can find out what happened to Summer Lighting. At least then we can try to get some money out of Lucinda Hunting-Baddeley. Maybe if we're lucky we can find the hamster and claim the insurance."

"Well, I don't have any better ideas," said Mike, "but what are we doing for money?"

"Sell anything and everything you can get hold of. Sell what's left of ancient Rome, sell your granny if need be, but we must be at that race; it's the key to everything. Summer

Lightning was due to race in it, so whoever stole him is sure to be there. They'll be expecting us." Hymie had never been more certain of anything.

"Well, I fancy a day at the races," said Mike. "We may as well go out with a bang as with a whimper."

Part Thirty-Five

'

March 18, Cheltenham sunrise. Aching limbs, sleep-flecked eyes. Yawn and stretch the waiting away. Threat of something in the air. A horse race? Kidnap, murder, lies? Dewy down on the Cotswold Hills, shining with irreproachable propriety. Smug in the Promenade, Regency façades, bathed in splendour, drowned in charm. A minute in the lives of two; unknown, unsung, unsavoury pieces of trash floating on the ebb tide of the Gold Cup flow.

Brothers and sisters of Eire and Kentucky, bright-eyed with the liquor of the moment, smother the trackside. Breathe smoke through the Arkle-haze, fête the weather, chew over form, odds and days long gone. Names lost forever, in time's sweet oblivion, untarnished return for their day in the sun. Eternal like heroes that live but a moment, but for *this* moment, their glory is all.

Millions of minions parade through their paces, a sea of essential irrelevancies; of patrols and permits, bright stalls and hoardings, all have their place in the great scheme of things. Gates, railings, cars, buses, fumes burning, noise blaring, focus shifting chaos. All is excitement; an electric current flickering through air.

The clock ticks so hesitantly back in the weigh-in room, waiting to weigh in the balance all things. Voices buzz and soar, swooping like gulls wheeling. Eyes smiling, laugh-crying, weighing and watching. Versace, St. Laurent and John Galliano all drive by for a fashionable killing spree.

Arms waving, touts shouting, course checking, tic-tacking drag on through the morning interminably. Clamour and tension build, high-rise deception climbs, stand at the pinnacle expectantly. To be *here* is everything, to be here; everywhere, up in the Stand let the circus begin. At the summit commanding; last seconds poised hungrily, wearily waiting, anticipating, silent with awe.

And they're off! In the thundering brightness they take flight. Flash Red, Flash Gold, Green, Yellow and Blue like flies impatient to meet their end; to cover time and space in a single thought, fly across the heavy turf, light as a feather poised on a knife edge of terror.

In the throng, Goldman like a flea; hunter and hunted: empty, nothing, free. Itch for his anger. Mock at those last vestiges of pride. Plumbed from the last dregs of hope. Was there ever a moment he was really there? In spirit, when the horse was drugged. In body, when the trap sprung. In mind? Never; away with the faeries, he.

Fleeting, flame flickering scorch-earthed infinity draws to a close as the clock stumbles forth. Still and forever, the chastened but wondering, hushed in their breathlessness, crowd clamours on.

Mike shook his partner by the collar.

"Hymie, Hymie, what's the matter with you? Did you

back a loser or something? I warned you not to overdo the prescription drugs. Did we find any answers?"

"…not untwist these last strands of man in me or, most weary, cry I can no more. I can; can something, hope, wish day come, not choose not to be."

"I thought not."

The man-mountain carried his seemingly deranged partner out of Prestbury Park.

In the distance an ambulance ferried away two injured spectators with bullet wounds, while a police van removed one livid-looking ex-butler, Alfred Jervis. His telescopic umbrella had a forty-five degree bend in the barrel and he was cursing the arresting officers as they bundled him into the back of the van. Mrs Timmins would never trust him again; Goldman was still alive.

Decca scratched his head. His scalp was itching and he'd noticed that of late it only itched when the name Goldman was mentioned.

"So, let's get this straight, Reidy, there's been a shoot-out at Cheltenham Racecourse on the day of the Gold Cup?"

"That's right, sir."

"And two suspicious-looking men were observed leaving the grounds; a short, shabbily dressed, overweight individual and his outsized accomplice?"

"That's what I was told."

"Why would Goldman and Murphy be at the Gold Cup though?"

"We can't be sure it was them, sir."

"I'm sure, Reidy; as sure as ever I can be."

"Shall we bring them in for questioning?"

"No, that won't be necessary. Just because they were there, doesn't mean they were responsible for the shootings. You should read your Sun Tzu; know your enemy. Well, I know Goldman like the back of my hand, so I know he can barely tie his own shoelaces unaided, let alone shoot someone. Let's just sit back and watch it unfold. There's precious little left for him to do now," said Decca.

"I don't follow you, sir."

"Goldman's a dead man, Reidy; a walking, talking, eating, breathing dead man it's true, but a dead man nevertheless. His time, if he ever had one, is all but over. His business is a failure, half the criminal underworld wants to bury him and he doesn't even have an office to hide in any longer. The sad thing is, he still thinks he's on the side of the Angels; that he can keep ducking and diving, wheeling and dealing and come up smelling of roses. He still thinks of himself as a private detective!"

"I see," said Reidy, who didn't see at all.

"Get me a report on everything that happened at the Gold Cup today. Leave it in my in-tray. In the meantime, get me Hu."

"Who, sir?"

"Eddie."

"Eddie who?"

"Exactly."

"Well, sir, if you don't know, I'll be blowed if I do," said Reidy, confused.

"No, not 'who', 'Hu' from Hong Kong; the Chinese detective."

"I'm sorry, sir, I'm not long back from hospital. You'll have to give me his name again."

"Listen, Reidy, Hu's a Chinaman."

"Bruce Lee's the only one that springs to mind, sir."

Inspector Decca stared morosely into space, while his brain re-played the conversation he'd just had with his junior officer.

"Sod off, Reidy, go and do some work. Send Potter to see me will you."

Looking peeved and confused, Reidy left the office.

Part Thirty-Six

The ancient and inscrutable face of Master Lau appeared drawn and irritated. He hated playing draughts, especially to lose, but he had to be civil to the old bat, at least for now.

"Well played, Mrs Timmins, you're an excellent draughts player."

"All games are alike to me. I play to win or not at all. I gather the Gold Cup proved profitable?"

"Certainly, madam. We made a very satisfactory return on our investment."

"Very gratifying. Was it enough to settle your outstanding debt to the Baron?"

"Of course."

"I'm glad to hear it. Which brings me to the small matter of Hymie Goldman. I understand he's *still* alive. What went wrong this time?!"

"I'm afraid you must take responsibility for that particular oversight yourself."

"How so?"

"Your own agent 'queered our pitch.'"

"My agent?"

"Please, give me credit for some intelligence. Your agent, Alfred Jervis, or 'Harry the Hit' as he's known in Teddington, was arrested by the police after bungling the job. I had an agent at the trackside ready to kill Goldman."

"Who? Steffanie Scarlatti?"

"Madam, I can't be expected to disclose the identities of my agents. In your interests as well as my own. What you don't know can't harm to you."

"I know very well you were using Scarlatti on the job."

"As you wish. I have no desire to get into a dispute over who was responsible when I know the answer very well."

"You forced my hand by your incompetence!" snapped Mrs Timmins.

"You insult me. Would you like me to refund the money on the contract or complete it?" He didn't care anymore, he just wanted to be rid of her.

"I'll give you twenty-four hours. Kill Goldman or give me my money back. Of course, if you fail, your reputation will suffer."

"I think not. Perhaps before Cheltenham, but now you've taken ineffective action of your own, my reputation is safe enough. Are you sure you wouldn't prefer your money back? Goldman's life is such a small matter."

"Small matter?! The man's a curse. He must die, don't you understand?! If not for him, Tiddles would be alive today. I can't rest easy in my own mind until the world is rid of him!" She'd clearly lost the plot where Goldman was concerned.

Scarlatti would see to it. It just seemed a little pointless, not to mention beneath him, having a hopeless idiot put to death just to placate a vindictive old woman.

"When do I get the money for the drugs?" she asked.

"I'll send it over by courier tomorrow." He smiled incongruously.

"Be sure you do. I expect you'll also be able to give me an update on Goldman."

"Certainly. Goodbye, madam," said Lau, still smiling.

As he sat in his pink velour armchair later that evening, enjoying his cocoa over an excellent new game-show, "Loadsa-Lolly", he was disturbed by a sharp rapping on the window. It was strange, because he lived on the fourth floor.

"Who's there?"

Perhaps it was a pigeon? No, pigeons didn't knock. He lifted the sash window and peered out. It was starting to drizzle and clouds were gathering over the dark streets.

A bird which had been resting on the grimy ledge of a neighbouring building fluttered past, shattering his calm and causing him to straighten up abruptly. Suddenly, the feline fingers of a black-gloved hand closed tightly upon his throat and pulled his head down to the sill. In a flash she was upon him, springing through the open window into the room and kicking Lau to the ground.

He lurched across the room, still gasping for air from his recent partial asphyxiation, barely managing to compose himself in time to meet her next assault. She slid her hunting knife from its scabbard and lunged at his chest in a vicious swipe. As shocked as he was, he'd had a lifetime of martial arts experience. Sidestepping her attack, he followed through with a power-punch to the ribs. She was fast, but not *that* fast. He caught her on the third rib and she collided with the corner of the hardwood dining table, breaking one of its legs off as she fell.

Lau unsheathed a five-hundred year old samurai sword from pride of place on the wall above the mantelpiece and leapt forward to finish the job.

"This is to avenge Chiu Mann," he cried, lifting his sword to deliver the coup de grace.

Like Mann, he had written her off too soon. Rolling sideways out of his path she pulled a small Derringer pistol from the back of her left boot.

"It's time for you to pay, Lau. With your life," she sneered.

It was her turn to underestimate him; for he was not called *Master* Lau for nothing.

Twisting a small packet of crystals concealed in his sleeve he disappeared into a purple haze. The smoke billowed out, filling the room with an all-pervading fog.

Yet she was not about to be denied her revenge so easily. Raising the pistol to shoulder height, she blasted away at the space Lau had occupied.

The smoke cleared. Lau's cape seemed to be suspended in mid air before her, torn in several places by bullet holes, and wet with something which looked like blood. The cloak fell to the ground and Lau re-appeared in a new silk-trimmed gown, apparently uninjured. He struck her hard across the head with his wooden stick.

"OOF! AARGH!" she spluttered.

"Never forget I am *Master* Lau and you owe me a debt of honour."

"I owe you nothing, Lau, nothing."

"You're bound to me like a slave to its master. Until you've completed our bargain I own you, don't you understand?"

She hated to admit it, but she was scared of him. All that psychological claptrap was messing with her mind.

"You swore to kill Timmins and Goldman, as the price of your freedom and so you shall. And yet, Goldman means nothing to me. There's no honour in killing an idiot. I reprieve him and excuse you. Mrs Timmins is another matter. Please deliver this briefcase to her tomorrow, then I won't have to set eyes on the miserable old bag again."

"Why, what's in the case?"

"Only something I promised her. Complete your mission and you're free," he said.

Outside in a shop doorway stood Mike Murphy, muffled against the cold and rain in an army-surplus trench-coat. He'd been waiting for several hours already, but seemed unmoved by the weather and the monotony of his assignment.

Scarlatti appeared at the ground floor entrance of the building opposite his vantage point and he prepared to follow her. He crossed the street and carefully followed at a distance as she crossed the foyer. He watched her enter the lift and clocked the indicator as it moved to the first floor before stopping, then he raced up the back staircase to the first floor, just in time to see Scarlatti's back disappearing into one of the apartments. He knocked on the door.

She eyed it suspiciously. Who could know she was here? Was she being paranoid? Better safe than sorry.

"Come in," she said.

The door flew open to reveal Murphy, blotting out the light from the corridor.

"Hello Steffie."

"Murphy? What are you doing here?"

"I've come about the golden hamster."

"I don't know what you're talking about. Are you delusional?" Who did he think he was, this doorman?

It would be difficult to miss him from where she was standing. It would be difficult to miss a target that big, period.

He removed his old service revolver from his trench-coat pocket and pointed it at her.

"Don't start any funny business, I just want the hamster."

Did she play dumb, or come clean? If she came clean it would probably mean killing him, but he'd started it. There was nothing childish about her; at least not on the glossy, hard-boiled surface.

She opened the top drawer of a filing cabinet, removed a tatty plastic bag and took out the golden statuette he'd heard so much about.

"Is this what you wanted?"

"Yes, although I hadn't expected it to be so small."

"Small is beautiful, although I wouldn't expect you to understand. Of course, the rule only holds for objets d'art." She smiled at him.

He could feel all his distrust melting away, yet he knew

that letting down his guard could prove fatal. There were many men who could testify to that.

"Put it back in the bag and give it to me."

"I'm intrigued to know the basis of your claim, Murphy. Is it just by force of arms?"

"I'm Goldman's business partner and I'm recovering it for the rightful owner."

She laughed. "You and Goldman? That's a hoot."

It wasn't the reaction he'd been expecting, but it made it easier to dislike her. It also made him angry that what had begun as a source of pride should have degenerated into something farcical. He *was* a partner, and he was here because he knew Hymie wouldn't stand a chance; she'd fooled him into thinking she was a seventeen-year-old trainee; as soon as she stopped laughing at him, he'd be toast.

"Just do as I say."

"Or what, you're going to shoot me? I can't see it, Murphy; you may be a dab hand at beating up tough nuts outside a club, but you won't kill someone in cold blood."

"Try me," he said.

He wouldn't kill her, he knew that; but he was willing to shoot her, if it meant he could get out of there alive.

"Pass me the bag, now!"

She started folding up the bag, but just as she was about to pass it over, she threw it at his head and dived for cover behind the settee.

He knew he may not get another chance.

BLAM! BLAM! CLICK

She screamed as she hit the carpet, clutching her left

shoulder; a searing pain was throbbing all down her arm. The scumbag had shot her. She removed her Derringer from its holster and aimed it at chest height just above the settee. Mike was struggling with concussion. The golden hamster had caught the side of his head and he was feeling decidedly groggy. He knew he had to get out of there, that the odds were turning against him and wondered if his gun was empty or if it was just the third chamber.

Lifting the statuette in the plastic bag, Murphy retreated down the corridor. He knew he wouldn't have time for the lift so started to head for the staircase. It suddenly dawned on Scarlatti that she was no longer the quarry, but the hunter and she reached the corridor just as Murphy was entering the stairwell. She ran after him, pulled open the door to the stairwell and fired down the staircase.

BLAM! BLAM! BLAM!

The bullets ricocheted off the staircase, their thunderous clamour echoing all around.

"AARGH!"

He was hit. A momentary pause, then he kept on moving. His only chance lay in flight. When she reached the bottom of the stairwell, he was gone. An occasional trail of blood spots marked his passing.

'An injured animal is a dangerous one' she thought.

She should know. She returned to her apartment and removed her jacket to examine the wound. She'd been lucky; it was no more than a flesh wound. No bones seemed to be broken and although it hurt like hell, it wasn't going to hold her back for long. She'd need a good plastic surgeon though, or she wouldn't be wearing any more topless dresses at Cannes.

Murphy would keep. Yes, he had the golden hamster, but he was injured, maybe even dying. If she kept her appointment with Edna Timmins, it would give him time to check into a hospital or bleed to death. Either way, he'd soon be dead and the hamster would be back where it belonged.

She dressed her wound with difficulty, needing to both staunch the blood and maintain her composure. Once Timmins was dead she could finish Murphy and disappear somewhere warm with the golden hamster. It was time to move on.

Part Thirty-Seven

Hymie was becoming a connoisseur of NHS hospitals. Like a trainspotter collecting numbers he'd started to keep a record of which ones he'd visited, perhaps with a view to publishing the definitive consumer guide. Not that anyone would want to read it, of course; most people tried to avoid them.

He lay comatose in Edgware General.

A nurse paused outside the curtains, looked inside briefly at the battered man of fortune and resumed her journey.

"What's the matter with him, doctor?"

"Nervous exhaustion, lack of sleep, too much fast food, caffeine and sugar in his diet. I could go on, but it would only bore you. Why don't I buy you lunch instead? Or better still, dinner?"

"You'll be lucky to get out of here long enough to eat dinner, Simon," said the nurse.

"Too true."

"They seemed to think he'd been taking drugs when they brought him in. Had he?"

"No. Well, not in the last forty eight hours anyway."

Meanwhile in Hymieworld a message was coming through from the Great Beyond.

"Hymie!"

No response.

"HYMIE!!" A voice like thunder.

The volume continued to grow until it filled his head, like a peal of bells.

"Yes, God. How can I help you?"

He was floating on the ceiling of the ward, looking down at himself in bed. His bruised and battered body looked old and tired, but somehow smaller than it seemed from the inside. His mind, his spirit, his soul were all alive and kicking, but that poor old body needed a rest.

"Just a social visit. You've been overdoing it, that's all."

"Can I have it in writing?"

"What do you think? I just thought I'd come and wish you well for the future."

"I'm not going to die, am I?"

"No, not just yet. You've got a business to run, haven't you?"

"That's right, I have. I've got a business partner now as well."

"Yes, a good man. Murphy isn't it?"

"You know it is."

"I suppose I do," agreed God, modestly.

"Have I still got to fight the devil?"

"Not today, no. You'd be amazed how often evil simply destroys itself. Still, it pays to be ready. Never go down without a fight. Always be the best you can. You know the rules. You even try to live by them in your own strange way. Good luck," said God.

Hymie lay awake in his hospital bed. He was alone and tired, but somehow at peace.

Part Thirty-Eight

"Take a seat, Lieutenant Hu."

"Please, call me 'Eddie', I'm not on duty now."

"Well, you can call me 'Ray' then. Thanks for sparing me some of your time. We've been making good progress with the Triad investigation, but we can't put names to all of the faces and I wondered if you could help us?"

"Happy to. My files are in the Bureau's offices in Hong Kong, but I can probably identify most of the operators from memory."

"Good. Now here's an interesting looking character; any idea who he is?"

"Yes, that's 'Master Lau'. We believe he's either in charge of one of the London-based Triads or is one of their senior generals. Despite that, we have nothing on him. He's at least sixty, has short grey hair and dresses like an old school Chinese Mandarin. You probably think he looks like Fu Manchu, right?"

"Funny you should say that, Eddie."

"Well, there's nothing funny about him. He's an organisational genius and ruthless killer, responsible for some of the bloodiest gangland murders of the past decade. He's also hard to find and harder to pin anything on."

"Do you know anything else about him? Addresses, contacts, hobbies?"

"Very little. He seems to be almost invisible, with more aliases than anyone alive. The little we do know came from an agent in Hong Kong. He was found knifed on the Star Ferry leaving Kowloon just a few days later," said Hu.

"Do you know anything about his activities in the UK?" asked Decca.

"No, that's outside my jurisdiction, I'm afraid. You probably know some of it."

"He was seen at a major crime scene on Beachy Head a couple of months ago, but no-one knew who he was, so when he disappeared we had no way of tracing him. He was mentioned in one of the witness statements though; a guy called Goldman claimed to have been kidnapped by him."

"Lucky for him you got there when you did."

"Try telling that to Goldman!" said Decca.

"He claimed that this Master Lau character was after a golden statuette of a hamster and that he'd do anything to recover it."

"Not the Golden Hamster of Wei Wei?!"

"Is it valuable?"

"It's a solid gold temple ornament. No-one's seen it for years. It was thought that one of the most violent drug barons had struck a deal for it and the buyer had reneged."

"I didn't credit the story much at the time; Goldman's an habitual liar."

"Who is this Goldman? and where is he now?" asked Hu.

"Oh, he usually shows up in one hospital or another if you wait around long enough. He's a walking disaster area; a no-account private investigator, blessed with unfeasible luck. I sometimes think he must have as many lives as a cat. It's a shame the same can't be said for those associating with him."

"Well, Goldman could use some protection if he knows anything about Master Lau."

"I guess you're right. I'll get Terse onto it straight away. Thanks for your help, Eddie."

"Thanks, Ray, perhaps our paths will cross again someday?"

"You never can tell."

Part Thirty-Nine

The discreet ring of a doorbell chimed in another overpriced West London apartment.

"That will be the courier with my briefcase, let him in," said Mrs Timmins.

One of her doormen opened the door on its security chain.

"What's the password?" he asked.

"Summer Lightning."

The door swung open to reveal Steffanie Scarlatti, dressed to kill.

They were momentarily stunned. Things can happen in a moment; bad things.

BLAM! BLAM!

Two heavy bodies slumped to the floor, the smiles frozen on their faces.

She lowered her pistol and stepped over the redundant doormen.

"I was wondering whether Lau would send you. I didn't think he'd trust you, but I can be wrong. It happens to the best of us," said Mrs Timmins, aiming a pistol at her guest.

Scarlatti said nothing.

"I assure you Miss Scarlatti, I rarely shoot at people, but never miss."

"It's Ms," hissed Scarlatti.

"Are you married?"

"Don't be absurd."

"Then it's *Miss.* I don't know *what* they teach young people today."

They faced each other across the room like two wildcats spoiling for a fight.

"Don't make any sudden moves, Miss Scarlatti, I'd be only too happy to shoot you."

"You say the sweetest things."

Mrs Timmins frowned, but then something occurred to her and she smiled.

"Sit down, but let me take your gun first; we don't want any more accidents."

Scarlatti dropped her gun on the parquet flooring with a dull thud.

"Did Lau ask you to shoot my doormen or was that your own idea?"

"They were a threat."

"What to? World peace? The ozone layer? You're not making much sense. You hold other peoples' lives cheap and I deplore that."

She poured two cups of tea from a fine white bone-china teapot.

Steffanie Scarlatti stared incredulously at the old lady. Could this really be the face of the ruthless gangland boss she'd heard so much about? Unlikely. She probably ran her crime empire through lieutenants; psychopaths with a grandma fixation. Yet who would have imagined herself to be a vicious killer?"

A flash of suppressed rage played about the lines of the old woman's face, like an electric current flickering around a circuit. It wouldn't take much to provoke her to anger, and then what? Was she capable of murder? In the final analysis, wasn't everyone?

"I'd like to play a little game now, dear," said Mrs Timmins.

"I don't play games."

"How sad, but you'll enjoy this one, I promise. I call it Serbian Roulette, it's like Russian Roulette only it's even more one-sided."

"What are you babbling about, you silly, old woman?"

Mrs Timmins was clearly annoyed, but held her tongue.

"You don't imagine I'd give you a gun for even one second, surely?"

"No, even you couldn't be that stupid," said Scarlatti.

"As I was saying, I do miss a good game of Serbian Roulette. No-one will play with me any more. They say I cheat."

"And do you?"

"Oh yes, shamelessly," confided Edna Timmins. "The aim of the game is to answer three questions correctly."

"Supposing I do?"

"You go home in a taxi."

"And if I don't?"

"You go home in a hearse."

"Ah, one of those games," said Scarlatti.

"*Those* games?"

"Strictly for suckers!"

"No matter, I only thought to give you a sporting chance. If you really don't want it I may as well just shoot you now."

"Now I come to think of it, I love Serbian Roulette," said Scarlatti.

"I'm so glad."

She was insane; completely and utterly bonkers. It took one to know one.

"May I have one last request, before we play your game? It's traditional, you know; before a big match."

"It depends," said Timmins.

"On what?"

"On the request. I'd hate to see you get an unfair advantage over me."

"Nothing could be further from my thoughts, Mrs Timmins. I simply wanted to see what was in the briefcase. I assumed it was either cash or drugs."

"Cash. Two million dollars worth. I approve; you're a woman after my own heart. It's a shame you have to die, but there it is. I'd offer you a job if I could, but you're far too dangerous. It gets very tiresome continuously having to watch one's back at my age." Edna Timmins lifted the briefcase and placed it squarely in her visitor's lap.

"Help yourself my dear," she said.

Scarlatti had been looking for something to throw at her hostess, but became genuinely curious to see two million dollars in bank notes. She pressed open the dual combination locks at the top of the case and flipped open the lid. She barely had time to notice that the case was full of scrap paper before the movement of the locks triggered the trembler device concealed in the case and the room was engulfed in a fireball.

Their screaming lasted a few short minutes and there was no-one to mourn their passing. Within an hour the apartment was reduced to a gutted shell.

Part Forty

They sat in their adjacent offices at 792A Finchley Road reading the papers. Hymie, as befitted a man newly enriched by a large insurance payout, was reading the Financial Times and finding it hard going. Apart from providing a use for the world's reserves of pink paper, what was the point? He turned to the Sports section and did a double-take. There *was* some justice in the world after all; Lucinda Hunting-Baddeley had been prosecuted for race-fixing. Let her laugh that one off. Lightning had been found safe and well behind a false wall in the stable block.

The Total Disaster Insurance Corporation, or 'Total DIC' as Hymie referred to them, had proved very appreciative of not having to shell out $2 Million for a golden statue of a hamster that most people wouldn't have given shelf-space to. Goldman Confidential had a bright and solvent future.

Mike, who was holding the Finchley News, was secretly reading Classics from the Comics, which he'd inserted inside the paper to maintain the illusion that he took an interest in the wider world.

Outside their offices, Janie Jordan; the new office junior cum receptionist, was busy cutting out newspaper articles relating to the firm's recovery of the golden hamster. They'd be dining out on it for years.

Mike glanced over the Finchley News and found an article on the discovery of two women's bodies in a burnt-out Kensington flat. The police were looking into it. He'd been over his final shoot-out with Steffie Scarlatti again and again in his mind and was now more certain than ever that he was lucky to be alive. Only his bullet-proof vest had saved him. He'd keep it on forever, although not in the shower, obviously. It looked as though she was finally dead, although the police weren't confirming anything until they'd checked her dental records.

The buzzer on the intercom sounded outside.

"Your nine-thirty is here, Mr Goldman" called Janie.

"Send her in please."

This time she'd see sense. Half a million quid for a business this good? It was preposterous! With a new high profile and successful case behind them surely the sky was the limit for Goldman Confidential. He could see it now; branches in every city, a call centre in Bradford and a string of Rolls Royces, platinum credit cards and glamorous assistants.

"Hello, Mr Goldman," said Sarah Chandar. "You're a difficult man to track down."

"I'm sorry, Sarah, I've been working deep undercover. So far undercover I thought I might never get out again."

"And now we know why. Congratulations on another successful case. Are you ready to talk terms on the sale of the business?" she asked.

"Of course, if that's what you're here for."

"Good. Now, Mr Goldman, or should I call you Hymie?"

He nodded.

"I've taken the liberty of drafting heads of terms; an outline agreement for your approval," she said.

He flipped over the pages and frowned. "But the price is only £500,000, Sarah, surely the business is worth more than that? With our new profile in the industry we ought to be looking for £1 Million."

"Not without a lot more investment, Hymie. There are only three members of staff and 24 hours in a day, after all. I represent Ceefer Capital, not the National Lottery."

Hymie tapped on the window for Mike to join them.

"Mike, this is Sarah Chandar from Ceefer Capital. She wants to buy the business."

Mike's face fell.

"Don't you want to know how much they've offered, and what your share is?" asked Hymie, surprised at his reaction.

"No, because you'd be making a terrible mistake, mate," said Mike. "This is our livelihood. If you sell it, you make us both redundant. Oh, you can live on the money while it lasts, but money isn't everything. Nowadays I get up in the morning looking forward to going to work. I'm a partner in the firm so I don't have to take any crap from anyone and I know that what I do makes a difference. I care about this firm, Hymie! If we worked for some big multinational corporation, all that would change; I might as well be a doorman at the Rainbow Rooms again, because whatever they offered me, I'd still be a wage slave. I'm surprised you can't see it yourself. Think of all the years you've struggled to get where you are, and for what? To give it away to the first venture capitalist that comes along? They're not running a charity, you know!"

Hymie fell silent. Sarah Chandar opened her mouth to speak, but stopped herself. This was *their* decision. It was a setback, of course, but there would always be another chance, people were basically greedy.

Mike shrugged. "It was good while it lasted," he said.

Hymie had looked forward to this moment for so long that he'd forgotten what was important.

"I'm afraid the deal's off, Sarah," he said. "Mike's right, we can't sell the business, it's all we have. It kept me going for the last few years, when otherwise I would have thrown in the towel." Tears welled up in his eyes, so he blew his nose quickly and surreptitiously wiped them away.

"I understand," said Sarah, and left them.

Later, Hymie began to doubt whether he'd done the right thing, but Mike was steadfast and the business couldn't function any longer without him. Instead of an ending, the meeting became a new beginning for the two detectives. Cases increasingly seemed to find them; good cases, providing interesting work and rich rewards. But all that lay in the future, and the future, as they said of the past, was another country.

Chronology Note

The events in "Revenge of the Red Square" take place after those in "Goldman's Getaway", although the stories are included here in order of publication.

REVENGE
OF THE
RED SQUARE

Featuring Hymie Goldman,
the Defective Detective

Part One

A strange way to make a living

In the leafy garden of a 1950's semi in Cricklewood, *The Amazing Harvey*, as he was professionally known, prepared to entertain an attentive and appreciative party of wide-eyed children. That, at least, was the theory. He stood at the far end of the immaculate lawn, past the potting shed by the strawberry beds, footling around with his props in the fruitless hope that his assistant, Boltini, would arrive in time to draw fire from the kids from hell. If the guy was half cut again, he'd have his guts for garters.

He'd never had much luck with assistants; the Lovely Leanne had run off with the man with the squint from the Job Centre while they were resting between bookings; the Daring Denise had broken her leg on the ski-slopes of Val Doonican or some other far flung resort, and Sharon had jacked it all in for the mystic allure of stacking supermarket shelves in West Croydon. Finally, he'd decided to get a male assistant, and *this* was the result; standing in a field in Cricklewood waiting for the pisshead to arrive. His real name was James Bolton - hence Boltini - and he'd seemed so promising at the start, when he ran into him behind the bar at *The Dog and Duck*, doing occasional card tricks for the punters. No wonder the guy had agreed to work for peanuts, when he wasn't monkeying around he was practically useless.

The lady of the house, Mrs Olga Flanagan, heiress to a Russian-Irish shipping tycoon, sailed down the path with an imperious air like a pocket battleship on manoeuvres. She had no time for children's entertainers, having always found something deeply suspect about men in their mid-forties who made a living from wearing fancy dress and deceiving minors.

"Well, Mr Harvey?"

"Just call me *Amazing.*"

She arched an eyebrow. "Have it your own way, but the children are getting restless," she said. "I think you should begin."

Harvey cast a last forlorn glance down the garden for Boltini, then resigned himself to his fate. He wouldn't have minded so much but he needed an assistant to divert the audience's attention away from his woeful performance.

"Can I have the money *now*?" he asked sheepishly.

"Surely it's customary to pay *after* the performance," she said.

"Not for me. The number of times I've worked for nothing..." Mrs Flanagan looked concerned. "...is few and far between," he added hastily, "but I do like to be sure of getting paid. I'd hate to have to drop by one night and turn your car into a heap of manure."

Two pencilled eyebrows were raised in mounting concern.

"Look, your money's safe in this envelope," said Mrs Flanagan, retrieving exhibit A from her cardigan sleeve, like a white rabbit from a hat. "There's nothing to worry about. You do the show, you get paid and you leave. Simple."

"Great," he said, without conviction. He walked back up the lawn to his makeshift stage, where a group of hyperactive eight-year-olds were beginning to disassemble some of his props with vandal-like glee.

Harvey tugged at the cuffs of his jacket and cleared his throat.

"Ladies, gentlemen, children. Well, children, anyway. Prepare to be astonished, prepare to be astounded, prepare to have your faculties disconfabulated, discombobulated and disconfusticated, as I mesmerise you with the magical, mystical enchantments of a thousand ages of wizardry. Way back in the mists of time… I tell a lie, it was last Tuesday."

He paused for the laughter that never came. Someone at the back of the audience blew a raspberry.

Harvey looked up with ill-concealed irritation. An anaemic youth with wire-framed glasses, an electric yellow tee shirt bearing the letter 'B' in fluorescent red and a purple cape appeared at his shoulder.

"Boltini, where the h…eck have you been?"

The assistant took an early bow, tripped over his untied shoelaces and fell headlong into the props so meticulously arranged on the magician's stage table. Rising unsteadily to his feet, Boltini made his way shakily past the potting shed and was violently ill in the strawberry beds.

Fourteen eight-year-olds laughed like drains, poked each other in the ribs and pointed at the less-than-magical figure of Boltini as he returned to join his mentor. Mrs Flanagan, meanwhile, bore a striking resemblance to a battleship which had come under fire in the midships and knew exactly what to do about it.

Harvey blundered on.

"Thank you most kindly. I appear before you today fresh from a thrilling expedition to the mythical isle of Maroonga, a voyage blessed with the discovery of a positive plethora of new and astounding tricks. As I'm sure you will know, on the isle of Maroonga, *everyone* is a magician and they have normal people like yourselves to entertain them. Why? I hear you ask. Well, it's a strange and mystical place. They all sit around in deckchairs wearing big hats and playing the bongos while watching people making tea and crumpets."

"Get on with it, mister. Do a trick or summat," chivvied an exasperated eight-year-old in the front row, whose patience had been sorely tested.

There's always one, isn't there, thought Harvey.

"Why are we waiting? Why are we waiting?" sang a boy with goofy teeth, in a tuneless wail.

Or two…

"Come on granddad, are you a magician or wot?" cried the teenager from next door, who had been standing on an old tea chest to see over the hedge. "This show's not even worth gate-crashing!"

But when it gets to three, thought Harvey, then it's definitely time to…

"Go!" shouted Mrs Flanagan. "And never darken my yew again."

Harvey had been about to pack up his remaining props and beat a hasty retreat, when he suddenly realised that she was talking to the interloper from next door. At least, that was the only inference he *could* draw from the sight of the stately Mrs Flanagan flinging a moth-eaten old tennis ball at the hedge.

"Thank you, thank you," he resumed. "Now without further ado, let me show you a miraculous card trick I learned from Houdini." Harvey reached into his trouser pocket and pulled out a deck of Bicycle playing cards. As he did so the packet opened, spilling half of them onto the floor.

"Surely he was an escapologist?" queried Mrs Flanagan, as the children began to laugh like a pack of hyenas at the collapse of the trick.

"Ah, no, I meant Sid Houdini, Harry's brother's grandson," said Harvey vaguely, as he tried to pick up as many cards as he could. "Now then, which of these delightful children is the birthday boy or girl?"

"Go on, Sophie, stand up," said the boy with the buck teeth.

A sweet little girl with her hair in bunches stood up.

"Happy Birthday, Sophie," said Harvey. "How old are you?"

"Eight."

"You know, I was *ate* once… by a lion at the circus, but the ringmaster cracked his whip and it spat me out in the nick of time."

Sophie smiled, in a vain attempt to humour the funny man, who was obviously nuts.

"Pick a card, any card," continued Harvey, offering a woefully small selection of playing cards to the little girl. Shyly, she took one and held it to her chest.

Harvey closed his eyes and walked clockwise in a circle three times. He put his hand to his forehead, feeling giddy. He'd forgotten to say the magic words! They could kick you out of the Magic Triangle for a lesser offence, if you were in it to begin with. Perhaps they wouldn't notice. He closed his eyes and put his finger tips to his temples. He was getting a migraine.

"It can only be the…eight of clubs. Am I right?"

Sophie looked at her card in confusion.

"I don't know, mister, I don't play cards, but it's got a funny man on with a curly hat."

"It's the joker, how apt," said Mrs Flanagan.

"That would have been my second choice," he said, hurriedly taking the card back from the little girl and placing it in his pocket. He lifted his collapsible hat from the props table, tapped it twice with his wand and the hat opened out with a 'pop'. He just needed a distraction, other than the sight of Boltini vomiting in different parts of the garden. He placed the hat on his head and smiled what he hoped was a winning smile.

"Now, who can tell me what a magician keeps in his hat? Can anyone? Mrs Flanagan?"

"In your case I'd hesitate to guess," she replied, frostily.

"Sandwiches?" wondered a boy in the second row.

"Chocolate biscuits?" asked Sophie.

"Cake!" cried another, as the food motif held sway.

The children had begun to lose interest and started picking their noses or dead-heading Mrs Flanagan's prize petunias. The boy with the goofy teeth was clearly in need of the toilet.

"Good ideas, but not the right answer I'm afraid. Shall we see?" added the magician. He lifted his hat to reveal a small and terrified white mouse. A couple of the girls screamed and the mouse took off like a rocket down the garden.

"This," said Harvey, gesticulating at the recently vacated space, "is Rover." He looked inside his hat in the vague hope of locating the rodent, but further probing of the top of his head revealed only a small pile of moist mouse droppings. At least he finally had their attention.

"Where's he gone, mister?" asked Sophie.

"Don't worry, kids, I expect he felt like a bit of exercise. It's quite cramped in my hat so he probably came over a bit faint. He suffers from claustrophobia, you know." He was babbling; he often did when there was nothing useful left to say. It was better than admitting that his act was a shambolic farce and that he should have stuck to teaching.

"Boltini! We have a mouse missing! There...over by the shed, quickly, get him, now!"

Boltini stared at him, green to the gills, with a look of sullen defiance on his pale yet uninterested face.

"The name's James, mate, and sod this is for a game of soldiers!" he said, walking off towards the house and his transport home.

"You'll never work in show business again!" called Harvey, after him.

Another raspberry wafted on the breeze, this time from Boltini. "I should have listened to them all," said the disgruntled assistant aloud, slouching off. "Never work with children or animals. Only there's a third category to watch out for…pillocks called *The Amazing Harvey*!"

Sweat broke out along Harvey's hairline. Disaster loomed. He was reminded of his first professional engagement; 'The Mendelssohn Job', when everything that *could* go wrong *had* gone wrong, resulting in the end of his career as far as Hendon, Golders Green and Finchley were concerned. In retrospect, it had been a walk in the park compared with *this*.

"Ladies, gentlemen, children, the kid with the goofy teeth, I'd like to say what a fantastic audience you've been…I, I …" he looked around for inspiration, but none was forthcoming. He felt like he was stranded in a wilderness of despair and all hope was lost.

"You're rubbish at magic, mister," said a girl with ginger hair and freckles. "Your assistant threw up, your mouse ran off and you don't even know any card tricks. I'd give up if I were you."

Mrs Flanagan looked at him with a combination of disappointment, annoyance and pity and returned the envelope she had been holding for safe keeping to her handbag.

"Out of the mouths of babes," she said.

Harvey opened his jacket to see if he still had anything left up his sleeve and was met by the flutter of wings and a face full of flying feathers as Maurice, his white dove, made a bid for freedom. Flying off into the wide blue yonder, Maurice dropped a message from on high, all down Harvey's shirt front. It seemed profoundly symbolic.

The children hooted with laughter. This guy may be a rotten magician, but he was a master of chaos and failure.

"Can you do balloon animals?" asked the kid with the buck teeth, on the basis that if they tried long enough they might be able to find *something* Harvey could do.

For the first time, *The Amazing Harvey* seemed to get really pissed off.

"Do balloon animals?! What do you take me for? I'm an artiste, not some drongo who ties *balloons* into funny shapes! I don't have a big red nose and long flapping boots, do I? No, I don't. Look, has anybody got any pets?" he asked.

"I've got a gerbil at home," said the girl with the ginger hair. "Timmy, his name is."

"What bloody good is *that!*" snapped Harvey. "I'm looking for an animal I can use in my act; a cat from Cricklewood, not a terrapin from Timbuktu!"

The girl started sobbing uncontrollably and Mrs Flanagan fixed him with an icy stare until he was forced to apologise.

"Sorry, young lady. I do apologise, it's just that as you may have noticed, one or two things have gone a little wrong with the act today, so I was hoping to show you some *real* magic to make up for it." He smiled to hide the pain.

"I've got a goldfish called Sammy," said Sophie, quietly. "Would he be any good?"

"Yes! Brilliant! Thank you, Sophie," said the magician. "Would you go and fetch him for me, please."

As she walked off up to the house, the long, lank figure of Boltini shuffled back towards the party.

"I knew you wouldn't desert the act, Boltini," said Harvey. "One day all of this will be yours," he said, gesturing grandiosely at the tatty collection of broken props. "All you need to do is fetch Maurice down off the neighbour's roof and track down Rover, and we're back in business."

Boltini looked at Harvey with a pained expression. "Has anyone seen the keys to my van?" he asked aloud, to no one in particular.

"Now, kids, while Sophie goes off to get her goldfish, let me entertain you with some juggling. I used to do this in the circus you know," said Harvey.

"What happened?" asked Mrs Flanagan, out of morbid curiosity. "Are they still in business?"

Harvey picked up three patchwork juggling balls and threw them into the air, one after the other until they formed a flying circle. Boltini wandered back over to the strawberry beds to see if he could locate his keys among the vomit spattered plants.

"Oh, yes. Uncle Henry's Flying Circus, it was called. We toured Army bases mainly."

"Poor devils," added Olga Flanagan, "dodging bullets all day and being forced to watch your act when they got back."

"This is rotten," said the kid with the buck teeth. "All you've done is lose things and a juggling trick my dad could do."

Harvey's self-confidence finally seemed to desert him. He was on the verge of throwing in the towel when Sophie returned with a goldfish in a bowl.

"Ah, yes, but can your father do *this*?" said Harvey, taking the bowl. His juggling balls hit the ground unheeded.

He took a large red handkerchief from an inside jacket pocket and draped it over the goldfish bowl. The audience fell silent. Even Boltini, who had been moping around looking for his keys, paused momentarily to watch and marvel. He hadn't seen this trick before.

"The illusion I am about to perform is technically impossible," said Harvey.

He lifted the hankie and removed the fish from the bowl with his hand. He placed it into a large brown paper bag and blew into the bag until it was fully inflated. Holding it out in front of him, Harvey passed his left hand over the top of the bag and recited the familiar incantation, "Hocus Pocus, fish-bones choke us." Then he placed the bag on the table in front of him and hit it three times with a wooden mallet. The silence deepened into a deathly hush. You could have heard a gnat fart.

Harvey picked up the paper bag and peered anxiously inside.

"And that, as they say, is magic!" he cried. "You've been a wonderful audience, thank you and goodbye!"

He fixed Boltini with a knowing look. "Here are your keys," he said, "get the stuff and meet me at the van in five," he added, legging it for the garden gate.

"Oi, mister, where's the fish?" asked the kid with the buck teeth.

"I'm sorry, I'm a magician, not a pet shop owner," said Harvey over his shoulder as he vanished.

Part Two

Meanwhile somewhere in North London.

In the ill-kempt offices of Goldman Confidential, Private Investigators to the Stars, Hymie Goldman and Mike Murphy sat amid the clutter with sour expressions, drinking a murky brown liquid. It was a substance whose composition had long baffled the finest forensic scientists of NW3, but was known to habitués of the Black Kat as 'coffee'. Certainly a medium sized dose precluded sleep for several days and had been known to stun an adult male gorilla but when you'd said that, you'd said everything.

"How's the case going?" asked Mike; the primate in question.

"I presume you're referring to the *new* case?"

"Well, I wasn't asking after your luggage, mate."

"The only baggage I have to lug around is you, Murphy. As for the case, it's too early to tell."

"Is there any money in it?"

"If there wasn't, I wouldn't be wasting my time, would I?"

"I hope not, but you're not even the best businessman at this end of the Finchley Road. I wouldn't trust your business nous as far as I could throw it. What's the client called anyway? You're being very secretive about it."

"Secretive? Pah! It's just that I have to respect client confidentiality."

"I'm not buying it. Who's your client?"

"Mr Redrum," said Hymie, quietly.

"Mr who?"

"Redrum."

"That's the name of a horse, you wally. You haven't gone and got mixed up with the county set again, have you? After all the trouble we had last time. Are you mad?"

"Look, Mike, this is why I didn't tell you about the case, because I knew you'd jump to conclusions, wrong conclusions. It's about the only exercise your feeble mind gets these days. Okay, so it sounds dodgy. No-one's called Mr Redrum. That's why I'm trying to find out how much baloney this guy's feeding me before I get in too deep. So how are tricks with you, my massive chum? Heard from the bird in Blackpool?"

Mike fell silent and took another sip of coffee. He winced.

"No, and I don't want to talk about it."

"I've always said women are a curse," said Hymie, insensitively. "They bat their eyelashes at you, you fall like a ton of bricks and then they hang you out to dry. It's only a question of time. Been there, done that, got the tee shirt."

"I never met your wife, did you love her?"

"Yes, but it was a long time ago," said Hymie. "Some things are best left in the past."

"Was she a looker?"

"As I said, it's best left in the past."

"I'll take that as a 'no' then. Did it hurt when she left you?"

"Blunt as a badger's arse, aren't you, Murphy. I don't need a bloody psychiatrist or a shoulder to cry on. I get along fine without all that hearts and flowers crap, so just leave it out. And if this is another diversion to stop me asking about *your* caseload, think again. How many new clients have *you* got?"

"Plenty, mate, plenty. I'm a client magnet. Ask Janie. Come to think of it, where is Janie?"

"Family funeral, I thought," said Hymie. "Her Uncle Len died."

"Couldn't have," said Mike. "She hasn't got an Uncle Len. Besides, she hasn't been in for weeks, just look at the dust on those files."

"I wondered why everything was in such a mess," continued Hymie, "but without Janie to point it out to me, it didn't really register."

"Maybe she had a better offer?" said Mike. "She is the best PA we've ever had."

"What? A better offer than Goldman Confidential? No, she'll have been kidnapped by aliens or won the National Lottery. We should call the police. No, on second thoughts..." he added hastily.

"Have you heard anything of Inspector Decca lately? He was your best buddy in Blackpool. It's funny how he's disappeared since we got back."

"It's like you said; what happened in Blackpool stays in Blackpool. Now, if you call the agency about a new receptionist cum bottle-washer, I'll go and earn the dosh to keep us afloat."

"That'll be the day," said Mike, heading for the peace and quiet of his own office to make some calls.

Part Three

Detective-u-(don't)-like

What *had* happened to Inspector Ray Decca? Did anyone know? Did anyone care? The *nearly* man of the Metropolitan Constabulary had seemed to be on the verge of total meltdown twelve months earlier, but after a short stay at a rest home for retired loonies in Blackpool, he'd become a completely different man.

Once he'd been a workaholic with a cast-iron commitment to the job, but after the collapse of his marriage, the promotion above him of a host of lesser men and the realisation that even terminal loser, Hymie Goldman, seemed to have a more successful career, he'd ceased to give a damn.

On his return to active service they'd put him in charge of the unsolved cases unit and assigned his arch-nemesis, Sergeant Barry Terse, to work for him on the basis that sometimes two wrongs could make a right. Even if they didn't, it surely made sense to bury the two least popular officers on the force in a small room in the bowels of HQ with a bunch of cases no-one wanted to hear any more about.

Decca sat behind his grey desk in a room no bigger than a portable toilet, poring over the crossword in *The Hendon Herald*. "Large flightless bird? Three letters? Sounds like the ex-wife! No, wait, it's on the tip of my tongue."

The grey phone on his desk trilled in the land that time forgot. He lifted the receiver.

"Hello, Decca."

"Oh hello, mate. Your ex-wife said I should give you a call. I'm trying to get the sports channel on your old satellite service and it keeps on coming up with an error message. Any ideas?"

"Who is this?" he asked, incredulously.

"Chaz Dipswell, I'm your ex's new partner."

"Well, Mr Dipstick, I suggest you take the remote..."

"Yeees."

"Press the red button three times..."

"Yeees."

"And shove it right up your arse. Good day to you!"

He slammed down the phone. The nerve of some people. As if it wasn't bad enough that his marriage was over, his career in tatters and he was working in a portaloo, everyone seemed to think he should be deliriously happy about it. When he wasn't stuck in this basement he was living in a bed-sit above the dry cleaners off Hendon Broadway.

The door flew open as if propelled by a hurricane, and the excitable figure of Barry Terse appeared like a dustbowl twister, clutching a file.

"Whatever happened to knocking, Terse?"

"It's still going strong, sir. There are knocking shops everywhere."

"Har, ruddy har. Why are you so upbeat today?"

"We've got a new case, Chief."

"Oh, just bung it over there with the stale doughnuts, I'm on my tea-break."

"Yes, but it's a real *live* case."

"Look, Terse…Barry, we're still only half way through 2002. I'm hardly likely to get excited about a new case from 2003, am I?"

"No, Chief, a *real* case. A homicide."

"Calm down, Barry. Let's have a reality check here; is that a flying pig I can see through the air vent? Who on earth would put *us* in charge of a homicide investigation? Has the whole force contracted beri beri?"

"Well, it's only a goldfish homicide, but it's a step in the right direction, isn't it?"

Decca banged his head on the desk then regretted his bravado.

"Are you taking the piss, Terse?"

"No, sir, Lord Tom O'Connor…"

"The guy who chairs the Police Complaints Authority?"

"Yeah, well, his granddaughter was having a kid's party in Cricklewood, when the magician they'd hired killed her goldfish then scarpered."

"And they want us to investigate it?"

"That's about the size of it, sir."

"And this is your idea of a golden opportunity? A case that clearly no-one else will touch with a bargepole because it's a bad joke and if we can't crack it we'll be hauled up in front of a complaints enquiry?"

"Now that you mention it, perhaps it's not a step in the right direction, after all."

"No, Terse. Come back 2002, all is forgiven."

"Yes, sir."

"Do we have any choice in the matter?"

"What do you think, sir?"

"I suspected as much. Ah well, it will be good to get out into the daylight again, I feel like I'm working in a cinema. See if you can get us a car, Terse."

"Will do, Chief," said the sergeant, backing out of the room.

Part Four

Conspiracy theories-r-us

It was a long way back from Cricklewood to anywhere, when all your magic tricks had failed, you'd killed an innocent goldfish belonging to the girl whose party it was and her mother hadn't paid you. *The Amazing Harvey* had never felt less able to live up to his billing. Even his assistant, Boltini, driving them back to Golders Green in the Magic Wagon, a purple Ford Transit with a giant rabbit painted on the side and a six foot wand stuck on the roof, seemed sullen and resentful. He'd have driven off and left him there if Harvey hadn't taken the keys to the van.

"Look, Harvey, no offence, mate, but you're rubbish. Really bad. You have to be the worst magician I've ever seen. And I'm your *assistant*... so, what does that make me? *Understudy* to the world's worst magician? Do you think I like following you around with a dustpan and brush? Do I look like a terminal masochist?"

Harvey looked at him dejectedly for a while. "Et tu, brute," just about summed up how he felt. When the whole world was against you, all you needed was a friend and confidante to stab you in the back.

"Listen, Jack,"

"James!" cried Boltini, irritably.

"Jack, James, whatever…we all have bad days. Don't you ever have them? You could have fooled me anyway. You looked like a bag of shit when you turned up at that party. I may not be the best magician in the world, but at least I take the act seriously. I'm always well turned out."

"Frequently turfed out!" snapped Boltini, resentful of such a gross slur on his professionalism. He swerved to avoid a traffic bollard. "I've always given the act 110% myself," he added.

"So have I!" snapped Harvey.

"Yeah, well, I just think that we should have more to show for 220% effort than a bunch of testimonials ending in 'off', don't you? We didn't get paid, I take it?"

"I was *that* close," said Harvey, holding up his right index finger and thumb, pressed tightly together. "The old battleaxe even showed me the envelope with the cash in to whet my appetite."

"I'll take that as a 'no' then."

The van pulled up outside 18 Elmcroft Avenue and Boltini switched off the engine.

"I'm sorry, old chap. Come in and have a drink, there's something I want to talk to you about."

Boltini wondered if he was trying to tell him that the act was over. Surely that was worth talking about, if only to confirm it was true. They got out and walked down the path. The house was easily the scruffiest in the road. Its facade seemed nearly as shambolic as its latest tenant. Inside, everything was scattered indiscriminately as though a particularly untidy burglar had been looking for valuables amidst a giant haystack of dross. In fact it always looked that way.

The only possessions Harvey owned with any discernible value were a cast bronze statuette of the Magic Triangle's first president, Derek Deviant, playing with his balls, which now adorned the grotty sideboard and an original advertising poster from the 1920's from one of the greats of stage magic. Boltini eyeballed it as he passed.

"Is that a genuine Po?" he asked.

Harvey followed his glance.

"No, even better, a genuine Pong," he said absently.

"Never heard of him. No, wait; it says Ying Tong Pong, the famous Chinese magician. I thought it was Po, not Pong," said Boltini.

"He was originally billed as *The Mighty Pong*, but soon learnt to his cost that his posters were more likely to attract the attention of the local public health inspector than the throngs of cheering crowds he craved, so he changed his name to Ying Tong Po and never looked back. You've probably heard the story of how he died on stage?"

"Tough audience?" asked James.

"No, for real, I mean. He was shot in the khazi at the Wood Green Empire."

"Tragic."

Harvey nodded. He sat back in his distempered old armchair and unscrewed the top from a half-empty bottle of scotch. In the artificial light of the standard lamp in the corner he could have passed for sixty, instead of his real age, whatever that was.

"Say when," he said, starting to pour.

The golden-coloured liquid was pouring down the sides of his glass onto the tabletop when Boltini finally said 'when'. It was just another exercise in brinkmanship.

"I didn't know you were such a drinker, Jack."

James let it pass. "Only since I started working with you, Harvey. I need something to help me sleep. It's the thought of all those ruined parties; sad, disenchanted kids and their disillusioned parents, wrecked props. Failure seems to follow you around. With all your empty promises you should have been a politician."

"Magic's a vocation, not a job. No-one said it would be easy."

"Actually, Harvey, *you* did. That's exactly what you said. I was pulling pints in The Dog and Duck, doing the occasional card trick to pull the birds and then one day, wham! *Blunder Man* arrives on the scene. Six foot two of hot air with dyed blonde hair, looking uncannily like BoJo after a night on the tiles, and telling me how I could earn the easiest hundred quid of my life as your assistant.

Join me, James, you said, and your fortune's in the bag. Was that the bag you lost that Cartier watch in last week, or the body bag that poor bloody goldfish died in this afternoon?"

"Jack, Jack. Wait."

"It's over. I don't want to be a laughing stock any longer. I don't want to exist on a diet of beans on toast, because I don't know where the next paycheck is coming from. Here are your car keys," added Boltini, dropping them onto the glass-topped table with a clatter. "I'll get a taxi home if you'll just point me in the right direction for the phone." He didn't actually have the money, but you couldn't make a grand exit by walking off in a fit of pique to catch the bus.

"The phone? Yes, I'm sure it's here somewhere. Try under that pile of laundry," suggested Harvey, vaguely. "Or wait till it rings."

Boltini sat down heavily. "If it only rings when we've got a booking, I could be here till next Christmas."

"It wasn't always like this though, was it?" said Harvey. "Remember the good times? Remember the 2005 Crouch End Police Ball? They loved us. They even tore up your parking ticket."

"*You* tore up my parking ticket," said Boltini, "and that damn fool desk-sergeant kept waiting for you to magic it back together.",

"Touching faith," murmured Harvey. "Now before you go, I need to tell you something."

"There's nothing you can say I want to hear. Tomorrow morning I'm going out to look for a *proper* job."

"That's fine, but I need to confide in someone. You see, *they're* after me and I want to make sure that if they catch up with me, there's someone to notify the Triangle," said Harvey earnestly.

"What's that then," smirked James, "the Cricklewood Knitting Triangle?"

"The Magic Triangle, of course."

"I see, Conspiracy Theories R Us now, is it?" said Boltini.

"James, please. This is a matter of life or death. You only know me as a not very good magician, a buffoon."

"Exactly, I couldn't have put it better myself."

"Well, what if I told you it was all a front and that I'm really a law enforcement agent working in conjunction with the Magic Triangle?"

"I'd think you were completely bonkers as well as being a crap magician."

"When I got back to the house yesterday, a parcel was waiting for me."

"Amazon?"

"Inside was this," said Harvey. He picked up a discarded jiffy bag from the sideboard and emptied the contents onto the floor.

"Two pieces of broken stick? Wow, I'm frightened."

"Look again. They're the two halves of a magician's wand. It's a warning."

"Yeah, but it could be from anyone who's seen your act; anyone who's paid for the dubious privilege anyway."

Harvey sighed. He recharged their glasses then took a sip of whisky.

"Have a drink, James, while I tell you about the Red Square."

"It's in Moscow isn't it?"

"As I'm sure you know, the Magic Triangle was founded in 1905 at Pinoli's restaurant in London by Derek Deviant, Claude Mastermain and Ying Tong Pong, the famous Chinese magician from St.Louis. But if you think they just set it up for laughs or to have somewhere to go on a Sunday afternoon after the pubs shut, you're sadly mistaken. It wasn't established to further its members' understanding of magic, but to provide an organisation powerful enough to counter the activities of the Red Square. The Square is an ancient order of thieves and vagabonds which came into existence in Rome in the year 1510. Originally, it was the creation of Pope Julius the sixteenth, who needed some papers recovered with no questions asked. He commissioned one of his cardinals, Carlo Benedetti, to form a special group of *illusionistas peculiares* which later became known as the Red Square. Each member was a skilled agent; a locksmith, acrobat, soldier, painter and decorator, sworn to absolute secrecy on pain of death and given a thousand ducats to seal his allegiance. There was no task they could not accomplish. Once they'd recovered the pope's missing papers and touched up the Sistine Chapel, they turned their hands to more lucrative pursuits; emptying bank vaults, highway robbery and blackmailing wealthy businessmen.

Too late the pope realised what a monster he'd created and excommunicated them all, hounding them out of civilised society. The outlaws went underground and dispersed across the western world. By 1850 they were active in London, gradually spreading their malign influence throughout the metropolis until, by 1905, the league of English magicians felt compelled to form the Triangle to counter the Square's illegal activities. At first the Triangle met with great success. By 1928 there were thought to be only three members of the Red Square left in the country; Rintizi the dwarf, Giovanni Prosciutto and Bram O'Reilly."

"Never heard of them," said Boltini.

"Exactly. They moved like shadows across the land, rarely drawing the attention of the authorities, but always being implicated in heinous crimes."

"So the Magic Triangle only exists to fight an underground organisation of gifted criminals?" said Boltini.

"Yes."

"And this secret society of master criminals is out to get you?"

"Yes."

"Well, I've never heard such a load of old tosh in my life. How many bottles of whisky did it take to come up with this?"

"I'm serious," said Harvey.

"So, what other signs have you had?"

"This afternoon, before I left for the show, I found a dead hedgehog on the path outside."

"Tragic, but what makes you think it has anything to do with the Red Square? Perhaps it just had a walk-on part in one of your tricks."

"The hedgehog is one of their mystic symbols."

"You're freaking mad, mate," cried Boltini. "I should get some treatment if I were you." He reflected again on what he'd been told and then began looking around the room suspiciously. "You're not winding me up are you, Harvey? It's not 'Candid Camera?'"

"I'm deadly serious. Believe me; anything is possible if you believe in magic."

"Yeah, I saw what you did to that poor bloody goldfish. Someone ought to set the RSPCA on you."

"There's no point in being glib about it, a broken wand can mean only one thing; death is stalking me. If I disappear sometime in the next few days you must go to the Triangle on Stephenson Way and tell the secretary that the Square is on the move. There's more at stake than our careers."

"That's lucky, 'cos mine's screwed!" cried Boltini, getting up from his chair and walking to the door. There was only so much bullshit he could take at one sitting.

"You know what they say," he concluded, as he buttoned up his coat, "don't call us, we'll call you. See you around."

"Goodbye, Boltini."

Part Five

The case is afoot

Sunday morning dawned on Marble Arch. Along the row of benches that stretched from the Arch to the edge of the park, a short well-built gentleman sat yawning alone. He opened the thermos flask by his side and poured himself a cup of steaming tea. He reached for his lunchbox then thought better of it; not even Hymie Goldman could eat lunch before eight in the morning.

Crowds of Sunday strollers, foreign tourists and gentlemen of the road drifted by like an elaborate tableau of city life. All ignored Goldman, as well they might; he had the perfect face for a private investigator: unappealing and entirely forgettable.

From across the park, a man-mountain appeared. With clapped-out red hair and an unfeasibly large overcoat, he bore a passing resemblance to a bull mastiff chewing a wasp.

"So, this is where you've been hiding!" said Murphy, as he squatted on the bench next to his elusive business partner, nearly tipping Goldman into a nearby waste bin.

"You haven't been working on a case after all, have you? Just hanging out by the Arch with all the other deadbeats!"

"Give me a break," said Hymie. "I didn't just come here to eat my sandwiches you know, I'm on a case. Anyway, this is hardly the time and place to discuss it."

"What?"

"My latest investigation"

"Oh, the racehorse case."

"Redrum," corrected Hymie.

"Shhh… don't give away any confidential information," mocked Mike.

Hymie fished in his coat pocket and removed a wad of fifty pound notes, which he waved in Mike's face.

"I suppose this is a fantasy too!"

"Blimey, Goldman, you'd better give that to me to hold. You could get mugged for a lot less than that around here. How much is there, anyway?"

"Ten big ones."

Mike stared at him dumbfounded. "From the Redrum case?"

"That's just for starters. If I can solve the case, there's a bonus too."

"What's to solve?"

"The whereabouts of a dud magician called *The Amazing Harvey*."

"Any luck so far?"

"No. He hasn't hit the big time yet so his act must be pretty poor."

"With a name like that, is it any wonder? Where have you looked?"

"Under various rocks. I'm on his trail, but it's a bit cold. He did a couple of diabolical gigs in North Finchley a couple of years ago then disappeared," said Hymie.

"And you suspect foul play?"

"No, it sounds like he was just too embarrassed to ever perform in Finchley again. I thought I might try Golders Green or Cricklewood next. I'm looking for the sort of place where lack of ability is no obstacle to getting bookings. Any ideas?"

"Britain's got talent?"

Hymie rolled his eyes. "I thought we might try the Magic Triangle. If he's a real magician, he's sure to be on their books."

"I'd better come along and protect the ten… ahem, *you* from any bother. You know you can rely on me to watch your back," said Mike.

"Yeah, but it's my front I'm worried about."

They ambled across the road to the nearest taxi rank. Hymie stooped down to speak to the cabbie, who was idly flicking through his racing paper.

"Do you know the way to…?"

"San Jose?" ventured the cabbie. "No, but if you hum it, I'll call the police."

"Ho, bloody ho! Everyone's a comedian."

"Where to, guv?" asked the cab driver, sensing his fare slipping away.

"The Magic Triangle," cut in Mike over Hymie's shoulder.

"Gorblimey, you gave me a start. Is this your trained gorilla?" he asked Hymie.

"You talk too much, mate," said Mike, "but I have a solution," he continued, flexing his knuckles ominously.

"Look, we just want to go to the Magic Triangle," said Hymie. "How about it?"

The cabbie appeared to be wracking his brain. "The Magic Triangle? *The* Magic Triangle? The *Magic*…"

"Yeah," said Hymie.

"Where's that then?"

"Look, *you're* the cabbie. When I go to a chip shop I don't expect to peel my own spuds. Take us to the flamin' Magic Triangle before I smash your face in!" snapped Mike.

"Why didn't you say so in the first place," said the cabbie, driving off without them. They had better luck with the taxi behind; not only had the driver heard of the Magic Triangle, but he even knew where to find it and was only too willing to take them there for a modest fee. They climbed into the back of the cab.

"You know, until a few weeks ago I'd never heard of the Magic Triangle," said the cabbie, "then all of a sudden every loony and nut job in London wants to go there."

Mike began to flex his knuckles again.

"Present company excepted, of course!" added the driver, suddenly catching sight of Mike's grim visage and furrowed brow in his rear view mirror.

"So, what's it all about?" asked Mike, as they trundled across the city.

"What's that, Mike?"

"Magic," whispered the big man.

"Ah yes, the old art of deception. Well, some would say it's entertainment in its oldest and purest form, but

279

personally I reckon they're just a bunch of crooks; they take your money and give you nothing in return."

"How long have you been a magician then?"

"Oh, very funny. Look, we're the good guys around here. We sort out people's problems and leave them with a smile on their faces. Where's the deception in that? We provide total commitment, sheer graft and all the legwork needed to get the job done; surely that still has value in this crazy world?"

Mike shook his head. "I reckon Ray Decca would disagree with you there. We may not be poncing around in flash suits pulling rabbits out of a hat or sawing some dolly bird in half, but as far as he's concerned we're still part of the problem, not the solution. Still, what would life be without a little magic every now and then?"

Hymie smiled and leant back in his seat. Mike may look like a man with no finer feelings but he could surprise you. At times he veered off the straight and narrow into the squashily sentimental.

The taxi pulled up in an empty alley near Euston Station.

"That's the place, there," said the cabbie, pointing at an ominous looking doorway with the number thirteen above the door. "Mum's the word," he added with a wink.

They paid him and got out of the cab.

"Quiet here, innit," said Mike. "It's hard to believe we're in the middle of eight million people."

"That's just what I was thinking. Yet down this insignificant street it's so quiet that practically anything could happen without anyone knowing."

"Come on, let's get on with it," said Mike, pressing the bell.

No response.

"What kind of a dive is this anyway, without a bell that works?" said Hymie. "Leave it to me, I'll soft soap them with the old Goldman charm." He hammered on the door with his fist. "Open up, it's a matter of life or death!" he cried.

Still no reply. Mike smirked. "So that's what you call charm is it? Leave it to me, mate, I do a great line in tact and diplomacy," he added, backing up to charge at the door. He started to run; twenty stone of ex-bouncer moving purposefully at high velocity. As he reached the door the wooden panels receded before him as someone opened the door from within. Mike continued on his course, speeding forwards until he collided with a hat-and-coat stand and ended up in a heap on the floor.

"Are you alright?" asked the man inside; a smartly dressed youth with a pointy face and horn rimmed spectacles.

"Huuurrrrr, hurrrrrrr... never better," said Mike, struggling for breath.

Hymie appeared, as if by magic, in the entrance.

"Can I help you?" asked the representative of the Magic Triangle.

Goldman swept his hand through his hair as though preparing for great oratory, cleared his throat and began.

"My name's Hymie Goldman and this is my business partner, Michael Murphy."

"That's as may be, but we're not open to the public. Do you have an appointment?"

"Ah, yes, I do," lied Hymie. "With Mr..er..." he continued, clutching for some shred of a credible name."

"Gordon Bennett?" suggested the youth with the spectacles.

"Yes, that's it, Gordon Bennett," said Hymie gratefully.

"Well, there's no-one here of that name," sneered the youth. "How about Walter Swinburne?"

"Ah, yes...that was it," said Hymie.

"No, never heard of him, he doesn't work here either," said the youth. "You're lying aren't you?"

"Huuuurrr... we're here to see Ali Bongo," said Mike, getting up belatedly from the carpet.

"I'm sorry, you're too late," said the youth.

"Not left already?"

"No, he died in 2009."

"Bugger!" said Hymie.

"I'd appreciate it if you would leave now," said the pointy faced youth. Some of us have work to do."

"Look, son," said Hymie, "what's your name?"

"Gerald."

"Look, Gerald, cards on the table. We're a couple of detectives looking for a magician called *The Amazing Harvey*. The sooner you help us out, the sooner we get outta your hair."

"Well, tempting though it is," said Gerald, "I'm just a lowly paid minion in the Magic Triangle, what's in it for me?"

"I'll tell you what's in it for you, punk!" cried Mike, pulling himself up to his full height as he lifted Gerald off the ground by the lapels of his suit, ripping one. "You tell us where we can find this guy Harvey, or you'll be spending the next few weeks drinking soup through a straw in the local hospital. Your choice!"

Gerald was clearly at a loss for words. His mouth was moving but no sound came out.

"Mike, put him down, for goodness sake," said Hymie. "I know he's an irritating little twerp, but he's hardly a threat, now is he?"

Gerald nodded in enthusiastic support of his saviour.

Mike lowered the shaken pen-pusher to the ground and the colour began to return to Gerald's face.

"So, you see, we're reasonable men," said Hymie. "We don't want to hurt you; it's just that we work in a dangerous business, that's all. Sometimes people try to hurt us, but we're men of peace as you can see. I'm sure you'll do your best for us, won't you, Gerald. As I said, all we need is a contact address for *The Amazing Harvey* and then we'll be outta here."

"Believe me, there's nothing I'd rather do than tell you," said Gerald, "but I've never heard of him. Simply practising magic doesn't qualify you for admittance to the Magic Triangle; we only take the best and brightest. At any time there are simply thousands of semi pro's plying their trade through small ads in newsagents shop windows. If you like I could ask around though. Just leave me your number and I'll call you if I hear anything."

"Do we look stupid?" snapped Mike, lifting Gerald up by the collar again and ripping his other lapel. "We give you our number and the next thing we know is the cops are on our doorstep giving us the third degree for roughing you up in the Magic Triangle. We weren't born yesterday, you nurk!"

"Mike…it's not worth it. Put him down."

Mike lowered the crumpled remains of Gerald to the floor. He promptly made a run for it.

"Thank you very much!" said Hymie. "That's why you should let me do the talking. We're supposed to be a couple of streetwise detectives solving cases with our wits and cunning, not a couple of mindless thugs scaring the crap out of unsuspecting members of the public who just happen to be in the wrong place at the wrong time. Gerald could have become a valued contact in this illustrious organisation instead of a new member of the 'We Hate Goldman Society.'"

Mike hung his head dejectedly and shuffled his feet.

"Anyway, we'd better get out of here before security arrives," added Hymie.

They legged it for the exit. As Hymie stepped out onto the pavement, a revving engine sounded out from somewhere nearby and a red sports-car raced down the street towards him. It hurtled along the road, mounted the pavement outside the doorway to number thirteen and sped on towards the startled sleuth.

CRUNCH!

Hymie reeled backwards into a world of silence and darkness. All Mike could see as he gazed down the street after the disappearing sports-car was the back of a woman's head. She may have had dark curly hair and been wearing a red jacket and scarf, but he couldn't be sure.

Part Six

All unquiet on the Cricklewood Front

There are parts of Cricklewood which are practically no-go zones for the working classes, assuming such people still exist. Streets where the Union Jack still flies over the manicured lawns of old Blighty and where Darjeeling and cucumber sandwiches are still *de rigeur* at four o'clock. It was into such a street that Inspector Decca and his chauffeur, Sergeant Terse, were decanted one sunny afternoon; two extraterrestrials on parole from Planet Portaloo.

For Decca, as welcome as it was to extricate himself from the bowels of Police HQ, a sense of foreboding had begun to trouble him; a feeling that it was all very well associating with the rich and powerful until it all went pear shaped and he was left carrying the can. Terse, blithely unaware of such possibilities, lived in a less rarefied world; a world in which a crook in a big house was still a crook, he just got away with it more often. He cared little for subtlety or sophistication, all that mattered was that he was *the law*. He would have felt right at home in Dodge City, but if it had to be Cricklewood, so be it.

They slammed the doors of the patrol car they'd commandeered and crunched their way down the gravel path to the imposing front door, inlaid with elaborate stained glass panels, no doubt nicked from the local church, thought Terse.

"OK, Terse, don't say *anything*," said Decca. "If you have to speak at all, try and stick to the weather or Andy Murray's chances at Wimbledon. On second thoughts, forget the tennis." Sergeant Terse reached out a sausage-like finger and pressed the doorbell three times in quick succession.

"Alright, sir," said Terse, who really wanted to shout 'Open Up! It's the Fuzz!'.

The door opened to reveal a mature and smartly dressed lady of a certain age, whose face, as she saw the police car, shifted down a gear from polite indifference to irked dismay.

"Don't you people drive *ordinary* cars nowadays?" she asked.

Decca flashed his credentials. "Inspector Decca, CID," he said, curtly. "This is my colleague, Sergeant Terse. And you would be?"

"Mrs Olga Flanagan, of course, who else would I be?"

Decca raised an eyebrow. Terse said nothing.

"Can we come in, or would you rather discuss matters on the doorstep?"

"No, please come in," said their reluctant hostess. "I take it you've come about the so-called magician?"

He nodded and they followed her through the house into a large and airy conservatory at the rear of the property.

"It was down there that it happened," she said, pointing to the end of the garden.

"I see," said Decca. "I've read the statement you made, of course, but it helps to see where the alleged incident occurred."

"There's nothing *alleged* about it," she snapped. "It was a despicable act by a depraved madman masquerading as a children's entertainer."

Decca coughed to suppress a smirk. "Yes, It must have been very distressing for you and the children. I hope you're feeling better now."

"Well, hardly. Poor little Sophie may never be the same again, not to mention Sammy, who was practically one of the family."

"Sammy?" queried Terse, flipping through his notebook, pencil in hand.

"Sammy the goldfish, of course! Why, when I think of his sweet little face pressed up against the glass when we had visitors it makes me so sad. Sad and angry…"

"So Sammy's the squashed goldfish," said Terse. "I see, now we're getting somewhere. Do you still have the body, madam?" he continued, forgetting Decca's instruction to be quiet at all costs.

Mrs Flanagan's eyes boggled. She couldn't believe what she was hearing.

"You see, madam," continued Terse, while Decca gaped like a goldfish out of water, "we need evidence; hard facts and reliable testimony from upright, respectable citizens like yourself. Kids just don't cut it in the courts. If you want us to put this sleazebag behind bars where he belongs, you'll have to show us a bit more than an empty bowl and a business card for *The Amazing Harvey – magic like you wouldn't believe*," he said, reading from the card. "I mean, come on, lady, by your own admission you didn't pay him so what are we looking at here? Criminal damage to a missing fish? He'll probably get off with a caution. He may even sue."

"Wu, wu, wu...yu..." was all the apoplectic Mrs Flanagan could manage.

Decca seized the opportunity to regain control of the interview.

"That'll be enough, thank you, Terse," he said. "Mrs Flanagan, please excuse my colleague. He's a very good officer but he's a little too used to dealing with hardened criminals. Clearly his sense of discretion has become a casualty of our difficult work."

He proffered a large white handkerchief.

Mrs Flanagan took it and blew her nose into it. "I do understand, Inspector," she said, with some effort. "Junior staff should speak when they're spoken to," she added, arching an eyebrow at the oblivious Terse.

"Nevertheless," continued Decca, "there's much truth in what the sergeant says."

Olga Flanagan drew herself up to her full five feet three inches. "That's simply not good enough, Inspector. This man, Harvey, is a menace to law abiding citizens everywhere and I fully intend to have him struck off as a children's entertainer. He should be exposed to the full force of the law. My daughter and the other children at her party may be emotionally scarred for life! Steps must be taken and they must be taken now. If you don't take them, then I will, and as I'm sure you know I have friends in some very high places."

Terse, who had friends in some very low places, stared out of the window.

Inspector Decca stood his ground. "I trust, madam, you're not suggesting that the law can be manipulated to serve the interests of a chosen few. I can assure you that the Metropolitan Police take these matters very seriously and we will be taking all the steps necessary to bring this perpetrator to justice. Although, in my experience, this kind of lowlife never sticks around anywhere long enough to suffer the consequences of his crimes."

"Have you thought about hiring a private detective?" asked Terse, impulsively.

"That'll do, thank you, Terse. Be quiet!" snapped Decca.

"No, Inspector, let the man speak. It's the first sensible thing he's said since he arrived."

Terse smiled fatuously. He'd been in this woman's company for less than twenty minutes and although he was no rocket scientist, he could already tell that she was a time-wasting, whinging old battleaxe with no conception of life outside the NW2 postcode. If he could palm her off on Hymie Goldman, he may just be able to avoid running around like a headless chicken on a pointless investigation for six months before being demoted to an even smaller office.

"You were saying?" prompted the Inspector, scarcely believing he was actually going along with this madness.

"We can't compete with private detectives on cases like this," began Terse. Decca closed his eyes.

"Our hands are tied," continued Terse. "You need someone who can give your case all the time and attention it needs, fight fire with fire, get their hands dirty. As policemen we have to abide by the law, we have to respect the human rights of scum like this, who really need a good kicking. Personally, I'd like to punch this guy's face in, but can I? Not ruddy likely, I'd be on the dole before you could say Jack Robinson."

"I like the cut of your jib, Sergeant," said Olga Flanagan at the thought of *The Amazing Harvey* having his face rearranged. "Can you recommend anyone?"

Decca quickly re-opened his eyes. This couldn't be happening; even Terse had more sense than that, surely?

"Officially, no. But off the record, madam, there *is* a man I've come across in the course of my duties who may fit the bill. He seems to have a way of inflicting a kind of natural justice on those he meets without any conscious effort. He's also cheap; you can usually beat him down to practically nothing."

"Excellent, Sergeant, and his name is?"

"Hymie Goldman. He works out of an office on the Finchley Road, above the Black Kat café. The business is called Goldman Confidential. No case is too small, nothing too much trouble. Mention my name, tell him I recommended him," said Terse.

"Thank you, you've been most helpful. Sammy must be avenged."

We're all going to hell! thought Decca. If we can get out

of here in the next five minutes I may just get back in time for the match, thought Terse. They said their goodbyes hurriedly and retraced their steps to the patrol car.

,

Part Seven

There's no people like show people

In a threadbare old theatre in North London, Marvin the Marvellous Mechanical prepared for his umpteenth comeback tour with barely concealed indifference. He was a dapper little man in his late fifties, immaculately dressed in faultless evening dress and a top hat, but he seemed listless as he went through his stage preparations.

"Five minutes to curtain up!" cried a voice backstage.

Marvin straightened out the props on his conjuring table and checked his pockets for the key to his once famous *Cabinet of Doom*, a rusting metal hulk, now painted lime green and concealed from view at the back of the stage. Boy, he'd played some dives in his time but this place took the biscuit. The masonry was crumbling, the lights flickered and the audience looked like they'd escaped from a day-care centre. In fact, they were simply sheltering from the downpour outside until the number 28 bus arrived.

Marvin wondered briefly how places like this could pay the rent, then caught sight of the posters for recent attractions, reflected on the pittance they were paying him and remembered. Ah, yes, *Harry Bosworth and Mr Jinks,* a dire ventriloquist act from Pinner which relied too heavily on the audience's ability to imagine it was being entertained. As for *The Peckham Pirouettes,* the critic, Roy Santiago, of *Then and Now* magazine had described them as 'a bunch of fat, bored, middle-aged women with no skill or training, sucking the life-blood out of local entertainment'. How he'd laughed when they caught up with him outside the newsagents on the High Street a few days later. You didn't hear so much of Roy these days; probably still in hospital.

The moth-eaten satin curtain sailed slowly away into the slips, leaving Marvin to his fate. As the scant crowd sat dripping in the aisles, suppressing a collective yawn of anticipation, he strode purposefully to the front of the stage to address them.

"Ladies and gentlemen, how do you do?"

Nothing. Not a ripple. Not a flicker. Scarcely a neuron connected.

"I'm Marvin the Marvellous Mechanical and I have an amazing magic show for you tonight to rival anything in the world. This act has been performed before the crowned heads of Europe. They hated it, that's why I'm presenting it to you tonight in this burnt out public lavatory. Only kidding."

"Before I begin the act for which I am rightly famous, let me introduce my assistant this evening; the lovely, the unscrew...sorry, inscrutable, Miss Lotus Blossom."

A short, blousy, middle-aged woman, flimsily disguised as a geisha girl in a cropped black wig, shuffled onto the stage, bowed and shuffled off again. Her real name was Doris Biggs.

"Thank you, thank you, Miss Lotus Blossom," said Marvin.

There was a half-hearted ripple of applause. A couple of people left.

He smiled then opened his mouth to reveal what appeared to be an egg. He carefully removed it and flattened it on the top of his hat. A cloud of white smoke appeared above him and a pigeon seemed to fly out of the top of the hat before fluttering down to the back of the stage, where it left a deposit on Lotus Blossom's wig.

The theatre was silent. You could have heard a pin drop, had the floor not been covered in chewing gum and empty sweet wrappers.

Unappreciative bastards, thought Marvin.

"I dare say you've seen stage magic before, that you think it's all sleight of hand and trickery," he said, "but tonight, ladies and gentlemen, I'm going to give you a performance you will never forget; a show of such power and ingenuity you may be excused for thinking me the devil incarnate."

The slow drift to the bus stop continued.

"Lotus Blossom, please to assist me," said the Marvellous Mechanical to his assistant, with a bow. The ageing geisha tiptoed across the stage and handed him what looked like a large red house brick.

He took it and held it out for the audience to see. "One common or garden house brick," he said.

"How do we know it's real?" asked a man in the third row of the stalls.

Marvin simply let go of the brick and watched it land on the stage with a crunch.

A young girl at the back of the theatre began to laugh hysterically but anyone looking around soon noticed that the right-hand side of her face was illuminated, presumably by her mobile phone.

Marvin stooped down to retrieve the brick, kicking away the traces of red dust.

"I think we've established that we're dealing with a real brick here," said Marvin, "but not everything is as it seems," he added. "If I were to tell you I could transform this simple brick into something entirely different by the sheer power of magic, what would you wish for, ladies and gentlemen?"

"A coupla hot biatches and some coke, man," called out a shady character at the rear of the stalls.

"Thank you, Chief Constable, but I'm afraid I'm only a magician, not a politician. Anyone else?" asked Marvin, scouring the auditorium for a sympathetic face.

"Well, I've been trying to get my hands on a Ford Cortina Mk 3 distributor cap for ages," said a balding middle aged man with his arms folded across his chest.

Marvin retrieved a large white handkerchief from his top pocket and blew his nose despondently. After all these years he never failed to be disappointed by his fellow man's complete lack of imagination. They simply had no sense of wonder.

"I'm sure you have, mate, but have you tried eBay?" said Marvin, dismissively. "Would anyone else care to wish for something?"

"A lovely big bunch of flowers," said a sweet little old lady in an aisle seat.

"A wonderful idea, my dear lady, and I shall be only too happy to oblige," said Marvin with relief. After all, how the hell was he meant to fit a Mk3 distributor cap up his sleeve?

"Abracadabra, super glue, roses are red and violets, blue!" exclaimed Marvin, dramatically.

Someone began to titter at the absurdity of it all.

"What goes up must come down," said Marvin, throwing the brick up into the air.

There was a loud popping sound and the brick vanished in a puff of white smoke, to be replaced by a cascade of paper daisies, which showered the stage in a blanket of coloured petals.

Marvin took his first bow and was gratified to hear the audience applaud warmly.

"Thank you, my friends."

Lotus Blossom tiptoed back across the stage, tapped her wristwatch and whispered something into Marvin's ear.

"Ladies and gentlemen, now for the pièce de résistance of this evening's performance, the moment you've all been waiting for; the *Cabinet of Doom*, featuring the *Pendulum of Death*." He nodded to Lotus Blossom to wheel the great hulking contraption to the front of the stage as he continued his patter.

"I'm sure you've all heard of the famous Harry Houdini, well the illusion I am about to present to you would have baffled even the great escapologist himself."

He carefully removed his jacket and hat and placed them neatly on the floor. He stretched out his arms and turned full circle on the stage before the audience to demonstrate he had nothing to hide.

"In a moment, ladies and gentlemen, I will be secured by official police-issue handcuffs inside the small compartment on the left-hand side of the *Cabinet of Doom*. Inside the cabinet itself..." he paused for effect and for Lotus Blossom to open the front of the lime green metal box, "is the *Pendulum of Death*; a razor sharp blade swinging back and forth inside the case. It is restrained from swinging for an absolute maximum of three minutes by these special retaining cords," he said, pointing to what looked like a couple of old mooring ropes. "If I fail to extricate myself from the handcuffs within three minutes and exit through the door at the back of the cabinet, the pendulum's blade will first slice through the restraining ropes and then through myself." He gazed intently into the auditorium.

The last few remaining audience members fell into a hushed silence.

Marvin covered his eyes with a blindfold and was escorted into place by his assistant, Lotus Blossom. She carefully attached the handcuffs to his wrists and left the chamber, closing the metal door firmly behind her. Finally she pressed the starter button on an outsized stopwatch mounted on a stand at the front of the stage and a drum roll sounded out across the theatre's ancient PA system.

As the seconds ticked by on the stopwatch, an increasing air of tension and anticipation gripped the remaining seven members of the audience. The atmosphere was electric. With thirty seconds to go there was a loud banging sound from inside the chamber, as though someone were desperately trying to escape. There was still no sign of Marvin. Twenty five seconds came and went, twenty, fifteen, the excitement was palpable. Lotus Blossom began to look more concerned than inscrutable. Ten seconds remaining, then five, then three, two and one passed and the audience gave an audible sigh as the sound of the pendulum swinging inside the cabinet grew louder. A trickle of dark liquid pooled onto the stage from the left side of the cabinet. Lotus Blossom ran to the wings and shouted for help. The safety curtain came down and the show ended abruptly.

As the last member of the audience stumbled out onto the street, stunned and fearful that he had witnessed the death of Marvin the Marvellous Mechanical, Lotus Blossom opened the door of the *Cabinet of Doom*, barely able to look.

Inside, everything was in a state of utter confusion. The pendulum had sheared through the retaining ropes and battered the sides of the cabinet, which were now protruding beyond their normal position. The trail of liquid which had trickled onto the stage appeared to originate from the pendulum's hydraulic system. The escape door at the back of the cabinet was wide open but there was no sign of Marvin, except for a pair of artificial arms hanging absurdly from the unopened handcuffs.

Down the corridor behind the stage, Marvin walked past the empty dressing rooms towards the stage door.

That bloody useless machine, he knew he should have had it serviced properly. It was just as well he'd been using those artificial arms or he'd be a goner by now. He pushed open the stage door and walked out into the dark street. There was a noise from overhead. He turned and looked up. The last thing he saw was a red house brick approaching at high speed.

Part Eight

A day in the life of Hymie Goldman

Goldman awoke to find himself in a strange bed with a severe headache. It wasn't even symptomatic of a wild and hectic social life, as he was well and truly alone. Where exactly was he? What had he been doing the night before and what day was this? he wondered briefly. He should have known better at his age. Ah well, he'd just have to pop out for some headache tablets from that new mega-chemist by the ring road, Hyper-Chondria.

The shapely rear of a woman in white overalls hove into view as she pulled open the blinds with a flourish. Aaarrrgghh! That was one sight he could do without, daylight! He'd never been a morning person.

"Nurse, please close the blinds, I'm not big on sunshine this early in the day," said Hymie.

"Sorry," said the girl, partly closing them. "Although it's gone eleven and I'm not a nurse. My name's Ruby. Mike asked if I could do a bit of cleaning, cash in hand." She looked at him curiously for a moment. She was a black woman of about thirty with playful brown eyes and a dazzling smile.

"I see," said Hymie. "So, where are we?"

"Don't you recognise your own office?" asked Ruby, laughing.

"Frankly, no. You're not trying to tell me this is 792A Finchley Road, surely?"

"Oh, but I am."

"I don't believe it. It's never looked like this in my time here. Where did this bed come from?" asked Hymie.

"Well, I must admit the place was in a real state when I got here. You wouldn't have believed the dust."

"There goes our filing system," said Hymie.

"As for the bed, it's just a convertible sofa that Mike moved in from reception."

Hymie smiled. "Well, thank you, Ruby, you've done a great job. Mike has some marvellous friends I never knew about."

He blushed slightly, despite his best efforts not to. He wasn't used to dealing with attractive cleaning ladies, only women who hated his guts or were trying to con him. "Would you be interested in a full time job?" he asked, as casually as he could manage.

"What, as a cleaner?" asked Ruby.

"Well, as you can probably tell, we're only a small business, we can't afford to pay a full time cleaner but if you can do office admin, answer the phone and make a decent cuppa too, the job's yours. If it works out you can even train as a private investigator one day."

"I don't know about that but the office manager's a good place to start. How much are you paying?" she asked.

He looked into her big brown eyes and forgot entirely what he was about to say.

"Err…what are you earning now?" asked Hymie.

"£18K plus overtime," she replied.

He realised too late he was in too deep but couldn't bear to admit it.

"Well, I'm sure we could manage an extra 5%," he said.

Ruby looked around the room dubiously. They couldn't afford to pay her nearly £19K a year. She'd be surprised if they took home that much themselves, but then she was between jobs and she hadn't earned £18K in the first place.

"It's a deal," she said. "When do I start?"

"Welcome on board, Ruby. Call me Hymie, everyone does."

The phone rang in reception. Hymie winced.

"No peace for the wicked," he said. "Why don't you make us both a cup of tea while I answer that."

"Hello, Mrs Flanagan…"

"No, this is Goldman Confidential, you've got the wrong number," he said, cutting her off. She rang again almost immediately.

"Hello, Goldman Confidential, no case too large."

"*This* is Mrs Flanagan. I'd like to speak to the manager please. I was just cut off by some idiot."

"Speaking, I mean I'm the manager, the proprietor in fact. Goldman's the name, Hymie Goldman, how can I help you, madam?"

"You were recommended to me by a policeman," she said.

Hymie's face fell. It damn near abseiled off a cliff. He tried to avoid the Fuzz wherever possible so the thought of being recommended by them made his blood run cold.

"Anyone I might know?"

"Yes, Sergeant someone or other, Tense I think. Yes, Sergeant Tense."

Hymie grimaced. Tense was an apt description of anyone having dealings with Sergeant Terse.

"I think you mean Terse, madam."

"Well, he *was* a little abrupt and to the point, but a good man all the same. He had very enlightened views on the punishment of offenders."

Hymie's mind boggled.

"What sort of case is it?"

"I want you to find someone and put the fear of God into him."

It sounded like a case for Terse. "And you're sure the sergeant recommended *me*?"

"He said it was right up your street. I think he'd have liked to handle the case himself, but his inspector said that their resources were a little stretched."

Hymie could imagine Decca saying it, yet why would they recommend *him* when they both thought he was a complete plonker? It all seemed a bit fishy. Still, as long as she was good for the money did it really matter? He'd long since given up expecting anything in his life to make sense.

"He seemed to rate you very highly, Mr Goldman," continued Mrs Flanagan, "he even said your charges were reasonable."

"How kind of him," he said testily. Either Terse was having a laugh or marking his card not to overcharge the old dear on pain of a social call. Or maybe she was just trying it on, you could never be sure. "Perhaps you'd like to arrange an appointment to come in and discuss the details?" he suggested.

"Is that strictly necessary, Mr Goldman? I simply want you to find a deranged madman called *The Amazing Harvey* who masquerades as a magician and children's entertainer and persuade him to retire immediately or else…"

"Or else what exactly?" asked Hymie.

"I'll leave it to your discretion," she said.

Hymie fell silent. He couldn't believe it. He'd spent years totally oblivious to the existence of *The Amazing Harvey* and then suddenly everyone he met was offering him money to find the guy. If only he knew where he was.

"I could pop you a cheque in the post."

It just got better and better. Hymie was on the point of pinching himself when Ruby returned with a mug of steaming tea to find him grinning broadly. She placed the mug on the desk in front of him, passed him a scribbled note then waved and left.

"Damn!" said Goldman. She hasn't resigned already?

"I beg your pardon, Mr Goldman, there's no need for that," said Mrs Flanagan.

"Sorry, Mrs Flannel…"

"Flanagan!"

"…my assistant just spilt a hot drink over my trousers," he said, as he tried to read the note which was upside down on his desk. It looked like 'need to arrange cat litter, see you tomorrow, R.'

"Did you say you wanted me to find *The Amazing Harvey*? The magician?" he asked. He'd always thought it must be impossible to get paid twice for solving the same case. Getting paid once was hard enough, but this seemed to open up all kinds of possibilities.

There was a snort of disgust from the other end of the phone. "Magician? Hah! That's what he calls himself, but he couldn't magic himself out of a paper bag. Do I take it you've heard of him, Mr Goldman?"

"No, but I think I can find him for you."

"Excellent."

"I normally charge £250 per day plus expenses but as you're a friend of Sergeant Terse, I'll do it for a flat fee of £1,000. Just send a cheque to Goldman Confidential, 792A Finchley Road, with your contact details and anything you can remember about Harvey and I'll get cracking."

"Well, it's a lot of money, but under the circumstances, you have a deal."

"Thanks for the call, Mrs Flanagan, and rest assured I'll do a good job for you," said Hymie, replacing the receiver.

"Yeehah! We're in the money..." he sang tunelessly to himself in the empty office. So what if the neighbours thought he was barmy? For once everything seemed to be coming up roses. Even his headache had disappeared.

Mike returned to the office and looked pensively at his dishevelled business partner.

"I suppose you know I saved your life again," he said.

"How do you work that out?"

"You don't remember me saving you from that sports car outside the Magic Triangle?"

"No."

"Typical! That's all the thanks I get. I yanked you out of the way at the last minute, but because you can't remember it, it never happened. Next time I won't bother, you ungrateful git. I expect you lost your memory when you hit your head on the doors."

"If you say so, Mike. By the way, I've hired a new receptionist cum bottle-washer."

"What are you paying her in? Green Shield stamps?"

"Don't you start, it's that bird, Ruby you sent round to do a bit of cleaning. I thought she was a friend of yours," said Hymie.

"Well, not exactly," said Mike. "I advertised for a cleaner for my flat and she was the only one who gave me a quote after she saw the place. The others ran screaming from the building or said they'd suddenly decided to give up the cleaning business for health reasons."

"Well, that's a sort of reference," said Hymie, a wistful look flitting across his face.

"You fancy her, don't you?"

"Don't be ridiculous," said Hymie, avoiding the question. "Besides, someone else has just offered to pay us to find *The Amazing Harvey.*"

"Now that *is* amazing. Who?"

"Some woman called Flanagan. She said Terse recommended us."

"Now we're in trouble.I thought we'd be in clover with

this case but if this guy Harvey is of interest to the likes of Terse and Decca, we'd better keep our wits about us."

"Never fear, Mike, we're a match for the whole lot of 'em," said Hymie.

Part Nine

In the Big Room

Inspector Decca walked resignedly along the tenth floor corridor and knocked at the Chief's door on the end at the left, next to the fire escape. The Chief was too important to fry if the office burnt down, thought Decca.

"Come in, Decca," said the wood-alcohol voice, seemingly through three feet of cotton wool.

The Inspector entered the room, approached the Chief's desk and awaited further instructions. He cast a glance at the collection of framed photos around the walls; the Chief being presented with a long service medal, the Chief winning his local golf club annual umbrella, the Chief outside Buckingham palace en route to a garden party; the Chief pissed out of his mind at some dinner for civic dignitaries, the Chief having a punch-up with Rod Hull and Emu.

"Sit down, Decca," said the Chief.

He sat, still wondering whether he was there for a kick up the arse or a pat on the back. He could swing for that idiot, Terse; nothing any good ever came of recommending Hymie Goldman as a private detective. It was so self evident as to be blindingly obvious to everyone, it seemed, but Terse.

"Well, Decca!" barked the Chief, a tall, heavily-built man in his late fifties with a blotchy red face and bright blue eyes. He directed his keen gaze at Decca like a search-light trying to spot an escaped convict.

"What have you been up to?"

"Well, sir..." said Decca. He wondered if he should blame it all on Terse, whatever it was, but realised it wouldn't do any good and simply smiled sheepishly.

"Bloody good job, Decca. Excellent work," blurted his commanding officer.

"Thank you, sir," said Decca, perplexed.

"I don't know how you did it, man, and I don't *want* to know but well done. I've been expecting to get it in the neck from Lord O'Connor over his granddaughter's goldfish for days but not only has this not happened, but I've actually had a call from the old boy congratulating me on your enlightened policing methods," said the Chief.

Decca could tell it had come as something of a surprise by the way the Chief kept scratching his head.

"Well, of course, sir, I have my methods," said the Inspector.

"I'm sure you do, Ray, and I'm sorry we haven't always seen eye to eye on everything. When you went barmy I had no choice other than to transfer you off the front line, but now I can see you're ready for a bigger challenge. You're a top man, Decca and you've been languishing in a pokey little office with dead flies...I mean files, for far too long. I want you back in Homicide tomorrow, Ray, and I always get what I want. To show that there's no hard feelings you can even take that loony sergeant with you. What's his name again?"

"Terse, sir,"

"Well, whatever. I'm sure we can just go back to losing the paperwork for those unsolved cases down the radiator like we used to." They had to cut costs somehow.

"Yes, sir, very kind of you, sir," said Decca. It was easier to put up with Terse than explain to the Chief that the man was a complete nightmare to work with.

"When you get back to Homicide, Decca there's a case I'd like you to investigate," continued the Chief. "One of those magician fellers turned up outside a theatre with his head bashed in; nasty business. Still, magicians are a damn funny lot; ripping up playing cards and hiding rabbits for a living, very strange."

"Yes, sir."

"OK, good job, Decca, now get lost."

Ray Decca stood up and walked to the door. There was a spring in his step once more, as he retraced his steps back down the corridor to the lift. Was his luck finally turning for the better? Was he about to join the greats of his profession at last?

Only the realisation that he was still lumbered with Terse and Goldman put a damper on things. Yet perhaps he could even do something about that.

Part Ten

The mystery deepens

Hymie Goldman sat picking his nose behind his desk at 792A Finchley Road. That was the beauty of having no staff, you didn't have to bother with the niceties of office life. He scratched his unshaven chin and retrieved a half-eaten bowl of cornflakes from the drawer in his desk. He couldn't remember leaving them there, but he supposed he must have done. The intercom buzzer sounded downstairs and he leant across his desk to answer it.

"Who is it?"

"Ruby, Mr Goldman, your new PA. I said I'd be here as soon as I'd sorted out a cat sitter."

A dreamy look passed across the scruffy detective's face as he recalled their meeting of the day before.

"Come in," he cooed, pressing the door release button.

She seemed to float into the room, a vision in a tight-fitting blouse and pencil skirt. His mouth opened involuntarily but nothing came out apart from a part-chewed cornflake. He brushed it away hastily and smiled.

"Where shall I start then, Hymie?" she asked.

"How about making us both a cuppa?" he said. "I'm sorry I'm in such a state, love, I lost track of the time. I'll go and have a shave and then we can get started."

As Hymie shuffled off to break the habits of a lifetime, Mike arrived.

"Hello, Ruby. Hymie told me you were joining us. I hope you know what you're letting yourself in for. He's a bit disorganised, to say the least."

"Oh, hi, Mike. Don't worry. He's paying me well. Besides, I've seen your flat, remember?"

"Okay, pot, kettle, black, sure," he said, but he still couldn't fathom why Goldman was splashing out cash they could ill afford on this girl. Was Mike - the Mug - Murphy now subsidising the old fool's love life? After all, this was the guy who wouldn't even shell out for a packet of chocolate hobnobs for a partners' meeting. Still, you couldn't say that to the new office junior.

Goldman returned from his ablutions, clean shaven and wearing a tie. Mike did a double-take.

"Can I help you, sir?" he asked.

Hymie frowned. "It wouldn't hurt you to smarten yourself up for once either."

In the time it had taken for Hymie to transform himself, Mike had put away the fold-up bed and Ruby had prepared the drinks.

Hymie beamed at them both with something akin to enthusiasm.

"Team," he began, "I've felt for some time now that we needed to put Goldman Confidential on the map. Of course, this takes time but every great journey starts with one small step; in our case, holding formal team meetings where we can pool our knowledge, hone our plans and get a real sense of team spirit going."

Mike stared blankly at him. It was news to him that Goldman ever thought about the business at all, let alone as anything other than his personal cashpoint.

"Otherwise," continued Hymie, "it's just me and him," he said, nodding at Mike, "sitting around trying to score points off each other."

"Completely pointless, you mean," said Mike.

"Exactly," agreed Hymie. "So if you'd care to pop out and get us some proper cakes," he said to Ruby, proffering a twenty pound note, "then we can start as we mean to go on."

Once she'd left, Mike looked through the blinds onto the street below. A smartly dressed Polish girl called Zuszka was mopping vomit off the pavement outside the Black Kat before any of their customers could tread it into the café.

"That Zuszka's a bit of alright. She can use a mop too. That's what I've been missing," said Mike.

"A mop?"

"No, you plonker! A bit of female company. Don't you ever miss it?"

"What, the abject poverty, the barely concealed hostility and the mutual loathing? I get enough of that here."

"So you're not interested in Ruby, then? It wouldn't bother you if I asked her out sometime?"

"I thought you fancied that Polish bird."

"I see," said Mike.

"See what?"

"Oh, nothing," said Mike. "We'd better start focusing on the case. We need results and we need them now, before this Redrum guy comes looking for his money back. How hard can it be to find a dud magician called *The Amazing Harvey*?"

"Surprisingly so," said Hymie. "If he was any good he'd have his name plastered everywhere, but as he's rotten, he seems to be virtually untraceable. Still, we haven't exhausted all the possible leads yet. What if I get Ruby to check through all the local papers for the last few years?"

"Haven't you already checked him out on the internet, then?" asked Mike.

"Yeah, well, I'm pretty good at investigations you can do from your own armchair."

"You can say that again," said Mike. "Tell me a bit more about the client. I know he's paid you a pile of cash, but what else do you know about this guy, Redrum?"

"There's not much to say, except the guy is seriously weird; a whole other level of odd. He just showed up out of nowhere, like some kind of ghost."

"When did he visit us?" asked Mike.

"Oh, he's never set foot in the office."

"So, where did you meet him?"

"It was a couple of weeks ago on a Tuesday. I remember 'cause I'd been to the flicks to see a late night showing of *The Killers* at the Freemont. I was standing in the entrance, trying to find my keys, when this shadow fell across me. I turned around and there was this tall guy wearing a black cape. It really scared the crap out of me."

"Like Batman."

"Yeah, that sort of thing."

"What did he look like?" asked Mike, feeling strangely sleepy.

"I couldn't really say," said Hymie. "I've never seen his face. He may not even have one, for all I know. You see he stood between me and the beam from the streetlamp. All I saw was his silhouetted shape behind the cape. Then, in a creepy Eastern European accent, he started telling me how he wanted me to find some magician called *The Amazing Harvey*. My first thought was that he must be an escaped madman and that I'd better humour him in case he pulled a gun on me, so I nodded a lot and said yes at the right moments, and at the end he gave me a case full of money and said he'd be in touch."

"Great. We've got another homicidal maniac for a client," said Mike, suppressing a yawn. "By the way, what's that buzzing noise outside and why are the lights flickering?"

"S'funny, I was wondering the same thing," said Hymie, leaning back in his chair.

"Zzzzzzzzz," said Mike.

"Zzzzzzzz," concurred Hymie.

Some hours later, Goldman was awoken by a wet rasping sensation on his forehead. His eyes flickered open. Everything was dark and he seemed to be alone in the office. Outside, the noise of the traffic suggested it was late in the evening.

Another wet rasping sensation tickled his face.

"Purrrrrrrrrr."

"Bloody hell, Bacon, thanks a bundle!" snapped Hymie, pushing the cat to one side.

Bacon was a street cat Mike had befriended in a moment of weakness. He occasionally sneaked into the office when no-one was watching and nicked any leftovers he found lying around. He'd earned his name after Hymie had caught him stealing his breakfast roll.

"Get the hell out of my office, you freeloading fleabag!" snapped Hymie, as he stood up to switch on the lights. He drew the blinds and sat down again. What the blazes was going on? He looked at his watch, which, if it could be believed, was showing 11pm. What had happened to Mike? And Ruby? How long did it take to buy a few cakes? It looked like he could kiss that twenty quid goodbye. Yet something inside kept telling him that it was worse than that; that Mike would never leave without saying goodbye or waking him up. So what had happened to him?

Bacon had retreated to Hymie's desk, where he sat licking himself conscientiously from tail to toe.

"Why didn't you do something, you useless feline!" cried Goldman, throwing his rolled-up tie at the cat. Bacon sprang down and as he did so, Hymie caught sight of a large white envelope with his name embossed on it in gold letters, sitting on top of his desk.

Inside was an invitation card which read:

'You are cordially invited to an extraordinary meeting of the Magic Triangle, tonight at midnight. Failure to attend may result in death.'

"Bloody magicians!" cried Hymie. This time he'd show them where they could stick their dirty tricks. He opened his desk drawer and retrieved a pair of heavy brass knuckle dusters that Mike had given him for Christmas. He wasn't much cop at fighting, but sometimes there wasn't any choice.

Part Eleven

Like Lazarus

Mike awoke, tied to a wooden chair with electrical cable, in a dark dank basement, poorly lit by a single low wattage light-bulb hanging from the ceiling above his head. He could smell the river and assumed he was in a tunnel somewhere in London. His head felt groggy and his nose and shirt seemed to have dried blood on them, although for once he couldn't remember being in a fight. He flexed his giant shoulders but the chair only creaked while the cable threatened to cut off the blood supply to his triceps.

"Hello! Hello!" he shouted. "Where the hell am I?" His words reverberated around the walls. "It's not that new West End club they're all talking about is it? *The Sewer*? Well, the service is bloody awful!" he cried, more to cheer himself up than anything.

There was a muttering in the darkness and a shuffling of feet. Suddenly, a dwarf appeared dressed for a circus performance.

"Welcome to the Carnival of Fools, Mr Murphy, my name's Rimbono. Sorry about the blood on your shirt by the way, you were heavier than expected, I believe they dropped you."

"Don't mention it. It looks like I'm the only one here; does that make me King of the Fools? Why didn't you invite my business partner, Hymie Goldman along? Now *he* knows a thing or two about fools."

Again, there was muttering in the darkness.

"He wasn't there when we collected you. At least, no-one answering his description. There was just a clean-shaven man wearing a tie."

Mike smiled. "Like you say, it couldn't have been Goldman. A right scruffy git he is."

"But we left him an invitation to join us. After all, we didn't want the great Hymie Goldman to feel left out," added Rimbono.

"He's used to it," said Mike. He couldn't quite believe anyone would refer to him as great though, even for a laugh. "He won't come, you know; he hates parties."

"Oh, he'll come to this one."

"So, if this is a party, where are the drinks and the cheesy nibbles?" asked Mike.

"All in good time," said the dwarf, removing five hand-grenades from the lining of his jacket and starting to juggle with them.

"I don't suppose you've heard of the *Carnival of Fools* before, have you?"

"No, it's not big in Finchley," said Mike.

"Hardly surprising, given that no-one ever leaves alive," said Rimbono for effect.

Another dwarf appeared from the shadows. He

looked identical to Rimbono and was presumably his twin.

"We were going to call it the *Carnival of Death*, but thought it sounded a bit naff, weren't we dearie?" said the newcomer, in an effeminate, high pitched whine.

Rimbono glared at his brother. "You always have to butt in at the wrong time, don't you, Malvolio; like the ham actor you are!"

"Ooh, get her!" snapped Malvolio. "She thinks she's the evil twin, but everyone knows it's me."

"Ladies, ladies, please!" said Mike. "Not in front of a stranger."

"Temper, temper, ducky. Still, they don't come much stranger than you, eh?" said Malvolio, giving their prisoner a cursory glance. "My name's Malvolio, matey, I'm famous. I've toured the world with all the *best* circuses as a juggler and acrobat; Malvolio the Magnificent they call me or Mal the Mag for short. He thinks he can juggle," he said, nodding at his brother, "but he can't!"

Mike looked blankly from one to the other.

"You *must* have heard of me," pleaded Malvolio.

Rimbono smirked.

"Nope…no, wait, yes, I *have*," said Mike. "I read about you some place. That was it, I read about you in *Juggling Balls Monthly* – Val the Fag they called you. They said your act was shit!" he added.

Malvolio removed a flick-knife from his jacket pocket and extended the blade.

"I don't think I like you any more, sunshine," he said.

Rimbono was laughing quietly to himself. "Wait,

brother, we haven't asked him any questions yet," he said.

Malvolio glowered venomously at Mike and with an effort of will put away the knife. "Your witness, Bono," he said curtly.

Mike was still trying to work out what he was doing there. Okay, so he'd been drugged or hypnotised or something and they'd brought him to this dump, but why? What did they think he knew? And who were they anyway?

Rimbono began juggling his hand-grenades again. It clearly helped him to relax. Mike considered asking him if they were live or not but thought better of it.

The dwarf looked irritably at his brother again then turned to face Murphy, still writhing in his chair.

"Where's Harvey?" he asked.

The question seemed to take Mike by surprise. "Harvey who?" he asked.

"Don't play games with me, Murphy; *The Amazing Harvey*. He calls himself a magician, but he's really a spy," said Rimbono.

"A spy?" said Mike. "Are you sure?"

"Look, who's asking the questions here, dummy? Either you're trying to hold out on us or you really are as stupid as you seem. Neither makes much sense. You see, I only have to pull the pin on one of these babies and walk out of the room for a moment and you'll be plastered all over the walls," said Rimbono.

Mike stared from one brother to the other, searching in vain for some trace of humanity. They looked like a couple of refugees from hell and he knew that if he didn't get out of there soon they would finish him for sure.

"Who are you working for, Murphy?" asked a voice from the darkness.

There was an intense pain behind Mike's eyes and he felt an overwhelming desire to answer any question they asked him. It was as though he were a tiny insect caught up in a maelstrom, powerless to resist.

"Who's asking?"

"Watch the grenades, Murphy. Watch them as they spin round and round. Watch them as they suck your mind into the vortex." Rimbono smiled a sardonic grin at him in the ghastly half light as the projectiles blurred into an arc of destruction.

"The pain!" cried Murphy. "For God's sake stop it!"

"It will end as soon as you tell us what we want to know," said the voice in the darkness.

"Okay, okay. I'll tell you anything!" shouted Murphy.

"Who are you working for?"

"Redrum," said Mike.

"What's he look like?" asked his interrogator.

"I dunno, I've never met him," said Mike, "ask Hymie, he's met him. He could be anyone for all I know. He could even be you."

The third man appeared from the shadows, an ominous presence of a man concealed behind a black cape.

"He could indeed, as you say, be me," said the man in a strange Eurasian accent. "But, of course, he isn't. Now, tell me about *The Amazing Harvey*; where does he live? Where does he hang out? Who are his known associates?"

"I've told you, I don't know!" cried Mike.

He slumped forward in his chair and tried again to loosen the cable binding him to it. The pain in his head was excruciating. He bit down hard on his lower lip until he drew blood. The sudden burst of pain in his mouth inexplicably helped clear the fog in his brain.

Any normal man waking from a nightmare, who found himself strapped to a chair and being interrogated by shadows and dwarves might despair, might give in to the encroaching madness and lose the will to live. Alone and in the dark, Michael Aloysius Murphy was different to others; not better or worse, just less inclined to quit and more inclined to fight.

"Look, I've had enough of this. I don't know who you think you are but there are laws against kidnapping and torture in this country, and when I get out of here I'm gonna push your face so far down your neck you'll be eating out of your backside!"

Mike's giant frame twisted and contorted like a huge serpent caught in the jaws of an enormous crocodile.

Snap! Crackle! Crunch!

The wooden chair disintegrated into splintered fragments beneath him as Mike stood up, several pieces of broken chair still hanging from him like Neanderthal jewellery.

"Oh shit!" cried Rimbono, freezing in fear as the grenades landed one after the other with a metallic clang on the basement floor. All but the last, which fell into Mike's outstretched palm. He pulled the pin and held on tightly to the release clip with his strong, thick fingers. The dwarves had already started running for the exit.

"Thanks, morons, I was trying to find out how to get out of here!" cried Mike.

He turned around to look at his arch-inquisitor, the man in the shadows, but there was no-one there.

"Oh well, waste not, want not," he said, throwing the grenade into the darkness at the far end of the room before running as fast as he could in the opposite direction.

Part Twelve

Too young to live, too old to die

At ten minutes to midnight, Hymie Goldman sat ashen faced on the bus to Euston station. He'd never make it, they hadn't given him enough time, but if anything happened to Mike, he'd never live with himself. Who else would do all the dangerous, boring jobs? You just couldn't find people willing to take them on. Mike was irreplaceable.

Outside the bus, neon-flecked tourists and drunken revellers jostled with late night commuters on their way to the late night kebab shop. London was no place for the old, the slow, the weak or the poor, and though Goldman permed three from four he had a steely, purposeful look in his eye for once. Damn it, the big guy needed him and how often did that happen?

"Eh, mate, got 50p for the bus?" asked a bearded tramp in the seat behind him.

"You're already on the bus, you scrounging git! What are you trying to do, save up and buy one?!" snapped Hymie.

A two-tone paper flyer, lying discarded on the floor at his feet, caught his attention. He picked it up and straightened out the creases.

'Marvo the Magnificent performs his death defying bullet catching feat for one night only. Thursday 7th at the Jack Raddish Memorial theatre in the Novotel, Hammersmith. Be there. Be amazed. Tickets £20 from all good agencies.'

Maybe he'd know Harvey? It was worth a try.

Several minutes later the bus ground to a halt at Euston and Hymie hopped off before the other passengers could alight. As he headed along the pavement towards Stephenson Way, he suddenly noticed a glow in the sky and a cloud of black smoke rising in a column above the street he was heading for. He started to run. Within a few yards he developed a stitch in his side, but he continued running through the pain. Mike would do no less for him and he could be in that building.

A fire engine rushed past, its siren blaring in the calm night air.

Hymie followed it at a distance as it turned into Stephenson Way. When he got close enough to see for himself, he was struck dumb at the appalling sight before him. The Magic Triangle building had been reduced to a pile of steaming rubble. He ran across the road to the cordon barriers. Flames flickered amidst the ruins. Charred timbers, posters and leather bound books smouldered on all sides and the battered entrance sign emblazoned with the Triangle's motto, *Age tuum negotium,* lay disregarded in the wreckage.

"Mike! Mike!! Where the hell are you?"

Goldman covered his mouth with a tatty handkerchief and closed his eyes to keep out the smoke fumes, but also to blot out the thought that no-one inside the building could have survived that explosion.

"Dear God, bring him back! Don't let the great lummox die. I swear on my mother's life I'll never expect him to do all the crappy jobs again!" wailed Goldman.

He couldn't get close enough to the building's main entrance to see anything so he skirted around the block to the rear, which hadn't been so utterly destroyed.

He was about to leave in the vague hope that Mike had been down the pub or out on the town with his new Greek bird, Bazookas, when Hymie noticed a rather tatty boot sticking out of a pile of rubble, and thought he'd better investigate.

He dug around the boot until a large hairy leg emerged, then clawed and scrabbled at the earth and shattered timbers with mounting excitement and fear. Could this person still be alive? Would they know what had happened to Mike or why the building had been so totally devastated? He continued to dig.

As he continued to dig, Hymie found a large piece of door pressing down across the top half of the poor devil. He lifted it with great difficulty before realising that there was a concealed air pocket beneath it, which had probably saved the guy's life.

The man was filthy and covered in ash but as the door came off his face he suddenly coughed and spluttered into life.

"Huuuuurrrgh!"

"You've had a lucky escape, mate," said Hymie.

"You could have fooled me! Where the hell have you been, Goldman?"

"Mike?"

"Well, who were you expecting? The Amazing Bloody Harvey?"

"It's great to see you… I thought you were dead."

"What? And let you get my share of the dosh!" quipped Mike.

"Same old Mike. I'll get us a cab back to the office and you can tell me all about it."

Part Thirteen

Clouds over Hammersmith

After a week of incoherent babbling about dwarves and men with no face, Mike was ready for a big night out and Hymie needed a change of scene, so they headed for the Novotel, Hammersmith with something verging on enthusiasm.

Outside, the letter 'v' in the green neon-lit sign appeared to have fused, leaving Hammersmith's only Novotel looking somewhat sorry for itself.

The detective duo pushed past the revolving door and headed for the concierge's desk, where a bored looking twenty-something was yawning and reading the local paper.

"Can I help you?" he asked.

"We've come for the big show," said Hymie.

"Right...er, would that be the International Parrot Fancier's Convention or the Magician?"

Mike looked bewildered at the reply. His life was getting stranger by the day and the last thing he needed was a run in with a bunch of exotic birds.

"The Magician, of course," said Hymie. "I saw a flyer

for it; Marvo the Magnificent and his amazing bullet catching act."

"Oh, you want the Jack Raddish," said the concierge.

"I beg your pardon," said Mike. "We came here to see a magician, not some prawn named after a salad."

"It's the name of the theatre," muttered Hymie, out of the side of his mouth.

"Yes, up two flights of stairs and along to the West Wing," said the concierge, picking up his paper again.

They headed into the voluminous interior of the building in search of the Jack Raddish Memorial Theatre, and hoped it had a bar.

"They're big on overblown stage names aren't they," said Mike.

"Magicians?" confirmed Hymie.

"Yeah, who else? *The Amazing Harvey*, *Marvo the Magnificent*…you never come across one called Average Sid or Just Bob, do you?"

Hymie smirked. When Mike was in his pseudo philosophical mood, you just had to let him talk it off.

"I suppose it's the posters…" continued Mike.

"Eh?" said Hymie, trying in vain to maintain the intellectual level of the conversation.

"Well, who's gonna go to see some bloke called Bob doing magic tricks? You just wouldn't bother would you? On the other hand, there's that guy…what's he called? Dave? No, Darren…that's it, Darren Brown. He's a big name these days even though he sounds like someone from down the pub."

"Actually, it's Derren," said Hymie.

"What, Darren Derren? Shows all you know, Goldman; sounds more like the Pink Panther theme tune."

"Have it your way, mate," said Hymie, handing their tickets to the usherette.

She smiled hesitantly at him. "I've been asked to let all patrons know that there's an escaped African Grey in the auditorium," she said.

"African Grey what?" asked Mike, with visions of elephants, rhinoceri and herds of wildebeest stampeding through the front stalls.

"Parrot," said the girl. "He's escaped from the International Parrot Fanciers Doodah," she added, by way of explanation, "but he's not dangerous."

"Not as dangerous as the fanciers anyway," quipped Hymie.

"They should have caught him before curtain up," said the girl.

"The fanciers should have been locked up years ago," said Hymie.

They walked down the aisle and took their seats, shuffling along row G past an irascible woman in a turquoise hat and a fat man with gravy spots down his tie. A recorded drum roll crackled over the PA system and the purple satin curtains parted to reveal a short, smartly dressed man with thinning hair and his tall, statuesque assistant, a blonde girl in her thirties who looked stunning in her gold lamé dress and fishnet stockings.

"Ladies and Gentlemen," continued the voice on the tannoy. "For one night only as part of his world tour, please give a big Jack Raddish welcome to the one, the only, the legendary…Marvo the Magnificent."

Three people clapped.

Marvo the Magnificent, or Bob Evans as he was known down the Goat and Compasses, looked a little underwhelmed. Nevertheless, he strode manfully to the front of the stage to address his audience.

"Ladies, Gents, Children, it's a great pleasure to be here performing for you tonight en route to the Hippodrome, Bradford. In a moment, I will perform the feat known to audiences around the world as the bullet catching trick; a trick which is as difficult and as dangerous to perform as any before seen on the magic circuit. But first, please put your hands together for my assistants this evening, the lovely Lavinia…"

The girl in the golden getup took an elegant bow, displaying her magnificent cleavage to the men in the plastic macs in the front row and generating an enthusiastic applause.

Up in the fly loft there was an audible squawking sound and a few grey feathers fluttered down onto the stage.

"…and ace marksman, Hugo Herschel," concluded Marvo.

A dapper man in a hunting jacket with a handlebar moustache appeared from the wings and took a bow. The applause continued in a lower key.

The noise seemed to disturb Einstein, the African Grey parrot, who had been resting above the stage and he flew out towards the back of the auditorium showering the audience below with bird droppings.

The lady with the turquoise hat took a direct hit and Mike was spattered with white splashes of bird muck across the shoulders of his jacket.

The woman stood up in disgust. "Someone call the manager, this is an absolute disgrace!" she cried.

"Perhaps Hugo can shoot that bloody bird!" shouted a heckler from the back.

Marvo beamed and directed his gaze at the lady with the ruined hat.

"I'm afraid Hugo would get into serious trouble if he started taking pot shots at poor defenceless birds. Never mind, dear lady, I'm sure the manager will recompense you for the damage. As for me, I can only sympathise," he said, pulling a bouquet of flowers from his jacket sleeve and passing them across the orchestra pit to her. He gestured to an attendant at the back of the auditorium for someone to capture the parrot.

"And now, ladies and gentlemen," continued Marvo. "Moving on to an illusion many have attempted but few survived, please be silent while I perform my world famous bullet catching act." He nodded to Lavinia, then walked to the centre of the stage and sat down on a specially prepared bar stool. Lavinia shimmied across the stage after him and then tied a specially prepared blindfold over his eyes.

"You will see, ladies and gentlemen, that I can see nothing of what may be about to happen," said Marvo.

The audience sat in hushed silence as ace marksman Hugo walked to a specially prepared spot on the stage and, removing a Smith and Wesson revolver from its case, carefully checked that it was loaded.

It was so quiet you could have heard a pin drop.

"Uh oh," said Einstein the parrot, from somewhere over the audience's heads, as two men in white coats approached him with a net.

A few members of the audience laughed nervously.

"Lavinia, if you please," said Marvo the Magnificent.

She pulled the cord on a small curtain which fell open to reveal a large stopwatch, mounted on a wooden board.

"When the countdown commences, I will have precisely sixty seconds of life left before Hugo pulls the trigger on that gun and we shall see, once and for all, if I really *can* catch a bullet in my teeth," said Marvo.

Lavinia pressed the release button on the clock and it began its countdown, every second audibly ticking away.

Marvo ran his tongue over the edge of the spent bullet inside his mouth and counted down the seconds, as he had done so many times before in rehearsal. To make his death appear authentic he had to take the dive at exactly the moment Hugo fired the blank round at him.

The seconds sounded out in Marvo's head as the time ticked away on the clock. Thirty seconds, twenty, ten. His leg muscles braced themselves to flick the stool forwards as he prepared to fling himself backwards across the stage. Five seconds, four, three, two, one.

BANG!!

The audience collectively seemed to stop breathing as they focused on the motionless figure stretched out before them on the stage. Marvo's arm twitched and the audience erupted through sheer relief into a thunderous applause.

Lavinia walked across the stage to the prostrate figure of Marvo to help him to his feet for his curtain call, but then stopped suddenly, her face frozen in fear. She signalled to the stagehand to lower the curtain and fell to her knees at Marvo's feet. He was bleeding badly and incoherent with shock.

"Bob, Bob! Can you hear me? What happened?" she implored him, leaning across his blood-soaked jacket to hear whatever he had to say.

He opened his mouth to speak but only managed to utter a couple of words before sinking back to the ground with dull and lifeless eyes.

Lavinia ran backstage, tears streaming down her face.

"Call the manager, he's dead! Marvo's dead," she cried.

Even on the other side of the curtain it was increasingly obvious to the audience that something was wrong. No-one performed a magic act like that without taking a large number of elaborate bows. Was Marvo injured? Was he *dead*? Surely they had all seen him move, surely he had to be alive, but if so, where was he?

By the time the news broke, the audience were queuing to get out.

Goldman, having been in more scrapes than most, had the presence of mind to get to the front of the queue.

"They're gonna lock us in and call the police, Mike. They're gonna need witness statements and that's the last place we need to be," he said, running for the exit before the manager could lock the doors. He oh so nearly made it.

"Hold on a minute, mate, where do you think you're going?" It was the assistant deputy relief bar manager, Dave Parsons.

Hymie drew himself up to his full five feet six inches and let him have it with both barrels.

"Ah, Mr...Parsnips," he said, giving the manager's badge a cursory glance, "I'm Arnold Stockhausen and this is my colleague, Kevin Fishbone," he added, pointing to a large man covered in bird shit who was rapidly approaching up the staircase. "We're from the Institute of Applied Parrot Studies. I was about to contact the RSPCB, the Freedom for Parrots League and the Health and Safety Executive about the worst case of parrot mishandling I've ever seen," added Hymie, "but if you let us out of the back door I may just be able to content myself with a strongly worded letter to the Parrot Breeders Gazette."

Dave Parsons' face fell. As aghast as he was at this tirade of verbal diarrhoea, he couldn't for the life of him think of anything appropriate to say and it was while his face was working overtime that Mike seized his chance and knocked him out of the way with a smart left hook.

Parsons fell to the ground like a sack of spuds and Goldman and Murphy hastily retreated from 'Novohell' the way they had come. Strolling along Hammersmith Broadway a few moments later, they happened upon two familiar faces hurrying along in the direction they had just come.

"Good God! It's Hymie Goldman," cried Inspector Decca.

"And Mike Birdshit," added Sergeant Terse sarcastically.

Mike glowered at him, but had learnt when to hold his tongue.

"Well, they always did have trouble with the birds," said Decca, laughing.

"Evening, Inspector," said Hymie. "Going somewhere nice are we?"

"Now that would be telling," said Decca. "I only hope you're not mixed up in it though."

"What? Us, Inspector?" said Mike.

"We keep a very low profile these days," concurred Hymie, as the two detectives made a beeline for the nearest cab rank out of there."

*

After a couple of hours of taking witness statements at the Novotel, Hammersmith, Decca and Terse managed to find some other mugs to finish the job while they returned to the police station for a supposed meeting with the Chief.

As they entered Decca's new office on the second floor of Metropolitan House, the phone started ringing.

"Get that would you Terse, I can't face any more pointless conversations this evening."

Terse nodded and lifted the receiver. "Inspector Decca's office; Sergeant Terse speaking."

"Can I speak to Ray Decca please, it's urgent."

Terse handed over the receiver. "It's urgent," he whispered.

"Hello, Decca here, who's speaking please?"

"About time mate, I've been calling for hours. It's Terry Longbottom, your ex-wife's new partner. Your central heating boiler has just packed up and I need to know who to call to get it repaired. I presume you have a comprehensive service agreement?"

"I see," said Decca, retaining his composure with some difficulty. "Well, Mr Large Bottom, I should call the Samaritans if I were you, because if you call me at work again I will personally see to it that the boiler's pipework is inserted so far up your arse that you have steam coming out of your ears. Go boil your head!" snapped Decca, almost smashing the receiver as he laid it to rest on his desk.

"Trouble at home, guv?" asked the sergeant.

"Nothing I can't handle, Terse. They must think I'm soft in the head," said Decca.

"Who, sir? The Gas Board?"

Ray Decca smiled sadly and sat down behind his desk.

"So, Terse, what did you make of this evening's events?"

The sergeant scratched his head briefly then sat down opposite his boss.

"Well, it's a funny business really. I've investigated plenty of homicides, but not where the victim was shot on stage in front of three hundred witnesses. At least it looks like an open and shut case; Marvo's assistant, Hugo Herschel was seen by the entire audience shooting him at point blank range. Everyone assumed the bullet he fired was a blank but it obviously wasn't. Why he did it we don't know, but perhaps he'll come clean when he thinks it over. Perhaps he'll plead guilty to manslaughter. Maybe it was just some terrible accident," said Sergeant Terse.

"Or maybe Herschel was just the patsy," said Decca. "Maybe when we look into it further the other assistant, Lavinia, stood to gain financially from Marvo's death."

"Yeah, maybe it was an insurance scam, but what I don't get are his last words."

"His last words?" queried Decca.

"Not Bolton."

"Are you serious, Sergeant? Marvo's last words were *not Bolton*?"

"Straight up. That's what that Lavinia bird said."

"So, were they due to perform in Bolton? Was there someone there with a grudge against him?" asked Decca, intrigued.

"That's the funny thing, she definitely said that they *weren't* appearing in Bolton."

"Well, he won't be now, that's for sure."

"The other thing that got me thinking, sir, was that it was way too much of a coincidence to run into Goldman and Murphy coming away from the crime scene when we arrived."

"You know, Terse, I think we'll make a detective of you yet," said Decca. "Come on, let's pay them a little social visit on the way to the curry house."

Part Fourteen

Puzzled of Finchley

It was late when Hymie and Mike got back to 792A Finchley Road after the concert. The lengthening shadows of dusk had departed, to be replaced by dark streets sporadically lit by the neon glow of the all-night mini-mart and the Taj Mahal curry house, successor to Benny Baker's celebrated Pizzeria.

Hymie tore off a calling card which had been attached to the weather-beaten woodwork of their front door with a nail-gun and squinted at it.

"Madame Za Za. Whether you're a giant or a dwarf, I'm the medium for you."

Mike chuckled. "A charlatan with a sense of humour," he said.

"Don't knock what you don't understand, Mike. I've been thinking we should contact a spirit medium for a while now," said Hymie.

"Well, I suppose they can't be any worse than your usual method; sticking the names of all the suspects on a dartboard and throwing darts at it until you hit one."

Hymie scowled. "You're only jealous. At least I *have* a method."

Once inside their squalid office, North London's second worst detectives broke open a bottle of Tizer and stretched out in their decrepit armchairs to piece together another seemingly insoluble puzzle.

Bacon the cat strolled casually across the room as though he owned the place and curled up on the moth-eaten settee, where he proceeded to lick his balls meticulously.

Hymie looked on in mute fascination.

"Okay, Mike, what do *you* make of this case?" he asked.

"I dunno, it's the strangest case I've ever seen and I've only ever worked with you, so strange is normal," said Mike. "You've got more chance of filling out your tax return correctly than cracking this one, Goldman."

"Tax returns? Hah, I don't have time to waste on that mindless bureaucracy. It's just gibberish submitted by the gullible to the unemployable who don't understand what they're looking at when they get it. Besides, we have accountants for all that crap."

"We have *accountants*?" asked Mike, impressed. "Who the heck are they?"

Hymie's brain raced as he glanced furtively around the room for inspiration.

"Furball and Mildew," he replied; alighting on the cat and their shambolic decor.

"That figures," said Mike. "I bet we've got Mildew."

"Speak for yourself," said Hymie. "Oh, they may not be the biggest or the best firm in town, but at least they show that we're legit. We're respectable businessmen not penny ante sharks like some of the cowboys around here."

"Leaving aside how, or whether, we pay Bodgit and Scarper for their creative accounting, how *are* we going to solve this case?"

"Mike, Mike, you worry too much. I've been thinking it over. Nothing could be simpler, we'll just tell Redrum that *The Amazing Harvey* has emigrated..."

"Yeah, to Russia," said Mike. "It might work."

"Russia? Niet, who's gonna believe that? I was thinking of France."

"Why? Do they like rotten magic acts over there? Pick a card, any card, monsieur, it doesn't matter which one 'cause they're all the Jack of hearts!"

"It just needs to be somewhere Redrum might *believe* Harvey might actually want to go. If he did his magic show in Moscow he'd either freeze his balls off or actually perform the flamin' act somewhere and wind up with a concrete overcoat at the bottom of the river Volga."

"It's not gonna cut it, is it, Hymie? Redrum isn't your normal client you can blag with stories about how you *nearly* found the missing magician but he got away. He's gonna be after us with a semi-automatic and no-one even knows what he looks like or where he lives. Even I'm a bit nervous about the guy and I don't scare easy."

"Okay, I get it, but that's not the only option on the table is it?"

"Glad to hear it," said Mike.

Hymie scratched his head. He needed more time, more money, and a bigger brain.

"Let's just re-cap on the facts so far," he said.

"If you think it will help."

"We were hired by some guy calling himself Redrum, who's publicity shy to say the least. In fact we've never seen his face."

"Perhaps he's a woman," said Mike.

"Or maybe he has some instantly recognisable feature like a birthmark, scar or tattoo which he needs to keep hidden."

"What else?" asked Mike.

"A rubbish magician," said Hymie, writing 'Harvey' in red marker pen on the wall. "Anything else?"

"The Magic Triangle?"

"OK," said Hymie, writing 'Triangle' on the wall.

"What about that parrot," said Mike. "I've never seen so much bird shit in one place."

Hymie thought about it briefly before writing 'full of shit' at the bottom of the wall.

"So where does that get us?" asked Mike.

Hymie read back the clues. "Harvey Triangle is full of shit." He looked mildly disappointed as though he'd half expected it to make sense. "Anything to add?"

"Not really, but while we're sitting around playing silly buggers, half the Magic Triangle is being snuffed out by a bunch of homicidal maniacs. It's no wonder we can't find this Harvey geezer; if he's got any sense he's probably keeping his head down to stay alive. We should just give Redrum his money back."

"I can't see him letting us go," said Hymie. "Even if we had the cash to pay him back,"

"Is there anything we've missed?" asked Mike.

"Ruby. It stands to reason she's mixed up in this

somewhere. No-one quits a job after one day of making tea."

"You did. Remember when you were an electrician?"

"You had to bring that up, didn't you? Well, it was a very long time ago. Still, there's no such thing as coincidence. If some bloke breaks wind in Kuala Lumpur you can be sure there'll be a typhoon in Tahiti before long."

"So who's been guffing in here then?"

Hymie took a swig from his glass with a pained expression. "Probably that bloody cat."

"What are we going to do? asked Mike.

Hymie thought about Ruby. There was no reason for her to be involved. She was no criminal, just a normal girl looking for a normal job. She'd just taken a long hard look at him and their crummy offices and decided to take a better offer.

"I dunno," said Hymie quietly. "I wish she'd come back with those cakes, though, I could murder one right now."

"Let's start again," said Mike. "What have we got? A guy who hates magicians. He certainly hates Harvey. What if he also bumped off that magician in Wood Green?"

"Marvin? Yeah, and Marvo the Magnificent," said Hymie.

"But why?" asked Mike. "I can't stand that crappy talent contest show on the telly but I don't go around popping off the contestants do I?"

"No, but you're not a homicidal maniac," said Hymie.

"True," said Mike. "So we're looking for a homicidal maniac who hates magicians."

"Very possibly," said Hymie, wondering if that was such a good idea.

"But how are we ever going to find him?"

"Maybe it's time to involve the police," said Hymie. "We could use their protection."

"What from Decca and Terse? They'd just stand by laughing while we got wasted."

Hymie picked up the calling card he'd discarded on the table by the door. "Then we'd better speak to Madame Za Za. I'll call her, there's no time to lose."

"You're nuts, Goldman, completely bonkers! Why don't you just read your freakin' tea-leaves or something?"

"Everyone needs an edge in this game, Murphy and you'd be surprised how many great detectives work with psychics."

"Yeah, just before they get carted off to the nuthouse, mate. We could always go undercover again," said Mike. "Set ourselves up as a magic act and see if we can draw Redrum's fire," he added.

"Count me out, Murphy. It's not that I'm chicken or anything," said Hymie, unconvincingly. "It's just that I don't look good in fishnet tights and you'd make an even worse-looking assistant than me. Besides, how would we get any bookings?"

The phone on Hymie's desk started ringing.

"Look's like they've heard about our magic act already," said Hymie.

"Goldman and Murphy, Magicians," he said.

"Good grief! Is that you, Mr Goldman?" It was a woman's voice; the voice of a woman used to getting her own way.

"it, it's that Flanagan woman again," hissed Hymie. "Solly, Chinese Laundree shut!" he cried, in his best Widow Twankey voice, before slamming down the phone.

Mike had wandered across to the window and was peering through the blinds.

"Unless you wanna spend the rest of the night down at Fuzz Central explaining what we were doing at the Hammersmith Novotel while a murder was being committed, I suggest we get outta here now," said Mike.

"The fire escape!" cried Hymie.

"I didn't know there was one."

"Well, not as such, but the builders never took that bit of old scaffolding down when they repaired next door's roof and beggars can't be choosers," said Hymie, climbing out of the rear window.

Part Fifteen

Fuzzy Night

They came from far and wide, from the four corners of the Metropolis; the greatest assemblage of senior police officers ever collected together, not for some must-see event, rather on pain of demotion and exclusion from the Met's inner circle.

No-one could remember the last time there had been a triple red alert, so they were all a bit sketchy about the protocol, but they all knew without any shadow of a doubt that they had to attend, come what may. Deep in the bowels of New Scotland Yard, in the lead-lined room with the biological warfare sign on the door, the Deputy Chief Constable, Jack Robinson, MBE, GCSE, NURK, stood at the lectern at the end of the gallery and tapped his baton for silence. A panel of the great and the good sat alongside him, screwing up their eyes to make out the faces of the assembled masses under the low wattage emergency lighting.

"Gentlemen, lady," began the Chief. "We are facing a major threat which I need your full support and cooperation to deal with. As you know from recent incident reports

347

and in the media, there have been a spate of attacks on members of the Magic Triangle. Only last week their headquarters in Euston were blown up and several of their members have been murdered. I need hardly say that this is no coincidence; we believe the Triangle's old adversary, the Red Square, is resurgent."

"What evidence is there?" asked a senior officer from the back of the room.

"The statistics are revealing in themselves," continued DCC Robinson. "Of the 365 registered members of the Triangle, fifteen have died in suspicious circumstances in the last six months and many of the others have disappeared without a trace. The Grand Wizard himself, J R Bowling, called me up a few days ago from his bunker in the Edinburgh suburbs to warn me that the Triangle could face extinction before the all important Police Ball season."

"Balls!"

"Who said that?" snapped DCI Donkin, a dinosaur of urban policing who'd survived numerous allegations of police brutality, as he struck the desk in front of him repeatedly with a six inch length of lead pipe he just happened to have about him.

"It was DI Cavanagh, sir, he's got Tourette's," explained an officer seated in the front row. "It's the new legislation, we're not allowed to ask about health issues at interviews any longer and the interview panel just thought he was refreshingly forthright."

The Chief rolled his eyes to where heaven should have been then turned back reluctantly to face the desk wrecker.

"That'll do, Donkin. That desk is coming out of your budget by the way."

"Hah!" replied Donkin, hitting the desk once more for luck from force of habit.

"No, what I meant was; how do we know it was the Red Triangle?" asked the officer at the back.

"Who the blazes are they anyway?" asked Donkin. "Red Triangle my arse, they sound like a right bunch of plonkers!"

"Gentlemen, DCI Perkins," resumed the Chief, smiling apologetically at the only female officer in the room, "this is intolerable. There are magicians out there being wiped off the face of the map and all we can do is sit around scratching our..."

"Balls!" cried Cavanagh.

"Heads," said the Chief.

"Are we sure we're not dealing with a serial killer?" continued the officer at the back.

"Who said that?" asked DCC Robinson. "I can't see you very well from here."

"DI O'Connor, sir," replied the faceless one.

"No relation to Lord O'Connor I suppose?"

"He's my father."

"A *very* good question, O'Connor," said DCC Robinson. "But I think we can rule out a serial killer for three good reasons. Would anyone like to name them?"

"Bloody Cornflakes!" snapped Cavanagh.

Robinson turned briefly to Donkin. "Get him out of here," he muttered, before continuing with the briefing. Donkin headed off purposefully.

"Firstly, fifteen homicides in six months seems a lot for one killer. It's not like some madman has gone on the rampage in a shopping centre, these murders were all carefully planned and executed. Secondly, if it *were* one perpetrator, we'd have some corroborating evidence from the crime scenes; the same gun or modus operandi. As it is, we have very little to go on; no credible suspects, no witnesses, nothing."

"And thirdly, sir?" asked O'Connor.

"Third? Did I say *three* reasons? Ah…yes…well."

There was a distant thudding of boots down the corridor outside, then the door flew open and Inspector Ray Decca appeared before the assembled masses, panting for breath and with a battered videotape in his hand.

"I was asked to give you this, Chief," he said to DCC Robinson.

An officer in the front row took the tape from him and, flicking a couple of red switches on the communications console in the central aisle, inserted the tape into it.

The tape began to roll. A grainy image of two dishevelled characters flickered across the screen above their heads. They appeared to be leaving a burning building.

"This film was taken on CCTV the night the Magic Triangle's headquarters were blown up," said Decca.

"Does anyone recognise those two men?" asked DCC Robinson.

There was a non-committal mumbling across the room.

"I do, sir," said Decca. "I'd recognise them anywhere. I know them like the back of my hand. The large gorilla in the smouldering donkey jacket is a former bouncer called Mike Murphy and the short scruffy one is his partner in crime, Hymie Goldman."

"Good work, Decca. Bring them in for questioning," said the Chief.

Decca smiled. "Leave it to me, sir," he said. He headed back to the entrance in a daze. He was back from the brink and this time he was back for good. You couldn't keep a good man down for long and they didn't come any better than Inspector Ray Decca.

Part Sixteen

AAAAA Cars for the discerning mug

On exiting Hendon tube station, if you hang a right then take a couple of lefts then perhaps another right and finally another left for luck, you could find yourself outside AAAAA Cars, just like Hymie did one cold and frosty morning. Having had enough of being treated like a sardine on public transport, of the timetables that made no sense and to which no self-respecting bus or train driver adhered anyway, Goldman had decided that enough was enough and he had to have his own wheels again. Yes, it was time to buy a car; a car that made a statement about him and who he was: that he was a class act, powerful, majestic and dignified; a tall order for £7,500.

Contrary to rumours, AAAAA Cars wasn't named after the punters who awoke screaming in the night once they realised what a heap of junk their cars were, but in the hope they'd appear first in any directory of car vendors daft enough to include them. Most people either called them 'Five–A' or tried not to mention them at all.

Five-A operated the kind of disorganised, sprawling forecourt that at first sight could have belonged to a scrap metal dealer. But the similarities didn't end there; if you couldn't see the vehicle of your dreams it was probably there somewhere, in bits, most likely, awaiting re-assembly to order. Hymie gave up looking after a perfunctory tour of the yard and headed into the low-rise 1950's pre-fab that passed as Five-A's office. Inside he was greeted, with complete indifference, by a man in his late twenties in a cheap suit and electric yellow tie. The office was old and tired looking with scruffy MDF furniture. Hymie felt right at home.

"Alright?" said the youth.

"Yes, I rang yesterday and spoke to a Mr Harris," said Hymie. "He said he could get me a collectable classic car at a price I could afford. The name's Hymie Goldman."

"That's right, it was me," said Mr Harris, holding out his hand. "Paul Harris. How much *can* you afford?" he asked, hastily removing his hand.

"Well, er…" said Hymie, totting up an imaginary budget on his fingers. "Not a penny more than £7,500."

'As much as that!' thought Paul Harris. This Goldman character didn't exactly reek of money, but seven and a half grand wasn't to be sneezed at either. "It won't be easy," he said, "but my word is my bond."

"Yes, Paul," began Hymie, "I see myself behind the wheel of a Bugatti, something in racing red with go faster stripes."

"With seven and a half grand I'm afraid you couldn't afford the steering wheel, let alone a whole car, but I may be able to get you a damaged hood ornament or a wing-mirror," said Harris, trying to inject a lethal dose of reality into Hymie's fantasy.

"Oh, right. A pity. So what do you have in my price range?"

"Well, Hymie, how about a classic American sedan?" he asked, trying to remember where he'd left the old two-tone rust bucket. "You'd have the birds jumping all over you," he schmoozed. "They love those massive yet compact, stylish yet functional, comfortable yet sporty, models."

Hymie, who'd already begun to worry about the fuel consumption and how he was going to park something as vast as a classic American car, was immediately taken with the idea of being a hit with the ladies and raised the white flag.

"When can I see it?" he asked, eagerly.

"Well, it's not that simple. It's currently owned by a well known international rock star who I can't name for legal reasons. He's a household name though and has a genuine reason for selling. If you'd like to see a picture of the car, I can show it to you on my computer," he said, calling up a grainy image with a few quick keystrokes.

Hymie squinted at the image then thought of the birds and the rock star life. "How many miles does it have on the clock?" he asked, for the sake of appearances.

Harris pressed another couple of buttons on his keypad. "237,000 genuine miles."

"And how many non-genuine ones?" asked Hymie, suspiciously.

"Believe me, Hymie, that's nothing. This car's a 1969 Fleetwood with an 8.2 litre engine. It'll practically run forever. Ask Bon...oh, sorry, I shouldn't have said that," said Paul Harris, suggesting plenty without actually saying anything.

"How much is it?" asked Hymie, his resistance crumbling.

"Well, he wanted £10K for it but I haggled him down. It was hard work getting him to lower the price but I finally got him to agree to..."

"£7,500," said Hymie, holding out an envelope full of readies.

"Done," said Paul Harris, taking it from him. "Just pop your address down on this piece of paper and we'll get it delivered with the keys and log book very soon."

Part Seventeen

A kick in the crystal balls

The stars shone down reluctantly on the dark streets of North Finchley as Mike and Hymie embarked on their quest for enlightenment. Hymie remained convinced that a trip to Madame Za Za's would shed new light on the case, while Mike just couldn't think of a good enough reason to change Goldman's mind or to get out of going himself. Setting out on foot again with only the prospect of public transport for relief made Hymie wish all the more for the arrival of their new car, but as the delivery date was uncertain he didn't think Mike would appreciate the good news just yet. He would have to pick his moment to tell him.

Trouble lurked in the shadows around every nook and cranny for those foolhardy enough to seek it and as usual, the fool Goldman and the poor man's Oliver Hardy, Mike Murphy, fit the bill.

"Are you sure you want to do this, Goldman?" asked Mike, as though checking his colleague were sure he wanted a kick in the bollocks.

"I mean, most mediums are a bunch of con-artists

who spin you a load of old tosh that on closer inspection could mean practically anything."

"Have faith, Mike. When have I ever let you down?" asked Hymie.

"How long have you got?" said Mike.

"Lately, I mean" added Hymie, to forestall yet another pointless bickering session.

"Besides, we don't have many other alleyways to explore at the moment."

As the words left Goldman's mouth, a tall shadowy figure in a cape emerged from a nearby side-street.

"I thought I'd find you here," said the stranger ominously.

"Ah, Mr Redrum," replied Hymie, nervously. "I was just about to call you."

"Call me what?" asked Redrum.

"Never mind," said Hymie.

"I thought I'd spare you the trouble, Goldman. Do you know the whereabouts of *The Amazing Harvey* or are you going to give me my money back?" he asked calmly.

Who do you think I am, Victor Kiam? thought Hymie. "We're very close to finding him," he said hastily. "Another week, perhaps two…" He glanced at the expressionless mask of the stranger for some hint of a reaction. "Or perhaps just a few days …" he added. "We've looked under most of the usual stones but it's hard to tell. Still, we'll get there in the end, we always do. Unfortunately it's company policy never to return money."

Redrum walked purposefully towards him, removing a folded knife from his coat pocket as he did so. "I'm afraid your time's up, Goldman. I'm going to have to terminate your contract," he said, flicking open the knife's gleaming blade. He flipped the knife between his hands, juggled with it briefly and then lunged at Hymie.

BANG!

Redrum collapsed like a punctured balloon into a crumpled heap in the alleyway.

"Bloody hell!" cried Goldman, not quite sure whether to be more shocked by his own narrow escape or the fact that Mike, from the best of motives, had shot their client stone dead.

Mike slipped the shooter back into his jacket pocket and walked over to the body. The sound of running footsteps and a police siren from a neighbouring street made him stop momentarily.

"I didn't know you were carrying a gun," said Hymie.

"Well, after that night in the basement with the poison dwarves I haven't been sleeping so well. Besides, you're not complaining, surely?" said Mike, as he stooped down to reveal the face of their erstwhile client.

"Not much more than a kid," continued Mike. "Do you recognise him?"

"No," said Hymie, looking down at the body with difficulty.

"Me neither," said Mike, "but it was you or him, Hymie, and I wasn't going to stand by and watch you get creamed, even if you are a bloody useless detective."

All the fight seemed to have drained out of Goldman. "Let's get out of here, Mike, before the Fuzz arrive. And thanks, by the way."

"It's okay, mate. Where to now?" asked Mike.

"The medium, where else? We need an alibi as well as some answers," said Hymie, leading the way briskly along the road towards the nearest bus stop.

Aspbury Towers, Palmers Green was a tired-looking Art Deco apartment complex which had seen better days. It had suffered from one too many urban redevelopment projects and was now cast into the shade behind the local *Save a Packet.*

"Look, twenty-five litres of mayonnaise for a fiver!" said Mike.

"Yeah, but it probably tastes like shit," said Hymie. "Here we are, Mike," he added, a moment later, pressing the buzzer for apartment number 21.

A crackling intercom buzzed in the still night air.

"Who is it?" asked a female voice.

"I thought she was meant to be psychic," Mike smirked.

"Shhhh, don't be so rude," whispered Hymie. "Hello, is that Madame Za Za?"

"Yes, who is it?"

"Hymie Goldman, I called to arrange a meeting."

"Yes, I remember; something about a missing person. Did you come alone?"

"No, I'm with my business partner, Mike Murphy. Can we come in?"

There was a pregnant pause while Madame Za Za considered her options or phoned a friend, before the intercom crackled into life once more.

"Yes, alright, I'm on the third floor, number 38."

"I thought you were number 21" said Hymie.

"You can't be too careful in this business so I give out a false address to keep the nutters away," said Madame Za Za.

There was a buzzing sound and a click as the door catch was released and then Goldman and Murphy entered the building. They walked across the lobby to a small lift in the corner. Hymie groaned, removing the 'out of order' sign from the door and discarding it behind him.

"How am I supposed to climb three floors with *my* knees!" he snapped.

"Well, you could always call up Madame Za Za to give you a piggyback," said Mike.

"You think she'd go for that?"

"No."

They dragged themselves up three flights of stairs and along two landings before arriving breathless outside number 38.

Mike pressed the doorbell and the door opened on a security chain.

"Can I see some ID please?" asked the feeble voice proceeding from a bundle of shawls behind the door.

"Ah, yes. What did you have in mind? Finchley Public Libraries or an old Oyster card?"

"Just something with a name and photo ID will do," said Madame Za Za.

Hymie proffered an old bus pass. The old lady took it from him and studied it for some time behind the door.

"You poor man, how you must have suffered," she said.

"I'll have you know that was taken a few years ago when I was fitter," said Hymie.

Mike laughed.

Madame Za Za removed the door catch and the two detectives followed her through a narrow reception room into the lounge. The décor was so outlandishly bright it could only have been designed by a colour-blind designer; an orange settee here, some purple curtains there and a garish patterned rug in the middle of the floor. In pride of place on the rug sat a large round table, covered in a black satin tablecloth. Madame Za Za herself was scarcely less eye-catching. The parts of her you could see, that is; mainly her hands, which were smooth, brown and covered in rings, while her body and face were swathed in silken robes and crowned by an almost totally opaque veil. For all they knew it could have been anyone under there.

"Sit down Mr Goldman, Mr Murphy, I've been expecting you."

"Well, you would have, I made the appointment a couple of days ago," said Hymie.

"No, I meant before that. It was foretold to me many moons ago that two men fitting your description would come in search of enlightenment."

Mike raised his eyebrows. This was the kind of baloney he'd been expecting.

"How do we know you have the power?" asked Hymie, suspiciously.

"Why else would you be here?" asked Madame Za Za.

Mike glared at Goldman as though he were wondering the very same thing. He started to get up from his chair.

"No matter," said Madame Za Za dismissively. "If you don't even have the sense to listen, then why should *I* care? Why should *I* care that Hymie Goldman and Mike

Murphy, detectives of 792A Finchley Road, North London have failed to find the whereabouts of a magician whose name begins with the letters A.H?"

Mike and Hymie gawped at each other in amazement and Mike sat back down.

"I see you were only testing me, gentlemen, but you need have no doubts about my gifts. I come from a long line of Romanys," said Madame Za Za.

She lifted the black satin cloth on the table with a flourish to reveal the tools of her trade; a large crystal ball, a deck of cards and some chicken bones.

"Cross my palm with silver or, shall we say, fifty quid, and I'll begin," she said.

Hymie paid her grudgingly, then had a pain in his wallet where fifty quid used to be.

Za Za passed her hands over the crystal ball, uttered an outlandish chant and appeared to enter a trance.

"I see you've been having a lot of trouble lately," she said.

"You never spoke a truer word," said Hymie.

"When *haven't* you been having a spot of bother?" said Mike.

"Please, Mr Murphy, your scepticism is interfering with my mystic aura."

"Sorry madam."

"The future is an open book to me," continued Za Za. "It's true that there are many possible endings but only I can see what will be. Que sera, sera."

"Go on, go on," said Hymie, half expecting her to burst into song.

"Are you sure you want to know what the future

holds?" asked Za Za. "No-one will think any less of you if you're not brave enough to face it. I mean, there's no shame in being a chicken, or, even if there is, at least you can sleep at night."

"Come on, Za Za, I've got fifty quid at stake here, what's going to happen to me?"

"Very well; I see two men in uniform, standing over a body."

"Whose body?" asked Mike.

"I can't see his face, he's wearing a mask," said Za Za.

"How convenient," said Mike.

"I can see a large man, surrounded by midgets," continued Za Za. "They are tormenting him until he snaps."

Mike's face became deathly white. "What happens next?"

"I see a magician in a cloak, casting spells over some large rocks," she concluded.

"What does it all mean?" asked Hymie, anxiously.

"I can't tell. The spirits only give us glimpses of the truth. It's up to each of us to make our own sense of those insights," explained Za Za.

"But there's so little to go on," said Hymie, irritably. "Can't you tell us more?"

"I'm afraid not, the crystal is clouding over again."

"Well, what about reading my tea leaves? What about those chicken bones on the table?" asked Hymie.

"Oh, they're just left over from my tea. I had Kentucky fried chicken tonight."

"You're sure there's nothing more you can tell us?" persisted Hymie.

Madame Za Za spread the deck of cards across the table before him.

"Pick one!"

Goldman tapped the back of a card and Za Za picked it up and looked at it.

"To find Harvey you must first visit the pyramid, but beware Bolton."

They left the apartment in something of a daze, not sure whether they had been duped or given vital clues to the mystery that enveloped them.

As they walked down the staircase, Mike noticed an apartment with a broken-down door and smoke streaming from the shattered windowpane. Ironically the number on the wall outside was 21.

As they opened the door onto the street they were met by a wall of headlamps. They were about to turn and run when a policeman with a megaphone hailed them.

"OK Goldman, Murphy, put your hands above your heads and lie face down on the pavement."

"I can't do both at the same time, I'm a sick man," protested Hymie.

"You do not have to say anything, but it may harm your defence if you do not mention when questioned something which you later rely on in court. Anything you do say may be given in evidence," said the policeman.

"You say the sweetest things, Terse," muttered Mike.

"The pleasure's all mine, guys," said the sergeant.

Part Eighteen

Musical Chairs

Click! Decca's finger pressed the record button on the interview room tape machine, leaving the rest of him free to depress his least favourite suspect.

"Interview with Hymie Goldman, 11.15 December 19th, Inspector Decca and Constable Potter in attendance," he said. Potter may as well have been taking a nap for all he was contributing.

"I'm no good at interviews," bleated Hymie. "I get all anxious, sweat breaks out along my hairline and I get a terrible itching in the small of my back," he added.

"All classic symptoms of a guilty conscience," said Decca.

"I wouldn't know, Inspector. Still, are you sure you wouldn't rather send me a questionnaire through the post? Or if you don't trust the mail we could always exchange texts or have a facebook chat," wittered Hymie.

Nothing good ever came of being interviewed by the Fuzz, he thought.

"Ho, ho, you will have your little joke, Goldman," said Decca, "but I don't want to be your web buddy, I'll settle for asking my questions here at New Scotland Yard if it's all the same to you, or even if it isn't. Now, let's begin with the end of your sorry career, shall we? Or are you still labouring under the delusion that you and that escaped gorilla, Murphy, are private detectives?"

"End of my career, Inspector? I don't mean to disappoint you, but you've been calling for that for some time without much success," said Hymie.

Decca frowned. "I've never denied your talent for chaos and destruction. I'm surprised MI5 haven't put a counter-terrorism unit on your tail to study your technique."

"It'll be the cutbacks," said Hymie.

"Let's not beat about the bush, we've got you on CCTV leaving what was left of the Magic Triangle's HQ on the night it was bombed. Terse and I can testify to seeing you leave a murder scene at the Novotel Hammersmith and we have witness statements from earlier this evening identifying you as the murderer of a man in a cape."

"Not Batman, surely?" quipped Hymie, feeling unequal to the tidal wave of circumstantial evidence against him. "OK, I realise it doesn't look good for me, I'm no fool. I know you've got a list of unsolved cases you're just itching to pin on me, but you know as well as I do that with the right brief none of it will stick in court."

"Do me a favour, Goldman, when could you ever afford decent briefs? You usually get the kind of nurks who can just about manage to get you a suspended sentence on a good day; losers like yourself. Tell me all you know and I may put in a word for you."

"Haven't you ever heard of client confidentiality?" asked Hymie.

"Yes, but I'm surprised that you have. Wake up and smell the coffee, Goldman! It's over. You're facing life behind bars. At this point I'd usually say 'and a pretty boy like you may never sit down again' but we both know I'd be lying."

"I never knew you cared, Inspector," said Hymie.

"I don't, but you will. Give me a reason not to stick you back in the cells, sunshine."

Hymie scratched the five o'clock shadow on his chin and tried to find a better solution than bloody-minded defiance.

"Look, Inspector, this case is just too big for Goldman Confidential."

"I thought no case was too large for you, Goldman?" smirked Decca. "At least that's what it says in your advertising."

"Don't get me wrong," said Hymie, defensively, "we get there in the end, we always do. We've got plenty of leads; naturally, it's just that we haven't cracked it yet. So, it occurred to me that if we pooled our resources we might get a result faster. Of course, for it to work you'll have to trust me. Can you do that, Inspector?"

Decca weighed him up noncommittally for a moment. "Tell me more."

"My client was a gangland killer who wanted to know the whereabouts of a third rate magician called *The Amazing Harvey*," said Hymie.

"So he hires a third rate detective…I'm with you so far," said Decca.

It was Hymie's turn to look narked but he said nothing.

"I couldn't find this Harvey character. He seems to be lying low, what with all those magicians being killed and the Magic Triangle itself being attacked. Anyway, the client turned up this evening wanting his money back."

"How inconvenient. What did you do?" asked Decca.

"I'm a man of peace, Inspector. I'm not cut out for violence. My client started threatening me with a knife when some complete stranger happened along and shot him. I was lucky it was a rough neighbourhood," said Hymie.

"Yes, very lucky!"

"Then I scarpered."

"Alright, Goldman, I can believe in you running away from a fight but tell me, what's the name of your client and can you describe the man who killed him?"

"I knew him as Redrum. I always assumed that was an alias."

"No kidding. So you never twigged that in addition to being the most famous Grand National winner of all time it was also 'murder' spelt backwards?"

It looked like all those hours spent poring over the crossword had paid off, thought Decca. Hymie gaped. Was it just a coincidence or had Decca actually stumbled onto a clue that he'd missed? It didn't seem to mean much, but it was enough to make him feel like a prize wally. "Very clever, Decca, but what difference does it make?"

"Describe this Redrum for me."

"I never saw his face, he always stayed on the other side of a cape whenever we met and he spoke with a strange accent," said Hymie.

"How strange? Walthamstow? Dagenham? Or from north of the Watford Gap?"

"He was a foreigner. I thought he might be from Russia," added Hymie.

"You mean the Kremlin?" asked Decca.

"I guess they could be in on it too."

"And who shot him?" probed Decca.

"It was too dark to see. Besides, I wasn't hanging around to find out, was I?"

"So it wasn't Mike Murphy then?" asked Decca.

"Good lord, no. Whatever gave you that idea?" asked Hymie. "Look, that's as far as I got, Inspector. My client's dead so I don't have a case any longer. Why don't you just save yourself the paperwork and let me go? If I can be of any further assistance please don't hesitate to call. You'll be wasting your time though," he added, helpfully.

"Let me be the judge of that, Goldman. There's more going on here than meets the eye. Even if I were to accept your story, which I have to say, I don't, that still leaves the inconvenient facts of your presence at the bombed out Magic Triangle HQ and at the Novotel, Hammersmith on the night Marvo the Magnificent was murdered."

"I'd love to help you, Inspector, I really would, but these are just coincidences. I was passing the Magic Triangle when it blew up so I naturally tried to help find any survivors, and there must have been thousands of people walking through Hammersmith on the night that magician died. Anything else is just a conspiracy theory. I'm just a hardworking private investigator, not one of the four horsemen of the Apocalypse."

"That's just where you're wrong," said Decca. "Death, Famine, Plague... and Hymie Goldman; what a lethal combination! Still, I don't have to sit here and listen to Jackanory when I've got a warrant to search your offices, do I?" he added, slapping the document down on the interview room table in front of him.

Goldman looked morosely from Decca to Potter and back again.

"You won't find anything there," he said. "I keep all my records up here," he added, tapping the side of his forehead with his right index finger.

"Well, I suppose it keeps the running costs down eh? I mean, why go to the expense of a filing cabinet when you only have two files and a selection of final reminders?"

They'd finally succeeded in annoying him; the arrogant Detective Inspector and his dumb stooge of a constable. Where did they get off taking the piss out of a hard working local businessman? His taxes paid their wages. Or, at least, they would have if he'd paid any.

"OK, so you want to know what gives with the Magic Triangle? Well, it'll cost you. I can blow open the whole damn case and see to it that you make Commander within the next couple of months, but Murphy and I walk out of here now." He eyed them like a card sharp holding a pair of twos.

"Interview suspended at 11.45," said Decca, switching off the recording machine.

"You'd better not be bullshitting me, Goldman or you'll never work in this city again."

"Promises, promises," replied Hymie, never an enthusiastic devotee of hard work.

"Come on then, what *have* you got for me?" asked Decca.

Hymie felt like a hedgehog caught in the approaching headlights of a truck. Now that it was finally time to put up or shut up he realised he'd already given away practically everything he knew. He could babble on about dwarves and parrots for a while but that would only get him locked up in a psychiatric ward. How could he possibly invent something big enough to get Mike and himself out of there? He decided to play for time and on the Inspector's Achilles heel; his craving for promotion.

"Hold it, Decca. Before I give your career the boost it so desperately needs, what guarantee do I have that you'll let Mike and I go free? I mean, you could be swanking around on the twentieth floor with the keys to the executive bogs while we're languishing behind bars," said Hymie.

A wistful look played across the Inspector's careworn face.

"What information is it you're *actually* offering me?" he asked. "You've already told me you don't know the whereabouts of *The Amazing Harvey*, so what *do* you know? Do you know who's behind the magician killings and where I can find them?"

It was Hymie's turn to look pensive. Oh, he could fabricate a ludicrous story with the best of them, but would Decca believe it and even if he did, would he let them go or have it checked out first? The latter could be fatal to his prospects of early release.

A thunderous knocking on the interview room door was followed by the appearance of a crew-cut head in the doorway.

"Chief, I need a word urgently."

"Now's not a good time, Terse."

"But it's *important*, sir," added the sergeant with conviction.

Decca stood up, collected his thoughts then strode out into the corridor, closing the door behind him. He was about to give Terse a piece of his mind when he noticed a huddle of ne'er do wells further down the corridor and thought better of it. In the midst of them all stood Mike Murphy like a bouncy castle at a funeral, handcuffed and surrounded by constables. Behind them on the bench sat two city-types in pinstripe suits and red braces, clutching a brief.

"I'm afraid we have a habeas corpus problem on our hands, sir," said Terse, lowering his voice in a stage whisper.

Decca gaped at the sergeant. Latin proceeding from Terse's gob had to be one of the most improbable sounds he'd ever heard; about as likely as the Chief Constable farting in Westminster Abbey.

"Eh?" said Decca.

"*Habeas corpus*, sir; it's a writ or legal action by which a prisoner can be released from unlawful detention," he explained.

"I know what it is, Terse! I just didn't expect to hear it mentioned in a conversation with *you*. GBH, yes, latin, no. Besides, we've only just arrested them, how on earth can we have a habeas corpus problem?"

"Well, sir," continued the sergeant, lowering his voice still further. "It looks like the case is falling apart."

"How can that be, Terse?" asked Decca, sounding like a small boy who'd had his ice-cream nicked and sand kicked in his face for good measure. "This time we've got them bang to rights. We've got the body…"

"Sorry to be the bearer of bad news, Chief, but it seems that the body is no longer in the mortuary. The victim wasn't quite as dead as we thought."

"That's the craziest thing I've ever heard!" groaned Decca.

"It's worse than that, though."

"Worse? How on earth can it be worse?"

"We can't find the weapon used to commit the crime."

"We *know* Murphy shot the guy, even if we don't have a body or a weapon, we can hold them on suspicion," said Decca.

"Sorry, sir," said Terse. "I did say it got worse. I've just had a call from DCI Donkin."

Decca closed his eyes and put his hand to his forehead. Whatever the sergeant was about to say scarcely mattered, it was well understood that no-one argued with Donkin. "What did he say?" asked Decca.

"He said he'd had a call from Goldman's lawyers," said Terse, nodding in the direction of the two suits on the bench. "He said they were a couple of legal eagles from the city; Fothergill and Dungannon, and we had to let them see their clients at once or we'd have to answer to him."

Decca shuddered. He'd sooner let the devil incarnate out onto the streets of London than answer to DCI Donkin. What he wouldn't give for something on the old dinosaur, like these city-types seemed to have.

"I don't believe it!" gasped Decca. "How the hell does Goldman do it?" he added, as his left eye began to twitch.

"Someone upstairs seems to like him," said Terse.

"But why?" snapped Decca. "Right then, Sergeant, better send in Fothergill and Dunmoanin. Presumably they'll want Murphy too?"

"That's what DCI Donkin said, sir."

"OK, what's the point in arguing, Terse? Before they go in let me just have a final word with Goldman. You never know, I may just be able to get a last piece of useful information out of the crafty sod."

Decca re-entered the room and invited Potter to leave them.

"Good news, Inspector? Am I free to go?" asked Hymie.

"Yeah, in some parallel universe perhaps," said Decca. "No, I thought I'd just check whether you had anything else to say before I returned you to the cells."

"I thought we had a deal, Inspector," said Hymie. "Putting me back in the cells wasn't part of it and the same goes for Murphy."

Decca stared across the desk at the battered man of fortune and frowned.

"It's true what they say, Goldman, the devil looks after his own. Apparently your lawyers have arrived."

"I have *lawyers*?" replied Hymie, incredulously. "Hah, I mean, yes, of course, where have they been all this time? Oh, and they didn't happen to mention the name of the firm, I suppose?" Hymie's mind was racing. Who could these *lawyers* be and why did they want to see him? Could he play it to his advantage and get out of jail or were they really a couple of hit-men come to silence him for good?

"I'm sure you'll find out when you get their bill," said Decca. "They didn't look like your usual low budget outfit though. Still, if anyone ever needed good lawyers it was you and Murphy. I'll send them in."

After a brief game of musical chairs, Hymie and Mike found themselves seated opposite two total strangers in smart suits.

"Allow me to introduce myself, Mr Goldman," said the senior of the two, a tall man of indeterminate age with dyed blonde hair. "I'm Fothergill and this is my colleague, Dungannon," he explained, indicating a pale youth with glasses who didn't look old enough to be a lawyer. "I expect you're relieved to see us," said Dungannon.

"Pleased to meet you," said Hymie, feeling slightly more confident that they weren't hit-men, but still wondering what they were doing there.

"OK, who are you?" asked Mike, getting instantly to the nub of the matter.

"We're your *lawyers*," said Dungannon, as though trying to convince himself.

"We don't have lawyers," said Mike, "although I didn't realise we had accountants until recently so I could be wrong," he admitted.

"Well, I'm Fothergill and this is Dungannon," said the elder man, clutching his brief. "We're living proof that you *do* have lawyers."

"Wait, yes, I see now," said Mike. "Decca thinks we've finally flipped and he's stuck us in a room with these two other delusional nutters while he phones for the dial-a-bus to Broadmoor. We can all share a padded cell!"

"I knew this was madness," said Dungannon irritably to Fothergill.

Fothergill was clearly made of sterner stuff.

"We are where we are, gentlemen. Imagine, if you will, that you're in a police interview room being observed through one way glass by a disgruntled police inspector and the two men sitting opposite you are your best chance of getting out of here."

"Yes, anything for a laugh, but who *are* you?" asked Hymie.

"Fothergill and Dungannon," repeated the elder man as though reciting a spell.

"I couldn't give a monkey's if you're Tom and Jerry if you can get us out of here," said Mike.

"All you need to do is nod at everything I say for the next few minutes while my colleague takes notes and you'll soon be walking out of here as free men," said Fothergill.

What was going on? wondered Hymie, nodding along to the imaginary conversation. They'd been hired to find a failed children's entertainer; a task at which they'd also failed, by a killer who they'd been forced to kill. Now they were trying to get out of a police station by pretending to answer questions for two men masquerading as their lawyers. They didn't look much like lawyers but then how would he know? They didn't have any lawyers. So who were these guys and what did they want? They'd failed to find *The Amazing Harvey*, but what if he'd decided to come looking for them? Hymie stared hard at Fothergill and Dungannon, but they simply shook their heads at him like nodding dogs in a rear-view mirror.

"Our work here is done," said Fothergill, standing up at last.

"About bloody time," said Dungannon.

"You wouldn't know anyone called *The Amazing Harvey*, I suppose?" asked Hymie, trying to catch the legal eagles off guard.

"No, sorry," said Fothergill.

"Nor his assistant, Boltini," said Dungannon as the fake lawyers left the interview room, still clutching their unopened brief.

In the observation room next door, Decca looked on with dejected fascination.

"I suppose we'll have to let those two idiots out now, Terse," said Decca.

"Unless you want to be the one to tell DCI Donkin, sir," said Terse.

"Well, if that's the way it's gotta be then so be it, but I want *everyone* watching them, do you understand? Homicide, Narcotics, the Fraud Squad, the Transport Police, Meals on Wheels, Finchley Public Libraries; in fact anyone in a blue uniform with a big hat. I don't want that pair to be able to take a leak in this town without me knowing about it. We're gonna bug them so hard they'll suspect us of being in the room with them. Sooner or later they'll crack, just you wait and see."

"Yes, sir!" said Terse vehemently. This was the kind of policing he'd joined the force for; no nonsense, twenty-four-seven harassment of delinquents and low lives, and they didn't live much lower than Hymie Goldman and Mike Murphy.

Part Nineteen

A Lambeth Walk

It was late in the evening by the time Hymie and Mike finally hit the pavement outside New Scotland Yard. Potter had needed the overtime so it had taken him even longer than usual to complete the paperwork. A host of passers-by flitted past in their own little worlds, oblivious to the two unsightly strangers.

"OK, let's just pack our bags and get away from here," said Mike. "Somewhere hot where the beer's cheap, the natives are friendly and there's no extradition treaty with the UK."

"What? We can't leave *now*; not now that things are finally starting to get interesting."

"You're insane, Goldman! Come to that I must be too, to have worked with you for so long. I've grown accustomed to the bizarre challenges of our working lives, to the prospect of meeting new and interesting people on a daily basis and to the fact that most of them seem to want to kill me!" snapped Mike.

"You exaggerate, Mike. No-one's tried to kill you in weeks. It's usually me they're after. Besides, I don't think we could avoid this case if we tried. Look up there," he said, pointing at the grim concrete facade of New Scotland Yard. Lights shone down upon them from numerous windows and a dozen blinds twitched as they walked on down the street.

"If Decca hasn't got us under close surveillance by now I'll eat my hat," said Hymie.

"I thought you'd eaten that during the last case," said Mike.

"It's just a figure of speech."

"So where *are* we going?"

"It's nearly Christmas, let's go and find a massive Norwegian Spruce with some twinkling lights. Covent Garden's only a short walk away, let's check it out and get something to eat while we're there," said Hymie.

Mike's stomach rumbled in agreement. "Excellent idea," he said.

Meanwhile, in Lambeth, the members of the local Rotary group had assembled in disguise as Santa and his elves for their annual Christmas charity collection. Eighteen normally law-abiding citizens and upright members of the community leant around sipping mulled wine and freezing their costumed butts off while their transport coordinator, a part-time elf called Geoff Scrivens, made his final inspection of the float.

A sixty-foot trailer, covered in fake snow and with an MDF sleigh on top, sat waiting at the kerbside. It was hooked up to an ancient Land Rover with shockingly bad suspension.

"Looks alright to me," said Geoff. "Where's our

designated driver? Has anyone seen Mr Patel?" A surge of Chinese whispers spread through the crowd like a Mexican wave; "Mr Patel? Mr K-Tel? Anyone seen Mr McTell?" before one of the group, Vicky Green, an elfette in sexy black stockings, suddenly remembered he'd phoned in sick.

"Sorry everyone, too much mulled wine." she said, giggling.

"You're kidding," said Geoff, "So we've got no designated driver and everyone's had a drink."

"Well it is Christmas," said Tim Wotherspoon, the local locksmith, as if that excused most things.

"There must be someone who can drive this thing?" asked Geoff. "After all, think of all those kids we'll be letting down if Santa doesn't pay them a visit. Not to mention all the money lost to good causes."

"It's terrible the way they commercialise Christmas these days," said Elsie Pickles, the local postmistress.

"I hope you're not referring to the Rotarians, Elsie, we do a lot of good work for charity you know," said Geoff.

"No, I meant everyone *else*," replied Elsie quickly.

"We could ask the Nelsons' new au pair," said an elfette with a half-full glass of mulled wine who was resting against the Land Rover. "She's over there," she added, pointing vaguely heavenwards. "I think her name's Nookie."

There were a few laddish guffaws from the predominantly middle-aged men in the group before Geoff silenced them with a frown and a shushing noise. "Nookie!" he cried. More guffaws.

"I think you'll find her name's 'Nuka', like *nuclear*,"

said Sam Nelson, enunciating clearly so as not to slur his words.

A tall blonde girl of twenty one with dazzling cornflower-blue eyes approached them. Her command of English was slight but she had already discovered that in her case it scarcely mattered.

"Yes, I'm Nuka. Can help, yes?" asked the blonde bombshell.

"You drive car, yes?" asked Geoff Scrivens, reverting to pidgin English as he always did when faced with a foreigner.

"Yes, just like that!" said Nuka, clicking her fingers. It was one of her favourite English expressions, generally prompting a smile from whoever she used it on.

"Great, thanks, Nuka. You see we've all had a few too many and we need someone to drive the Land Rover," explained Geoff.

"Few is many? Drive? Yes, just like that!" she confirmed, cheerfully. How hard could it be? She'd been driving her father's tractor for years.

"Thank God for that," muttered Geoff under his breath.

"Here are the keys," he added, handing them over to her, "I've programmed the satnav so you only have to follow the instructions. Just stick to ten miles per hour and take it easy around the bends and you'll be fine."

"Round the bend," repeated Nuka, smiling.

She looked at the keys in her hand, then at the smiling faces of the group and decided to go with the flow. After all, what had it said on the au pair agency's advertising poster? 'Travel abroad, meet new people, learn new skills', and why not?

"OK, everyone aboard the float who's meant to be!" cried Geoff. "Donation collectors grab a bucket and follow on behind."

"It's a float, not a ruddy cart-horse," quipped Terry Jones, a builder in a baggy Santa costume, as he struggled onto the back of the float. He was soon joined by half a dozen slightly inebriated elves and elvettes.

"When you're ready, Nuka," said Geoff merrily.

Nuka opened the door of the 1976 vintage Land Rover, settled herself into the driving seat and turned the key in the ignition.

VrrroooMMM!!

Yes, just like that! thought Nuka, just like papa's tractor. She revved the ancient diesel engine again and lifted her foot off the clutch.

VrrrrrrrrooooOOOMMM!!!

Geoff Scrivens blanched beneath the rosy cheeks of his elf costume as the Land Rover lurched forward before thundering down the road, at thirty miles an hour, away from the small industrial estate which had hitherto been its home.

A gaggle of bucket-carrying elves looked on aghast as Nuka waved to them in the car's rear-view mirror. "Now turn left" said the satnav, causing Nuka to swerve to the right as she looked perplexedly around the car. The float disappeared rapidly from view, weaving drunkenly in and out of the scant evening traffic with the screams of those fairy-folk still clinging on for dear life drowned out by the jolly sound of 'Jingle Bells' blaring out over the society's clapped-out PA system.

Having arrived at Covent Garden and finding no Christmas tree with or without festive lights, Hymie and Mike had adjourned to the nearest pub, *The Marquess of Anglesey*. They sat stuffing themselves with mediocre food and quaffing overpriced beer for over an hour, while the flow of reason stagnated into monosyllabic grunts. Finally Hymie leant back, replete in his creaky chair.

"OK, Mike, I'd better level with you, I didn't drag us over here to see a Christmas tree after all," he said.

"No kidding, Goldman? Thank God for that," said Mike, "I thought all that time in Scotland Yard must've softened your brain. So what *are* we doing here?"

"I've been thinking over what Madame Za Za said."

"What, about the magician with the large rocks?" asked Mike.

"No, about having to visit the pyramid to find Harvey," said Hymie.

"Look, mate, I'm not going to Egypt for you or anybody. I'd come down with the Pharaoh's revenge on the first night and spend the rest of the time in the bog."

"Mike, there are pyramids all over London if you did but know it. That's where I think Madame Za Za meant; London, not Egypt."

"Oh, good," said Mike, distractedly pulling on his left earlobe. He fell silent then started tugging at his lower lip for a change. Funny what boredom makes you do.

"So, don't you want to know about the London pyramids? asked Hymie, crestfallen. He was about to explain his theory, when the pub door flew open and a group of five Elvis impersonators came in from the cold.

Three wore white jumpsuits with gold embroidery down the front, one wore a tight-fitting jacket, black slacks and blue-suede shoes and the fifth was just out walking his hound dog. Would-be leader, Dan Evans from Braintree; he of the BS shoes, approached the bar and started back-combing his hair in the mirror. One of the barmaids sidled up.

"Are those your own sideburns?" asked Odette.

"Ahuh, they sure are; 100% genuine Memphis horsehair. Are you lonesome tonight, honey?" asked Dan. "Ambition's a dream with a V8 engine", he added, apropos of nothing.

"Maybe later, Elvis. Can I get you a drink?"

"Strong liquor never passes my lips."

A skinhead stood next to him at the bar. "Know whatcha mean, mate, down in one eh?"

"Ahuh. No. I'll have a lime cordial please," said Dan, "with maraschino cherries and a little umbrella."

"We're out of umbrella's," admitted Odette.

"Well I'd just like to be treated like a regular customer, so I'd better have a bag of pork scratchings," said Elvis.

After she'd found a pack and placed it on the counter, she noticed one of his blue-suede shoes lying on the bar beside his drink. "What's this?"

"It's one for the money."

"Returned to sender!" she said, chucking it at him.

Mike and Hymie strolled up to the bar for a refill.

"Has anyone ever told you, you look just like Barry Manilow?" asked Mike.

Dan looked horrified. "You can knock me down, step on my face…" he sang.

"If you insist," said the skinhead.

"Slander my name all over the place..."continued Dan.

"Cut to the chorus," said Hymie.

"You can do anything, but lay off of my blue-suede shoes!!" sang Mike, Hymie, Dan and half the people in the bar.

"Thank you very much," said Dan, taking a bow.

"Do you know Copacabana?" asked Mike.

"Look, mate, I'm not friggin' Barry Manilow, right!" cried Dan, annoyed. "The Lord gives and the Lord loves his takeaways, but unless you like hospital food I suggest you hop it!"

The barmaid hastily attempted to clear away everything breakable from the counter.

The other Elvises gathered around Dan and started practising their karate moves. The man-mountain had come to Elvis, but the Elvises would be ready, willing and able to hand him his ass on a silver platter.

"Blimey, look at the time, Mike, we'd better be leaving, eh? How about going somewhere else for a nightcap?" said Hymie.

"Sorry, I just can't chicken out," said Mike, standing up. "It's an old personality defect." He flexed his knuckles then clenched and unclenched his ham-like fists while the pub interior seemed to grow darker and smaller.

"Oi, Elvis!" said Mike. All five of them looked up.

Hymie stood up in solidarity. "Gents, gents, my friend has a highly developed sense of humour, as you can see, but he also has serious medical issues. Forgive us, but we can't stay and chat, we have to attend Outpatients."

Murphy waded into them regardless, but was kicked from pillar to post by their co-ordinated karate moves. Finally, he landed a punch on Dan Evans, sending him flying like a sack of spuds across the room towards the bay window. He landed in a crumpled heap on the floor.

At that moment, Nuka and a dwindling band of elves; still clinging onto the wreckage of Santa's float with grim determination, bowled along the Strand at forty miles per hour with Jona Lewie exhorting passers-by to 'stop the cavalry' from the last remaining speaker in active service. Presumably, Jona was referring to the squadron of police cars trailing along in their wake with festive lights a-flashing. Demolishing a bicycle stand, a red phone booth and two lamp posts, Santa ploughed on into Wellington Street although Santa, aka Terry Jones, was too preoccupied to do much waving. Smoke was now pouring freely from the Land Rover's engine compartment, but Nuka kept going in the misguided belief that she was 'doing her bit for charity', whatever that meant.

As the sleigh approached the *Marquess of Anglesey* the satnav suddenly piped up "now turn right." She applied the brakes sharply and swerved left. As she did so, a nut on the Land Rover's front right wheel pinged off, bringing Santa's goodwill mission to Covent Garden to an abrupt halt. The battered old four-by-four mounted the pavement and smashed into the front of the pub, flattening Elvis and hospitalising an elf. Nuka climbed out of the car unscathed. 'Land Rover not tractor,' she thought.

A traumatised Santa was later spotted running screaming into the night with a couple of shell-shocked elves limping after him, while two dishevelled men fitting the descriptions of Goldman and Murphy hobbled away down Wellington Street, away from the *Marquess of Anglesey* pub.

One thing was certain: Elvis had left the building.

Part Twenty

Cadillac Heights

Dawn arrived at 792A Finchley Road with the thundering of the corporation dustcart and the plaintive cries of the local wildlife, coughing and spluttering their way into a new day. Mike arose irritably thanks to the cumulative aches and pains of narrowly escaping from a collapsing pub and sleeping on a settee which was simply too short for his great hairy legs. He peeked through the yellowed blinds and froze. A broad grin spread across his craggy face.

"Hey, Goldman, look at this!" he cried.

Hymie, as usual for the time of day, was asleep and snoring.

"Zzzzzzzzzzzzzz."

"Stop the snoring and come and have a deco at this, mate!" said Mike, shaking the scruffy sleuth from his slumbers as he dozed in his favourite chair with his overcoat buttoned up to his chin.

"Eh, wassermarrer? Is there any more toast, love?" asked Hymie.

"Love? Who are you calling *love*, you nurk?" snapped

Mike. "Look, Goldman, you've gotta come and have a look at this pile of motorised crap someone's left outside."

Hymie stood up, stretched then slumped back into his chair again like a lifeless blob. He shared ninety-nine percent of his DNA with a jellyfish and it showed.

"What time is it?" he asked, as an afterthought.

"Oh, I dunno, seven? seven thirty?" said Mike, without looking at his watch.

"I rest my case," said Hymie, closing his eyes.

"That has to be the biggest piece of shit I ever saw on a pavement," said Mike. "Hah, now he's getting a parking ticket," he added gleefully. "Hah, hah, serves him right, the prat. Imagine the cheek of the guy; first he buys the biggest all-American rust-bucket he can find then he dumps it in *our* street. There should be a law against it. Maybe there is. I can't wait to see the guy's face when he realises that not only does he have the worst car for miles around but he's got a parking ticket to go with it! C'mon, take a look at this car, and I use the word loosely. It's two different colours. I bet it's two old bangers welded together; they'd never paint it like that otherwise. I bet they'll be towing it away soon and you'll have missed it."

At the thought he might be missing out on something good, Hymie slowly regained consciousness and stumbled over to the window.

"What are you on about, Mike? Who's towing what, eh?"

"Maybe it was a decent car in its day…" continued Mike, "maybe it was *two* decent cars, but now it's just a wreck."

Hymie stared out of the window. His mouth opened and closed spasmodically but no sound came out. Mike watched him, first in surprise, then out of curiosity and finally with a dawning sense of realisation.

"It's yours isn't it?" he asked at last. "You actually bought that piece of junk."

"Ours, Mike, ours, and she's a 1969 Fleetwood, by the way," said Hymie. "A genuine classic."

"So are you," added Mike. "A genuine classic, one hundred percent proof, idiot."

"Well, we needed a new company car and they said they could deliver in a hurry," said Hymie, looking for a bright side.

"I'll bet they did. They wouldn't want that eyesore cluttering up the forecourt for long," said Mike. "Probably had it on the back of the trailer the moment they'd got the dosh."

"Isn't she a beauty?" continued Hymie, regardless.

"I can think of a few good words for it, mate, but *beauty* isn't among 'em," said Mike. "More to the point, I thought we'd agreed there'd be no more big spend items without talking to me or the accountants first."

"What, Furball and Mildew?" asked Hymie.

"Yeah," said Mike.

"Oh, I made them up," said Hymie, quietly.

Mike ground the knuckles of his right fist into the palm of his left hand in annoyance. "I knew it. I *knew* you were lying, I mean, what kind of firm calls itself Furball and Mildew?"

"Exactly," said Hymie. "They'd have been rotten, even

if they did exist." He stared at their new wheels on the pavement below to forestall further conversation. "Look, Mike, do you want to stand here bickering while they tow away our vintage motor or shall we take her for a spin?"

"Well, when you put it like that," conceded Mike, "where are the keys?"

"They said they'd leave them behind the sun-visor," said Hymie.

They eyeballed each other in startled amazement momentarily before running at full tilt down the stairs and out onto the street.

"Well, no-one's nicked it, it *must* be junk," said Mike.

Hymie just climbed into the driving seat and revved the V8 engine like a geriatric boy racer.

"Music to my ears!" he mused.

Mike climbed in, belted-up and they roared off down the Finchley Road with the CD player blaring out 'No More Heroes' by the Stranglers.

"Can't you switch that racket off?" asked Mike, half a mile later.

"Ah, no, sorry," said Hymie, "the CD's stuck inside."

Mike punched the display on the front of the player and the band sounded like they'd fallen off a cliff. At any rate the music died.

"You need to control your aggression better, Mike," said Hymie.

"What chance do I stand, working with you?" said Mike.

The road took them north through a dozen congested suburbs until the car had nearly guzzled all their petrol and Goldman needed a leak. He pulled off the road into a lay-by and relieved himself in the bushes, thoughtfully left there for the purpose.

"So, why on earth did you buy this pile of junk, eh, Goldman?" asked Mike.

"Shhh, she'll hear you," replied Hymie. "Besides, I needed some wheels to pull the birds. I've been getting a bit lonely lately," he confided.

"I thought you'd given up on women," said Mike. "Let's face it, you've never had much success with them, have you?"

"Whereas you've been a right Casanova, you mean?" quipped Hymie. He didn't have to take abuse about not pulling birds from King Kong.

"I was only quoting you," said Mike. "I remember what you said after that last bird took you to the cleaners... Drearie? No, Deirdre. You said, 'Mike, if I ever look like I'm even thinking about chatting up another bird, stop me...whatever it takes, stop me.'"

"Yeah, well, I didn't mean it, did I?" said Hymie.

"You never do, mate," said Mike. "So who's the unlucky girl? Anyone I know?"

Hymie shuffled his feet. "Ruby," he said. "I was going to call Ruby and ask her out."

"What, the cleaner you hired who disappeared weeks ago with our petty cash?"

"We don't know that, for sure," said Hymie. "She went out in search of cakes."

"Fair enough, with a mission that tough she could be gone for weeks."

"So, I err…was wondering if you had her number?" asked Hymie.

"Well, yes, as it happens, it's on my mobile," said Mike, removing the handset from his jacket pocket and passing it over. "I can't wait to see your legendary bird-pulling technique in action," he added, smiling.

Goldman looked blankly at Mike then climbed out of the car and disappeared into the bushes again. He needed privacy if was going to crash and burn over a woman again; Mike taking the piss would only make it hurt all the more.

Mike twiddled with the knob on the CD player, but the Stranglers had taken offence and weren't coming back. Only the sound of Goldman mumbling in the bushes gave him away. Finally he emerged smiling and returned the phone to Mike.

"Thanks, buddy," said Hymie.

"What did she say?" asked Mike.

"I'm seeing her tonight," said Hymie.

"Yeah, but what did she say?" repeated Mike.

"Well, I didn't actually talk to her but her auntie said she'd pass on the message and that Ruby would be sure to meet me tonight."

Mike smirked. "Yeah, and I'm the flying Dutchman."

Part Twenty-One

A Hot Date

Hymie sat at a small table inside *Hotcha Mocha* and stared regretfully into his full fat latte with chocolate sprinkles. It had cost him a tenner, but since he'd arrived an hour early for his hot date with Ruby and it was chucking it down outside, he didn't have a lot of choice.

Would she get his message? Would she bother to come? And what had happened to that twenty quid he gave her for cakes all those weeks ago? You could buy an awful lot of cakes for twenty quid. Or two coffees. He caught sight of himself in the café window and wondered if he would pass muster. He'd certainly taken more care than usual over his appearance; he'd showered, shaved, combed his hair and pressed his best suit overnight under the mattress. What more could any woman want?

"Excuse me, but is this seat taken?"

It wasn't Ruby but a tall thin man in a pinstriped suit with keen blue eyes, greying hair and a parrot on his shoulder. Hymie did a double-take. Ah, no, the parrot was on a poster of the Amazon rainforest on the wall behind him.

"It's a free country," said Hymie sarcastically, his ten pound cup of coffee weighing heavily on his mind. It seemed a bit much that in an empty café these wandering loonies still singled him out.

The man placed his cup on the table top and sat down opposite him. Close up he looked more like a fugitive merchant banker than an escaped nutter, but you could never tell.

Hymie looked intently at the stranger, who smiled back.

"Do I know you?" Hymie asked.

"No, but please let me introduce myself," said the stranger in a mid-Western accent, producing a business card from his inside jacket pocket. "My name's Lafarge, Cranston Lafarge the third."

"Is it some kind of hereditary title then?" asked Hymie, "or are there two others?"

"Oh, no, it's just a family tradition, you know. I represent the Farmer's Union Collective Insurance corporation of Texas."

"FUCIT?" asked Hymie.

"Pardon?" said Lafarge.

"I'm sorry, I never buy insurance in cafés," said Hymie. "Or anywhere else, come to that. I'm just not the insurance type," he added.

"What, nothing's ever gone wrong in your life?" asked Cranston.

"Oh, all the time," sighed Hymie, "I'm just too skint to buy insurance," he confided. That usually did the trick, but not on this occasion.

"Please, Mr Goldman, don't worry. I'm nothing if not well informed and even if I were a gambling man, there are few people I'd be less likely to insure than you."

Hymie felt strangely insulted. Where did this guy get off? Coming in here refusing him life insurance; why, he could get comprehensive cover anytime, anywhere, no questions asked. He was about to give the guy a piece of his mind when it dawned on him that he didn't even want the blasted insurance.

"So, how do you know my name and how did you know where to find me?" asked Hymie, suspiciously.

"I made it my business to find out, Mr Goldman. You see, I have a serious proposition for you."

Hymie reflected on the last time he'd had professional dealings with an insurance company and shuddered. It had been an elaborate set up by an organised crime syndicate which had nearly killed him. He'd need to be mad to get involved with another insurance company.

"So, how much are you paying?" he asked.

"Don't you want to know more about the investigation?" asked Lafarge, surprised.

"What, with coffee at ten quid a cup?" replied Hymie, eyeing up the baristas bitterly. "I need every pound I can get."

"Well, I can assure you, sir, if you can deliver on your reputation, there's a big cheque waiting for you at the end of it," said Cranston.

Hymie flinched. Had this poor fool confused him with someone else? Or had he, Hymie 'Megabucks' Goldman suddenly acquired a reputation for something other than failure? And while he was asking big questions, why was his life becoming so random?

"Well, Mr Cranston the third, what can I do for you?" he asked.

Lafarge leaned forward in his chair and lowered his voice."We want you to recover a certain device from the Red Square," he said.

Hymie weighed up the suited wonder for several seconds. No, there was no other explanation, he was plain nuts. He wondered briefly which high security establishment he'd escaped from and then decided to play along for laughs.

"What kind of device are we talking about?" asked Hymie.

"A Quark bomb," replied Lafarge.

"I've never heard of it," admitted Hymie.

"I'm not surprised," conceded Lafarge. "Let me fill you in. You know, I presume, that the Red Square is in the employ of the Millennium Group?"

"What, the hotels and conferences group?" asked Hymie.

"Hah, very good. No, the group of religious fanatics and anarchists based in Wacko, Texas," said Lafarge. "They've been planning an 'end of the world' party for some time now and, unlike some other groups of crazed madmen who confine themselves to forecasting the date of Armageddon, have sufficient resources to make it really happen. The Quark bomb has long been rumoured theoretically possible, but now we believe it may actually exist."

"And what can it do, this Quark bomb?" asked Hymie.

"Only suck the earth into a black hole."

"Pretty bad, then," said Hymie.

"The end of life, the universe, everything as we know it," confirmed Lafarge.

"And you want *me* to get this bomb away from Red Square?" asked Hymie, incredulously.

"Not Red Square, *the* Red Square; the terror organisation who have been trying to kill the magician you're investigating."

"*The Amazing Harvey*?"

"Exactly."

"I see," said Hymie, wondering why he hadn't stuck to lost pet investigations. "So what's Harvey got to do with it?"

"He's just a fly in the ointment," said Cranston.

Poor devil, thought Hymie. The world's gone mad and a bunch of terrorist nutters are out there trying to kill a harmless magician.

"Is there anything else I should know?" asked Hymie.

"Only that the Millennium Group has forecast the end of the world in forty-eight hours, so you haven't much time to find the bomb."

Hymie looked around the café for the hidden camera but it didn't seem to be there.

"So, the world's about to end and I'm the only person trying to stop it?"

"No, of course not," said Lafarge. "We've got the FBI, CIA, MI5, 6 and 7, and every other intelligence organisation in the world looking into it. It's just that we've been getting a bit desperate," he conceded.

The be-suited wonder passed an envelope across the table to Goldman. "They asked me to give you this," he said simply.

Hymie opened it and removed what appeared to be a blank cheque.

"It's signed and dated," said Lafarge, "but the amount's blank. If you can find the bomb and return it to me within the next forty-eight hours, you can put any number you like in the box. If not, it probably won't matter."

Hymie had been about to make his excuses and head off for his hot date at the Freemont cinema, but now that the world was about to end it suddenly seemed embarrassing to admit it.

"Consider this my top priority," he said.

"Thank you, Mr Goldman," said Cranston Lafarge, holding out his hand.

Hymie shook it vigorously.

"And may the hopes of the world be with you," added Lafarge earnestly. He stood up and walked off into the night, leaving Hymie to finish the last few gulps of his ludicrously overpriced coffee.

Nah, just some nutter, he thought, as he drained his cup to the dregs. I wonder where he got the joke cheque from and who put him up to it?

Checking his watch, Hymie discovered to his horror that the film was due to start in five minutes so he hastily scattered a few old coins onto the tabletop and ran off in the direction of the Freemont.

Once inside the lobby, hot and dishevelled and with his date nowhere to be seen, he flattened down his hair and straightened his tie. Ruby was the kind of girl you often dreamt about, but rarely met, and when you did you could never find the courage to ask out. He wondered again if she'd received his invitation and whether she would come. After all, he was scarcely love's young dream.

As he was on the point of giving up hope she arrived, breezily pushing through the revolving door and giving him an encouraging peck on the cheek.

"Hello Hymie, I nearly didn't make it," she said.

"I'm glad you did, Ruby," he replied, blushing.

"Well, I thought I owed you an explanation."

"It can keep," said Hymie, smiling.

"So, what are we seeing?" she asked.

"*This Gun for Hire,*" he said. "The classic film noir, c'mon or we'll miss the start."

He paid for the tickets and a large bucket of popcorn and they made their way silently up the stairs that led to the auditorium. Inside the theatre everything was pitch black, but the movie had already begun so they found their seats by the flickering images on the screen. They shuffled along the back row in the half-empty theatre and took their seats together. Hymie had grown up watching vintage detective movies and they still held a fascination for him. He sat riveted to the screen as Veronica Lake began her familiar song and dance routine.

"I've got you and I'm enjoying it fine," she sang.

"I love this scene," said Hymie, his eyes glued to the film.

"I've got you right where I wanted you," sang Veronica.

"I'm over here, Hymie," whispered Ruby.

He turned to face her and she startled him with a passionate kiss on the lips. The bucket of popcorn fell unnoticed from his hands, disgorging its starchy contents across a wide area of the theatre floor. Suddenly the film he had loved for so long seemed to fade into the background as he gave himself up to the warmth of her embrace. Time stood still then raced ahead and left him gasping for breath. All the clues and blind alleys of every case he'd ever worked on drained away and left him feeling as light as a feather.

Part Twenty-Two

Home, home and deranged

In the penthouse suite of a skyscraper in downtown Dallas, Tex Avery, oil billionaire, evangelist and owner of the world's largest collection of cartoons, held court as Chairman of the Millennium Group. The Board meeting was attended, as usual, by an assemblage of sycophants and yes-men, recruited for their ability to agree to any ludicrous statement Tex cared to make, without so much as a murmur.

"Laydees and gentlemen, the day of our deliverance approaches," said Tex, chewing on a cigar the size of a small baguette. "In forty-eight hours a cute liddle Quark bomb called *Daisy-Belle* is gonna suck this planet into a black hole twice the size of Texas and those unbelievers are gonna look like a bunch of damn jackasses," he continued. "Boy would I like ter see Walt Disney's face when he realises he's been stuck in a freezer like a packet of frozen peas fer nuthin' this past fifty years!" cried Tex, with fervent glee.

He looked around the room to make sure all the dogs were nodding and smiling contentedly. They were.

"Yeah, and those scum-suckin' losers in the Davidian

Cult of the Seventh Coming are gonna be kicking each others' butts to kingdom come when we get the date right for the end of the world, after they've been gittin' it wrong fer years!" added Tex, graciously. "The Mayans got it wrong, the Egyptians got it wrong and *they* got it wrong but Papa Tex, he knows!"

"Hallelujah, Papa Tex!" cried Sybil Cronk, Head of Marketing.

"Amen, oh Great One!" cried Forrest Hawks, Head of Resources.

"Praise the Lord!" exclaimed Verne Crapowski, Head of Stationery.

Tex gazed expectantly around the room for further rapturous applause until his eyes alighted on Dave Clarke, Head of Accounting and Finance, who was busily tapping away on his pocket calculator. Dave stopped and looked up momentarily.

"Oh, that is good news," he said. Dave, who was British, had always struggled to overcome his natural reticence, even for a fat pay-cheque. Truth be told, he'd faked the whole evangelist thing just to get a decent job in a strange and alien country.

"How are we doing fer subscriptions, Dave?" asked Tex. Surely even a Limey bean-counter could be relied on to count to ten billion.

"Still coming in nicely thanks, Tex," said Dave.

Tex pulled the cigar out of his mouth and blew a large mushroom-cloud shaped smoke ring over his head.

"You betcha goddamned ass, Dave," said Tex. "We've gotta pay fer that darned Quark bomb somehow and I don't see why I should have ter pay fer it after all I've done for this organisation."

What had he done? wondered Dave. Only made an absolute fortune out of oil, gone round the bend and decided to blow up the planet to satisfy some demented form of megalomania. Someone had to stop the guy before it was too late. He looked around the room for support but they were all clearly deranged or high on narcotics. It had been all too easy to just keep taking the money and hope the madman would prove delusional but now the doubts were beginning to set in. What if he really had a *Quack* bomb, whatever that was?

"Any questions?" asked Tex.

This was Dave's chance to stand up and be counted. He shuffled in his seat and stuck his hand in the air.

Tex looked at him in surprise like a teacher getting a question from the remedial kid at the back of the class.

"Where exactly is this Quack bomb?" asked Dave.

"Quark," corrected Tex. "Our agents in the U.K. have built it for us," said Tex. "When I give the word, they'll press the button and poof! Game over," he added.

With British engineering there was hope for them yet, thought Dave.

"But, aren't they members of the Millennium Group themselves?" asked Dave. "Because, if not, how do we know they'll set off a bomb that will destroy themselves as well as all life on the rest of the planet?"

"Why, we have back-up, of course, Dave," said Tex. "We weren't born yesterday. We've hired a guy called Square, Red Square, he's an expert in his field."

Tex fixed him with a steely glare to forestall any further questions.

"Thank you, laydees and gentlemen. Now, if we've all finished, please join me in our communal prayer."

They all closed their eyes while Tex recited some dreadful bilge about the birds and the bees, parrots squawking in the trees and a large impending explosion putting an end to all living things on the planet. Dave made a mental note to get a proper job while he still could and the Board members all filed out of the room to attend other pointless meetings with other sycophants.

Part Twenty-Three

The Sound of Distant Thunder

Outside 792A Finchley Road it was snowing; big fat soft snowflakes that muffled the sound of your footsteps and blanketed everything in a dazzling layer of brilliant white. Mike sat inside, shivering on the tiny leather-effect sofa as their ancient central heating system had chosen that precise moment to pack up. It was almost as if, like Hymie, it had planned to down tools just as the real work was beginning.

Mike could have sworn he'd heard the rumble of distant thunder; either that or his stomach was playing up again. And where was that bum, Goldman? On the morning of December 21st he was nowhere to be seen. Not that he needed him, heaven forbid, but where else could he be? Despite his endless complaints on the subject, Hymie habitually slept in his office chair; it was as much a part of him as the five o'clock shadow and the fast food stains down his shirt.

There was a loud knocking at the door downstairs. Mike edged over to the window to see who it was, but the windows were all misted up.

Carol singers? Jehovah's Witnesses? Who else would be daft enough to come calling in a snowstorm? wondered Mike. Of course, it could be Hymie, having left his car in a snowdrift and having lost his key.

"Coming!" shouted Mike as he lumbered down the stairs. He opened the door and looked out into the street. There on the step were two men in snow-covered coats like a couple of door-to-door snowmen.

"Did we call at a bad time?" asked the taller of the two, brushing the snow from his dyed blonde hair while his colleague attempted to defrost his glasses.

"It depends what you came for," said Mike, cagily. "You see, I was thinking it was about time I started putting up my Christmas decorations so if you came here to try and sell me something or collect the payments on Goldman's car, I should beat it now, while you still have your teeth."

"Don't you remember us?" asked the man with frozen specs, anxiously.

Mike took a long hard look at the pair of them and then a faint glimmer of recognition dawned.

"You're those flamin' lawyers…Mildew and Muldoon. You haven't come for the money, have you?" asked Mike, suspiciously.

"No," said the taller man. "That's to say, we haven't come for the money and we aren't in fact lawyers but a couple of magicians."

"No kiddin'," said Mike. "We've been looking for a magician, called…"

"*The Amazing Harvey*," said the taller man, holding out his hand.

"And Boltini," said the man with the glasses.

"Yeah, that's it," said Mike, "know where we can find 'em?"

"Sorry, Mr Murphy, *we're* Harvey and Boltini," explained Harvey.

"Oh, I see," said Mike, who, after searching half of London, couldn't quite believe that they'd just turned up on his doorstep.

"If you'll let us in for a minute we can explain everything," said Harvey.

"Goldman's not here at the moment," said Mike.

"It's a matter of the utmost urgency, I assure you," added Boltini.

"Well, I was gonna put my feet up with a beer in front of the telly, see. It is Christmas, after all," said Mike, hesitantly.

"My dear Murphy, time is running out. If we don't speak to you now there may be no Christmas for you or anyone else, not this year nor any other," said Harvey.

"Well, I suppose you'd better come in then," said Mike.

They re-assembled upstairs in the office and the two magicians shook the snow off their coats while Mike boiled the kettle.

"Help yourselves to a seat," he said.

Mike passed out some mugs of tea and took up residence in Hymie's chair.

"So, what's this all about?" he asked.

"It's a long story and we don't have much time," said Harvey, "so stop me if I'm not making any sense."

"Oh, I'm used to that," said Mike, "I work with Hymie Goldman."

"As I understand it, Mr Murphy, you were hired by Redrum to find me," said Harvey.

"Yeah, but it doesn't matter any more," said Mike. "He's dead, I shot him myself."

Harvey smiled. "I'm sure you did, but he's not *dead*."

"Sure he is," said Mike. "I saw him lying there on the pavement."

"Redrum is a master of the dark arts, Mr Murphy. I've seen him jump from a burning building and fight off a small army of assassins without sustaining so much as a scratch," explained Harvey. "Whoever you saw lying on the pavement wasn't him. Or if it was, he wasn't dead but simply deceiving you with a skilful deception."

"Impossible," said Mike.

"Did you take his pulse or inspect his wounds?" asked Harvey.

"Well, no. There wasn't time," said Mike.

"That's all the opportunity he would have needed," said Harvey.

Mike felt confused. On the one hand it was a relief that he hadn't actually killed the guy but on the other, he couldn't quite believe it was true.

"So, where's Redrum now? And what's he up to?" asked Mike.

"He's trying to wipe out the Magic Triangle," said Boltini.

"Well he's not doing too badly so far," said Mike. "I was nearly killed in that explosion at the Magic Triangle's HQ in Euston. Are you saying that he was behind it?"

"Almost certainly," said Harvey.

"And is he working alone?" asked Mike.

"Almost certainly not," said Boltini. "He's one of the leaders of a terror organisation called the Red Square."

Mike sipped at his tea. "This isn't a wind up is it?" he asked, "only I've had enough wind ups to last a lifetime."

Harvey assured him that it wasn't.

"The Red Square and the Magic Triangle are sworn enemies," explained Harvey. "It was believed that the Square had been eradicated in 1938 when their last leader, Dan McGrew, was hung for murder, but somehow they've come back from the dead and they're intent on revenge. Someone must be funding them, we don't know who, but it's clearly some evil madman with deep pockets as they're rumoured to have dozens of new agents and some kind of atomic bomb."

"Great," said Mike, "just in time for Christmas. So what are *you two* doing about it?" he asked, taking a leaf out of Goldman's book on how to pass the buck.

"It's funny you should ask," said Harvey.

"Oh, hilarious," agreed Mike.

"Because that's why we came to see you. You see, the Square won't rest until every last member of the Triangle is dead and when they achieve that they'll come back and tie up the loose ends," explained Harvey.

"Like Hymie and me?" asked Mike.

"Precisely," agreed Harvey.

"So we may as well join forces now as wait for a knock on the door or an A-bomb through the letterbox later," said Mike.

"I couldn't have put it better myself," said Harvey.

"One thing I don't get," said Mike, "is how you, not being rude but, a *crap* magician, should know so much about what's going on. How is that?"

"It's a fair question, Mr Murphy," said Harvey.

"Yeah, so what's the answer?" asked Mike.

"Because I'm not nearly as bad a magician as I appear, my friend," said Harvey. "In fact I have the honour to be one of the sleeping dragons of the Magic Triangle. There are only a handful of us and we spend most of our time…"

"Sleeping?" wondered Mike. It sounded like a good job for Hymie.

"In a way, yes; living on the very edge of normal society…"

Definitely one for Hymie.

"Watching and waiting for the re-emergence of dark magic with all its attendant evils," concluded Harvey.

Mike took another sip of his tea, which had now gone cold. "You don't say," he said.

"I thought as much," said Boltini, standing up and removing an ugly-looking revolver from his jacket pocket. He pointed it at Harvey who instinctively started backing away.

"Stay where you are, both of you," snapped Boltini. "This little charade has gone on long enough. You see, I'm not the pathetic magician's assistant you think I am but a senior member of the Red Square. I've been working undercover as Boltini since Harvey's last assistant disappeared but now the hour of reckoning is upon us, or rather you. Tonight heralds the arrival of the winter solstice and we're planning a farewell party for the Magic

Triangle at Stonehenge. All the missing magicians will be there, and you're both invited, naturally."

"I thought there was something funny about you," said Harvey, looking down his nose with disdain at his former assistant. "Just something sinister behind the specs."

"Is this a private argument or can anyone join in?" asked Mike. "After all, it is my gaff." He stood up and started to walk over to the window.

"I said stay where you are, Murphy, or I'll shoot," barked Boltini.

"What and alert the police?" asked Harvey. "Just take a look outside, Boltini, there are police surveillance men everywhere. Didn't you notice the green florist's van or the Mr Sloppy ice-cream van with no ice-cream or the team of road-menders around the corner? When did you last see a real road-mender out in the snow, eh?" he added.

"Or at all," said Mike.

Boltini walked over to the window. It seemed to be true, at least they were all out there, but could it just be another illusion? "Nice try, Harvey, but no coconut," he said. "Now sit down while I tie you up."

"I've had better offers," said Mike, starting to walk back to the settee.

Suddenly, there was a curious scratching noise at the window from behind them as Bacon made a bid to come in from the cold. Boltini turned instinctively towards the sound and Mike, seizing his chance, leapt across the room at him, knocking the gun to the floor. In the tussle that followed, Mike's size and strength quickly gained him the upper hand and as Boltini desperately reached out to retrieve his revolver, Mike knocked him cold with a well-aimed uppercut.

"Bravo, Mike!" cried Harvey.

Mike shrugged. "So, what shall we do with him?" he said, pointing at the crumpled figure of Boltini. "Were you serious about the police surveillance boys being outside?" he asked.

"Well, I can't say that they are and I can't say that they aren't," replied Harvey, "but it's probably best to leave first and then tip them off about the break-in later."

"Break-in?" asked Mike.

"Well, what else was he doing here?" asked Harvey.

"True, true," said Mike. "I'd better make sure the only prints on the gun are his," he added, as he retrieved the revolver from the floor with his handkerchief.

Part Twenty-Four

Under surveillance

The whole point of surveillance is to watch someone closely without being detected. In this way you gather reliable intelligence and can make informed decisions. Too much intelligence, however, and you can't see the wood for the trees. This is how it seemed to Inspector Ray Decca as he sat at his desk trying to sift through the huge pile of dead trees generated by his 'Get Goldman' campaign. In mobilising the mighty police surveillance machine for this purpose, he'd inadvertently brought Goldman and Murphy to the attention of those within the intelligence community who'd previously never heard of them, nor ever wanted to. Like Chinese whispers the story had spread, grown like wildfire and morphed into something beyond extraordinary; the Russian Secret Service believed Goldman to be an Israeli Special Agent with superhuman strength, the CIA, NSA and a host of other American acronyms believed him to possess incalculable psychic powers and the Chinese now ranked him as the fourteenth most dangerous man on the planet.

It would have amused and dismayed Decca to learn this, as he still had Goldman's card marked as an idiotic and persistent pain in the neck.

Terse burst into the room deep in the bowels of New Scotland Yard, brandishing his files like a machete.

"Do you wanna hear the latest on Goldman, Chief?"

Decca placed the last piece of his prawn mayo sandwich into his mouth, chewed it briefly and swigged his tea.

"Only if it's going to help us convict him," he said.

"Convict him of what, sir?" asked Terse.

"Anything will do," said Decca. "Preferably all the unsolved crimes on the books, given the amount of time and money we've spent watching him!" he added.

"Well, I've been working twenty-four seven, as you know, sir," said Terse, yawning. "And most of the other lads on the team haven't been home in days."

"Yeah, I've seen their takeaway expenses," said Decca. "I'd be surprised if they had time to do any surveillance, the amount of food they've put away. So, what's the latest, Terse?"

"Well, Chief, we tapped his phone but it looks like he only receives incoming calls and there were precious few of those. We also encountered some radio-wave interference on the remote receivers from that dodgy taxi firm around the corner, Ram-A-Jam Taxis."

"Yeah, I've heard their adverts on the local radio, they claim to be the cheapest cab firm for miles because they only use cheap crappy taxis. Why that would induce anyone to use them I can't imagine. Most of their cabs have been built from spare parts salvaged from insurance write-offs," said Decca.

"Shall I shut them down, Chief?" asked Terse.

"Go for it, Terse," said Decca. "Treat yourself. What else has been happening?"

"We've had 792B Finchley Road wired for sound for weeks now sir, but there's nothing to report."

"Probably because Goldman's office is at 792A, Terse," groaned Decca.

"Oh, yes, sorry, sir, I meant 792A," said Terse, although he clearly had his doubts.

"What about the rest of the cast of thousands working on the case? What have they come up with between takeaways, Terse?"

"Plenty, Chief," said Terse. "Constables O'Keefe, O'Toole, and Reidy are stationed at the back of the premises, disguised as road repairmen."

"Disguised, Terse?"

"Yes, sir," explained the sergeant. "They're wearing grubby boiler-suits, hard hats and haven't shaved for forty-eight hours. They haven't seen anything of Goldman, but O'Keefe's most insistent that there's a dangerous pothole that needs fixing."

"I don't believe it," said Decca.

"No, it was a genuine pothole, sir, he sent in some photos," said Terse.

"So, is that all we've got to show for hours and hours of overtime and a pile of paperwork, Terse? There's a dangerous pothole just off the Finchley Road?

"Ah, no, sir, I was forgetting constables Jones and

Jackson. They took up position in the apartment opposite 792A Finchley Road with the thermal imaging camera," said Terse.

"Yes? Anything *hot* to report?" asked Decca.

"Well, apparently Mike Murphy spent twenty-five minutes in the loo, sir."

Decca shook his head in disbelief. "What about the eye in the sky?" he said. "Surely they've come up with something?"

"You mean the lads in the chopper, sir? Yeah, apparently they followed Goldman driving his new car for a couple of miles up the Finchley Road and then had to leave pronto to deal with a burglary in progress in NW3," said Terse.

"Oh, he's got a new car, has he?" asked Decca. "Ferrari? Porsche? Citroen 2CV?"

"No, some hideously deformed heap of American junk that looks like two old shoe boxes stuck together," said Terse, who had no soul when it came to cars.

"Discreet and understated like the man we know and loathe," said Decca.

Terse smiled and nodded.

"So, to sum it all up," said the Inspector, morosely, "after spending the entire departmental surveillance budget for the next three years, all we can say for sure is that Mike Murphy's had a dodgy takeaway and Hymie Goldman's still got appalling taste in cars! They're going to kill me, you know that Terse, don't you."

Terse observed a respectful silence at the imminent demise of Decca's career.

"Anything else I can do, Chief?" he asked.

"Well, Terse, I know Goldman of old," said Decca. "Something big's going down and I don't mean down Mike Murphy's toilet. Now's not the time to retire injured from the chase. Hit them with everything you've got; an extra man, tracker dogs, the Police and Criminal Evidence Act, tear gas, anything. I can probably get the overtime approved on the nod for a few days longer. We may as well be hung for a sheep as for a lamb, eh, sergeant?"

"Er, yeah," said Barry Terse, wondering what the Chief was wittering on about.

Part Twenty-Five

Ram-A-Jam ding dong

There are businesses in London that could only exist in London because they couldn't get away with it anywhere else. They provide services below the radar of official recognition; so shoddy, cheap and nasty that their clients assume they must be getting a bargain. Ram-A-Jam Taxis was just such a business and given their commitment to the cheapest possible fares using the cheapest possible vehicles, their customers were literally taking their lives in their hands by getting into the back of one of their cabs.

The proprietor and general manager, one Mehmet Demirok, was a Turkish immigrant who'd pursued the dream of UK citizenship back in the nineties, circumventing the government's 'Look, no borders!' policy on the basis that it seemed too good to be true, by marrying a mentally unstable girl from Macclesfield. It had never been a love match, the relationship had gone horribly wrong almost immediately and he'd loathed the climate, with its perpetual rain and grey skies, even more than his new wife. Undeterred and unafraid of hard work, he'd set off late one night with a suitcase full of readies to make a better life for himself in the metropolis. Ram-A-Jam Taxis had been the result.

Despite all Mehmet's hard work, Ram-A-Jam Taxis was a zombie firm; living proof that you did actually need to know something about the business you were in if you ever expected to succeed. If they broke one regulation concerning the commercial conveyance of passengers in a taxi or private hire vehicle, they probably broke the lot. However, it was their creative use of a proscribed radio frequency to transmit messages between base and their drivers which finally put them on a collision course with Sergeant Terse of the Metropolitan Police. They'd buggered up his surveillance operation and made him look a complete berk in front of the Chief and they were about to learn that some kinds of crime didn't pay.

On the morning in question the deputy controller, Larry Martin, sat hunched over his clapped-out console dishing out assignments to the great unwashed on their cash-in-hand payroll. "Pico, can you pick up Mrs Goodbody at 1 Bryanston Mews West, Marylebone," said Larry over the transmitter.

"Roger and out," came the reply.

Pico Villalba, a Venezuelan, held the record for the most jobs completed in a single day; ninety-eight, although it was rumoured that he'd been high on coke at the time and that thirty-six of the jobs related to the same little old lady whom Pico had refused to let out of the cab. Most the drivers were desperate, unhinged or on the run. Pico was all three.

"No show, Larry," came a distant voice from the ether. It was new driver Tommy MacDonald, who they'd taken to calling Ronald or Ron for short.

"I waited outside the Fat-Busters meeting for ten minutes but when I asked inside at the desk they got quite shirty," said Ron.

"What was the client's name, Ron?" asked Larry.

"Mr Jarse," replied Ron, "Hugh Jarse."

During the course of his first month the poor sap had been sent to a massage parlour to collect Norma Stitz, to a cosmetic surgery clinic looking for Ivor Biggun and now to a diet club in search of Hugh Jarse.

"You've fallen for it again, haven't you, Ron?" smirked Larry. "You're a hopeless case, mate. Just go and sit outside Kings Cross station till it wears off. You never know, you might strike it lucky," he added, laughing.

"Right-o," said Ron, "over and out!"

The door flew open and in swaggered Sergeant Terse, like a sheriff from the old Wild West, with deputies O'Keefe and Reidy scuttling along behind. Reidy had only recently returned to active service, having spent some months convalescing after a nasty incident involving a deranged female gangster. He'd only been persuaded to return to work by a gypsy fortune teller, who'd told him he had a 'lucky face' and sold him a sprig of 'lucky heather'.

"Where's the manager?" asked Terse in his usual no-nonsense manner.

"He's out," said Larry. "Can I help?"

"Are you in charge?" asked Terse.

"Yes."

"And you would be?" asked Terse.

"Larry Martin, cab controller."

"You'll do," said Terse, handing him a warrant. "As I'm sure you know, Larry, this is an illegal private hire firm. We've got a court order to remove all your radio equipment and to arrest all your staff. Any questions?"

Larry gaped. Mehmet, who'd been smoking his hookah pipe in the back room and who'd overheard everything, emerged in a blue funk holding a baseball bat.

"Get out of my office, you heathens!" cried Mehmet. "Or I'll kick you out! Ram-A-Jam Taxis provide a good service, ask anyone. Everyone loves Ram-A-Jam."

"Look, mate," said Terse, "I'm only doing my duty. You hand over the transmitter and come quietly and everything will be fine."

Mehmet took a swipe at him with the baseball bat. Terse ducked and the bat connected with Reidy, who was looking the other way at the time.

"Aaaaahhh! Me head!" cried Reidy, doubled up in pain.

"So sorry," said Mehmet, "I was trying to hit the other policeman."

"You shouldn't have done that, sunshine," snapped Terse, removing the baton from his belt and swinging it at Mehmet's head. Mehmet jumped out of the way just in time and the baton came crashing down on the end of the controller's console, smashing part of the equipment.

"What have you done to my expensive equipment, you mad fool!" wailed Mehmet. Larry meanwhile had jumped onto the floor and started crawling away into the back room, heading for the exit.

"Grab the equipment, lads!" cried Terse.

"Oh no you don't!" cried Mehmet, taking another swipe at Terse with his bat.

Terse sidestepped the attack with his usual aplomb and as Mehmet sailed past him he swung a well judged kick after him, deflecting the bulky Turk into the crouching figure of Reidy, who was just getting up from the floor.

"Ooofff!" exclaimed Reidy as he collided headlong with the wall.

Mehmet collapsed into a heap, groaning, and Constable O'Keefe quickly slipped the handcuffs on him and read him his rights.

"Get the rest of the equipment together, Reidy, there's a good lad," said Terse. "I'll collect that joker, Larry Martin from the back room," he added. While Reidy was trying to recover sufficiently from his injuries to carry out the sergeant's orders and Terse was in action down the corridor, the radio transmitter crackled briefly into life.

"No show, Larry," said a familiar voice. "I'm sitting outside the *King's Head* in Crouch End, but there's no sign of any Al Caholic."

Part Twenty-Six

Love is a many splendored thing

Mike arrived back at 792A Finchley Road to find the front door off its hinges but held loosely in place by, what looked like, a complete roll of red and yellow crime scene marker tape. There were boot marks all over the door's paintwork so he assumed that the police had paid them a call. Climbing the stairs to the office he wondered what had happened to Boltini and when he could expect a return visit from Terse.

Mike sat in Hymie's chair and put his feet up on the desk. Ah, the joys of being your own boss. The chaos of the last few weeks was finally beginning to coagulate into some kind of deranged sense. As so often before, the simplest explanation, however absurd, was nearly always right; what had seemed at first to be just another missing magician investigation, had turned out to be a battle royal between two groups of wand-wavers who hated each other's guts. His only concern was that the final punch-up had yet to take place and, as brave as he was, it wasn't really *his* fight. He was a great believer in minding his own business and Stonehenge had never been on his list of places to visit before you die, especially if it became last on the list.

The door downstairs collapsed loudly against the wall as Hymie breezed in with a huge devil-may-care smile on his face.

"This is it, Mike, I'm in love!" exclaimed the mushy detective.

"Hymie, we need to talk."

"But first, I've gotta tell you about the girl of my dreams," continued Hymie. "She's simply stunning in every way."

"That's great, mate, but I have urgent news. The magicians have been round."

"Magicians? Who cares about magicians when you have a cool car and a beautiful girlfriend?" enthused Hymie. "By the way, what happened to the front door? We're not made of money you know."

"It turns out that those *lawyers* who got us out of the police station were really *The Amazing Harvey* and his assistant, Boltini," said Mike.

"Really?" said Hymie, throwing himself down on the settee.

"Yes, although it turns out that Boltini bats for the other side."

"You mean he's gay?" asked Hymie.

"No, he works for the Red Square," explained Mike.

"Have you been sniffing the Domestos again?"

"Look, there's no time to lose. We've got to go to Stonehenge and it's gotta be now."

"Since when were you interested in ancient history?" asked Hymie.

"Just listen, there are two organisations, one called the Magic Triangle, the *good guys*, and one called the Red Square, the *bad guys*, right? They're both full of magicians and they hate each other's guts. Now, the guy we were trying to find…"

"Harvey?" asked Hymie.

"That's right, Harvey; well, he's one of the good guys. Redrum and Boltini on the other hand…"

"Boltini?"

"The skinny guy with glasses who pretended to be Harvey's assistant."

"Oh, him," said Hymie.

"Yeah, well, he's working for the bad guys. Anyway, it seems as if the Square…" began Mike.

"Bad guys?" interrupted Hymie.

"Yep, as I was saying, the *Square*, which was behind the recent magician murders by the way, has kidnapped a load of magicians and is planning to polish them all off tonight at Stonehenge. Now, I know what you're thinking," said Mike.

"You mean, when are we gonna run into the *Green Rectangle*?"

Mike fixed him with a look so belligerent that Goldman quickly fell silent. "Some of us have been working our butts off while you've been chasing birds," he snapped.

"Hold on there, Murphy!" exclaimed Hymie. "For a start, she's not a *bird* but a wonderful, divine, angel in human form, and for the record, I've been working too. I ran into some nut job last night in a coffee bar who also started blathering about the Red Square. He gave me a blank cheque and asked me to help him find a bomb. I didn't take it seriously at the time, why would I? Besides, why would *anyone* want to go looking for a bomb? But now it all seems to fit into the shambles that is this case."

"It just keeps getting more and more mysterious," said Mike. "But one thing's for sure…"

"I agree," said Hymie. "This isn't a job for us any longer, it's a job for Inspector Ray Decca of Goon Squad."

Mike nodded. He'd narrowly avoided admitting that Boltini had held him at gunpoint in their own offices because he could imagine the effect it would have on Goldman.

"Only a damn fool policeman chasing promotion would be stupid enough to follow a group of madmen with a bomb to Stonehenge," said Hymie. "But how are we gonna get Decca to believe what's going on?"

"That's what I was wondering," said Mike, "but then Harvey mentioned that we were being tailed by about half the police in North London."

"Are you sure?"

"Just take a look out of the window," said Mike. "Can you see a green florist's van?"

"Check," said Hymie.

"Well, at 12.15pm a guy from Domino's Pizza delivered three of their finest to the occupants of that van so, unless cut flowers need Margheritas, I'm guessing there are three cops in there," said Mike.

"Hah!" said Hymie. "Well I never."

"And that's not all," said Mike. "Do you see an ice-cream van?"

"Mr Sloppy?" asked Hymie.

"That's right, soppy," said Mike. "Well, apart from the obvious question of who buys ice-cream when it's minus three degrees out there, some kid actually did try to buy one earlier and a big guy with a crew cut opened the serving hatch and told him to piss off."

"Great," said Hymie. "So we just have to open the window and shout down to them that we're going to Stonehenge, and we're in business."

"No, I'm afraid we'll have to go," said Mike. "It's the only way to be sure they get there. If we're lucky we'll be able to take a detour out of there when we get near."

Hymie looked doubtful. "You know I'm not much of a traveller," he said.

"We're talking Wiltshire, not Outer Mongolia. Besides, I thought you loved driving that new heap of junk of yours," said Mike.

A blissful look flitted briefly across Hymie's face. "That's true," he said, "the Fleetwood could do with a spin." Then his face clouded over again.

"But don't you remember Madame Za Za's prediction, Mike?"

Mike had forgotten every word of it five minutes after leaving her flat. "Nope," he said. "It was all a load of baloney...something about a giant midget throwing stones at two policemen," he said.

"Nonesense, she was right on the money; two policemen standing over a body while a magician casts spells over some giant rocks," recalled Hymie.

"Exactly," said Mike. "It was the kind of vague meaningless bullshit that could mean practically anything."

"Mike, get real, buddy. Giant rocks? Where else could it be but Stonehenge?" asked Hymie. Mike fell silent. He knew when he was beaten and didn't see the point in arguing any longer.

"OK, Goldman, I get it, but that just means we need to go now and quickly. That's the only way we'll get the Fuzz there in time," said Mike, standing up and putting on his coat. "Have you got sat nav in the all-American rust bucket?"

Hymie frowned and lowered his head. It wasn't so much that he was fed up of having his dream car abused as the realisation that he simply didn't want to go. He didn't want to walk into a trap or put his life at risk now that he had something, or someone, to lose. He looked cagily at Mike, now heading for the stairs, and finally realised that he didn't have any choice.

"It's OK, Mike, there's a road map in the glove compartment."

Minutes later the two unlikely heroes climbed into the Fleetwood, revved up its monstrous engine and disappeared down the Finchley Road in a cloud of green smoke.

Part Twenty-Seven

The need to know

Inspector Decca lay asleep across the desk in his office in Met Towers. His eyelids twitched uncontrollably as he dreamt about the rise and rise of data. Everything came down to data; more and more people, creating more and more reports on more and more other people, engaged in more and more pointless activities. Take the internet: when he was a kid, all the lads played football down the park. Now they sat at home in front of a screen playing computer games. What was that all about? Even Goldman had more sense than to waste his time playing computer games and he was virtually retarded. Then there was all the social media; more and more people making contacts they'd probably never meet and would probably loathe if they did. None of it was *real*. Eventually humankind would evolve into a race of blobs with two fingers to operate a computer console.

"Chief, Chief, wake up!" cried Terse, shaking the inspector awake.

"What?" snapped Decca. "What is it, Terse?"

Terse looked terrible. Leaning against the wall to stay upright, with bloodshot eyes and bedraggled hair, he looked like a man who'd been living on takeaways and hadn't slept for three days, which strangely enough he hadn't.

"Good news, sir. We've found Goldman and Murphy. They seem to be heading for Stonehenge," said Terse.

"They haven't become hippies have they?" asked Decca, who hadn't slept for a week.

"Not as far as I know, sir."

"No, they probably haven't got enough hair between them to make one hippy," said Decca. "They weren't dressed as druids, I suppose?" he asked.

"Druids?" said Terse, "I wouldn't know, sir. They just looked like the scruffy gits of old," he added, gazing with concern at the Chief, who seemed to be losing the plot.

"Where are they now, Terse?" asked Decca.

"Heading down the M3 towards Salisbury. We've got a helicopter and a couple of unmarked cars following them," added Terse.

"So what makes you think they're headed for Stonehenge? It doesn't sound like one of their regular haunts to me," said Decca.

"They left a note on the door of their office at 792A Finchley Road, Chief," said Terse.

"I suppose it said 'Gone to Stonehenge, Back Soon' eh Terse?" said Decca, sarcastically.

"Yes, sir," said Terse, "how did you know?"

Decca looked at him doubtfully. "So, they're expecting us to follow them, I suppose."

"I expect so, sir," agreed Terse.

"But, why?" snapped Decca. "What are those two

idiots up to now? It all seems a bit odd to me, but I dare say we'll find out soon enough. Get onto the Wiltshire Constabulary and tip them off that we're expecting an Alpha One emergency at Stonehenge later today. You never know, they may already have it under observation. Even if they don't, where Goldman leads can trouble be far behind?"

"No, sir,"

"Then get me an unmarked car; something fast, and ask the special weapons officer to join us. We'll need to be suitably tooled up; if Goldman's going to Stonehenge we could be on the verge of World War Three. Either that or a punch-up with some hippies."

"Yes, sir," said Terse, who liked nothing better.

Decca's phone began to ring. It was sure to be some smart-alec boyfriend of his ex-wife's trying to wind him up or the Chief Inspector bugging him with questions he didn't have the answers to. Nothing made sense any more: his ex-wife, his job, the football results. Nothing. He didn't have to answer it though, did he?

"Let's go and kick some ass, Barry, and if it's Goldman's, then so much the better."

"Yes, sir!" replied Terse enthusiastically.

Part Twenty-Eight

Flotsam and Jetsam

If you want to drive from North London to Salisbury in a hurry there's no finer road than the M3. Frankly, you'd be mad to go any other way, even if you could find another route. Other roads may be more scenic, less noisy and less damaging to the environment but nothing so far invented can surpass it for directness and speed of travel. If you're fortunate enough to have already passed Farnborough and thus to have broken the back of your journey, and are in dire need of a shot of caffeine before the ordeal that is Basingstoke, then you couldn't do better than to visit Fleet Services.

It's true that the ambiance leaves something to be desired; with its grim, functional, shed-like architecture, like a headlong collision between Bauhaus, Hammer horror and a nissen hut. With the fragrant aroma of diesel wafting tantalisingly over the half-empty lorry park and the hordes of screaming kids dragging their dispirited parents off to McDonalds for a happy meal, nowhere could be more alluring to the seasoned metropolitan traveller of today's Britain.

What better place to enjoy cold fries and warm sandwiches? The chance to refill your tank with super-taxed petrol or your bladder with anaemic coffee? What price the chance to take a leak in the convivial surroundings of the world class toilets or the range and quality of the well-stocked shops? These things are beyond price and perhaps it's best not to ask the price as a shock is surely bad for the digestion.

At Fleet Services you can buy a newspaper, a book of twenty-year-old crossword puzzles, some over-boiled sweets or a packet of tin tacks (not to be confused with the mints with a similar name for obvious reasons). Sit in the cafeteria and watch the world go by; fat and poor, rich and thin, hirsute or follically challenged, famous or unknown, the flotsam and jetsam of humanity; all desperate to get off the motorway for a break and shortly afterwards all too desperate to re-join it.

Fleet Services never closes, Fleet Services welcomes all. Fleet Services is more than a place, it's a state of mind; rather like the prison of the same name or the *Hotel California*, 'you can check out any time you like, but you can never leave'.

Hymie and Mike sat staring at the froth on top of their coffees in Fleet Services, wondering what on earth they were doing there at the world's end and when the government had introduced the new super-tax on coffee.

Outside on the tarmac, three unmarked police cars pulled into the service station car park. In the black Vauxhall Insignia V6, Sergeant Terse turned off his ignition and flicked a switch on his police radio.

"Bravo One this is Charlie Three, can you read me, over?" he said.

"Come in Charlie Three, this is Bravo One," came the reply. "Stop pratting around, Terse, I'm parked right next to you," said Decca. "Get off the police radio frequency and see if you can find Goldman and Murphy. They're inside that square building over there," he said, pointing, "probably having a cup of coffee. How hard can it be, Terse? It's *Goldman and Murphy* not Al-Qaeda and this is a ruddy motorway service station not central London!"

"Right you are, sir," said Terse into his handset. "Over and out, Bravo One" he said, switching his radio off. He climbed out of the car to speak to his junior colleague DC Collins, who was already returning from a foray into the main service station concourse.

"Two men answering the description of the suspects just crossed the footbridge to the eastbound carriageway," said Collins.

"What, a tall well-set guy and a short scruffy bloke in a tatty leather jacket?" asked Terse, taken aback.

"Yes, sarge," confirmed Constable Collins.

Terse scratched his head. This made no sense at all. "You mean they've got wind of the fact we're here?" he asked.

"Could be, sarge. They looked like they were planning to climb into the back of a lorry heading back to London. Shall we apprehend them?"

"You can tell all that can you, Collins? You can tell what they're thinking just by their shifty behaviour?" asked Terse.

"Well, I've got a psychology degree," said Collins.

"And you know where you can stick it, mate," said Terse. "I dunno where they get 'em from, I really don't." He signalled to his remaining colleagues to join him.

"Collins has spotted Goldman and Murphy heading over the footbridge. Quickly, everyone over there to collar them before they hitch a ride back to the Smoke," barked Terse.

Decca wound down the window of his car. "Carry on, Sergeant, I'll just grab a cuppa and be with you in a minute" he said.

"It's OK, Chief, I'll get them," said Terse, sending the five other officers off in pursuit, so he could have a breather. They ran into the concourse, raced up the stairs to the footbridge and disappeared out of sight while Terse walked over to the kiosk to collect two teas.

Hymie and Mike sat watching incredulously as the coppers ran past them without any hint of recognition. Fortunately, Terse had missed them too as he'd blundered into a group of Japanese tourists on the way back to their coach and narrowly avoided spilling all of his drinks as he passed them.

"I think we'd better go," said Hymie, as the last policeman passed.

"I haven't quite finished my coffee," said Mike, raising his cup.

Suddenly Inspector Decca appeared at the main entrance in search of Terse and his tea. Mike squatted down behind a plastic pot-plant, pulling Hymie with him.

"I've finished now," he said, placing his cup inside the plant pot.

Decca crossed the concourse floor to inspect the detective novels in the news kiosk when Terse appeared with his half-empty cup of tea. While they exchanged pleasantries, Mike and Hymie slipped past them, holding newspapers in front of their faces. They reached the doors undetected, crossed the car park and climbed into the Fleetwood. Decca and Terse returned to the car park shortly afterwards. They were standing on the tarmac watching the road bridge when Terse's police radio crackled into action with the latest news from Collins.

"We've apprehended the suspects, sir," said Terse.

Goldman and Murphy drove slowly past, heading for the feeder lane to the M3 West, and waved at Decca.

"I can see that, Terse," said the Inspector, irritably. He stood seething at the kerb, but could do nothing to stop them.

"Well, at least we know they'll be following us," said Mike.

"Yeah, but it was dangerously close. If they'd arrested us there we'd have never made it to Stonehenge, and those magicians are depending on us."

Part Twenty-Nine

In Stonehenge no-one can hear you scream

I t was late in the afternoon and the sun was beginning to set as the Fleetwood coasted down the A303 to Stonehenge. Hymie and Mike sat in silence, lulled by the sound-dampening snow outside and the faint hiss of slush running off their tyres.

"I wonder where the Fuzz have got to?" wondered Mike. "We haven't seen 'em since leaving Fleet Services."

"Oh, they'll turn up. It's not as if they don't know where we're heading," said Hymie. "Besides, how hard can it be to tail a multi-coloured American car the size of a small town?"

"I did see a chopper in the distance as we left the M3, but it's been eerily quiet ever since. Anyway, as you say, if they wanted to find us they'd have no problems."

"It's about time we turned off this road and headed back to civilisation," said Hymie. "I mean, we don't want to find ourselves at Stonehenge by accident, do we? Have a look at the map."

Mike shrugged. "I kinda thought we'd have to go through with it."

"But you *agreed* we'd hightail it out of there," said Hymie. "We were only trying to lead the police to Stonehenge."

"Yeah, but how else are we gonna be sure the Red Square don't do something stupid?"

"Why is that *our* problem? The world's full of loony organisations doing daft things, most of them governments, but what chance have we got of stopping them?"

"We have to try," said Mike. "We'll just go and have a look, wait until the police arrive and then push off, right?"

Hymie tightened his grip on the steering wheel and sighed. It didn't look like he had much choice. It was always the same; as one door closed, another slammed in your face! He nodded reluctantly.

When they reached the turn off for Stonehenge, via the A344, the road had been closed. A makeshift barrier had been erected in the middle of the carriageway and a red warning sign said 'Chemical Spill, Keep Out!'

"Whadda ya reckon?"

"I've been ignoring 'Keep Out' signs most of my life, so it's a bit late to start now," said Hymie, putting his foot down on the accelerator. The old Fleetwood groaned, then roared, then lurched forward with its wheels spinning, demolishing the sign and the barrier as it ploughed on through the slush.

"Goldman, your driving sucks!"

"Kicks ass, don't you mean, Mike?" corrected Hymie.

Mike smiled. "They're not that far apart really," he said. He retrieved his old break-top Webley revolver from his inside pocket, flicked it open and loaded each of the six chambers with a bullet from his right hand jacket pocket.

"Look, Mike, I don't want no-one getting shot, right?"

"Fine, I'll just have to shoot everyone we meet then," agreed Mike, "that ought to do it," he added, putting the loaded weapon back in his jacket pocket.

They arrived at the car park and climbed out of the car. The place was deserted and eerily, almost deathly, quiet. As they walked along the pathway in the fading light the monument hove into view; four groups of snow-covered stones like giant snowmen, enclosed in a circular ditch. The blue sarcen stones seemed to stand guard in the chill winter evening against some unknown terror, as they had for centuries and would, in all likelihood, for many more.

"So, is this it?" said Mike. "Just a bunch of giant rocks in the middle of Salisbury Plain? I was expecting something more."

"More?" scoffed Hymie. "What did you expect? A bevy of naked virgins pole-dancing around the stones while a bunch of drunken druids looked on, chanting ancient football songs? Or a chorus of dancing girls perhaps, high-kicking their way across Salisbury Plain? Or maybe even a herd of marauding wildebeest? This place is a World Heritage Site, Mike, you have to take it as you find it."

"Well, you can't really miss it, I suppose," conceded Mike, grudgingly. He patted the Webley in his pocket for reassurance. "Come on, let's get this show on the road."

Hymie looked stricken. "What, without Decca and Terse?"

"Well, they haven't done us a whole lot of good so far."

"I know, but at least they have plenty of back up," said Hymie. "They've always got my back up anyway," he smirked. "All we really have is you and a gun. I'm a spent force once I've made a few wisecracks and run off to hide."

"Don't sell yourself short, mate, your wisecracks would stop an army of psychopaths with uzis dead in their tracks at fifty paces," said Mike.

Hymie looked surprised.

"Only kidding," said Mike, "don't try it, will you? At least you're good at hiding," he agreed. "As for myself, I'm cold, wet, and in the middle of nowhere and I just want to get World War Three over so I can go home and enjoy what's left of Christmas!" He pulled out the Webley and walked off towards the centre of the stone circles.

"Mike, come back. You can't leave me here on my own. What about the Red Square? What about the chemical spill? It could be toxic. You know I break out in a terrible rash at the slightest trace of chemicals."

Mike paused briefly, looked blankly at his pitiful colleague then headed off again. Hymie shrugged then ran after his outsized business partner, eventually catching up with him as Mike suddenly fell to the ground.

"Ah, the old army training eh?" said Hymie, squatting down beside him.

"No, I'm tying my shoelace, mate, how about you?" said Mike.

"I thought I heard something," bluffed Hymie, in a whisper.

They gazed out across the historic vista of the standing stones. Backlit by a large orange sun, gradually setting in the west, they appeared less like a part of the real world and more like some outlandish dreamscape. A thin plume of smoke began to rise from a fire in the distance.

"I don't like the look of that," said Mike.

"Me neither, we really should call for back-up," said Hymie.

"Here," said Mike, handing Hymie a rubber cosh and a heavy brass knuckleduster. "Stay close behind me," he said, walking slowly forwards. Through the lengthening shadows, the two detectives slowly crossed the field that lead to the stones, attempting to keep a low profile. Soon a semi-circle of tents appeared from out of the gloom. One tent stood out from the others by the opulence of its scarlet satin trim, its grandiose scale and by the two armed-guards posted outside with sub-machine guns.

The tents were pitched on the far side of the stones with a large bonfire immediately in front of them, emitting the same thin trail of smoke they'd recently observed. The fire itself could only just have been lit as the flames hadn't spread to the main section yet. The core of the fire seemed to comprise a stack of old wooden furniture, dotted about with bizarre hooded figures, like dinner-suited scarecrows.

"We don't have any grenades, I suppose?" asked Mike, hopefully.

"No, I gave the last one to my Auntie Ada for Christmas," said Hymie.

"Shame," said Mike. "How is she?"

"Still recovering in hospital," said Hymie.

As they inched forward to the edge of the outer stone circle, they realised that they were already in too deep and had passed the point of no return. There's never a cop around when you want one, thought Hymie, who'd never wanted one before.

An army of red-coated minions milled around the stones, like a swarm of red ants in the centre of the circle. On their left flank, a kangaroo court seemed to be in progress, passing sentence on the Square's enemies without recourse to evidence, facts or presumably, justice. On the right, a bedraggled line of convicted magicians in dinner suits were being led in chains to the altar stone to meet their doom. Dumbstruck, Hymie and Mike watched in horror as the grand inquisitor, robed entirely in red and wearing a devil mask, asked the magician at the front of the line if he wanted to say anything before his sentence was carried out.

"I'm no criminal, I'm Domino Dave," said the cringing character in the dirty dinner jacket. "I'm a children's entertainer for Christ-sakes, let me out of here!"

Dave started fishing desperately in his pocket for something to support his claims but could only produce two dominoes.

"Sadly deluded right till the end," sneered the grand inquisitor.

Suddenly incensed, Dave pulled a concealed wand from his back pocket and rammed it up his tormentor's left nostril. "Take that, you red bastard!" he cried, before he was clubbed to the ground by a baseball bat-wielding henchmen.

"Aaaaargh!" shrieked the grand inquisitor in agony. "I saw his act once, it was an abomination!" he cried, callously, once he'd collected himself together. Dave collapsed unconscious to the floor. Two attendants picked up his crumpled body, covered his head with an old sack and dragged him away.

A tall well-dressed man with white hair followed him in the queue. As he approached the grand inquisitor, Mike recognised him as *The Amazing Harvey*.

"Afraid to show your face, eh?" said Harvey, contemptuously. "I'm not surprised, but don't expect to have it all your own way. We have reinforcements coming any minute and it's the Square that will burn in hell before the day is out, not the Triangle!" he cried. He pulled a deck of Bicycle playing cards from his jacket pocket and spread them in a fan. "Pick a card, any card," he said, proffering them to the grand inquisitor from force of habit.

The inquisitor removed his mask with a flourish and cursed him.

"Damn you, Harvey! I've waited a long time for this day and there's a special place reserved for you on top of the bonfire," he snarled, removing his spectacles to wipe away the condensation. It was Boltini.

"I always had my doubts about you, James Bolton," said Harvey, calmly. "I think it was the fact that you never once blinked in all the time we worked together."

"You're blinking mad, mate," said Boltini, with a sneer. He nodded twice and a gang of red-coated henchmen descended on Harvey, crushing him to the ground. He was dragged away with a sack over his head, pulling the flags of all nations from his coat-sleeves, as he disappeared to join his colleagues.

"My God, they're building a funeral pyre!" cried Hymie.

Mike was ahead of him. "Not for much longer," he said, standing up. "I've got a plan."

"There's nothing wrong with our usual plan," said Hymie. "You shoot the lot of them while I run off and hide," he added, trying to lighten the atmosphere.

Mike smiled. "Not this time, mate, we're massively outnumbered. Look, I'll try and work my way around to the leader's tent and see if I can get a hostage while you go and get the police. No pressure, but if you don't make it back in time I should jack in the detective racket if I were you and go back to being an electrician."

Hymie shook his head. "You've never seen my re-wiring," he said, dismissively. "It's more lethal than your left hook. Don't worry though, you can count on me, Mike." Then he turned and ran, as fast as he could, back to the car.

Once inside the Fleetwood he called Decca on his mobile phone and told him in as few words as possible what was happening. Decca confirmed that they were already on their way to Stonehenge and told him not to do anything stupid, which made Terse laugh uproariously in the background.

The smoke plume was beginning to rise more prominently into the chill night sky. Hymie clenched his fists until his knuckles stood out white in the car's dark interior. Damn it! He couldn't sit idly by while those poor magicians fried, or while the best business partner he'd ever had, was in mortal danger. He may be useless, but he'd have to do *something*! If not, he may as well be the tea-boy as the proprietor of Goldman Confidential. He strode out across the field once more with the steely glint of determination in his eyes. Red Square? Hah! he'd soon hammer them into a mangled oblong sort of shape. Too late, he realised they'd been watching him the whole time.

"You'll never take me alive, you red devils!" cried Hymie.

"That's the general idea, ducky!" snapped the dwarf at the front of the group, who seemed to be in charge.

"You're not Mal the Fag, by any chance?" asked Hymie. "Mike said you were a waste of space."

Seething with rage the diminutive figure leapt at him, grabbing him by the throat and throttling the wise-cracking detective until he could hardly breathe. Hymie lunged out with the rubber cosh and knuckle-duster Mike had given him, narrowly escaping strangulation, but before he could escape the rest of the gang set about him. Something hard struck the back of Hymie's head and a searing pain shot through him. He staggered forward a few feet and wondered if this was the end. He was drifting in and out of consciousness now, reeling unsteadily on his feet. He could have sworn he heard the whoop whoop sound of a chopper blade overhead and then a blinding spotlight fell on him from above.

If it was the police, they'd arrived too late. For him it was all over. He fell with a thud onto the cold hard ground and lay still.

Mike battled on, all unknowing. Overcoming the setbacks of being large and unwieldy, he'd skirted around the edge of the stone circles until he'd arrived at the head honcho's tent. One of the guards was taking a leak behind a standing stone a short distance away, so Mike seized his chance and quickly pistol-whipped the solitary guard with the butt of his trusty Webley. He waited in the shadows for the return of the second guard before repeating the process and leaving the two of them trussed up like a pair of Christmas turkeys. As every second passed, the flames on the bonfire snaked ever higher and the prospects of rescuing the magicians receded.

Mike pulled back the hammer on his Webley Double Action, pushed through the tent flaps with it held tightly in his shooting hand and prepared to deliver his ultimatum to the Square's commander.

Inside the tent, a vivacious young woman with dark curly hair sat behind a fold-up table in her red jump-suit, watching him coolly.

"You!" he said.

She smiled bemusedly at him. "Who were you expecting, the Wicked Witch of the West?"

"If the name fits," said Mike.

Their voices were lost in the cacophony outside the tent as the police made their grand entrance with three helicopters, an armoured car and a fleet of patrol vehicles. Sirens blared, chopper blades whooped and gallons of water were jettisoned onto the bonfire from above as the perpetrators ran in all directions like headless chickens. Decca was determined to wreck the Red Square's parade. Promotion beckoned.

Mike poked his head through the tent flaps to see

what was happening. The police! Goldman had made it. He turned back to gloat over the Red Square's imminent defeat, but all he saw was a cloud of red dust. The woman in red was gone.

Outside, Decca and Terse had been pinned down by gunfire. Three of their patrol cars had exploded into flames and several police officers lay injured on the ground.

"Terse, take half of the men and get behind the tents," cried Decca. "We need to trap them in a pincer movement or we'll lose them in the dark."

Terse headed off with a dozen officers in riot gear. He was in his element, now that the gloves were off and the adrenaline pumping. He quickly deployed his troops to best effect, forming an outer perimeter fence around the tents.

"Don't forget, men," cried Terse, "wait till you can see the whites of their eyes. Then beat the crap out of them!"

The choppers flew in, dispersing tear gas canisters in the centre of Red Square operations. The gang members scattered and ran, either into the waiting batons of Terse's team or towards Inspector Decca, still crouching by the burning police cars.

A few of the gang members were still firing at the police and Decca became increasingly concerned, not only for the safety of his men, but about the damage to the ancient stones. He lifted his loud hailer and stood up behind his car.

"Oi, you lot!" he cried. "Don't you realise this is a *World Heritage Site!* Put down your weapons and give yourselves up or it'll be so much the worse for you!"

As the choppers flew over the battlefield again, shining their spotlights on the assembled gang members, it was clear they were thinking about it. Decca continued to exploit his theme. "Do you *really* want your families to know you wrecked Stonehenge? It's been here for several thousand years. When you get to court even the judges will take a dim view."

After some grumbling and dissent in the ranks, the Red Square finally laid down their weapons and surrendered. Although there had been casualties on both sides, Decca and Terse could take satisfaction in a job well done and look forward to the promotion they so richly deserved.

Mike, meanwhile, who'd been scouring the pre-historic building site looking for Hymie, finally came upon his prostrate figure in the mud. He knelt down beside his body and tried to take his pulse. For a moment time stood still in that desolate place.

"He's dead!" cried Mike, pounding on the snow covered ground with his massive fists. He stood up, consumed with rage, and glowered at the retreating ranks of the Red Square. "You've killed him, you bastards!" he shouted, tears welling in his eyes. "He may have been the worst business partner in the world and his personal hygiene may have left a lot to be desired, but he only came along because I asked him!"

A police medic walked over to Goldman's body, stooped down and checked again for signs of life. "Actually, he's alive!" he cried. "Get him a stretcher, someone."

Mike fell silent. "Oh, well, my mistake, no-one's perfect," he said at last, blowing his nose to conceal the tears. "Thank God the dopey sod's still with us, 'cause if there's one job I definitely wouldn't want, it's his," he added, following the stretcher to the waiting helicopter.

Part Thirty

Quark, Quark, Quark!

At New Scotland Yard the evidence had finally begun to catch up with the Red Square. Weapons, finger-prints, bodies, dental records, every one told a tale. No longer just a bunch of faceless ghosts, the Red Square had become a list of suspects on the run. Most importantly, they were all men and women with bank accounts who'd been paid by electronic bank transfer, and in this computer-controlled world every payment left a tiny digital trail behind. While the identity of its leaders remained a mystery the net was rapidly closing in on the Square's financiers, the Millennium Group.

As for Hymie and Mike, the powers that be had decided that the last thing they needed was a media circus and that the best way to avoid one was to keep those two clowns out of the courts. They were told to keep out of trouble or else and quietly shown the door. At least, *Mike* was shown the door; the door to the Fleetwood, and told to piss off. Goldman, who'd been reduced to a semi-vegetative state again, was having a job identifying how many fingers Terse was holding up, in the Royal Free Hospital. After several days of hospital food and daytime TV therapy, however, his self-preservation instinct kicked in and he phoned Mike, pleading to be picked up in the Fleetwood.

With Mike at the wheel and Hymie fiddling with his bandaged head in the back of the car, the conversation finally returned to Stonehenge.

"So, what happened to you?" asked Mike.

"Someone hit me."

"I can't blame them for that, I've often felt like doing it myself," said Mike, "but what were you doing at the time?"

"I'd just spoken to Decca on my mobile and I was coming back to find you."

"You were?" asked Mike, surprised.

"I was, and then wallop, all I saw was stars."

"So, I suppose you'll want to know what happened next?"

Hymie opened his mouth to speak then paused. "You know, Mike, I don't believe I do. You see, I'm tired, my head aches and I'm sure knowing how close we came to total disaster, as usual, won't make me feel any better."

Mike fell silent. He'd lost count of the number of times he'd had to sit and listen to Goldman waffling on about something and now that *he* knew what had happened, while Goldman didn't, it seemed a bit much that the dope didn't want to hear it.

"After you fell on your face," began Mike, "I battled my way into the leader's tent."

"It's OK, Mike, it's not necessary, really," said Hymie.

Mike fixed him with a stare that said 'shut up and listen or you're going straight back to A&E'.

"Fantastic," said Hymie.

"Exactly," said Mike. "Well, when I got in there, who d'ya think was there?" he asked.

"Father Christmas?" wondered Hymie.

"No, Ruby," said Mike.

Hymie's face fell. "You mean she was working for the Red Square?"

"I'm afraid so," said Mike. "In fact, she seemed to be in charge. Oh, and Harvey and Boltini were there too," he added. "Boltini turned out to be some kind of bigwig in the Square."

Hymie seemed to have lost all interest in the conversation. "Oh, I see," he said quietly.

They drove the rest of the way back to 792A Finchley Road in silence. Mike parked on the pavement outside and turned off the Fleetwood's eight cylinder engine.

"Did we have to come back here?" asked Hymie. "I thought, under the circumstances, you might let me crash at your flat over Christmas."

"Yeah, well, as long as you're paying for everything," said Mike, reluctantly. "I just need to check on Bacon first."

"What, that damned flea-bitten moggy?"

"I know, I just can't bear to think of him being shut up in the office over Christmas," said Mike.

"Good point," agreed Hymie. "Imagine the smell if he was locked in for a few days, let alone a week."

"You're all heart," said Mike.

"I know," said Hymie. "I'm my own worst enemy."

They made their way up the threadbare stair carpet and into their empty office. There was no sign of a cat anywhere. What there was; slap bang in the middle of Hymie's desk, was a large cardboard box with a card label attached.

"Looks like Decca's sent you a Christmas prezzie," said Mike.

Hymie smiled. "We'd better check it's not ticking. I don't have a lot of well-wishers, as you know."

"You can say that again," agreed Mike.

Hymie lifted up the attached card and read the inscription.

"This isn't much use to me any longer, Hymie, but it could make you a rich man, love Ruby X."

A far-away look played briefly over Goldman's gormless face before Mike called him back from his fool's paradise.

"Hellooo! Goldman! She was working for the *bad guys*, remember. It's probably a bomb or something similar," cried Mike in disbelief.

"There's nothing *similar* to a bomb, Mike," said Hymie. "Either it goes BOOM or it doesn't."

"Well, let's not put it to the test, mate," said Mike.

Hymie lifted the lid off the box to discover a large silver-coloured brick inside with one large red button in the middle. Engraved in italics next to the button were the words 'Do Not Press'.

"What do you think it is?" asked Mike. "A sandwich toaster?"

Hymie picked up the metal brick and examined it more closely. "Errr… it's quite heavy," he said. "It might even be solid silver; we could sell it for scrap. I wonder what the button does?"

"I dunno, H, but if I were you I'd leave it well alone." Mike reached out to take it from his loopy partner but Hymie was already pressing the button.

"Noooooo!" cried Mike, jumping behind the settee with his fingers in his ears.

"Hello, I'm Daisy-Belle. Congratulations on activating me," said the device, as Mike hit the deck like an oversized sack of spuds.

"Hello, Daisy-Belle," said Hymie, a little surprised to find himself talking to a silver brick. "Are you a telephone answering machine?" he asked.

"Why, no, I'm a Series Alpha Quark Bomb," explained the device.

"No kidding," said Hymie with a hint of sarcasm. "Wouldn't you rather toast us two cheese sandwiches?" he asked, hopefully.

"No, my sole function is to create a black hole triggering complete gravitational collapse, whereupon all matter on earth will be sucked into a void for all eternity," said Daisy-Belle.

Mike had regained his composure sufficiently to stick his head above the back of the settee and gawp at the device.

"Oh my God, it's *that* bomb!" said Hymie.

Mike looked at him with a pained expression in which curiosity, outrage and utter confusion battled without resolution. "You mean you knew there was a bomb on the loose and you *still* pressed the button?" asked Mike, aggrieved.

"Yeah, well, it was an easy mistake to make," said Hymie, defensively. "It didn't look like a bomb."

"You mean it didn't have the word 'BOMB' written on it in large capital letters?"

"Hang on a minute," said Hymie, "if this is a bomb, why hasn't it gone off?"

"Five minutes to detonation," said Daisy-Belle, helpfully.

"Ah," said Hymie, "how far away do you think we can get in five minutes, Mike?"

"However far it is, it won't be enough!" snapped Mike. "The only thing we can do is try to deactivate it. Try pressing the button again."

"What do you think this button is, Mike, a flamin' light-switch you can just turn on and off?" Hymie, pressed the button again just in case.

"You have already activated me, thank you," said Daisy-Belle.

Blind panic gripped Hymie. His short-lived career as an electrician had been something he'd always tried to forget but now he was beginning to contemplate opening up Daisy-Belle to cut through the wires, assuming there were any. There had to be a better idea.

"Listen to me, Daisy-Belle, can you be de-activated?"

"Yes, my detonation sequence can be terminated if you tell me the eighteen digit code," said Daisy-Belle.

"Eighteen!" spluttered Hymie. It might just as well have asked him to climb to the top of Mount Everest while giving Murphy a piggyback.

"Four minutes to detonation," added Daisy-Belle, with complete indifference.

Hymie decided to try reasoning with the device. He removed his bandages to show how seriously he was taking matters. Mike meanwhile seemed to have lost the plot and was busily rummaging around in the cleaning cupboard.

"OK, Daisy-Belle, listen to me," said Hymie. "Why do you want to create a black hole?"

"It is my function."

"Yes, OK, but what purpose does your function serve?" asked Hymie.

"I am not programmed to answer your question, only to detonate," said Daisy-Belle.

Typical bloody woman! thought Hymie. "Look, I only activated you by mistake," he said, "so if you detonate you won't be providing a satisfactory service."

"Let me think about that," said the bomb. For what seemed an eternity nothing happened. Mike continued to rummage while Hymie sweated.

"This is hopeless," said Hymie, at last. "I'm going to call the bomb squad like I should've done in the first place."

"Step away from the telephone, fatso," said Daisy-Belle. "One minute to detonation."

"So what was all that crap about 'let me think about it'?" said Goldman, resentfully, seething from the unjustified personal abuse.

"Does not compute," said Daisy-Belle.

"Mike! It's all over! Curtains!" cried Hymie.

"I'm more of a blinds man, myself," said Mike, storming back into the room with a bucket full of warm soapy water, right on cue. He placed it on the floor by Hymie's desk before grabbing the Quark bomb and quickly dropping it into the water. It sank to the bottom, fizzing merrily as it went. Daisy-Belle's last words were "You bast…. Fzzzzzt!"

"How on earth did you know that would work?" asked Hymie, when it became clear that it had.

"Oh, intuition," said Mike. "I dropped my mobile phone down the bog last year and it never worked again so I assumed it would work with a Quark bomb too."

"You never cease to amaze me, Murphy."

"Oh, it was nothing," said Mike.

"So, about Christmas at your flat."

"It'll cost you, but I do have a new dancing Santa decoration that I know you're gonna love," he said, leading the way outside to the Fleetwood.

Part Thirty-One

A very personal Black Hole

In the penthouse suite of the tallest skyscraper in downtown Dallas, Tex Avery sat in the boardroom, drumming his fingers on the table with boredom, surrounded by his puppet Board. He was lamenting the failure of *Project Daisy-Belle,* as he had christened his scheme to destroy the world by sucking it into a black hole. A few days earlier they'd all been gathered at the appointed time at a hog roast on his ranch, waiting to meet their maker. However, other than the consumption of a tonne of scorched pork, nothing earth shattering had happened.

"D'ya think the bomb went off after all and we're just sitting here in heaven dreaming?" wondered Tex, removing his Stetson.

"Well, Papa Tex, wouldn't there be Angels or something?" asked Sybil Cronk, Head of Marketing.

"You're right, we've been let down again by those darn foreigners. I should've known they couldn't be trusted. Next time we'll use our own, home grown talent. Why, show me a man from anywhere in the world who can blow things up better than an American and I'll show you a damn liar!" snapped Tex.

He was gratified to see the rows of nodding heads around the table as he surveyed his fellow Board members.

"Hallelujah!" cried Forrest Hawks, Head of Resources, emphatically.

Tex's glance alighted on Dave Clarke, their British Head of Accounting and Finance, and his face fell. There was something not quite right about the guy; he wasn't from Texas.

"How much money have we got left, Dave?" asked Tex.

Dave pressed a few keys at random on his calculator to lend weight to his prognosis. "It's not looking good, Tex," he said, quietly. How did you tell a Texan oil billionaire he was broke? wondered Dave. Preferably on a long distance call.

"Not good? But you're in charge of the finances, Dave, why not?" thundered Tex.

Dave toyed with the idea of telling the truth; that he just did as he was told like all the other muppets in Tex Towers, but realised it would be verging on insanity.

"Well, er, Tex," he replied, chewing his nails briefly, "I managed to stop some of the payments to the Red Square but someone in London's frozen our assets."

"Goddam Limeys!" cried Tex, glaring at Dave.

"And we've started getting calls from some heavy duty agencies in the US," added Dave.

"Such as?" queried Tex.

"The CIA, the NSA, the FBI and the IRS," said Dave.

"But I have friends in all these organisations on the payroll," said Tex.

"Yes, but we can't access any funds to pay them," blurted Dave.

"Dave, deal with it, buddy, or you'll be leaving us very soon!" said Tex.

"The CIA said they wanted to interview you *today*, Tex."

"Well, that's a terrible shame, Dave, 'cause I'm busy washing my hair. Why don't they interview you, instead?"

"Er, well, I don't know…" said Dave, who suddenly had a desperate desire to be elsewhere.

"It wasn't a question, Dave," said Tex. "Thank you laydees and gentlemen, I'm now calling this Board meeting to order." He stood up, put his Stetson back on his head and smiled at the assembled crowd of sycophants and hangers-on as he headed for a cupboard at the back of the room. Removing a key from the fob attached to his belt he unlocked the cupboard and removed a gun belt containing two bright shiny Colt revolvers. He strapped on the belt and turned to face the Board.

"Blessed are the peacemakers, for they shall be called the sons of God!" cried Tex. "And what I got me here are a couple of Mr Colt's finest peacemakers!" he added.

"Why, Papa, what you gonna do?" asked Sybil Cronk, anxiously. Like others on the Board she'd reluctantly signed up for being sucked into a black hole for all eternity, but drew the line at dying in a hail of bullets.

"Why, child, this is Texas, and in Texas it's your God given right to defend your home from intruders," said

Tex, checking that every chamber in each of his revolvers was loaded and ready to roll. "If the CIA think they can just waltz in here without an invitation they have another thing coming!" he added.

"Three black sedans just pulled into the car park," said Dave, who'd asked the security guard on the desk downstairs to text him as soon as any strange visitors arrived.

"Shred everything, Dave!" cried Tex. "Anything those goddamned heathens from the CIA could misconstrue as non-charitable activities anyhow! The rest of you good 'ol Texan boys, go getcha guns out of your desks, cars and offices and meet me in the lobby in ten. Let's give the CIA a warm Texan welcome."

The rest of the Board members filed out in a daze, leaving Dave to consider his dwindling career options.

Tex hurried out of the room and headed down the corridor to the elevator. He pressed the call button then waited. As he stood there he noticed something black on the floor that looked like a broken stick. He picked it up and threw it into the chromium-plated garbage can. Those cleaners are getting slack, thought Tex.

The elevator arrived to the muted strains of Mozart's Requiem. He made a final inspection of his matching pair of Colts then stepped into the dark void. Inside the shaft the lift was noticeable by its absence. By the time Tex reached the thirteenth floor he was travelling at over eighty miles per hour.

"Yeeeeaaaahhhh! I'm comin' Lor..." were his last euphoric words before he splattered into the ground.

Later, at his memorial service, it was remarked by those who knew him best that Tex had been a man of devout faith and religious conviction. His gross stupidity was allowed to pass unremarked for fear of offending his trigger-happy relatives.

Part Thirty-Two

An arm and a leg

Inspector Ray Decca sat at a table in *Hotcha Mocha* one evening with his eyes glued to the door. He felt like a fish out of water in café society, but this was where his informant had asked to meet so he couldn't do much about it. He'd rejected the early advances of the baristas on the grounds that he was waiting for someone, but as the clock ticked relentlessly by, they increasingly looked like they didn't believe him.

Finally, a tall man with a stooping gait, a large floppy hat and long beard entered the café and approached his table.

"The red cow is flying tonight," said the stranger.

"Thank God, for that," said Decca. "Have a seat."

"No, I said *the red cow is flying tonight*," repeated the stranger, more emphatically.

"Oh, I see, yes, of course," said Decca, remembering the coded response. "How udderly ridiculous!" he added, looking around him to ensure there were no witnesses to his embarrassment.

The stranger sat in the chair opposite Decca, gesticulated to a waitress behind the counter to join them and removed his hat. He had long white hair, although the beard was clearly false.

"Two coffees, please," said Decca to the waitress, ignoring the proffered menu. He looked intently at the man facing him for a moment.

"Haven't we met somewhere before?" asked Decca.

"Well, it's perfectly possible, of course," began the stranger, "but I don't think it's at all likely."

"I see," said Decca. "So, what should I call you?"

"Mr Smith," said the stranger.

"Right, no names, no pack-drill," said Decca, tapping the side of his nose.

"No, my name's Smith, Harvey Smith," explained the stranger. "Although I'm not in the phone book," he added.

"You said you had some information for me, is that right?" asked Decca.

"Yes, very valuable information," said Mr Smith.

"In my experience, Mr Smith, Harvey, there's no such thing as a free lunch, so what do you want in return?" asked Decca.

"Why, nothing, Inspector. Surely it's my duty as a law abiding citizen to keep the police informed about illegal activities that come to my attention," said Harvey.

"Well, I'm delighted to hear it," said Decca, relieved.

"Besides, it's always useful to have a friend in high places," added Harvey, cryptically.

Their coffees arrived and Decca picked up the bill. He glanced at it casually.

"Twenty quid for two coffees!" he spluttered, feeling as though he'd received a blow to the solar plexus. He wondered briefly if he could find a disguise; perhaps even borrow Harvey's false beard, and leg it out of the toilet window, but then remembered he was an Inspector in the Metropolitan police. At least he'd been right about the free lunch.

"So, what did you come here to tell me?" asked Decca.

"You have in your custody a certain dangerous criminal," began Harvey.

Decca smiled. "We've got loads of the buggers," he said, "you didn't drag me here just to tell me that, surely?"

"Please," said Harvey, "let me finish. The criminal in question masquerades under the name of James Bolton."

"Yeah, we picked him up at Stonehenge recently, what of him?" asked Decca.

"His real name is Karl Bielefeld and he's the Head of Operations for the Red Square," explained Harvey. "At various times he's been a double, triple and even quadruple agent for the Square, then the Triangle and then the Square again. He'll try to confuse you with his hard luck stories about being the assistant to a failed magician, but believe me, he's a ruthless killer. He arranged all of the recent spate of magician killings in person, although he frequently works with a lady called Ruby Murray."

"I see, well that's all very interesting, of course, but what evidence do you have?" asked Decca.

"I'll send you a file through the mail, Inspector, with all the evidence you need to put him away for life," said Harvey.

"Excellent, excellent, Mr Smith. I look forward to receiving it. Incidentally, why didn't you bring it with you tonight?"

"Just a little security precaution, you understand," said Harvey.

"I see," said Decca. "Just one more question: what do you know about something called a *quark* bomb? It came up in conversation when we were interviewing some suspects."

"Ah, yes, the quark bomb," said Harvey. "I came to the conclusion that it was an elaborate hoax. You see, the Square's resurgence was funded by selling a mythical explosive device, the quark bomb, to a bunch of religious fanatics who wanted to blow up the world.

The Red Square sold them a silver box containing some sophisticated communications and voice recognition software, but they weren't planning to blow themselves up, were they? Not even for a few million quid," concluded Harvey.

"No, of course not," said Inspector Decca. Only a fool would have thought otherwise.

They shook hands and Harvey disappeared into the night, leaving Decca to struggle up to the till with a heavy heart to settle the bill.

Part Thirty-Three

A short walk to freedom

It was 11.45 pm on New Year's Eve. Hymie lay scratching himself on the sofa in Mike's apartment with the television blaring in the background. Crowds of people were having immense fun doing silly things in Piccadilly and Times Square; some things never changed. He imagined how they'd all feel if they knew how perilously close they'd come to being sucked into a black hole. Probably none of them would believe it, and he couldn't really blame them for he didn't quite believe it himself. Probably some of them would blame *him* for depriving them of a new experience. You could never please everyone, that was why so many people ended up just trying to please themselves but it didn't have much to commend it as a way of life.

Mike was asleep and snoring in his armchair after consuming a dozen beers and a whole ham.

"Oh well, Mike, another year's about to end and what do we have to show for it?" said Hymie. "A few empty beer bottles and the same old crap on the telly. Next year I'm going abroad; somewhere warm and inviting where the women are friendly and the booze is cheap, or vice versa."

469

"Get lost! I never touched your stinkin' diary!" shouted Mike, in his sleep.

"What the hell are you on about, Murphy?" asked Hymie, resisting the urge to throw something hard at his somnolent buddy.

"I dunno what station it was at," said Mike "but it was definitely a Class 56."

"My God, Mike, I never had you down as a closet train-spotter," said Hymie in mock horror. He struggled to his feet and put on the outsized raincoat that Mike had left draped over the bannister. He needed some fresh air to clear his head and take away the corrosive sense of hopelessness that always afflicted him at that time of year.

Outside on the street it was raining. Hymie turned up his collar, put his hands in his pockets and simply walked. What was his life all about? he wondered. Was it all about finding someone special to share his time and energies with or just about keeping going? He had been so sure that Ruby was *the one* that he couldn't switch off his feelings for her just because she'd turned out to be some kind of terrorist nutter. Even giving him a bomb for Christmas had seemingly been well intentioned. Certainly no-one had ever given him anything so valuable before.

He laughed at the thought of such a strange love token and at his own ability to twist the truth to justify her actions, but soon found himself crying in the rain. It didn't matter that it was a cliché, it helped release him from the fundamental sense of loss he'd never managed to express. How else could he reconcile himself to carrying on as normal with his shattered dreams of love and happiness heaped up on all sides? Had she loved him? Would he ever know? In the cold light of day, did it really matter? Were love and happiness just illusions that offered relief for a while from the pain and tedium of existence? And why was he so hung up on the thought that there must be more to life than this?

The rain was pelting down harder now and as Hymie stood beneath a streetlamp offering no shelter and precious little light, the hostility of the elements seemed to pummel him out of his gloom. With an effort of will, he drew back from the emotional precipice of despair and began to focus on the facts that were his stock in trade. Mike and he had saved the world. Few people could claim as much. The Quark bomb was even now sitting de-activated in a bucket of soapy water at 792A Finchley Road. They'd stopped a criminal gang from murdering their rivals and they'd helped the police to catch the bad guys. As for the money, he still had that blank cheque from the insurance company somewhere and they couldn't complain too much if he filled it out for a few hundred thousand quid to tide them over. When you thought about it like that, life didn't get much better. In the distance, Hymie could see and hear Barnet council's entire annual fireworks budget going up in flames. Those guys had the right idea; so what if it *was* raining? He couldn't have been happier if he'd been sipping margaritas on Copacabana beach.

DIAMONDS
FROM
OUTER SPACE

FEATURING HYMIE GOLDMAN,
THE DEFECTIVE DETECTIVE

Prologue

The carbonado or "black diamond" is a polycrystalline diamond found only in alluvial deposits in the Central African Republic and Brazil. Its origins are uncertain but one school of thought holds that it was created from the impact of giant asteroids before falling to earth billions of years later. Nothing happens quickly in outer space.

Part One

Tiger, Tiger, Burning Bright

Stamford Raffles could scarcely have imagined what it would become when he founded the Zoological Society of London in 1826, but today London Zoo is one of the truly great landmarks of North London, located at one end of Regent's Park near Camden Town. With a design first laid out by Decimus Burton in 1828 and overflowing with listed buildings designed by a formidable array of architects over subsequent decades, the zoo has garnered a proud reputation for animal welfare and conservation. Of course, any team is only as strong as its weakest link.

On any given day you'll find the Zoo fit to bursting with visitors; with the happy smiling faces of raucous children. Children delight in the strange and the new, in the thrill of wild animals up close and dangerous, so it's just as well that the inmates are incarcerated behind six-inch-thick glass and bars or they might just make a light snack of one or two.

On the evening of June 13th the Zoo's latest attraction, Kitty, a 300lb tigress recently flown in from Jersey, was pacing the length of her holding pen awaiting the arrival

DICK FOR HIRE

of the keeper to release her into the comparative luxury of her permanent quarters. Except that something had gone wrong; the usual keeper, a man called *Jiggers*, had phoned in sick and the superintendent had drawn a blank on any sensible replacement. There was only old Tam left.

Tam McMurdo was the last of a dying breed of zookeepers; without a single solitary qualification in animal husbandry and knowing next to nothing about animals in general, he'd joined them in the Sixties when all you needed was a peaked cap and a willingness to shovel shit. Truth be told, that was *still* all anyone needed, but qualifications were everything nowadays. Eventually they'd even have degrees in shovelling shit, although they'd probably market them as the new professional standard in excrement rehabilitation and charge a fortune for the right to use the designatory letters after your name, Dip.STIC.

The superintendent picked up the phone on his desk and rang the crabby Scotsman on his mobile. Amazingly, he answered.

"Who the buck's callin' me noo? De ye no ken the pub opens in fife minutes, ya Glaikit bodie?!"

"Is that you, Tam?"

"Och, no, it was someain else answerin' mah phain, the rascal. Is that you Superintendent Davy?"

"Tam, we need you to stand in for Jiggers, he's been taken ill. Would you please head straight over to Big Cats and let the new tigress into her enclosure. Just settle her in for the night and she'll be fine till the morning."

"I was jist in th' wey o goin' aff duty," said Tam, "and I haven't worked with the Big Cats for some time."

478

It was true; they'd progressively transferred him to slower and slower animals over the years; from the cheetah to the water buffalo to the three-toed-sloth, until he was finally working with the only creatures slower than himself – the giant tortoises. You could leave them alone with the gate open for half an hour while you went for a drink or a pee without any worries at all.

"I'll make it worth your while, Tam" continued the superintendent. "An hour's overtime at double pay," he added hastily.

"Och, okay," said Tam. He wasn't going anywhere special anyway as his only hobby was collecting empty Scotch whisky bottles and they didn't come cheap.

The superintendent replaced his handset and headed off home for the day, while Tam made his way slowly across the park towards the Big Cat enclosure. He waved at the pygmy hippos and made faces at the bearded pigs as he passed by; they reminded him uncannily of Superintendent Davy.

Outside the Big Cat enclosure, Tam paused and leant on the wooden handrail of the perimeter fence to give the new tiger an appraising glance.

"My, my, you're a bonnie wee moggie!" he said, under his breath, as the tigress bared her teeth at him before stretching out on the floor of the cage once more.

The old keeper opened the security gate and entered the enclosure cautiously. He was still one cage away from those teeth and claws and, as slow as he'd become, he wasn't about to forget his basic training. He picked up a metal pole with a wire loop on the end and lifted the catch on one end of the pen then retreated into the keeper's den to check if there were any outstanding instructions. He screwed up his eyes to read the scrawled handwriting and as he did so his mobile phone went off again like a crackerjack in his jacket pocket.

"Ruddy heel! Is that you Ali?" Ali Khan, one of the Zoo's security guards, was the closest thing Tam had to a friend in the place. While Tam drank to forget, with some success, Ali, who had no social life whatsoever and hadn't had a girlfriend in five years, fancied himself as an animal rights vigilante, fighting for justice in a world of oppression and indifference; a rebel without a clue.

"Yeah, I just wondered if you fancied a few jars after work?" asked Ali.

"Och, let me hink it ower, mon," said Tam, with a smile. "Ah was gonnae go anyway, when dae ye finish, Ali?"

"I just did, mate. See you in *the Pit* in five," said the security guard, alluding to their local pub, *The Gorilla's Armpit* by its more appealing nickname.

Tam pressed his nose against the viewing panel to check on Kitty only to realise he was one wild animal short of an exhibit. He wondered briefly if he could have lifted the wrong latch on her pen but let it pass. After all, at this stage of the proceedings what difference did it make? Now, the tiger is one fantastical creature for sure. The Tungusic people of Siberia consider it part god, the Chinese regard it as the equal of the dragon and the Hindus of India know it as the mount of Durga the invincible, but one thing's for sure, if you leave 300lb of Panthera Tigris next to an open cage door it won't hang around for long.

"Holy Jobby!" cried Tam. "Ah've lost ma wee beastie!" This was what came of doing favours for Jiggers and that daft bloody Superintendent, he thought.

"How far can it have gone?" cried Ali, "it's only a flamin' tortoise!"

Tam put his hand over his eyes and groaned. How bad could it be? At least the Zoo had just closed for the day. Perhaps he could find it before morning or come up with a good excuse before the tiger ate someone. But it *wasn't* a flamin' tortoise!

"Och, weel, there's the thing, Ali. They were short staffed y'see…"

"Short staffed? How do you mean, Tam?" asked Ali.

"Jiggers was off sick," added the Scotsman, with uncharacteristic reticence.

"But Jiggers is in charge of the…"

"Tigers. I know," said Tam.

"Bugger!" said Ali.

"Precisely," concurred Tam.

"So, what are you going to do?" asked Ali.

"Well, I thocht I might get bladdered and pretind it niver happened," said Tam.

"Look, Tam, you don't want to throw away your pension after 50 years service now, eh? Leave it to me. I'll get the rifle and the tranquilliser darts and be there in a jiffy," said Ali, who was basically a decent bloke even if, at 43, he still lived with his widowed mother and three cats; Rambo, Kurt and Clint. He could see himself now, in his safari jacket and pith helmet, tracking down the dangerous escaped tiger, putting it to sleep with an expertly aimed dart and receiving a citation for bravery from the Zoo's Chief Executive. They might even make him a freeman of Regent's Park.

Ali crept into the security office, slipped past big Reg, who was asleep with his feet up on the desk and, unlocking the rack on the wall, removed a rifle, loaded it with a tranquiliser dart and headed for his electric buggy. Of course there were protocols to be followed and a shed-load of forms to fill out but the true man of action couldn't allow himself to be bogged down with all that crap. He'd show them there was more to Ali Khan than a pen-pushing mummy's boy!

He mounted the electric buggy, turned the key in the ignition and prepared to set off on a tiger hunt.

"Neeeeeeeeerd, neeeeeeeeerd!" groaned the electric motor as Ali shot off in hot pursuit at two miles per hour.

Back in the eye of the storm, Tam was considering his options. Maybe he should call the police? After all, tigers were dangerous wee beasties. If only he'd ignored his mobile phone when Superintendent Davy had rung! He could have said the battery was on the blink again or that he'd dropped his phone in the Galapagos tortoise enclosure and one of the dopey buggers had eaten it…but no, that's what came of being too conscientious.

Eventually Ali hove into view, like a refugee from Daktari on an overgrown lawn mower.

"I came as quickly as I could, Tam," said Ali.

"Any sign of the tiger?" asked Tam.

"I've searched all over the place but there's no sign of it anywhere," said Ali.

"Och, weel, if ye canna find her with your correspondence course in animal tracking, Ali then no-one can," said Tam, graciously, although it occurred to him that even a Galapagos tortoise with a dodgy leg would have given the great hunter a run for his money on that buggy. "Thanks for tryin' anyway."

Ali shrugged. "I'm just sorry the trail was cold when I got there," he said. "I've an inkling she'll be over the wall and into the park by now," he added. "Perhaps I could track her down with a little more time. She'll have to poop sometime."

"Weel, if it's time yer after," began Tam, "ah've bin thinkin' while ye've been searchin' and it may be that we have more time than we first thocht. Y'see ah've never known Jiggers to tek a day off sick when he could tek a week so if ye think ye can track the wee beastie doon in a few days, then all we need's somethin' stripey to stick in the pen till Jiggers gits back."

Ali stared at the deranged Scotsman in slack-jawed amazement. Then he rallied and latched back onto his dream of fame and glory, like a drowning man catching sight of a dinghy as he went down for the second time.

"Well, I'm owed a few days leave," said Ali, who never took a holiday. "And there's nothing I'd like better than to show them all what I can do," he added, wiping the barrel of his rifle. This was the big one; the chance of a lifetime, perhaps the only chance he would ever have to go deep undercover in the wilds of London and pit his wits against those of the tiger.

"I'll do it!" said Ali, with conviction.

Part Two

Old Soldiers Never Die

A few hours later and a few short miles across London from the zoo, night fell like a black shroud upon South Hill Park. Even the stars gave up the unequal task of lighting a sky blighted both by a drifting veil of pollution and gathering storm-clouds. It was as though some divine hand were trying to draw a curtain over something foul.

In "The Old Manor", one of the larger brick piles along the tree-lined avenue between Parliament Hill and Hampstead Heath, a distinguished elderly couple were preparing to go to bed; Colonel Algernon and Lady Caroline Wittering had been retired for some years and had settled into a series of domestic routines so mundane as to be virtually coma-inducing. The Colonel had disappeared upstairs at 10.15pm precisely, ostensibly to clean his dentures while his wife made the Horlicks in their "His" and "Hers" Royal Horticultural Society mugs and opened a packet of Bourbon biscuits. She tutted quietly to herself as a loud thudding sound filtered down from upstairs, loosening a few particles of plaster from the ceiling into the Colonel's mug. 'Oh well, the old bugger won't notice with his eyesight,' thought his wife.

A house is a funny thing. Over the years it takes on the personalities and foibles of those who live in it. Its furnishings and décor reflect their lives, their accomplishments and their aspirations. After a career spanning some thirty years in the British Army, in which the Colonel had served in some of the most dangerous and forbidding places on earth, his private study had become one of the darkest places imaginable. Located immediately above the kitchen, it had two small windows which were never open and a pair of black velvet curtains which were always drawn. Even the cleaner knew better than to go inside the room and as for the lady of the house, she had always assumed it was full of stuffed animals and shrunken heads or vice versa and left well alone.

Upstairs in his study the Colonel, a powerfully built man of 73 with white hair and a limp, known to his comrades the world over as *Nutter* for his cool head under fire, was desperately searching for something. The drawers of his bureau lay upended on the floor, their contents scattered on all sides, while the man himself, plainly distrait and losing his customary sang froid, feverishly threw piles of papers, boxes and jars around in a blind panic.

"Where are you, you evil hearted bitch!" he cursed.

A cold chill ran down his spine as he noticed the curtains were blowing freely in the wind.

"Who's opened the bloody windows!" he cried, lurching towards them. As he reached the open casement he froze in his tracks as a low growling sound emerged from the shadows in the dimly-lit room.

The Colonel turned to face the intruder like the man of action he was, grasping a souvenir from Nepal; a razor sharp Kukri knife, from the contents of the drawer on the carpet next to his Turkish tobacco-pouch slipper.

"You won't find me an easy target, damn you!" cried Nutter as he brandished his knife in the general direction of the umbrella-stand.

Between the aspidistra and the tatty elephant's foot umbrella-stand in the corner a wild creature crouched ready to pounce, then hurtled across the room at the old soldier with the pent-up aggression of a coiled spring being released.

The room momentarily became a war-zone with flailing limbs and murderous cries as the two figures clawed and grappled for their very lives across the cluttered room. The Colonel's framed collection of endangered butterflies fell from the wall, shattering into dust as it hit the carpet, while his antique swivel-chair was upended and smashed into his collection of rare blue and white china. Even his treasured Ming vase was knocked from pride of place on its pedestal, crashing into an old pair of army boots lying on the floor. Eventually, the intruder prevailed and escaped through the open window, leaving the Colonel's battered body oozing life on his hand-woven Persian rug.

"Peeeeeeeeeeeee!" squealed the kettle in the kitchen downstairs.

Caroline Wittering prepared their bedtime drinks, then ascended the stairs with the tray of Horlicks and biscuits. As she reached the landing it struck her that something might be wrong. After all, how long did it take to clean your dentures? The study door was wide open and the howling gale outside was blowing freely through the open windows, tossing the curtains aside like yesterday's limp lettuce.

"Algy!" she cried. "Is everything alright?"

She stumbled into the room and switched on the light. There on the floor lay the bloody and disfigured body of her husband, his red-raw face shredded and unrecognisable. Who or whatever had killed him had made such an appalling mess, it could almost be anyone lying there.

"Dear God!" she exclaimed, as the tray slipped from her trembling hands and the mugs and Bourbon biscuits clattered onto the Colonel's broken belongings on the floor. Her gaze fell on the flapping curtains. Who or whatever had done such a terrible deed could scarcely have been human. Thank heavens it had gone.

Part Three

Paparazzi Powers

The sun rose over the concrete coffin of New Scotland Yard to remind the oppressed forces of law and order that it was British Summertime. For one day only. Miss it at your peril. The scent of freshly baked cakes wafted along the corridor, accompanied by the sound of doughnuts being dunked into coffee. Now that the building had been evacuated of nicotine the detectives were forced to rely on caffeine and sugar to get them through the day, let alone the interminable night shifts.

In the Chief's office on a floor which may or may not exist and which, if it does, must not be named for fear of breaching the Official Secrets Act, that popular double act of quasi comedians, Inspector Ray Decca and Sergeant Barry Terse, were waiting to see the great man. The sound of a flushing toilet from the Chief's en-suite facilities heralded his return. He slammed the door shut forcefully behind him to keep his office odour-free, then sat at his enormous desk and squinted at them from behind a bank of telephones. The Chief refused to use mobiles on the basis that they melted your brain; or at least that was his theory.

"Is that you, Decca?" asked the Chief, screwing up his eyes to see across the world's longest desk. He needed some new contact lenses or perhaps a telescope.

"Yes, sir, you sent for us," admitted Decca. "Terse and myself, or so I was told."

"Ah, yes. Decca and Terse," said the Chief, thinking of Morecambe and Wise and then of Abbott and Costello, with a sigh.

"What can we do for you, sir?" asked Decca.

"Sit down, the pair of you," said the Chief. They sat.

"Well, that's a tricky one, Decca," he continued. "You see, last week I was going to call you in for a commendation after you wrapped up that Red Square case so brilliantly…"

"Thank you, sir," said Decca.

"But before I could find a slot in my schedule you went and blotted your copybook," said the Chief, frowning.

"I can explain, sir," said Decca, wondering which indiscretion he was referring to.

The Chief opened the right-hand drawer of his desk, removed a well-thumbed copy of a tabloid newspaper and threw it down on the desktop in front of the two officers.

"This won't do, Decca!" barked the Chief. "Super-cop in sex orgy with Philippino Lady Boy!"

"I was framed, sir," said Decca, lamely.

"I suppose you're going to tell me it was a vice bust which went wrong, aren't you, Decca?" said the Chief, tapping the side of his nose and winking.

"Er…yes," said Decca.

"I thought so, but what about *this*?" asked the Chief, retrieving another newspaper from the drawer on the other side of his desk.

"Top Cop beats up ex wife's live-in lover!"

Terse sniggered. He'd warned the Inspector not to shove that TV remote up the guy's arse but he had to admit that Decca's ex had a talent for dating annoying wind-up merchants.

Inspector Decca fell silent and stared into space. It was the final frontier after all.

"Look, Decca, I know it's hard to believe but I was young and insane once," said the Chief, brightly.

The silence was deafening.

"No-one's saying that being a policeman's a picnic but you can't go around getting press coverage like that without it playing havoc with your career prospects. Basically, you've got to keep your head down, Decca, if you want to get on. Quite frankly, Sergeant Terse here has got more of a chance of becoming the Duke of Edinburgh than you have of getting a promotion right now."

Terse smirked.

"Thank you, sir," said Decca, trying to wrap up proceedings as quickly as possible.

"As for you, Terse," said the Chief, turning his attention to the crew-cut sergeant.

"Arsenal," said Terse, whose mind had been elsewhere while the spotlight fell on Decca.

"Arsenal, Terse?" said the Chief, looking for some kind of explanation.

"Great, team, sir," said Terse, with a hint of a smile.

When inspiration deserted him, as it frequently did, he often resorted to verbal or physical abuse but even Terse could see that punching the Chief's lights out was an even worse career move than the Inspector's sordid foray into the pages of the tabloids.

"The jury's still out on you, Terse," said the Chief, a Fulham supporter. "You're either the worst officer on the force or one of the very best," he added cryptically, staring hard into Terse's untroubled blue eyes.

Here at last was something the Sergeant could relate to: a staring contest. So what if the guy was his boss's boss? *No-one* intimidated Barry Terse. Terse stared back, unblinking.

"Was there anything else, sir?" asked Decca.

"Of course there was, Decca!" snapped the Chief, returning his attention to the Inspector. "Do you think I just called you in to tell you what a pig's ear you've been making of your life recently? I'm your commanding officer, man, not Jeremy Kyle!"

The Inspector held his tongue. Long experience had taught him that when the Chief was in one of his moods the less anyone said to him the better.

"I'm transferring you both onto a murder team investigating a highly unusual and sensitive case," said the Chief, looking at his watch. Surely the tea-trolley was due at any minute. "Consider it an opportunity to prove to me that you're both the first rate officers I believe you to be and not a couple of right Charlies who can't even be trusted to find a missing pet."

"Thank you, sir!" they cried in unison.

"That's better," said the Chief. "Now, about this case. The day before yesterday a retired Army Colonel was torn to pieces in his own home in Hampstead Heath. A terrible business. His wife found him. A real mess, they'll never get the carpets clean. Still, there you go, it's not our job to clean carpets. Catch criminals, yes, clean floors, no," said the Chief, gazing vacantly around the room until he noticed Terse was still staring at him.

"So, we're going back to M.I.T.?" queried Decca.

"Yes, M.I.T., Homicide, call it what you like," confirmed the Chief, "but that's where you're going. Just one last thing, Decca," he added.

"Anything, sir, just name it," said the Inspector.

"Tell your idiot sergeant to stop staring at me before I have him busted. He can serve out the rest of his career as a community officer in Dulwich!" snapped the Chief.

Terse shuddered and stopped staring.

"Now get out of here and keep your noses clean," added the Chief.

Decca and Terse stood up and headed for the door, relieved that this time at least they hadn't been for the high jump. You never could tell with the Chief; it was like working with a dormant volcano.

Part Four

Round another bend

What was it with Hymie Goldman? Despite being North London's second-worst private detective and having abysmal dress sense, he'd solved another big case; stopping international terror organisation, the Red Square in their tracks and walking off into the rain with a large cheque for his trouble. But was he happy? Of course not. Some people never are and he was one of them. He'd convinced himself that everyone was out to get him and decided to consult a psychiatrist to prove the point. On the NHS, of course; he wasn't daft enough to pay Harley Street prices. His GP, or the locum who'd been standing in for him while he sunned himself in the Mediterranean, had been only too happy to refer him; anything to get him out of the surgery, and now he sat in the waiting room at Edgware General, with his oversized business partner, Mike Murphy sucking on a boiled sweet for moral support.

"I don't believe you, Goldman! Of all the places you've dragged me along to; Edgware Psychiatric Clinic has to be the most ridiculous. You can't *afford* to be bonkers, mate we've got a business to run. Psychiatrists are for the well off."

"Well that's where you're wrong, my dumb chum," said Hymie, listlessly discarding the Christmas 2004 edition of "Woman's Own" onto the waiting room table. "Mental health is vital to a healthy, balanced life," he added, reading the tagline from a faded poster on the wall.

"Tosh," said Mike.

"Mr Goldman? Is there a Haitch Goldman here?" asked the receptionist.

"Yes, I'm here!" cried Hymie.

"Doctor Guanajuato will see you now. Room 2."

Hymie and Mike entered Room 2 with difficulty. It had the approximate dimensions of an undersized broom cupboard and smelt of disinfectant. After a few minutes of scrutinising each other more closely than they had in years a very thin balding man in a white coat appeared, with a stethoscope around his neck.

"Doctor Guano?" enquired Hymie.

"I see," said the man in the white coat, "it's going to be one of those days again." He sat behind the desk in the corner which looked like it'd been acquired from a junior school in their closing down sale.

"I'm Hymie Goldman, and I'm nuts." He clearly thought it must be something like Alcoholics Anonymous; you had to admit you had a problem before you could move on.

Mike laughed. "I couldn't have put it better myself."

"Pleased to meet you, Mr Nuts," said the doctor. "How long have you been wearing those clothes?"

Mike and Hymie exchanged glances and there was a knock at the door.

"Go away! I'm busy counting my marbles," said Doctor Guanajuato. "One, two, three…" he began.

'As many as that?' thought Hymie.

"Now roll up your left trouser leg and say ahhhh," said the psychiatrist, fiddling with his stethoscope.

Mike stared hard at the poster on the wall and tried to keep a straight face while Hymie began rolling up his trouser leg with a bemused smile on his face.

"Is this really necessary?" he asked.

"No, it's just a test to see how gullible you are," conceded the doctor. "You passed with flying colours," he added, brightly.

The door opened and a security guard appeared in their midst. The receptionist stood behind him, neither willing nor able to join them in the cramped room.

"That's him," she said, pointing at the doctor. "He's an escaped mental patient with a history of impersonating doctors. I've just had a call from head office. We should have known he was an impostor; he never took any holidays," she explained.

The man known as Doctor Guanajuato picked up his stethoscope and ran; past Goldman and Murphy, past the security guard and off down the corridor. For a small man he was making rapid progress. Suddenly, however, a male nurse appeared from around the corner, wheeling another patient, bandaged from head to toe. The phoney doctor collided with the unfortunate man, gambolled over the top of his wheelchair and came to rest in a heap on the floor. The security guard grabbed him firmly by the collar and led him away.

"Sorry for the inconvenience, Mr Goldman," said the receptionist, "I'll see if I can fit you in with one of our other consultants."

Hymie looked at Mike. "No thanks," he said. "If he's half as crazy as the last one, I think I'll pass," he added, making his way down the corridor towards the exit.

Part Five

Meet the Witterings

It had taken Decca and Terse some time to find their new cubicle in the beehive of New Scotland Yard but scarcely any time at all to personalise it. They both travelled light. They collected the files on the Hampstead Heath murder case then headed to the crime scene, stopping off at *The Garden Gate*, a nearby pub, for lunch on the way. Decca blanched and stopped eating when he caught sight of the victim's photo; it was more like a piece of meat than a human head. Terse simply ordered another burger, extra rare with tomato ketchup on the side.

"Have you met any of the other officers on the team, Terse?" asked Decca, in a vain attempt to stop him eating.

"What did you say their names were?" queried Terse, spraying sesame seeds down the Inspector's tie.

"Sutherland, Payne and Del Monte," said Decca.

Terse smirked. "Well, I met DC Sutherland once, he was a right twat, and Payne always lived up to his name, but I've never heard of Del Monte, he must be new."

"Why do you say that?"

"Come on, Chief; he wouldn't be able to stand the piss-taking for long with a name like that. They'd be calling him Peaches. That or Pineapple Chunks…yeah, Chunky for short."

"I don't know why I bother talking to you, Terse," said Decca, shaking his head.

He resumed reading the case notes. "It seems that Colonel Wittering was something of a hero. He had medals and honours up to his armpits. Whoever did this clearly must have hated him to leave the poor devil in that state."

"I'm sure you're right, Guv," agreed Terse, washing down the last of his burger with a mouthful of *Olde England Ale*. "But we don't know much about him, do we? He may have been a wrong 'un. They do say that bad things happen to bad people."

"Thank you, Mystic Barry," said Decca, sardonically. "Are you going to solve the case using old wives tales or do you remember something called *police work*?" added the Inspector. He pored over the case notes again. "There's a note here from DC Sutherland. Apparently the family is gathering at the house today."

"Probably trying to find out if the Colonel left them anything in his will," said Terse.

"Well, the timing's perfect; we can meet all of the old boy's relatives at the same time," said Decca.

They left the pub and slowly wound their way up South Hill Park, taking in the atmosphere of affluence and isolation as they went. There was no real sense of community any more, reflected Decca, just a row of disconnected houses and people, young and old, gay and straight, married and divorced; each family, couple or individual locked in their own private cage. As usual, it was up to him to make sense of it all, assuming there was any sense to be made. A gentle breeze blew across his face and he smiled. What a charming place, thought Decca, then turning back to the investigation his eyes alighted on an enormous turd lying on the edge of the pavement.

"What an impressive pile," said Terse, gaping at the entrance to "The Old Manor".

"It just looks like a heap of shit to me, Terse," replied Decca.

"Look, Guv, you've seen where I live, now *that's* a heap of shit, this is your genuine, one hundred percent proof stately home," said Terse.

"Where you make your mistake, Sergeant, is in thinking I'm talking about the house. I'm actually talking about that pile of excrement on the pavement behind you."

Terse turned carefully around and whistled through his teeth.

"Now *that's* what I call a turd!" he agreed. "I wouldn't like to meet the dog that did that."

"Me neither, Terse, only I can't help wondering if it actually came from a dog at all. Bag it up, Barry, there's a good lad," he added, with the mock bonhomie he adopted when asking junior colleagues to perform unsavoury tasks.

After searching each of his pockets in turn, the Sergeant finally managed to find an evidence bag and gingerly scooped up a large sample of the excrement, being meticulous to avoid touching any of it himself. He sealed the bag and, carrying it by his side, rang the bell of The Old Manor.

After a while a member of the domestic staff appeared before them in a black waistcoat.

"Hello, may I help you?" he asked.

"Police," said Terse, flashing his badge. "I'm Sergeant Terse and this is Inspector Decca of the Met. We'd like a word with Lady Wittering. I believe she's expecting us."

"I see," said the domestic. "You'd better come in. Can I take your hats and coats?"

"No, but perhaps you could put this in your fridge for me," said Terse, offering him the evidence bag.

The man took it reluctantly, then disappeared into the house.

Shortly afterwards a tall, elegant lady appeared from the drawing room.

"You must be the police," she said. "I'm Caroline Wittering." She held out her hand to Decca. He shook it very formally.

"Yes, Inspector Decca," he explained, "and this," he added, in brief acknowledgement of the inexplicable, is Sergeant Terse."

Terse nodded like a plastic dog in the rear window of a car. He took out a notepad and pen from his jacket pocket and started taking notes.

"We'd like to ask you a few questions about the death of your husband."

"Very well. I suppose you have to get the facts straight," said Caroline Wittering, "although I did give a statement to the local police."

'Might as well have written it on bog roll and flushed it down the loo', thought Terse.

"Thank you for being so understanding, Lady Wittering," said Decca. "It must have been a terrible shock for you, finding your husband dead like that."

"It was, and in such dreadful circumstances," she agreed. "He was barely recognisable."

"I see," said Decca, "but you're sure it *was* your husband?"

"Who else could it have been, Inspector? He was wearing my husband's clothes and lying on the floor of my husband's study."

"Yes, I'm sorry, your ladyship, but we have to explore every possibility. This is a murder enquiry after all."

"Yes," she said, quietly. "I just can't come to terms with it. One minute he was cleaning his dentures, the next he was gone. He hadn't even drunk his Horlicks."

"Tragic," said Terse.

"Thank you, Sergeant," said Decca, dismissively. "You didn't see who killed your husband, Lady Wittering?"

"No, Inspector, as I told your colleagues, there was only the open window and no trace of anyone else in the room except for the mess."

"Was anything taken?" asked the Inspector. "I mean, at the moment we appear to have no motive for the attack."

"Nothing I know of," she replied.

"Is it possible the Colonel had enemies?"

"None that I know of," said Lady Wittering. "Perhaps you should ask his fellow members in the club," she added, as an afterthought.

"Club? What club would that be?" asked Sergeant Terse.

"The Kit Cat Club."

"Some kind of biscuit appreciation society?" asked Terse, writing something in his notebook. Decca gave him a withering look.

"No, Sergeant, it was a club of some of his old army pals. They used to get together every so often over dinner at the Savoy. They used to talk about the old days, I think. I didn't like to ask."

"Could you provide us with the names and contact details of the members?" asked Decca.

"Yes, I expect so," said Lady Wittering. "I may even have a photo of them in the drawing room, if you'd care to follow me," she added, leading them across the spacious hall and into a large wood-panelled room where three adults sat around drinking tea and bickering. At the arrival of the two strangers all conversation ceased.

"Hello children, Inspector Decca and Sergeant Terse are from the police. They're here to find out what happened to Daddy," said Lady Caroline.

"He's been murdered, any fool can see that," said a tall, slim man with an eye-patch over his left eye, wearing a long black leather coat and laced-up boots. "Even a man with one eye can see that!" he snapped.

"Maurice!" cried his mother, "there's no need to be rude, we must do all we can to help the police find Daddy's killer."

Maurice stood up and walked towards the policemen.

"I'm sorry," he said. "It was something of a shock." He held out his hand for Decca to shake.

"I understand entirely," said the Inspector. As he shook

Maurice's hand he noticed that his right index-finger was missing. He wondered what other body parts he was missing.

"What happened to your..?" began Decca.

"Eye? I lost it in a fencing accident," said Maurice.

'You had to watch out for those pressure treated fence panels,' thought Terse, 'they could spring back at you.'

"And your finger?" asked the Inspector?

"Shark attack," said Maurice. "I also have a titanium-alloy foot," he added. "Like they use on jet aircraft. They offered me plastic but I told them where they could stick it."

"How did you lose your foot, then?" asked Terse, curious despite himself. He looked at the laced-up boots, trying to work out which foot was the fake. Maybe it was both of them.

Maurice looked at the sergeant, then at his mother and siblings, trying to gauge their reaction, then shrugged and began. "It's a long story…" he said.

"Which he's not going to bore us with today!" cried his sister, jumping up out of her chair. She was in her thirties, tall and tanned with long black hair and sparkling eyes. "I wouldn't mind but it gets more ludicrous every time he tells it. He's never been near a shark and his foot's made of carbon fibre, like an old canoe, not titanium alloy. He does like to exaggerate," she concluded.

"Thank you, Delilah, that's enough," said Lady Wittering. "The children have never got on well together, Inspector. They can just about manage the pretence at Christmas but getting them under the same roof twice in one year is simply asking for trouble," she added.

"That's not entirely fair, you know, mother," said the third of the children, a man in his forties wearing a pinstriped suit, prescription specs and brogues.

"No, I know, darling," said Caroline Wittering. "This is Handley, he's always very sensible, bless him. He's something in the City."

"We're not quite sure what exactly," said Maurice, "but knowing Handley, it's sure to be very boring."

"We're very proud of him," said Lady Wittering, simply.

"He's only jealous because Handley has a proper job," said Delilah.

"Children, please. Your father's dead, show some respect," said Lady Wittering.

They all fell silent. Terse doodled on his notebook.

"Thank you, Lady Wittering," said Inspector Decca. "Perhaps you could all tell me where you were on the night of June 13th?"

"I was at my desk in the City," said Handley. "If you leave before midnight they regard you as a lightweight."

"And what is it you actually do in the City, sir?" asked Decca. The other family members all looked at Handley as if it was a question they'd always longed to ask but couldn't bring themselves to.

"Ah, well, I'm a derivatives trader, Inspector. I trade in, er…derivatives," said Handley.

'Whatever *they* are,' thought Terse. He was interested to note that even Handley seemed a little vague on the subject.

"I was in Paris," said Delilah.

"On holiday, miss?" asked Decca.

"No, I work there, Inspector," she explained. "I'm a buyer for a French fashion house."

"A *trainee* buyer," corrected Maurice, still narked at her remark about his foot.

"And you, Maurice?" asked Decca. "Where were you on the night your father died?"

"In a pub somewhere, I expect," said Maurice, "drinking to forget…what exactly, I can't remember."

"Hopefully you can do a bit better than that, sir," said Decca. "I'd hate to have to ask Sergeant Terse to write 'whereabouts unknown' next to your name in his diary."

Terse happily obliged.

"Well, er…it was the Black Sheep in Camberwell," explained Maurice. "I'm at an art school nearby; the UAL."

"It keeps him off the streets," said Lady Wittering. It was worth every penny; she couldn't face having him around the house again.

"I'm just waiting for them to recognise my huge talent," said Maurice.

'Aren't we all,' thought Terse.

"I see," said Inspector Decca, gravely, watching Maurice as though he were half expecting some other body part to drop off before his eyes. "So none of you has any idea who killed your father. You don't know who his enemies were, and you can't shed any light whatsoever on anything which may help with our enquiries. Well, frankly I'm disappointed." He handed a card with the office contact numbers on to each of them. "If anything occurs to you after we've gone, then call. I don't care what time of day it is; morning, noon or night and I don't care how trivial it seems, Sergeant Terse will be waiting for your call. This is a serious crime and we won't rest until the perpetrator is safely behind bars."

"Won't you join us for a little light lunch, Inspector?" asked Lady Wittering. She walked over to a writing desk by the wall, opened the lid and removed a photo of a group of elderly men in dinner jackets, all smoking massive cigars. They all seemed to have masses of facial hair as though they were trying to conceal their identities. "You wanted a photo of the Kit Cat Club," she said, passing it to Decca.

As she spoke a waitress appeared in their midst carrying a tray of canapés.

Terse was about to lift one from the tray when he caught a whiff of something unpleasant.

"Gorblimey! What's that?" he asked.

"I thought the paté was off as the chef was preparing it but he had a cold and couldn't smell anything," said the waitress.

"Thank you, your ladyship but we've already eaten," said the Inspector.

"Oh, well, perhaps another time, Inspector," said Lady Wittering, escorting them back to the front door. "Did you have hats or coats?" she asked.

"No, ma'am," said the Inspector.

Suddenly Terse piped up, a bemused expression on his face, "although they did put something in the fridge for me," he said. "It was a bag of something." Lady Caroline sent one of the staff to recover it and handed it to him with a quizzical look. Decca eyed him warily.

"Thank you, your ladyship," said Terse. He could have sworn the bag was lighter than it had been before.

As they walked off down the street, Decca stopped. "Did you capture all the salient facts, Terse?" he asked. The sergeant flipped open his notebook to reveal a drawing of a biscuit, a doodled pair of breasts, a cartoon sketch of a man with a wooden leg and the words 'whereabouts unknown' written in a bubble coming out of the top of his head.

"Yes, everything seems to be in order, sir," he said.

Part Six

An office called 792A

To the vast majority of the city's inhabitants London's Finchley Road is just one of many dreary commuter routes; anonymous, noisy, congested with traffic, nothing out of the ordinary. Yet in a certain semi-derelict office at 792A Finchley Road, downtrodden and delusional private investigator, Hymie Goldman had managed to work his detective magic in not one but two highly improbable and dangerous cases in just a few short years. Reflecting on his success with the Golden Hamster and the Red Square only made him resent the squalor of his grotty office all the more. It had once been apartments; 792A to F but after the back of the building had collapsed in a freak storm, reducing 792C, D and E to a heap of rubble, the landlord had converted what was left into offices, all with the lowest possible build spec. The walls bore more than a passing resemblance to cardboard and the carpets had been salvaged from a fire damaged hotel. When he signed on the dotted line, Goldman had been attracted by the cheapness of 792A, although as he often managed to avoid paying the rent for months at a time, it scarcely mattered.

Hymie sat behind the pock-marked desk in his office, reading *The International Enquirer*. He took a swig from a disposable cardboard coffee cup and winced. The Black Kat café downstairs had started trying to emulate the success of the big coffee shop chains but unfortunately it only extended to the cups, not the coffee.

The door to his office shook on its hinges and the head and shoulders of a large man in army-surplus clothing appeared through the frame, like a stuffed moose-head coming to life. Mike Murphy, ex soldier, doorman and bodyguard was army surplus himself but had still managed to save Goldman's worthless hide on numerous occasions when it mattered. Even Goldman had recognised the fact and made him a partner in the firm.

"What's that you're reading, *The Beano*?" asked Mike.

"Just keeping a breast of international developments," said Hymie.

"Right," said Mike, thinking that his business partner had always been a bit of a tit. "So, what's happening in the world?"

"Elvis has been sighted again, in a kebab shop in Honolulu."

"Yeah, but who by?" queried Mike, "some gutter-press journo with a drug habit and a deadline to meet?"

"I shouldn't wonder," said Hymie, closing the magazine.

A tall, attractive girl in her twenties appeared in the doorway. She was clearly only there by mistake and would eventually realise it.

"What's up, Charlie?" asked Hymie. He'd been amazed when she'd accepted the job as their new PA cum receptionist as she seemed to be genuinely bright and ambitious. Something truly awful must have happened to the economy.

"There's a client here to see you, Hymie," she replied, handing him a tie and an electric razor.

"What am I supposed to do with these?" asked the scruffy sleuth.

"You put one around your neck and have a shave with the other" said Charlie, leaving him to deduce which was which.

"There's a mirror in the toilet," she added.

"Is there?" said Hymie, who'd never noticed before.

"Yes, I put it up yesterday," explained the helpful PA.

"Just for the record, Charlie, who's the client?" asked Hymie as he headed for the toilet. It wasn't so much unisex as squalid and they generally tried to keep clients out of there, for fear of losing business, by the simple expedient of an 'out of order' sign on the door. It was easier than getting it repaired.

"Lady Wittering," said Charlie, brightly. "She said you came *highly recommended*...even if you did work in the world's most appalling offices. I tried to explain it was all a front."

Hymie smiled. She was what they'd been after for years; a PA with initiative who didn't mind being economical with the truth. It was only to be hoped that she didn't turn out to be a homicidal maniac like the last two. Of course, she was tall, blonde and had an hourglass figure so he was more than willing to take practically anything on trust.

Goldman shaved hurriedly in the garish half-light of

the toilet, missing a few patches of bristles, attached the clip-on tie at his neck and returned to his office. His PA reappeared silently at his shoulder.

"By the way, Hymie," said Charlie, "the screen on my desk doesn't seem to be attached to anything. It's almost as if the office is just designed to *look* like we use a computer system."

Then again, thought Hymie, initiative was often overrated.

"Oh, didn't the last PA connect it back up again?" he said, innocently.

She shrugged. "Shall I show in your client?" asked Charlie.

"Yes, please. Also, see if she wants a drink and rustle one up, that would be great." Where he supposed it was going to come from never crossed his mind.

Moments later, the tall, elegantly-dressed figure of Lady Caroline Wittering was shown into the office with Charlie in tow, carrying a cup of tea. She was perhaps fifty-five to sixty years old, striking looking with high cheekbones and a slightly stooped gait, presumably from carrying that heavy designer bag. Hymie jumped up from his chair to greet her.

"Lady Wittering, I presume?"

"You must be Mr Goldman," she said, looking at him with a combination of surprise and concern.

"Call me Hymie," he said. "Everyone else does. And this," he said, waving in the general direction of Murphy, who'd taken up residence in a chair in the corner, "is my business partner, Mike Murphy."

Mike made a sound like he was clearing his throat then fell silent again.

Lady Caroline did a double take. They had to be the unlikeliest pair of chancers she'd ever met. She wondered if Goldman was really a detective or just using it as a cover for something less salubrious, like body snatching. Hymie meanwhile was wondering if she'd be alive for long enough to pay his bills. Too many of his clients had found out the hard way that hiring him was like booking a one way ticket to the morgue.

"How's your health, Lady Wittering?" he asked.

"Fine, Mr Goldman. How's your *business*?"

"Your business is my business," said Hymie. "How can we help you?"

She weighed him up with a thoughtful gaze.

"Well, you were recommended by the Major, so I can only assume that he knew what he was doing," she said.

Hymie had long since given up wondering who recommended him or why. Life was too short and some things just never made sense. Besides, he needed the money.

"Tell me how we can help and I'll give you an estimate," said the former electrician.

Lady Wittering's eyes welled up. Hymie took a tissue from his desk drawer and offered it to her.

"A touch of hay fever, Mr Goldman, nothing more, I assure you," she said, taking the tissue and blowing her nose into it.

"Of course, your ladyship," replied Hymie, attentively. "All in your own good time. You're among friends here; anything said in this office stays in this office."

She looked at the paper-thin walls dubiously. "I'm glad to hear it," she said. "I don't know quite where to begin, but I suppose it should be in Africa. It was 1964 and my husband and I were newlyweds. He was a junior officer in the army and we were posted to Uganda just after it had been granted its independence. The country was plagued with rebels in those days so a couple of regiments of the British Army were sent in to assist with the transition to peace and democracy. Of course, we all know how that ended up…"

"Amin ?"

"Yes, that's what I mean," she said, nodding. "But even so, there was such a spirit of optimism at the time."

"They were difficult times," said Hymie, thinking back to his miserable schooldays in darkest Finchley.

"My husband, the Colonel, was in charge of a unit monitoring illegal arms trafficking across the Congo border. The Ugandans wanted gold to support their fledgling economy while the Congolese rebels needed guns and ammunition to overthrow the ruling regime. It was a marriage of convenience and our poor bloody troops were stuck in the middle as usual."

Lady Wittering sighed and dabbed at her eyes with the remains of the tissue.

"I remember it as though it were yesterday," she continued. "It was in the rainy season and Algy and the boys had been out on a mission for days when suddenly he returned alone late one night. He was drunk and babbling and in such high spirits that he couldn't sleep. We sat up for hours talking about our plans for the future. In the morning, he shut all the blinds in the small sitting room at the back of our bungalow and removed a bulky, sack-wrapped package from his pocket. Inside was the largest, blackest rock I'd ever seen. At first I thought it was a lump of coal."

"But it wasn't?" queried Hymie.

"No. It was a huge uncut black diamond; a superb carbonado."

Hymie whistled softly under his breath.

"Algy told me there were plenty more where that came from and that once we got back to England we would be made for life, everyone in the unit would be well taken care of and that no-one else must know about it."

"And you kept it a secret?" asked Hymie.

"Yes," replied Lady Wittering, "for all these years. He smuggled the gems out of the country in the back of a military jeep and within a year we were back in England, living the high life."

"So what went wrong?" asked Hymie. "Presumably the gems were protected by some voodoo curse placed on them by a tribal witch doctor in the deepest Congo and its savage retribution has only recently caught up with you," said Hymie, revealing a taste for sensational action adventure fiction.

"How did you know, Mr Goldman?" wondered Lady Wittering, aghast. Perhaps the major had been right about him after all.

"It's the age old story, I'm afraid," explained Hymie. "Soldiers find fabulously valuable but cursed gems in the jungle, steal them in contravention of a mystical tribal curse and return home to spend their ill-gotten gains only to find their nemesis stalking them. Why, if I had five pounds for every time a client had told me that story…"

"He'd have a fiver," muttered Murphy, from the back of the room.

"So how has the curse manifested itself, your ladyship?" asked Hymie, intrigued.

"A week ago Algy was horribly murdered in his study and the black diamond stolen," she said.

"The carbonara?"

"Doh! Mr Goldman, carbona-do," said Lady Wittering, as though dealing with a remedial child.

"Yes, of course. I'm sorry to hear it," said Hymie. He couldn't think of anything else to say as there wasn't a nice way to be murdered. "I expect you've already contacted the police?"

"Yes, they've put one of their top men on it, an Inspector Decca."

"I see," said Hymie, looking at Mike, who resembled a bulldog chewing a wasp. "So, what can *we* do for you, Lady Wittering?" he continued. "I mean, with a *top man* like Decca investigating the crime, we don't want to be getting under his feet now do we? You know what they say, two's company, three's a crowd. Besides, even if we were to go looking for the carbonado, we'd be taking our lives in our hands, wouldn't we. It's cursed as you said yourself."

"The Major said you were a man who laughed in the face of danger, Mr Goldman."

Mike suppressed a snigger.

"Well, as true as that may be, Lady Wittering, what do you want us to do? Recover the diamond?"

"Precisely so, Mr Goldman. Let the police catch Algy's murderer, all I want you to do is recover the black diamond and keep my family's name out of the papers."

"Yes, there's nothing worse than having your reputation tarnished by the tabloids," agreed Hymie. "Please bear with me, just a few more questions and I'll be able to tell you if we can help and what it will cost. Firstly, do you have any idea who could have killed your husband?"

Lady Wittering removed a faded photograph from her bag and slid it across the desk.

"The short answer is no, I don't know who killed him, but these men were his comrades in arms. If anyone can tell you, it will be one of them. They were all members of a club they called the Kit Cat Club."

Hymie stared hard at the grainy image. It was a group shot of some old soldiers. Someone had written their names in biro above their heads. One man had a cross drawn over his face.

"Major Daniels, Sergeants Travers and Pettiman, Corporal Cholmondeley and a man with a cross. What does it mean?" he asked.

"That's Captain Bonser," said Lady Wittering. "He died last year in a hang-gliding accident in Chile. I've written the last addresses I have for the rest of them on the back of the photo next to their initials."

"I see. Excuse me for asking, your ladyship, but what is this diamond worth? If we're going to be putting our lives on the line to recover it, we need to know."

"Well, for obvious reasons it wasn't insured, but I should say it would cost at least a six figure sum to replace, possibly more."

Hymie cast a glance at Mike, who was grinning broadly from the corner of the room.

"A thousand pounds a day plus expenses," he said. "We'd need an advance of £20,000."

It was Lady Wittering's turn to look thoughtful.

"That's rather a lot, Mr Goldman," she said. "After all, what guarantee do I have that you'll find it? I was thinking more along the lines of a reward. You bring me the carbonado and I'll give you your £20,000, no questions asked."

It was tempting but he'd learnt the hard way not to accept the client's first offer.

"We're not a charity, your ladyship," said Hymie, "we have bills to pay like everyone else." Boy, did they ever, he thought. "Make it £30,000; a £10,000 non-refundable deposit payable today with the balance of £20,000 payable on delivery and we have a deal," he said, narrowing his eyes.

"How long do you expect it to take?" she asked.

"There's no way of knowing," said Hymie, "but if you appoint us today we'll start straight away."

Mike's stomach started gurgling from the back of the room, like the plaintive cry of a mastodon trapped in the primaeval swamp.

"Well, after lunch anyway," added Hymie.

"Good heaven's what's that? The plumbing?" asked Lady Wittering.

"Yes," agreed Hymie. "You won't find a better firm of private investigators around these parts, you know," he confided.

"Well, like I said, if you're good enough for the Major, you'll do for me," said Lady Caroline, removing a cheque-book from her bag and writing out a cheque for £10,000.

"You won't regret it, your ladyship," said Hymie. "Incidentally, who is this major you keep referring to?"

"Oh, just an old friend from Blackpool," she said.

Hymie looked thoughtful. He didn't believe in coincidences or Father Christmas any longer.

Part Seven

The Ass-felt Jungle

Ali Khan had begun to entertain serious doubts about his mission to recover the lost tiger, Kitty. There was no getting away from it, a City and Guilds in animal tracking may equip you to identify at least 22 varieties of shit but it didn't prepare you for the travails of the past few days. Early on he'd written off Regent's Park on the basis that there wasn't enough ground cover and redirected his efforts to Hampstead Heath. He'd parked his motorised transport in the bushes, correctly surmising that if he did strike it lucky he'd never be able to drag a fully grown tigress very far, even in a camouflaged body bag. However, what they neglected to tell you on the tracking course was the necessity for looking inconspicuous while hanging around in broad daylight in a safari suit with an air-rifle slung over your shoulder. Oh, you could pretend to be admiring the flora and fauna or whistle nonchalantly until you were blue in the face, but you couldn't blend in to save your life. He'd had to hide in the bushes himself on several occasions simply to avoid being apprehended by the police. The other thing they'd failed to mention

519

was that after dark the Heath became a magnet for every pervert and fetishist in the neighbourhood. After three nights on the mission he'd already been propositioned by two men in plastic macs, a fireman, a traffic cop and a native American, complete with feathered headdress. The disguises seemed to get more bizarre as the days dragged by.

Needless to say, Ali's feelings towards that useless Scots git, Tam, as he now regarded him, had undergone a radical change for the worse. How could anyone be stupid enough to lose a tiger? He smirked at the thought of Tam trying to convince Superintendent Davy that Kitty's non-appearance was down to her natural shyness or some form of jet lag caused by her flight over from Jersey Zoo. Then he stopped smiling at the realisation that he was a bigger fool. After all, how could anyone be gullible enough to go looking for the tigress in a public park on their day off, dressed like a great white hunter! He jumped back into the bushes at the sound of approaching voices and wondered how much longer he could endure this ordeal. He'd give it till daybreak then he was out of there for good, let the chips fall where there may.

As he scanned the horizon from his shrub-covered vantage point Ali's gaze suddenly alighted on something stripey moving suspiciously about fifty metres away in the bushes. He lowered his rifle from his shoulder, checked that the tranquiliser dart was loaded in the breech and then stooped down to take aim. A low snuffling sound could be heard from the direction of the striped creature, a sure sign of a tigress hunting for food. Ali lifted the rifle to his shoulder, took aim and paused with his finger on the trigger. He couldn't afford to get any closer in case she turned on him but he'd only get one shot before the tigress knew he was there. It could only be a matter of seconds before she caught a whiff of mothballs from his safari suit. He squeezed gently on the trigger. There was a faint whistling sound as the tranquiliser dart flew through the bushes and then a muffled crash as a large, striped creature hit the ground.

"Gotcha!" cried Ali, delighted with his marksmanship. He pushed his way carefully through the undergrowth and approached the somnolent animal with extreme caution. There before him lay a badger with a dart hanging out of its backside, asleep and snoring; at least, that's what it sounded like. He should have known! His colour blindness had already put paid to his career in the navy and now it had caused him to shoot a badger instead of a tiger! He pulled the dart out of the badger's rear end, returned it to its case and scooted off to find his electric buggy. Sod this for a game of soldiers, he was going to take a proper holiday, somewhere warm and trouble free. Let that dozy Tam do his own dirty work!

Part Eight

A strange smell in Kensington

Mike turned the key in the ignition of the 1969 Fleetwood and the monstrous 8 litre engine roared into life.

"Where to?" he asked, slipping the automatic gear stick into the drive position and pulling away from the kerb.

Hymie clicked his seatbelt into place then rummaged around in his pockets for the photo of the Kit Cat Club. When he found it there was a part-sucked mint stuck to one man's face and a large crease along the top right corner.

"Oh well," he said, philosophically, at least the boiled sweet has only covered up the face of the guy with the cross on his head. Yeah, the hang-gliding guy, and he's already dead.

"No big deal," said Mike, "when you're dead, you're dead. So, where *are* we going, Goldman?"

"I thought we'd visit Sergeant Travers first," said Hymie, checking the addresses on the back of the photo.

"Yes, but where is he? I'm not a bleedin' mind reader."

"Calm down, mate, I was just about to tell you, wasn't I," said Hymie. "Here we are, 12 Troy Court, Kensington High Street."

"Right, I'll head down to the Edgware Road then hang a right at Hyde Park," he said, swinging sharply on the steering wheel and flooring the accelerator pedal.

"I reckon we'll have this case solved in a fortnight and then be able to take it easy for a few weeks," said Hymie.

"No offence," said Mike "but you're no Hercule Poirot are you? You've got the physique alright but you're a bit short of the little grey cells. I'm just hoping we don't run into any more bother this time. I'm tired of dodging bullets and punching people."

Hymie looked shocked. It wasn't so much the insults, which he'd been learning to ignore, as the prospect of a pacifist ex-bouncer watching his back. "But that's what you do, Mike," he said. "You're one of the best there is at punching people. I know it can't be easy dodging bullets when you're *that* size but you're pretty good at that too."

Mike shrugged his acknowledgement of the compliment. "So, what's the plan, Hercule?"

"We don't need one. One of these old soldiers is going to know something," he explained, tapping the photo. "Why else would these old scroats set up a club together after leaving the army if it didn't have something to do with the diamonds?"

"Sorry, H. I just don't buy it. These guys were comrades in arms. They've known about the diamonds for years. They've done alright out of them too. So why would they suddenly start killing each other? I don't think we can assume anything. All we have is a dead Colonel, a missing diamond and an old photo. It could take ages."

Hymie shook his head. "Just leave the thinking to me, Mike. You'll see, one of these old guys will lead us to the diamond and then we'll collect the reward. If not, we'll just pocket the ten grand and put the case in the 'unsolvables' pile."

Mike looked dubiously at his business partner. "You don't understand. These guys are old soldiers, retired veterans. They live by their own code, take the rough with the smooth, look out for each other. They're not gonna tell you anything."

"No, but they'll talk to you," said Hymie. "After all, you've spent time at Her Majesty's pleasure too."

"I was in the army, mate, not the nick," said Mike, aggrieved. "I was proud of serving my Queen and Country, something you'll never understand."

"You're right," said Hymie, "but that's just why they'll talk to you; you're one of them."

"I wouldn't be so sure," said Mike. "It's not like everyone who ever served in the army is the best of pals or something, you have to have served with them, been through the same battles and wars, survived the same shit," he explained.

"Well, if the old army baloney doesn't work, you can just threaten them. After all, no-one messes with mad Mike Murphy," said Hymie.

"You've got no respect," said Mike.

"Yes, I have, for pound notes, mate. Do you want a share of that twenty grand or not?"

They fell silent as the city slid past to the hum of the ancient Fleetwood's massive engine. The car suited them down to the ground; old and knackered and built for comfort not speed. It stood out like a sore thumb, but kept going regardless, sustained by a meagre diet of petrol fumes and body filler.

Eventually they hit Kensington High Street and Mike, catching sight of a red-brick building with the sign 'Troy Court' outside, swerved off the road onto the pavement, nearly squashing a little old lady, loaded up with shopping bags. She seemed to be mouthing obscenities at them so Mike wound down his window to check.

"Are you alright, love?" he asked.

"Well, if I am, it's no thanks to you!" she cried. "You nearly killed me with that ruddy great pile of rust!"

Hymie leant across to try to placate the woman, who seemed about to explode.

"Madam, please accept my sincere apologies. We're from the Special Branch, on a top secret mission under the Official Secrets Act. I'm Inspector Tree and this is my colleague, Sergeant Bush," he said, flashing his Finchley Public Libraries card at her with a winning smile.

Mike rolled his eyes. You could always trust Goldman to make a crisis out of a drama.

"In fact, madam, this man is completely off his head," said Mike, nodding at Hymie. "Take no notice of anything he says as it will only get you into a terrible mess and believe me, I should know," he confided, getting out of the car and slamming the door.

The woman looked up, aghast, as Mike towered over

her. Suddenly remembering she'd left a cake in the oven, she legged it for home.

The two detectives crossed the road, walked up to the main entrance to Troy Court and pressed the buzzer for apartment 12. There was no response.

"Maybe he's out," said Mike.

"Or the buzzer's broken," said Hymie.

"We could be here for ages," said Mike. "Why don't we just leave him a message to give us a call?"

"Because he won't," said Hymie. "Not if he's the kind of guy you seem to think he is. Besides, the last thing we need to do is leave calling cards lying around with our names and phone number on. Don't forget, Decca's investigating the Colonel's murder. If he gets wind…"

Mike smiled.

"…that we've been messing around on his patch," continued Hymie, "then it's goodnight Vienna."

"Not to mention Finchley," said Mike.

"Exactly," said Hymie. He was about to press the buzzer again when a smartly dressed young woman appeared inside the lobby and gave them a long hard stare through the glass partition.

"Are you from the Public Health Department?" she asked.

"Yes, that's right, I'm Hendersby, and he's French," said Hymie, nodding at Mike, who gave a Gallic shrug.

"Thank goodness for that. There's a terrible smell coming from apartment 12 and we've been waiting for someone to do something about it for days," said the woman.

"I see," said Hymie. "Well, we'd better take a look for you. Which floor is it on, miss?"

"The fourth floor," she said, pressing the door release catch. "An old chap lives there but I haven't seen him recently. Perhaps there's something wrong with his plumbing."

She led them up the stairs to the apartment, waiting at regular intervals for them to catch up with her.

"I always take the stairs, don't you?" she asked, when they got to the fourth floor landing. "It's such a good aerobic workout."

Hymie and Mike, virtually doubled up in a desperate attempt to catch their breath, were unable to find suitable words, but looked at each other as if to say 'you mean we had a bleedin' choice?' Once Hymie's face had returned to its normal shade of puce and his heartbeat had stabilised, the foul stench which had been haunting the landing outside apartment 12 gripped his nostrils with extraordinary violence. He almost retched.

"Gorblimey, it smells like a dead badger," cried Mike.

"I think you're right, Mr French," said Hymie. "Not a lot of people know this but they crawl into lift shafts and ventilation pipes to hibernate in the summer and sometimes die there."

Mike just looked at him in dismay.

"Leave it to us, miss," said Hymie. "We'll handle it from here," he added, helpfully. They waited for her to go. Fortunately she seemed to be in a hurry to get away.

"Thank you, Mr Hendersby," she said. Hymie smiled at her. "My pleasure," he said. "And Mr French," she added.

Then she rapidly descended the stairs to get as far away as possible from the terrible smell.

Once they were sure she'd gone Hymie knocked hard on the door of apartment 12.

"I've got a bad feeling about this, H.," said Mike, "Dead badgers don't smell like that, surely?"

"Well, I had to tell her something," said Hymie. "Either something died or Sergeant Travers is in dire need of a bath."

Repeated knocking seemed to achieve nothing so Mike opened the door with a shoulder-barge. The shattered door collapsed onto the floor of the darkened apartment and they both peered cautiously inside.

There on the rug in the entrance hall lay the blackened and decomposing body of a dead man, his face contorted with pain.

"Are you alright, Sergeant Travers?" asked Hymie.

"I expect he's feeling a bit peaky," said Mike, "he looks like he's been dead for a few days."

The stench was unbearable. Hymie stumbled to the top of the staircase in a daze and vomited over the handrail, showering the lobby downstairs.

"I think the Grim Reaper got there first," said Mike. "There's nothing we can do now except get the hell out of here before the Police arrive." The burly ex-bouncer lifted his business partner under the armpits and carried him bodily down the first flight of stairs until he remembered what his legs were for and they made a swift exit to rejoin the Fleetwood waiting outside.

Part Nine

Home Sweet Home

Back at 792A Finchley Road, Hymie Goldman sat shaking like a leaf in his office chair. Although he could no longer protest that he hadn't seen a dead body before there was no denying that he still couldn't cope with a corpse, at any level. With a shaking hand he poured the black coffee Charlie had made down his shirt front and jumped up as it scalded him.

"Aaargh!"

Mike raced into the room to find Hymie dabbing at his shirt front with a grotty handkerchief.

"I thought you were having a heart attack," said Mike, "not some minor coffee spillage."

"I could have been disfigured for life."

"Look, we both know that this has zippo to do with a hot coffee and everything to do with a dead suspect, right? You need to toughen up a bit. These things happen. We don't even know if Travers was murdered or died of natural causes; he was no spring chicken after all."

"*I* know," said Hymie. "No one ever died by accident on one of our investigations!"

Mike raised his eyebrows.

"Look, Mike, I can't hack it, alright. I think we should send Lady Wittering her money back and see if we can't find some more missing pet cases. You don't get killed looking for lost pets."

"Now, that's not gonna happen, is it?" said Mike. "For one thing we've already started spending the money, and for another, we're private investigators not boy scouts. If we start sending people their money back just because the going gets tough, the word will soon get around and we'll become a laughing stock in the business."

Hymie hated it when Mike was right. "So, what do you suggest?" he asked.

"We go to see the rest of the Kit Cat Club while they're still alive, just in case someone really is bumping them all off," said Mike.

"Or, alternatively, we wait and see who the last man standing is and then tip off the police," said Hymie, climbing out from the massive shadow of his yellow streak.

"Yeah, right," scoffed Mike, "and wave goodbye to the £20,000 reward. No-one gives away that much dough if they don't need to. No, we're gonna find that diamond if it kills us."

Hymie gulped.

"Just an expression," said Mike, quickly. "I know; why don't we go out on the town to celebrate?" he added, changing the subject.

"Celebrate what?" queried Hymie, who rarely needed an excuse for a slap up meal and a few beers.

"Who cares?" said Mike, "a hundred and seventy shopping days left till Christmas? the end of *Celebrity Big Brother*? Anything you like."

Hymie could tell·when he was being humoured but knew he didn't really have a choice. The only direction left was full steam ahead. Sooner or later Decca was going to hear about their trip to Troy Court to visit Sergeant Travers and whatever daft names he'd given that woman wasn't going to change their descriptions. Take any photofit picture you like, there was only one Goldman and Murphy.

"What are we going to do about Decca?" Hymie wondered aloud. "One way or another he's going to find out we're involved in this case and when he does, I wouldn't like to be in our shoes."

Mike studied his outsized brogues and looked thoughtful. "Well, the only other option is to go and see him ourselves and let him know we're just trying to help. Appeal to his better nature."

They exchanged dubious glances then simultaneously burst out laughing.

"Yeah, like that's gonna happen," said Hymie.

"Better nature? Hah, we may look daft, but we're not that stupid," agreed Mike.

There was a knock at the door.

Shit, that'll be Decca, they thought simultaneously. Hymie looked out of the window at the pavement below before accepting the futility of attempted flight. Running away would just make them look guilty and Decca could outrun him anyway. It was pointless.

Charlie poked her head around the door. "There's a man here to see you, Hymie."

"What kind of a man?"

"Kind of old, in a tweed jacket with a walking stick," she explained.

"Did he give a name?" asked Hymie, relieved. It didn't sound like Decca and that could only be good news.

"No, but he said it was urgent; a matter of life or death, in fact."

"You'd better send him in, then," said Hymie, taking out a notepad and pen from his desk drawer.

Moments later a small, nervous man was shown into the office. As Charlie had stated, he looked to be over the hill, slimly built and wearing a tweed jacket and cap. His eyes were a piercing blue and never rested, flitting busily around the room as he stood there awaiting further instructions.

"Please, sit down, Mr…?" began Hymie.

"Are you Goldman?" asked the old man.

"Yes, please take a seat," repeated the man from Finchley.

"My name's Harry Pettiman, Mr Goldman, formerly Colour-Sergeant Pettiman of the King's African Rifles," he confided, standing more upright as he said the words.

"Well, I'm pleased to meet you, Harry. Call me Hymie, everyone else does. And this," said Hymie, pointing at the bulky form of Murphy at the back of the room, "is my colleague and business partner…"

"Yes, I know," said Harry Pettiman, "Mike Murphy. I also know you're working for Lady Wittering," he added.

"I wouldn't go that far," said Hymie.

"I'm a member of the Kit Cat Club, you see, along with Colonel Wittering, Captain Bonser and Sergeant Travers. At least they *were* members but now they're all dead and I was worried I might be next."

"Why would you be next?"

"I've just received a postcard from Ulan Bator," said Pettiman, as if that explained everything.

"I don't know him, I'm afraid. Is he a friend of yours?" asked Hymie.

"Just take a look for yourself," said the Sergeant, handing over the postcard.

"It's a picture of a goat," said Hymie, confused.

"Try the other side," explained the Sergeant.

On the other side of the card, to the left of Sergeant Pettiman's name and address was a postage stamp from Mongolia bearing a picture of a yak, with a brief scrawled message next to it which read simply "You're next!"

"And you think this may be a death threat?"

"Yes, of course," said the Sergeant, wondering if he was always this slow. "Perhaps I shouldn't have come," he added, "You don't seem to know as much as I thought."

Hymie decided to come clean. "Wait, a minute, Sergeant, you were right, we are working for Lady Wittering. Not on the murder investigation mind; that's a police matter, but to recover some stolen property."

"The black diamond?" asked the Sergeant.

"What do you know about the black diamond?"

"So it *is* missing," said Sergeant Pettiman, triumphantly. "I assumed it'd been taken when the Colonel was killed but getting information out of his old lady was like trying to get blood out of a stone."

"So, who took it?" asked Hymie.

"That'd be telling."

"So, you don't know either," said Mike, walking over from the back of the office.

Pettiman shrugged. "Like I said, I'm just trying to stay alive. I haven't got it and I don't suppose Bonzo Bonser or that poor slob Travers had it. If the Colonel had it they'd have killed him without a second thought to get hold of that diamond. They don't care what you say, y'see. They shoot first…"

"And ask questions later?" said Hymie.

"No, they don't bother with questions, bless you. They just kill you and turn over your house, your possessions, anything they can find," explained Pettiman.

"Who do?" asked Mike.

"Why, the Uzbegs, of course," said the Sergeant. "If the Uzbegs come looking for you then may God have mercy on your soul. Why'd you think I came looking for protection?" he asked. His eyes fell on Hymie. "Though I think you could use some yourself."

"Look, Shorty, I handle the protection around here," said Mike, glowering at Pettiman, "so, if you want to stay in one piece, tell us what you know about the black diamond and where it's likely to be now."

The Sergeant could see that Mike at least wasn't to be trifled with.

"I'm guessing she didn't tell you much," said Pettiman. "The Colonel and a bunch of the lads stole it from a sacred temple in the Congo; the biggest carbonado you ever saw, as big as a man's fist and worth a fortune. They also took everything else they could find; gold, silver and a mountain of precious stones. Then they set fire to the temple and disappeared into the African jungle. Oh there have been rumours, tall stories about how a certain troop of the King's African Rifles have been living on easy street for years but no-one was ever able to prove anything. Then the Uzbegs appeared, bringing retribution and death in their wake."

"Who are the Uzbegs?" asked Hymie.

"Only the most ruthless and successful diamond smugglers the world has ever known," said Sergeant Pettiman. "They're also known as *the Oz*. Don't be fooled by the herds of goats and the furry hats, they're organised, they're deadly and they have informants everywhere."

Mike scratched his head. "Never heard of them," he said. "Are you sure you're not just making it all up?" he asked, clenching his fists ominously. "We may not look so sharp; me and the witless wonder," he said, pointing at Goldman, "but the cemeteries are full of people who underestimated us."

"So I've heard," agreed Pettiman. "That's why I came to see you."

"So, what do you want?" asked Mike. "We don't know where the diamond is any more than you do, but we want it just as much. It sounds like we're in competition."

"How much has she offered you to recover it?" asked the Sergeant. "Ten grand? Twenty?"

Mike smiled. "I'm not telling," he said.

"Well, I'll give you fifty thousand for it," said Pettiman. "Pounds sterling; none of your Euro rubbish," he added.

Hymie was definitely beginning to enjoy this case.

"But you don't own it," said Mike.

"Neither did the Witterings," said Pettiman. "Why else do you think *you're* looking for it instead of the police and every insurance agent this side of Timbuktu? Besides, my need is greater," he continued. "If I don't get that diamond to the Oz before they get to me, it's curtains."

"We'll think about it," said Hymie. "Leave us a deposit of ten thousand pounds and a contact number and we'll be in touch." It was worth a try.

Sergeant Pettiman removed a cheque-book from his inside jacket pocket and wrote out the cheque without a murmur. "Don't worry about the number," he said. "I'll call you. I've suddenly decided to go on a tour of the British Isles for my health. I won't be back until the diamond is recovered. I'll be travelling light and staying in cheap hotels under an assumed name, so don't bother trying to contact me. I pray to God you find the thing before the Uzbegs find me. Good luck, lads, all the hopes and dreams of a poor old soldier go with you!"

"One last question," said Mike. "How do the Uzbegs know of the existence of the black diamond?"

"It was rumoured that the Colonel used them to help smuggle the stash out of Africa and then reneged on the deal," said Sergeant Pettiman. So saying, he collected his walking stick and cap and set off to the bus stop for who knew where.

Part Ten

Toxicology

Deep in the refrigerated basement of the Royal Free Hospital on Pond Street, Inspector Decca and his partner in crime, Sergeant Terse were keeping an appointment with one of the consultants in the Pathology Department. Professor George Irwin, the medic in question, had just popped out for a cup of tea and a warm before they arrived, leaving them to make their own introductions to the bodies which were spread out on all sides, like slabs of meat.

"I hate these places, they give me the creeps," said Decca, shivering in the cold.

"I love 'em myself, sir. There's nowhere more exhilarating than a good mortuary, especially on a hot day," said Terse, lifting the corner of a sheet to examine the chilled corpse beneath. "Poor sod," he added.

A large man with white hair, white clothes and a white lab coat which didn't quite fasten up at the front emerged silently through the swing doors behind them.

"Jesus H. Christ!" exclaimed Decca, jumping half out of his skin at the sight of the apparition. "I thought you were a ghost!"

The Professor smiled. He'd had more flattering comparisons, but he'd had worse too; ever since he'd started working with the police.

"Don't worry, man, there are worse things down here than ghosts," said the Professor, cheerily.

Decca looked at his watch, as though he were being kept from something more important, like washing his socks. He produced his police badge from an inside pocket and waved it at the Professor.

"Inspector Decca, M.I.T.," he said, "I've come to see Colonel Wittering's body."

"What is it about the Colonel's body?" asked the Professor. "You're the third person who's asked to see it in the last few days. I wouldn't mind, but most of the time we have enough trouble trying to persuade the next of kin to identify them."

The Inspector seemed agitated. "Can we just get on with it, please," he said, directing a withering look at the Professor.

The man in white led them across the floor to a three drawer refrigerated cabinet and pulled out the top drawer. "Here you are then," he said, "Caucasian male, aged around 70, cause of death...cut to pieces by something sharp."

Terse lifted the sheet and studied the Colonel's last human remains.

"He's definitely dead, sir," he said, gravely.

"You don't say, Terse," said Decca, pushing his colleague out of the way so he could inspect the body himself. "Is this it?" he asked, revolted. "Only it looks more like a wholesale order from the butchers than a corpse.

Whoever killed him made a right mess of the poor devil.
How did you identify the body?"

"By the name in his jacket," said the Professor, lamely.
"That and a positive ID from his wife, the Wittering
woman. Though heaven knows how she recognised him."

"What about dental records?" asked Decca.

"Well, Inspector, you may not have noticed, but he has
no teeth. The lower part of his skull was entirely missing,"
explained the Prof.

"So we can't really be sure it's him," said Decca. "And
as far as the cause of death is concerned, 'cut to pieces
by something sharp'? I take it that means we don't know
what killed him either," he added. "OK, Doc., give it to me
straight, what's your best guess?" concluded Decca.

"I'm not in the business of guessing, Inspector, I
leave that to you, but for what it's worth it looked to me
as though he'd been eaten by some large predatory wild
animal."

"But what could have done that?" asked Terse, "a lion?"

"Possibly, yes," agreed the Professor. "A lion or a tiger
could have made a mess of him like that, but how could it
have come to be in his house?"

"We simply don't know," said Decca. "Has anything
else funny happened lately?" he asked.

"Well, it depends what you mean by *funny*," said the
Professor. "We did have another old soldier in yesterday, a
Sergeant Travers."

"Travers? Are you sure it was Travers?" asked the
Inspector.

"Yes, with a heart like an Ox," said the Professor. "No

sign of any pre-existing illnesses. At the moment it looks like poisoning, although we won't know for sure until the blood tests come back."

"My heart aches, and a drowsy numbness pains my sense, as though of hemlock I had drunk," murmured Decca, absently.

"Precisely so, Inspector," said the Professor. "I didn't have you down as a Keats aficionado."

"We're not all philistines and ignoramuses in the police force, you know," said the Inspector.

"Who's this Keats, geezer?" asked Terse, "Has he got any form?"

"No Terse, but we may just have found a lead after all."

They thanked the Professor briefly and returned to their car.

"Let's get back to the station, Terse," said Decca. "I want everything we have on Sergeant Travers, formerly of the King's African Rifles," he added.

Part Eleven

The men in furry hats

Mike opened the blinds in Hymie's office and sunshine flooded into the room as if to say 'Cheer up, guys, it's going to be OK.' Of course, no-one ever trusted the British weather and with good cause.

"So, which of the Biscuit Boys are we visiting next?" asked Mike. "Assuming they're not all six feet under by now."

Hymie frowned. "They can't all be dead," he said, without conviction.

"So, what theory are you working on now?" asked Mike. "Come on, who stole the diamond and where is it?"

"Well, on the plus side, the list of suspects is getting shorter by the day," said Hymie.

"And on the minus side?" asked Mike.

"The list of suspects is getting shorter by the day," repeated Hymie. "Soon there'll be no-one left to ask."

"Except the killer," said Mike.

Hymie didn't like the way the conversation was going so he changed the subject. "What I don't understand is where the Uzbegs come into all this. They seem to have scared the crap out of Sergeant Pettiman, so I'm in no hurry to meet them, but no one else has even mentioned them, so do we believe in them or not? Do they really exist? What do you think, Mike?"

Mike smiled. "Well, I've heard plenty of tripe since I've been working with you, Goldman, but I've never been asked to believe in a tribe of furry-hatted Mongolian diamond smugglers before. How do they make their getaway? By motorised Yak?"

Hymie laughed. "When you put it like that, Mike I don't believe in them either," he agreed. He pulled the photo of the Kit Cat Club out of his pocket and placed it on the desk in front of him. The mint which had stuck to Captain Bonser's face now had a piece of fluff attached to it, making him look like he had a long white beard.

"The trouble is," said Hymie, "that we don't know which of these old scroats to believe. We can't even be sure they're dead when they're supposed to be. Take Old Father Time here," he said, pointing at Bonser, "how are we ever gonna prove or disprove that he died in a hang gliding accident in Chile? I'm buggered if I'm going out there to find out."

"No, I'm with you there, H." said Mike, who didn't like cold climates.

Suddenly Charlie appeared in the room. It was as if she'd been listening at the door and, tripping over an untied shoelace, had fallen against it and landed on the carpet. Uncanny. Hymie looked suspiciously at her. "Anything we can do for you, Charlie?"

"I was wondering if you needed anything? Cup of tea? Bacon roll? It's just so quiet out there," she confided.

"Sounds great," agreed Hymie.

"No but thanks, Charlie," said Mike. "We're going out for a meal soon."

Hymie turned to Mike, suddenly losing all interest in the case. "So, what's it to be? Curry or Italian?"

"I thought we'd try that new place off Piccadilly Circus, the *House of Meat*," said Mike.

"There's nothing like a balanced diet," agreed Hymie. "Call us a cab, Charlie."

Moments later the decrepit duo were standing on the pavement outside the Black Kat café, waiting for a taxi. There was a constant stream of vehicles but no sign of any black cabs. Suddenly a battered green transit van pulled up next to them, the back doors flew open and a gang of men in furry hats and hand-woven shawls emerged, smelling of goats and brandishing strange implements.

"What?" was all Mike managed to utter before one of the gang hit him in the face with what looked like a large custard pie but was probably an anaesthetic as it sent him reeling onto all fours on the pavement. Hymie was bundled into the back of the van just before it sped off into the evening traffic.

In the van's dark interior, Hymie wondered what on earth he was going to do without Mike. One of the gang held him in a vice-like shoulder grip, eventually releasing him once he ceased to resist.

"What do you want with me?" asked Hymie, indignantly. "I was on my way to the *House of Meat*."

"Yu Hansi?" said one of the men in the furry hats, a large, foreign-looking gentleman with a massive moustache.

"Eh?" said Hymie.

"Yu Hansi?" said the man, louder.

"I heard you the first time, squire," said Hymie, "I just didn't understand what you were saying."

The man struck Goldman across the face, making his nose bleed.

"Ow!" cried the man from Finchley.

"Yu Hansi Globdan?"

Hymie was faced with the age old dilemma of either admitting that he actually was Hansi Globdan or claiming to be someone else entirely. He was adept at creating new and surprising identities. The only problem was that for once it might be safer to tell the truth. If they believed he was someone else they may let him out with a curt apology or they may just kill him to avoid leaving witnesses. What had Pettiman said? They shot first but didn't bother asking questions later.

The man with the moustache appeared to be growing impatient.

"Yes, that's me, Hansi Globdan," admitted Hymie, reluctantly.

The man with the moustache nodded and his associates burst out laughing like fiends from hell.

"Yu hab dimon?" continued the furry-hatted one.

"No, I'm afraid not," said Hansi.

The man struck him again. Goldman winced as the pain shot through his face.

"Yu wan lib or di?"

"Lib," said Goldman, picking up the stranger's lingo with a speed born of the will to survive. He could see why they didn't ask many questions.

"So wher dimon?"

Goldman tried desperately to remember the names of the members of the Kit Cat Club.

"Captain Bonser?" he ventured.

"Ded."

"Oh, yes, sorry, the hang gliding accident," said Hymie, but the man with the moustache only laughed scornfully at him as though only an idiot would believe that.

"Colonel Wittering?" continued Hymie.

"Ded."

"Sergeant Travers?"

"Ded," repeated the man with the moustache. "Yu no lot ded peeple, Hansi."

"Sergeant Pettiman?" volunteered Hymie, still trying to avoid joining the ranks of the deceased.

"Wher him?" asked the Uzbeg, suddenly interested.

Now he was in trouble. He didn't know where Pettiman was but whatever he said had to be plausible; plausible and a long way away, obviously.

"He in Blackpool," said Hymie.

"Blak poop? Hahahaa," laughed the Uzbeg, not sure what to make of Hansi Globdan. Was he really as big an idiot as he seemed or was there more to him than met the eye?

"Yu dicktecktiv, Hansi?"

"Yes, very good dicktecktiv," said Hymie, modestly.

"We see," said the Uzbeg with a sneer. "Yu have wik to fine dimon," he said.

"You want me to work for you?" asked Hymie, incredulously. "How much you pay?"

The van pulled up at the kerb suddenly and Hymie wondered if this was the end of the line.

"Yu wan lib?"

"Yes!" cried Goldman, frantically.

The van's rear doors flew open again and Hymie was pushed out onto the pavement. There, lying in a groggy heap, was Mike Murphy, still wondering what had hit him.

The van pulled off into the traffic, quickly disappearing from view.

"I think we can safely say they exist, Mike," said Hymie, nursing his injured head in his hands.

Part Twelve

Welcome to the House of Meat

When they'd recovered from the shock of their unexpected meeting with the men in the furry hats, the men from Finchley decided to stick to Plan A and go out for a meal.

After all, as Hymie observed, a "wik" or a week may not be long enough to find a valuable black diamond, but it was certainly long enough to go into hiding.

They sat at a table for two in the House of Meat and studied the décor. The walls were covered with a garish mural of every kind of wild animal you could think of; it looked like a group of seven-year-olds had been asked to paint a zoo.

Hymie studied Mike's unsightly face. He was sporting a pair of black eyes and looked like a giant panda.

"Well, you seem to fit in for once, Murphy. By the way, how did you get those shiners?"

"Look, Goldman, let's not go there, alright. They took me by surprise. It happens. Just shut your cakehole before it happens to you," he added, irritably.

Hymie zipped it. He felt sorry for Mike. Whereas he'd always been rubbish at fighting and had tried to avoid punch-ups, Mike had made a career out of hitting people and it must have shaken his self-confidence big time to find himself out for the count so quickly. "Don't get me wrong, my massive chum, I'm with you," said Hymie. "My number one priority right now is to keep as far away as possible from those ruddy Uzbegs. Pettiman definitely had the right idea."

Mike didn't want to be drawn on the subject so he resumed his study of the menu. Hymie joined him.

"Aardvark surprise?" wondered Mike.

"Yeah, the surprise is there's no aardvark in it," quipped Hymie.

"How about a nice Kangaroo Vindaloo?" asked Mike. Hymie shuddered.

In the end it all sounded so unappealing that they simply ordered two "meat specials" and trusted to luck. They sat munching on a bizarre array of dead things for the next hour. Pork, beef, wildebeest, llama, giraffe and alligator, it was all seemingly as one to the clientele of the House of Meat, incorporating Anatole's exotic pet emporium, which had recently gone into liquidation.

"Funny how it all tastes like chicken after a while," said Mike.

"That's what I was thinking," said Hymie. A passing waiter stopped and put his finger to his lips. "It's hamster," he whispered. "Amazing what you can do with a good sauce, eh?" he added, retreating through the swing doors to the kitchen.

Finally they were too full to eat anything else and, loosening their belts, resumed their conversation.

"You know we can't go back to the office for some time," said Hymie.

"I'm with you there," agreed Mike. "Those guys were deadly. No threats or banter, just wham! Game over. You'd better tell Charlie to take a few weeks off too," he added. "We don't want her getting a visit from the Uzbegs."

"True," agreed Hymie. "Besides, after that business in Kensington we're overdue for a visit from Decca and Terse. Maybe I should give her a call. More to the point, I really need some time to think. It's all in there somewhere," he added, tapping his forehead with his index finger. "I'm convinced we must already know where the diamond is if I can only work out what all the clues mean."

"We don't have *that much* time, H. We need to get out of here fast. Perhaps we should even think about leaving London. What do you think?"

"Hiding out's just the opposite of finding things," said Hymie. "We just have to work out where no one's gonna bother looking for us."

"I'm not going back to Blackpool," said Mike.

Hymie looked at Mike's black eyes again. "That's out of the question," he said. "They think Sergeant Pettiman's hiding there."

"What makes them think that?" asked Mike.

"Oh, you know..." said Hymie, shrugging. His eyes followed the assembled crowd of wild animals around the walls in search of Noah. "Wait, I have it!" he cried.

"Well, let's hope it's not contagious," said Mike, "I've got enough troubles as it is."

"When was the last time we went to the zoo?" asked Hymie.

"I can't remember," said Mike, humouring him.

"Exactly, never!" cried Hymie. "So why would anyone go looking for us at the zoo?"

"They wouldn't," agreed Mike, "unless they were as barmy as you."

"Precisely," agreed Hymie. "Tomorrow we're going to the zoo. Tonight we'll have to stay in some grotty hovel nearby. Have you still got the flat, Mike?"

"No, I got evicted months ago," admitted Mike. "I've been floating between 792A and my Auntie Vera's place."

Hymie smiled at the thought of Mike floating anywhere.

"We could always stay at the Kings Hotel, Bayswater," said Mike.

"Very funny, Mike but we have to draw the line somewhere. Let's just take pot luck close to the zoo," said Hymie.

They took a cab to the cheapest hotel they could find near Camden Town and drowned their sorrows in the bar until closing time, polishing off a bottle of Jeff Daniels, a Southern Whiskey substitute made in China by Jack's less talented cousin.

Part Thirteen

Zoo Mania

The following morning Goldman and Murphy rose early, fully dressed from the night before. Viewing the world through the haze of a hangover is never ideal but when you've only been given a week to live by homicidal goat-herders in furry hats, it's nigh on compulsory. Mike attempted to brush his teeth with a soapy finger while Hymie completed the briefest of ablutions by running his palm over his depleted locks. They shared a conversation-free breakfast of cornflakes and toast and were soon back pounding the streets of London en route to the zoo. After a couple of blocks, Mike hailed a cab and once they were safely belted up in the back, Hymie continued to ignore him by calling the office on his mobile. Mike gawped morosely out of the cab's grubby window as Goldman mumbled away in the background. Eventually Hymie switched off the handset and stuck it back into the bulging right pocket of his coat.

"What was that all about?" asked Mike.

"Oh, just telling Charlie we'd be out for a few days and to keep a look out for men in funny hats," said Hymie, jovially. "I gave her a few tasks to get on with too. There's nothing worse than leaving them with nothing to do. They get bored and leave."

"She's a bright one, that Charlie," said Mike. "Where did you find her?"

"Well, in actual fact she found us," admitted Hymie. "She just appeared in the office one morning and said she'd always wanted to work for a firm of private investigators and could she have a free trial."

"So she's working for free?" queried Mike.

"Just at the moment," agreed Hymie, "although I did put her in charge of the petty cash."

Mike smiled. "So she's in charge of about fifty pee and a pile of old receipts."

Hymie nodded.

Mike looked thoughtful. Either that or he was suffering from indigestion. "I don't get it," he said after a while, "why would an attractive, intelligent young woman be working for *us* for free? I mean we don't have a very good track record with staff, do we? Remember the one who tried to kill you…and the other one; who was running an underground terror organisation from our office? I hope you took up references on Charlie?" said Mike.

It was Hymie's turn to look thoughtful. "Not exactly," he said, quietly.

"What does that mean?" asked Mike, knowing full well he wasn't going to like the answer.

"Well, Bacon liked her," said Hymie.

"I see," said Mike, "so who put the cat in charge of recruitment?"

"Also, I had a good feeling about her," added Hymie.

"Yeah, you, me, and ninety-nine percent of the male population of London have a *good feeling* about her, but that doesn't make her employee of the month," said Mike. "Goldman, you have to be the biggest idiot ever to employ anyone!"

"It'll be alright, Mike, just you see," said Hymie, dismissively, as the cab pulled up outside the entrance to London Zoo. He paid the fare and they disembarked through the dreary plastic façade for a day of lying low among the wildlife of NW1.

Once inside the metropolis's premier animal exhibit the two deadbeat detectives trudged around the park looking for inspiration. Mike's first encounter was with a 400lb African mountain gorilla, which looked suspiciously at him from behind the glass as if to say 'how did you get out, mate?' Hymie read from the plaque in front of the enclosure;

"The mountain gorilla is listed as Critically Endangered in the International Union for Conservation of Nature's *Red List of Threatened Species*. There are only around 780 surviving in the wild and 4 in captivity. Their numbers are split between the Virunga volcanic mountain range, which spans the border area of Rwanda, Uganda and the Democratic Republic of the Congo, and the Bwindi National Park in Uganda. They're primarily vegetarian."

"Eats shoots and leaves?" said Mike.

"Much like yourself," agreed Hymie. "And the Uzbegs," he added, lest Mike should think he was being compared to a gorilla.

"So this big fella came from the same place as the black diamond," said Mike. "It makes you think, eh?"

"It certainly does, Mike," said Hymie, who'd already begun thinking about lunch. "You mean, if only gorillas could talk?" he added.

A man in a long black leather coat, with laced up boots and an eye patch walked rapidly past them, carrying a sketch pad and some pencils. Mike looked at him suspiciously.

"You get some funny types in here," he said.

"I know," agreed Hymie. "Still, perhaps he's a famous artist who comes to do some sketching. I told you a trip to the zoo could be inspirational."

"Yeah, you're also the guy who told me he had a *good feeling* about Charlie. Mark my words, Goldman, she'll turn out to be a wrong 'un, just like all the others."

Hymie frowned. "I suppose I'd better just ignore the snide remarks and get on with solving this case," he said. "I mean, you've never been big on thinking, have you?"

"OK, Brains, where do we go from here?"

Hymie removed the crumpled black and white photo of the Kit Cat Club from his inside coat pocket and scanned the names written above the images of the old soldiers. "There aren't many of them left, Mike," he said, "just Major Daniels and Corporal Cholmondeley."

"Well, we'd better get a move on before they join the others in the cemetery," said Mike. "Assuming one of them isn't the culprit, of course. Who's next on your hit list?"

"Cholmondeley," said Hymie, "although I think they pronounce it *Chum-ley*, like the dog food."

The two shabby detectives walked slowly along the footpath past the penguins and the butterfly house before approaching the tiger enclosure. There, sitting on a shooting stick and with his sketch pad on his lap, sat the man in the long black coat. He seemed to be peering at something at the back of the enclosure, unable to make it out properly or believe his eye, as his left eye was hidden beneath an eye patch.

"Can you see anything in there?" he asked Hymie, who leant against the glass and looked inside.

"No, not really," admitted Goldman. "What's it meant to be?"

"A tiger," said Mike. "This is the tiger enclosure, after all."

The man in the black coat nodded. "Well, that's what I thought," he said. "You see, I'm an artist and I particularly wanted to sketch the new tiger but all you can see is something striped hiding in the bushes. It's not even moving. If I didn't know better I'd think it was one of those dogs-on-wheels toys that had been painted orange with black stripes."

Hymie smirked. "What, in London Zoo?" he said. "I very much doubt it. This place is la crème de la crème, mate. What did you say your name was?"

"I didn't, but it's Wittering, Maurice Wittering, and one day my name will be the toast of the art world," he said, tossing his head back.

Mike and Hymie exchanged glances. The glances said that this guy was definitely living up to his name and wondered if he could be related to Colonel Wittering. Hymie studied the long black coat, the laced up boots and the eye patch and shook his head. No, this guy was clearly barking. They made an excuse and walked off hurriedly towards the flamingos.

In the bushes at the back of the tiger enclosure Tam McMurdo was busy trying to keep up the pretence that there really was a tiger in residence. Ali had set out to recover Kitty from the neighbouring parks over a week ago now and although he'd checked in once or twice via walkie-talkie early on, Tam hadn't heard a dickey bird, let alone a tiger's roar ever since. At least the regular keeper, Jiggers, was still off sick but how much longer could he take off work with diarrhoea? When he got back the shit would really hit the fan. Tam pressed the play button on his old tape recorder, strategically placed beside him on the floor and a soulful wail proceeded from its tinny speakers.

"Meee Oooowwww!"

Maurice looked distinctly unimpressed. It sounded more like an injured moggy than Kitty, Queen of the Jungle. He wondered why they'd bothered to transfer such a pathetic specimen all the way from Jersey.

"It's nae ruddy guid, th' games ower," said Tam to himself, kicking the tape recorder in disgust. Sparks leapt out of the battered machine but Tam took no notice. He removed a packet of cigarettes from his jacket pocket and lit one. "Ah main an aw be hung fur a sheep as a lamb," he muttered, drawing on the cigarette and puffing out smoke rings over the makeshift model tiger. He knew he should have camouflaged the wheels a bit better but after a few jars in the Pit he'd convinced himself that no one would notice.

"Hey! There's smoke coming from that tiger!" cried Maurice in disbelief, still sitting on his shooting stick watching the striped object in the bushes.

On hearing this, Tam decided that he'd better scotch the rumour that London Zoo was setting fire to the animals before there was a public backlash. He dropped his cigarette and left the enclosure via the keeper's office, where he met the agitated Maurice at the door.

"Dinna fash yersel, it's only an auld stuffed dug!" he cried.

Maurice looked blankly at him, gave up the unequal task of trying to fathom what he was saying and pushed his way past the weary Scotsman. There on the wall inside the keeper's office hung a fire extinguisher, which he lifted down and carried anxiously to the smouldering figure in the bushes.

"I knew it!" cried Maurice. "I knew it wasn't a tiger."

The toy dog on wheels was ablaze now. The bushes themselves had caught fire too, whether from Tam's cigarette or the sparks from the tape recorder wasn't clear. Maurice pressed down the lever on top of the extinguisher, expecting to deluge the flames in foam or water but all that came out was a low hissing sound. He turned around to look for the deranged Scotsman but Tam was nowhere to be seen. Then Maurice realised that his coat had caught fire. He flapped wildly at his coat tails to extinguish the flames but all it did was fan them higher. There was nothing for it but to find some water. Screaming and cursing he ran back to the entrance and fled in the direction of the penguin enclosure.

Moments later a man in a long black coat with flames lapping around his backside was seen vaulting over the low wall of the penguin enclosure and diving into their pool, scattering the colony of startled residents in all directions as he did so. A large cloud of steam arose from the pool as he disappeared below the water.

Mike and Hymie looked on in dismay from the nearby flamingo enclosure and shook their heads disapprovingly as the zoo's fire engine arrived to deal with the blaze in the Big Cat enclosure.

"Artists will be artists, I suppose," said Hymie.

Part Fourteen

A quiet word with Goldman

In a tiny office in New Scotland Yard the not so tiny Inspector Ray Decca pored over the police file on the recently deceased Sergeant Travers. It was a very short file because the first time he'd come to the attention of the police was as a suspicious death in a block of Kensington flats.

"Good Lord!" cried Decca, "Would you believe it, Bazza?" he said, handing the file across his desk to the hunched figure of Sergeant Terse. The sergeant read the notes.

"Travers' body was found after some bogus health inspectors called and smashed in the door to his apartment," read Terse. "Would you believe it, what's the world coming to?"

"Yeah, just read the descriptions of the *health inspectors,*" said Decca.

There was a pause while the sergeant found his place in the narrative.

"One was a short, overweight, scruffy man, aged between 35 and 70 with verbal diarrhoea and the other was a large brooding man of about 6 foot four, weighing something over 300 pounds," said Terse.

"Does that remind you of anyone we know?" asked Decca.

"Goldman and Murphy, Guv!"

"Exactly, who else could it be?" said Decca. "Get the car, Barry, we're going to pay them a social call."

"On my way, sir," said Terse, heading for the car park.

Forty-five minutes later, the patrol car pulled up outside 792A Finchley Road and Sergeant Terse led the charge into the grotty detectives' offices. He pulled up abruptly, however, at the sight of an attractive young woman sitting behind the reception desk. He looked at the number on the door again to make sure he was in the right place.

"Are Goldman and Murphy in?" he asked.

"Who wants to know?" asked Charlie.

"Look, cut the crap, Love," said Decca, "we're policemen, and they're expecting us."

"I'm sorry to disabuse you of that notion, *Love*," said Charlie, "but they aren't expecting you. I'm their PA and I've never heard of you, so unless you have a warrant, I'd advise you to leave immediately."

Decca's jaw dropped. He was used to all kinds of evasive action from Goldman and Murphy but a receptionist with attitude was the last thing he'd expected, especially one who looked like a real woman.

"Er…yes, sorry, miss," said Decca. "Who are you?"

"Charlotte Finch," said Charlie, "and who would you be?"

"Inspector Ray Decca of M.I.T," said Decca, flashing his badge at her, "and this," he began, before thinking better of it, "…is Terse. He can't help it, poor chap; he's always been like it."

Decca goggled at Charlie. He clearly hadn't seen a young woman with curves and a devastating personality for some time.

"So, I suppose you'll be leaving now?" asked Charlie.

"Look, you don't want to upset the police, surely?" said Decca. "We may not have a warrant but we can get one easily enough, you see this is a murder investigation." He gawped at her again in the hope of impressing her, but Charlie just filed her nails.

"I just want to ask them a few questions, that's all," explained the Inspector, as reasonably as he could manage.

"Well, they're out," said Charlie. "I haven't seen them since yesterday evening when they went out for a meal."

"Anywhere nice?" asked Decca.

"I don't know, Inspector. I did get a call from Mr Goldman this morning though. He said they were going undercover for a while and asked if I would make some enquiries for them."

"What enquiries?" queried Decca.

"Just routine administrative matters," said Charlie.

"I see," said Decca. "Well, the next time you hear from them would you let them know that Inspector Decca would appreciate a word urgently. Oh, and ask them what they know about dead badgers." he added, mischievously.

Decca and Terse headed back onto the Finchley

Road and drove off empty-handed. You had to hand it to Goldman; he seemed to have some kind of sixth sense, allowing him to avoid police interviews. Still, the night was young, he couldn't run very fast and he couldn't hide forever.

Part Fifteen

The trouble with Cholmondeley

The sun rose again, finding Finchley's second-worst private detectives still on the case. "The trouble with Cholmondeley," said Hymie, "is that he's got a posh name. It's spelt Chol-mon-deley and pronounced Chum-ley. The other thing wrong with him is, according to Charlie, he seems to be living in a mental hospital."

"Well, there but for the grace of God…" said Mike.

"Charming," said Hymie. "Still, nuts or not, we need to cross him off the list. If he's genuinely looping the loop at twenty-thousand-feet then we can discount him, but it may just be a cover story."

"Yeah, I mean there must be dozens of master criminals hiding out in asylums, right, H?" said Mike.

"Exactly," agreed Hymie. "The other thing I don't get is how someone with a poncy name like Cholmondely is only a corporal. With a name like that he should be running the show."

"I can see you know all about the army," said Mike, sarcastically.

They walked along the street to the nearest taxi rank and Hymie leant in at the driver's window.

"I'd like to go to Hanwell Asylum, Southall," he said.

The driver looked cautiously back at him. "I can believe it. Are you visiting or staying there?" he asked, clearly inclining towards the latter view.

"Just visiting," said Hymie, "although I don't see how it matters."

"No, you're right," agreed the cabbie, "as long as you can pay the fare, you can be as mad as a box of frogs. It's a fair old way, mind, it'll cost you," he added.

"How much?" asked Hymie.

"Fifty quid, maybe more, it depends," said the cabbie.

Hymie resisted the temptation to quibble and climbed into the back of the cab. "We're men of means," he said, as Mike joined him.

"So, it looks like the corporal's got a few mental health issues," said Mike. "These days, who hasn't? It's almost become fashionable."

"Well, I hope he's nuts," said Hymie. "They've put him in the John Connolly Wing."

"Never heard of it," said Mike.

"Me neither, but apparently he was some famous loony doctor."

They fell into a silence borne of having spent too much time together in a grotty and claustrophobic hotel and only snapped out of it when the cab pulled into the driveway of the Hanwell Asylum.

"Drop us anywhere," said Hymie.

"I was going to," said the cabbie. "That'll be fifty five quid, please."

"Charming!" said Hymie, grudgingly unrolling the sum from a wad of notes secreted in his inside coat pocket. They made their way across the tarmac to the imposing entrance to the hospital and stopped outside.

"What's the story today, Goldman?" asked Mike. "We're a couple of escaped loonies looking for a bed for the night?"

"Mike, please. Give me credit for some intelligence." He'd thought about it, of course, he just hadn't reached any conclusions. "Nothing so obvious. I mean, the place must be full to bursting with patients and doctors. We need a different angle."

"Such as?" asked Mike.

"I was thinking we could be from his…publishers!" said Hymie, picking a business at random. "Yeah, that's it, he's written a book and we're from the publishers."

"He's really written a book?"

"No, well, maybe. Look, he's bonkers, how's he gonna remember?" said Hymie.

"Oh, he'll remember, alright."

"Even if he does, the staff won't know any different," said Hymie. "Right, I've got it. It's all falling into place. He wrote his memoirs, all about his time in Africa. He sent us the first few chapters and we've decided to commission it. It's perfect, we can ask him anything we like…"

"Like, did you ever steal a massive black diamond or kill half your platoon?"

"Exactly," said Hymie.

"He's gonna answer a stupid question like that? He may be nuts but he's not crazy!"

"It's the element of surprise, Mike. We'll lull him into a false sense of security with a load of questions about the weather or the wildlife and then wham! We slip in the tricky questions and watch his eyes. You can always tell by the eyes."

Mike looked into Hymie's eyes with concern. "Yes, I can see what you mean. You've been overdoing it."

"I'm a grafter, Mike."

"I meant the booze and the carbs."

"I see," said Hymie. Honesty was important in a friendship but you could have too much of a good thing. He looked up at the clock tower, looming over the entrance to Hanwell Asylum. It seemed to have stopped at 11:59. Clearly time didn't mean much within the institution's walls. His own watch, the high spec. Casio MTP-1259D with the all important 50 metre water resistance, was showing the time as 12:15 precisely.

"Come on, we're late."

"We have an appointment?" asked Mike, incredulously.

"Certainly," said Hymie. He strode forward through the large double doors and breezed up to the reception desk with the air of a man for whom time meant money. Mike followed.

"Good afternoon," said Hymie.

"Hello, can I help you?" replied the receptionist. She was a woman of about forty with thick glasses and dyed blonde hair.

"Yes, I've come to see one of your inmates," began Hymie.

"We call them patients," corrected the receptionist.

"Sorry, I meant patients," said Hymie. "A Mr Cholmondeley," he added. "I believe he's in the John Conolly wing."

"And you would be?"

"Mr Mann," said Hymie, "and this is my colleague," he continued, "Mr Booker. We're from his publishers."

The receptionist looked surprised. "Do you have an appointment?"

"Yes, of course," said Hymie, dismissively.

The receptionist tapped a few buttons on her keypad and looked at the screen in front of her. "Well, there's nothing here," she said.

"That's impossible," said Hymie. "My PA booked it weeks ago. We've been travelling for days to keep this appointment and my diary for the next forty-eight hours is stretched to bursting point. We *have* to see him."

"I'm sorry," said the receptionist, "I'm only doing my job."

Hymie stooped down to the desk and rested his arm on the counter. "Has anyone ever told you, you bear a striking resemblance to Marilyn Monroe," he said.

"No, really?" said the receptionist, amazed.

"Well, I'm surprised," said Hymie. "Don't you think so, Michael?" he asked, implicating Mike in another of his underhand schemes.

"Oh, yeah, definitely," agreed Mike, "Marilyn for sure," he added, thinking more of Manson than Monroe.

"Perhaps the appointment was booked through one of your colleagues?" suggested Hymie.

"Can you remember who you spoke to?" asked the receptionist.

"As I said, it was arranged by my PA, Charlie and she's usually very reliable," said Hymie.

The receptionist looked thoughtful. "It wasn't Yvette, was it?" she asked.

Hymie could sense he was winning. "Very probably," he said.

"She was temping with us for a while but we had to let her go."

"Poor attendance?"

"No, just useless," confided the receptionist.

"Well, anything you can do for us would be greatly appreciated," said Hymie with a wink.

She picked up the phone on her desk, tapped in a short extension number and spoke to a colleague in hushed tones. "Excuse me, but where did you say you were from?" she asked Hymie.

"Mann Booker, the publishers," said Hymie. "We were hoping for a few words with our new signing, Mr Cholmondeley. He's written what could easily be the next big blockbuster!"

"Really?" said the receptionist, impressed, before continuing to whisper animatedly into her handset. Shortly afterwards she replaced it on her desk and smiled triumphantly at the bogus publishers. "You can have ten minutes," she said. "A porter will be along to collect you shortly."

"You're a marvel!" said Hymie. Mike nodded.

The receptionist beamed.

The porter, a man of about one hundred and fifty, with a stooping gait and blue overalls, led them through the desolate corridors with all the enthusiasm of Quasimodo showing day trippers around the bell tower at Notre Dame.

"Who did you want to see again?" he asked, for the second time in five minutes.

"Mr Chol-mond-eley," repeated Hymie.

"I know, I know, I'm not an idiot, you know," said the porter, wiping his nose on the sleeve of his jacket. Having exhausted his limited conversation he set off again through the sunless corridors and into the dark heart of the asylum. They passed day rooms, nurses' stations, treatment rooms, toilets and even a cafeteria with no sign of human life anywhere. It was as though they had passed through the gates of reality into the twilight world of institutional care. Finally, when it felt to Hymie that he'd been walking for days and that all hope was lost, they arrived at a small room with bars in the window, through which they could dimly discern the slumped figure of a man in pyjamas, sitting in front of a television.

"He's not dangerous, is he?" asked Hymie, pointing at the bars.

"They're to keep people out," said the porter, "not in."

The porter unlocked the door to the room and beckoned them in. "I'll be back in ten minutes," he said. "There's an alarm on the wall if you need it," he added, walking off.

Mike and Hymie seated themselves opposite the man in the pyjamas and coughed to attract his attention.

"Who the hell are you?" asked Mr Cholmondeley, startled at the sudden appearance of two strangers in his room.

"We want to publish your book," said Hymie.

"What, 'Fly fishing in Malawi'?" asked Cholmondeley.

"Yes...I mean no," said Hymie, temporarily flustered.

"But I sent it off twenty years ago. Heaven knows what became of the manuscript," said Cholmondeley.

"No one will read it now anyway," said Hymie, "not after 'Salmon fishing in the Yemen'."

"Why not, the miserable bastards!" cried Cholmondeley.

"Maybe you have another book in you?" suggested Mike.

"Yes," agreed Hymie, "about your time in the Congo with the diamond smugglers."

"I don't like the look of you," said Cholmondeley, "and I've never been to Africa."

"But you just said you'd written a book about Malawi," said Mike.

"Not me. Must have been some other stinking fisherman."

"Look, Mr Cholmondeley," explained Hymie, "we have it on good authority that you were in the Congo in the 1960's with the King's African Rifles."

"No, I never touched his rotten rifle and only the devil was in the Congo in the Sixties. Did he send you?" asked Cholmondeley.

"No, we're trying to find out what happened to Colonel Wittering. He's dead, you know," said Hymie.

"Good riddance to the old bugger!" said Cholmondeley.

"Didn't you like the Colonel, then?" asked Hymie.

"Tra la-la la-la la-la, tra la-la la lah lah, Tra la-la la-la la-la, tra la la la la lah..." sang Cholmondeley, doing a perfect imitation of *The Archers* theme.

"We only want to know what happened, corporal," said Mike.

"Tra la-la la-la la-la, tra la-la la lah lah…" continued Cholmondeley, putting his fingers in his ears.

Hymie tried to pull Cholmondeley's hands away from his ears.

"Nurse! Nurse! They're trying to kill me. I won't go back there, they can't make me go back! The horror of it! Aaaaaargh!"

The door to the room opened and two male nurses appeared in their midst.

"That's enough," said one of them, "I'm afraid you'll have to leave now, you're upsetting the patient," he said, addressing the publishers.

Hymie shrugged. "I guess there isn't a book in everyone after all," he said.

The porter re-appeared from the corridor and escorted Hymie and Mike to the nearest exit.

"Every one a winner," said Mike as they stood outside on the drive again. "How many more of these dopes have we got to see?"

"Only the one," said Hymie, "Major Daniels, but I've a feeling we've saved the best till last."

Part Sixteen

The road to Greenwich town

Very few people get asked to leave Hanwell Asylum because they're upsetting the patients but Mike and Hymie had somehow managed it. Not that it was a matter of pride, in fact they'd dearly have loved to have had a full and frank exchange of views with Corporal Cholmondeley but he'd had other ideas.

Walking off down the road towards Ealing Common in the drizzle they couldn't have been more disconsolate.

"So, where's this Major Daniels live, H?" asked Mike. "I'm betting it's nowhere near here, am I right?"

"In the scheme of things, you couldn't be more wrong, Mike," said Hymie. "He only lives on the other side of town."

"Yeah, but London's a big town," quibbled Mike.

"Oh, pardon me," snapped Hymie, "anyone would think I was asking you to walk to Timbuktu instead of taking a couple of poxy tube rides down the District and Jubilee Lines.

"Come on then, where exactly does he live?" repeated Mike.

"Well, if the text I received from Charlie is anything to go by," said Hymie, "he's living at the Holiday Inn in North Greenwich."

"And I thought she had some common sense!" said Mike. "How can he be *living* in a Holiday Inn? A couple of nights are enough for anyone. Are you sure she's not winding us up?"

"Personally, I believe her. She says he's been living there since it opened in 2000. Let's face it, it's gotta be an improvement on the asylum."

"That was Cholmondeley," said Mike, "but, I suppose we'd better see the last guy on the list. How far is it to the nearest tube station?"

"Ealing Common's just down this road," said Hymie.

"How far?"

"No more than a couple of miles," said Hymie, pulling his collar up against the rain. "I can't keep shelling out for cabs, you know!" They trudged down the road in virtual silence, lost in their personal thoughts and the shared misery of the walk.

When they got to Ealing Common tube station there was a gathering of tribal warriors outside, in full war paint, carrying placards saying "Give it back! Now! Or else!"

"What's all this in aid of?" Mike asked a bystander.

"It's the M'Bongo," said the man. "Apparently they're a well known tribe from the Congo. They want their sacred black diamond back, and they want it now."

Hymie looked horrified. "But how do they know who's got it?"

The man shrugged. "Beats me, mate, but I wouldn't

like to be in his shoes when they find it. Those spears aren't made of rubber, you know!"

A small group of policemen broke up the demonstration while the two morose detectives slipped into the tube station and shortly afterwards appeared on the eastbound platform heading for North Greenwich. Once safely ensconced in the rickety old tube they relaxed and sat back in their seats.

"That was a bit weird, H. I mean, how many different groups of people are there looking for that black diamond?" asked Mike.

"I dunno, Mike, but it couldn't have been a coincidence; there's no such thing."

Mike looked thoughtful and fell silent. He didn't have a clue what it all meant but now wasn't the time to ask tricky questions. There was no such thing as privacy on the tube and any one of their fellow travellers could be working for one of their rivals. The same thing had seemingly occurred to Hymie, who had started doing his impression of a scruffy overweight man sleeping on the tube. It was a virtuoso performance, complete with snoring.

The tube rattled its way laboriously along the District Line to the accompaniment of hissing brakes, sliding doors, flickering lights and the ghost of a breeze. Strange people got on, sat down, stood up and disembarked like fleeting shadows, but none of them were stranger than Goldman and Murphy. After what seemed like hours they changed lines, platforms and trains in the strange subterranean world of London's living arteries and finally rolled into North Greenwich station, tired and subdued at 3:15pm.

"Let's hope it's worth it," said Mike.

"Have faith," said Hymie. "This guy's a major so he's sure to know something."

"We'll see," said Mike.

Part Seventeen

Crowd Control for Major Daniels

In the spacious lobby of *The Holiday Inn Express*, Greenwich, Hymie struck the top of the brass bell on the counter with the palm of his hand and waited with ringing ears for something to happen. A smartly-dressed Indian man appeared from out of the ground on the other side of the desk. Perhaps he'd been tunnelling under the floor or simply having a nap.

"Good afternoon," said the receptionist, with a smile.

"Good afternoon," replied Hymie, not wishing to be outdone in the politeness stakes. "We've come to see…"

"Major Daniels, "said the receptionist. "I know. You must be Mr. Goldman and Mr.Murphy. The Major is expecting you."

Mike and Hymie exchanged puzzled looks. "He is?" queried Hymie. It seemed as though everyone else involved in this case had a better idea of what was going on than he did. But then he was forgetting Mike, if you could forget anything quite so large.

"Oh, yes," continued the man from Calcutta, smiling again. "He said you'd be arriving some time this afternoon and gave me a very accurate description of you both."

"But he's never met us," said Mike.

"The Major is always very well informed," said the receptionist.

"So, what have we come to see him for?" queried Mike.

"Well, if you've forgotten, Mr. Murphy, I'm sure the Major will tell you, but he hasn't confided that in me."

Mike glowered from under beetling brows.

"Please, gentlemen, the Major asked me to send you through to his suite," explained the receptionist. "He's in room 21, just down the corridor on the right."

The two detectives collected their thoughts and walked down the corridor to the Major's suite. Hymie reached out to knock on the door.

"Come in!"

"How did you know we were here?" asked Hymie, facing Major Daniels across the vast expanse of his sitting room. For a member of the Kit Cat Club he was looking uncharacteristically well. He was in his sixties, tall and distinguished-looking with sleek grey hair and wearing an old green smoking jacket and slippers.

"Gupta phoned to say you were here," confessed the Major, "and it only takes about two minutes to reach my door from the lobby. Have a seat," he added, indicating two large armchairs. They sat.

"You must be tired after your long journey from Hanwell," said the Major.

"You're unusually well informed, Major," said Hymie.

"Oh, I keep my ear to the ground, don't you know,"

said the Major. "Try to keep an eye on old Cholmondeley too, poor old bugger. Did he mention me?"

"No, but he did a good impression of being completely round the bend," said Mike. "He kept singing the theme tune to *The Archers*."

"Yes, he's quite a fan," agreed the Major.

"Well, I don't suppose there's much fun in the asylum," said Hymie.

"No, you're probably right," agreed the Major. "It was thoughtful of you to pop in though," he added, as though their visit to Hanwell had been a social call.

"Look, Major, cards on the table time," said Hymie, "we're here on a case and we'd like to ask you a few questions."

"I know exactly why you're here, Mr.Goldman. You're here because Lady Wittering hired you to find a large carbonado which she believes to have been stolen from her husband's effects. You've traipsed around half of London in pursuit of shadows and been threatened by the Uzbegs and now you don't really know what to do next. Am I right?"

"Lucky guess," said Hymie.

"Well, you've come to the right place at last," said the Major.

Hymie looked unconvinced. He surveyed the room around them. It was a bit more spacious than the norm for a hotel room but when you'd said that, you'd said everything.

"You're also wondering why a man of my calibre would choose to live in a bog-standard hotel room."

"It may have crossed my mind," said Hymie.

"It's just so deliciously *anonymous*, don't you think?" said the Major. "I could check out tomorrow if I wanted to; no notice, no nothing, but I'd miss the cooked breakfasts and the laundry service. I've been here since the place opened, you know. It's more like home than any home I've ever known."

"OK, Major, cut the crap! Where's the black diamond?" asked Mike, who'd had enough of officers wittering on. The major looked at Murphy with mild disdain.

"You were a sergeant, weren't you, Murphy?" asked the major. "Why doesn't that surprise me? Good at getting difficult jobs done I expect, but lacking finesse."

Mike clenched his fist and crossed the room towards the Major.

The Major smiled. "You can't threaten me, Murphy, you're too late. You see, I'm immune from threats, I'm dying."

Murphy stopped in his tracks and sat down again.

"How long have you got to live?" asked Hymie, looking at his watch.

"Oh, long enough to put a few things right," said the Major. "No one knows for sure. We all sleepwalk through our lives, imagining we're immortal, but when they tell you you only have a short time left to live it focuses the mind wonderfully," he added, leaning back in his armchair.

"We didn't come here to threaten you," said Hymie, secretly wondering how on earth they were going to get anything out of him any other way.

"So what *do* you want, Goldman?"

"Well, you were right when you said we were working for Lady Wittering and she did hire us to recover the black diamond," said Hymie.

"The carbonado? It's certainly something special," admitted the major. "Have you ever seen a black diamond?"

Goldman and Murphy shook their heads.

"Even if you had," explained the major, "this one's unforgettable; as big as your fist and with so many sparkling facets that a man could lose his mind gazing into them. It has an 'otherworldly' quality which comes from the fact that it fell to earth from the sky a few million years ago. It's no wonder it bewitched Wittering. From the moment he set eyes on it, he was a lost soul."

"How did he acquire it?" asked Hymie.

"He stole it, of course," said the major.

"Who from? The Uzbegs?" asked Murphy.

The major laughed at the big man's folly. "The Uzbegs have few virtues," he said, "but they suffice as the instrument of divine retribution."

"Did they kill the Colonel?" asked Hymie.

"I think you're missing the point," said Daniels.

"Which is?"

"That Colonel Wittering never had any legitimate right to the carbonado. Worse than that, he murdered the people that did. We were in the Congo," explained Daniels, "tracking some gunrunners near the border when we stumbled upon a little stone temple in the middle of nowhere. It was guarded by perhaps a dozen men from the M'Bongo tribe and there were some women and children nearby in a native village. I was all for going around the settlement but Wittering wouldn't hear of it. He sent Travers and a couple of the lads out to do a recce of the site and when he found out there was treasure in the temple he ordered them to blow the natives to kingdom come. Not a man, woman or child was left alive and that bastard has had it coming to him ever since."

"Well, until he was horribly murdered in his own home," said Hymie.

The major looked at him thoughtfully. "Well, that's one interpretation," he said quietly.

"So, where's the diamond now?" asked Hymie.

"That's what everyone wants to know."

"And you're sure you don't know?"

"If you want an answer to that particular question, Mr.Goldman, I suggest you attend the final meeting of the Kit Cat Club," said the major, cryptically.

"I thought most of the members were dead," said Hymie. "In fact, the only ones left are you, Pettiman and Cholmondeley. Pettiman was last heard of en route to the Outer Hebrides and Cholmondeley's still a few buns short of a picnic, so who could have called the meeting if it wasn't you?" asked Hymie, studying Major Daniels' face.

"Oh, it wasn't me, I assure you," said the major, "but someone called it alright. Gupta informed me a few days ago that an orange had been placed in the mouth of one of the lions at the base of Nelson's Column and that can only mean one thing; that there's to be a meeting of the Kit Cat Club on Hampstead Heath on the 23rd "

"But that's tonight," said Hymie.

"Yes, we meet at 10pm. Well, we're not as young as we used to be and it'll be dark by then," said Major Daniels.

"Where's the meeting?"

"Like I said, Hampstead Heath," said the major. "It's near the old boathouse on Highgate Ponds. You'll see when you get there. I'm expecting a big turnout tonight," he explained, "so if you decide to come, do come prepared." A strange look came into his eyes as his mind wandered to another time and place.

"When you run out of options in life, you too might find yourself swearing strange oaths in some god awful monkey temple in darkest Africa," said Major Daniels, closing his eyes.

The two shabby detectives sensed that the interview was at an end and made their way back to reception, where a cab was ready and waiting outside to take them back to 792A Finchley Road, via Trafalgar Square. After all, it wasn't every day you got the chance to see a bronze lion chewing an orange.

Part Eighteen

The Cat and the Canary

When Hymie and Mike got back to the office, Charlie was busy reading the latest erotic gardening bestseller, 'Fifty shades of Green'. She surreptitiously slid it into her desk drawer as they entered. The office looked much tidier than usual, so much so that Hymie rubbed his eyes in disbelief three times before he was prepared to accept what they were telling him.

"No, it's definitely 792A, Mike," he said. "I recognize the stains on the carpet."

"Well, I'd say Charlie's worked miracles on this dump, while we've been out. Nice job, Charlie," said Mike.

Hymie scowled. He didn't like to admit that the place had ever been a dump, even if it had.

"Did we miss anything, Charlie?" he asked.

"What, apart from the junk mail deliveries and the police?" she queried.

"Obviously," said Hymie.

"No."

"Well, we're going into conference now," said Hymie. "If anyone asks, you haven't seen us and we aren't here."

"I was just about to go home. It is nearly five."

Hymie looked at his watch. "See you then," he said, breezing into his office. Once inside, he tipped up his swivel chair to evict Bacon the cat, who seemed to have taken up squatter's rights. "Sling yer hook, furball," he cried, uncharitably. The cat made only a token miaow of protest before heading off for a night on the tiles. Mike pulled up the other chair and stretched out in it.

"What did you make of Major Daniels, H?" asked the big man. "Was he for real or what? I can't really see him flying out to the Congo to give a massive diamond back to the M'Bongo, can you? Even if he is dying."

"Nor me, Mike," agreed Hymie. "And as for that crap about only having a few hours left to live, I'm not buying that either. He looked as well as you or me," he added, with a hacking cough.

"Still, I don't suppose we can get out of that meeting tonight," said Mike. "It's the only lead we've got."

"Yeah," said Hymie, "It's sure to be a pretty lame meeting too. By my reckoning there'll only be two of the old duffers there, Daniels and Pettiman. Even Pettiman's only a maybe; the last time we saw him he was busy running away from the Uzbegs. As for old Cholmondeley, he couldn't get out of the funny farm if his life depended on it. That only leaves Wittering, Bonser and Travers and they're all dead.

Suddenly there was a terrific splintering noise and the door to Hymie's office collapsed onto the floor of the room. There in the doorway stood four men in hand-woven shawls and furry hats. Two of them were brandishing baseball bats.

"Hewo Hansi," said their leader, a walking moustache with a man attached at the back.

He sounded pleased to be renewing an old acquaintance. Hymie looked stunned. He'd hoped to avoid meeting the Uzbegs again in this world and the next. Mike leapt out of his seat as though he'd spilled hot coffee in his lap and scoured the room for something heavy to hit them with. All he could find was a tattered copy of *War and Peace* which Hymie had bought from one of the local charity shops to fill up his bookcase. He hurled it across the room at an advancing Uzbeg, who swatted it away with a disdainful swipe.

"Yu funny man, fatty," said the man with the moustache. "Now shit!" he added.

Hymie sat down leaving Mike to consider his options. He could either sit, shit or get his head bashed in; tough choice.

The leader of the Uzbegs clicked his fingers and the two batsmen set about rearranging the room with wild abandon, reducing the office to a pile of broken furniture and battered office equipment. Mike glowered at them and seemed ready to make a move.

"Leave it, Mike," said Hymie. Reluctantly, Mike sat down.

"Wher dimon, Hansi?" asked the man behind the moustache.

"Yu give me wik," replied Hansi, in his best pidgin Uzbeg. "Me got two days lift."

"Ha, ha, haaa! Two days in lift," laughed the Uzbegs.

Hymie tried to smile but only managed a rictus grin.

"Yu big dicktecktiv, Hansi. No need wik. Wot yu fine?" asked the chief Uzbeg.

"Well, we've been talking to people, investigating new leads, travelling around London looking for oranges," began Hymie. Oh, what was the point? he thought, the vicious bastard wouldn't understand anyway. "I wurking on it," he said.

"Wan infurmashun," said the Uzbeg. "Now!"

Hymie was about to say that he didn't have any information, that the office was under police surveillance and that Murphy was a black belt in karate then he caught sight of the wreckage that remained of his office and realized that the Uzbegs really didn't give a damn.

"There's a meeting tonight," he said.

"Wher?"

"On Hampstead Heath at 10pm," sang Hymie the canary. "Major Daniels and the rest of the Kit Cat Club are meeting for the last time."

"Hamster Heat, ten pee," repeated the Uzbeg. He squinted at Goldman, trying to decide whether to believe him or not.

"Near the boathouse," added Hymie, desperately trying to convince him.

"Neo Butthoose," repeated Ghengis Khan. "Yu tell tru, yes Hansi?"

"Yes!" cried Hymie, emphatically.

"Gut," said the Uzbeg, evidently satisfied that the last of the great dicktecktivs was too scared to lie to him. So saying, he turned and led his furry-hatted followers down the staircase and out onto the Finchley Road. As they left the building they passed two burly men in overcoats coming in the opposite direction. They exchanged incredulous glances. It looked like Goldman was working with circus performers now.

Upstairs, Hymie and Mike sat amid the carnage wondering what on earth had hit them. The Uzbegs seemed to come from another planet. The clumping tread of heavy shoes on the stairs announced the arrival of Decca and Terse but Goldman and Murphy seemed oblivious.

"My god, you've let this place go, Goldman," said the inspector, surveying the wrecked office with mild amusement.

"It's funny," said Hymie, "but we were just lamenting the fact that there's never a policeman around when you need one." Privately he was wondering how much shit one man could take before it buried him. They said it never rained but it poured.

"Really, Goldman? *You* needed a policeman?"

"He's only kidding," said Murphy, tipping Hymie a meaningful wink. Hymie rallied quickly, "Just my little joke, inspector," he said. "In fact, we were just experimenting with a new office layout."

Decca stared at him. "You must think we came down with the last shower," he said.

"Pickfords don't make this much of a mess, someone's trashed the place. It wasn't those circus performers we met on the way in, was it?" asked Terse.

"Circus performers? Do I look like Billy Smart?" quipped Hymie.

The two policemen laughed. "No one would ever accuse you of being smart," said Decca, "except a smart arse, of course, but they did look distinctly like they were coming out of your office."

"And one of them had a baseball-bat," said Terse.

"Now you come to mention it, they *were* here," said Hymie, crumbling under the weight of circumstantial evidence. "They called themselves the amazing Karamazov Brothers; a troupe of fairground acrobats from the Steppes. They said they'd had some money stolen and wondered if I could help."

"Did they think you'd taken it then?" asked Decca, examining the broken furniture.

"If they came to see you, they must like losing money," said Terse.

"What I don't get," said Decca, "is why they came to see you instead of the police?"

Hymie shrugged. "Ours not to reason why…" Mike sat in silence and continued to stare sullenly out of the window. The Uzbegs had caught him by surprise twice now. Was he losing his touch?

"What's the matter, Murphy?" asked Decca. "Cat got your tongue?"

"Always a pleasure, Inspector," said Hymie, distractedly.

"Yeah, like contracting herpes," muttered Mike, suddenly back in the here and now.

Terse glared at him, inviting him to make something of it, but Mike just sat there.

"So, what can we do for you, Inspector?" asked Hymie, as though he'd only just noticed him.

"I'd heard you were interfering in police business again, so I thought we'd pay you a visit to warn you off."

"Very thoughtful of you, Inspector," said Hymie, "but we don't have the faintest idea what you're talking about."

"You know full well what I'm talking about, Goldman; the Wittering case. Colonel Wittering was murdered and a little bird told me his wife had hired you to recover something valuable that disappeared at about the time he died."

"Wittering? No, it doesn't ring any bells with me, Inspector. How about you, Mike?" asked Hymie, all innocence.

"No, me neither," said Mike.

"Have it your way, perhaps you'd like to tell us what you know about badgers then?" asked Decca.

Mike laughed. "Nothing, he's allergic to the countryside."

"That's not what I heard. Two men answering your descriptions and claiming to be public health inspectors turned up at Troy Court on Kensington High Street just before a dead body was found. When questioned, these jokers started babbling on about badgers hibernating in the air conditioning vents," explained Decca.

"I see," said Hymie.

"It could've been anyone," said Mike, "loads of people look like us."

It was Terse's turn to laugh. "I don't think so," was all he finally managed to say.

Meanwhile, Hymie was busy considering all the angles. They needed to stay out of the police cells for long enough to attend the last meeting of the Kit Cat Club and recover the carbonado or they could wave goodbye to their reward. Besides, having just invited the Uzbegs to join the party they needed some serious protection.

"OK, Inspector, I'll talk," said Hymie. "What do you want to know?"

"Everything," said Decca, "omitting no detail, however trivial it may seem to a numpty like you."

"If I tell you everything, I'll need your solemn word you'll keep us out of it," said Hymie.

Decca looked sceptical.

"Have it your way, Inspector, only there's a big showdown tonight and if you don't know where it is you'll miss the best chance you ever had of solving the Wittering case. It may be your only chance."

Decca frowned. "If this is a hoax, you two clowns will be behind bars faster than Terse can say Jack Robinson."

Hymie nodded. "Firstly, you were right. We *were* hired by Lady Wittering; to recover a collection of gold and precious stones stolen from her husband when he was murdered. And yes, we knew you were investigating the murder, but we thought we could keep out of your way and we needed the money. Anyway, Lady Wittering gave us an old black and white photo of her husband's comrades in arms. They were all members of some geriatric boys brigade called the Kit Cat Club, dedicated to sitting around in pubs talking about the good old days. So we went around talking to some of them. When we went to see Sergeant Travers we found him dead in his flat. As for the rest, we met Sergeant Pettiman briefly before he set off on a tour of the highlands and islands in a bid to avoid the Uzbegs.

"Who or what the hell are the Uzbegs?" asked Terse.

"Those four men you passed coming out of here when you arrived were the Uzbegs," said Hymie with a shudder. "They were the ones who did this," he added, pointing at his shattered furniture. "They're lethal."

"How about the rest of the old soldiers?" queried Decca.

"Captain Bonser's dead. We never met him. Cholmondeley's in the asylum at Hanwell and Major Daniels is the only one who seems to know what's going on. He's living at the Holiday Inn Express in Greenwich," explained Hymie.

"And he's the *brains* of the outfit?" queried Decca.

"You'd be surprised," said Hymie, "it's really very nice."

Decca looked at him dubiously. "I don't know why I should continue to expect anything you tell me to make sense, Goldman. It never has before."

"To cut a long story short, there's a meeting of the Kit Cat Club arranged for 10pm tonight on Hampstead Heath," said Hymie.

"Where on Hampstead Heath?" queried Terse. "It's a big place."

"Near Highgate Ponds, by the old boathouse."

"Why?" asked Decca. "I mean, I'll take it as read for now that someone's told you about the meeting but what's the purpose of it?"

"Now that, I don't know," admitted Hymie. "It could be to divvy up the valuables, it could be just to say goodbye, I mean, they're all pretty old and knackered these days, or…" Hymie looked blankly at the Inspector. For once he'd run out of bullshit.

Decca looked thoughtfully at him. He couldn't say he liked the guy but for once he didn't think he was lying to him. "Alright, Goldman," he said, "we'll take it from here. Just make sure you're nowhere near the place when this meeting starts or we'll book you for loitering with intent. If this turns out to be a wild goose chase, we'll be back, with a charge sheet as long as your arm. Do I make myself clear?"

"Yes, Inspector," said Hymie, feeling he'd got away lightly. "Just a word of warning; keep an eye out for the Uzbegs. They may talk gibberish but they're fast and deadly."

"So's Terse," said Decca as the two policemen walked off down the stairs.

"So, what now?" asked Mike, once he was satisfied they were alone again.

"We're going to Hampstead Heath, of course," said Hymie.

"But you just told Decca we'd stay away."

"Not exactly," said Hymie. "I said I understood what he meant when he advised us to keep away from the place, but there's still a case to solve and this is still the only lead we have. We'd better go equipped this time, Mike." Mike nodded.

Part Nineteen

The Big Showdown

Night had fallen on the sleepless city of London and through the dark streets Hymie and Mike had driven the stately old Fleetwood out to Hampstead Heath and left it there; camouflaged beneath the trees and shrubs of Highgate Ponds. They were dismayed to find that due to an unseasonal fog around the lake they could hardly see more than a few feet in front of them.

"This is hopeless. We may as well forget it and go home," said Hymie. "In this fog we won't have a clue who we're dealing with."

"Hold your horses, Goldman, neither will anyone else. If they can't see you they can't hurt you, can they? It stands to reason."

"Good point," said Hymie, tripping over his shoelaces and hitting a tree. "Oof!"

Mike placed a firm hand over Hymie's mouth and pulled him back from the footpath to the edge of the bushes. Up ahead they caught a glimpse of five shadowy figures, huddled together near the boathouse.

Mike signalled to Hymie to keep the noise to an

absolute minimum so as not to give them away and the two detectives crept snail-like along the edge of the path, carefully utilising every inch of cover afforded them by the low hanging branches of the trees and bushes. Eventually both the shapes and voices of the group of men came into sharper focus. Hymie removed a pair of infra-red binoculars from his inside coat pocket and studied the men more closely.

"It's the Kit Cat Club," he whispered.

Mike raised his eyes to the heavens as if to say "you don't say, Brains!"

"But you don't understand, Mike," continued Hymie. "It's nearly *all* of them; Daniels, Pettiman, Cholmondeley… even Colonel Wittering. The bugger's not dead at all, damn him!" he muttered. "Wait a minute, who's that guy with the long white beard? He looks just like the bloke in the photo with the fluff stuck to him. It can't be. It is, you know; it's Bonser, the ex-hang glider."

"He's not dead either then," said Mike.

"No," agreed Hymie.

"What are they saying?" asked Mike.

"How should I know," whispered Hymie, "I'm not a ruddy lip reader."

Suddenly a red light started flashing on the top of Hymie's binoculars and a faint beeping sound could be heard.

"What the devil's that?" cried Colonel Wittering, staring intently at the bushes Hymie and Mike were now hiding in. Mike grabbed the binoculars and flung them into the lake. There was a loud plopping sound and then the flashing light and beeping noise disappeared below the surface of the water.

"Those cost me a small fortune!" hissed Hymie.

Mike glared at him. "You're about as surreptitious as an explosion in a fireworks factory!"

"It was only the battery warning light. I didn't realise it made a sound as well," explained Hymie. "I've never had to change the batteries before."

"Good evening, gentlemen." It was Major Daniels. In the time it had taken Goldman to blow his own cover the five old soldiers had tracked them down. Mike and Hymie stepped out of the bushes.

"Who the hell are you and what the hell are you doing here?" asked Colonel Wittering, with his customary old world charm.

"They're Hymie Goldman and Mike Murphy," explained Daniels. "The private detectives your wife hired to find the carbonado," he added.

"Well, who on earth invited them?" asked the Colonel, clearly aggrieved at having his private meeting invaded by a couple of wandering idiots.

"I did," admitted the major.

"You bloody fool!" snapped Colonel Wittering.

"Yes, the short scruffy one's completely off his rocker," said Cholmondeley, the escaped mental patient. "They came to see me in Hanwell, claiming to be a couple of itinerant publishers. I'm surprised they let them out."

"Perhaps one of you would be good enough to explain what's been going on while I've been dead," said the Colonel.

"I think I can explain," began Pettiman.

"I doubt it," said Cholmondely, "You're as thick as two short planks."

"At least I'm not round the bend," said Pettiman, aggrieved.

"Guys, guys, chill out, man. Why can't we all get along like brothers, eh man?" said Bonser, who had spent some time in a hippy commune since hang-gliding out of the army.

"Shut it, Bonser!" barked Colonel Wittering. He began to unbutton the holster strapped to his belt but Mike was too quick for him, removing his own revolver from his coat pocket and aiming the barrel at the Colonel's chest.

"Hold it!" cried Mike. "Now, let's be a good officer and leave our gun where it is, shall we?"

Wittering buttoned up his holster carefully and watched Mike with a combination of annoyance and caution while his comrades fell silent.

"Thank you, Michael," said Hymie, before directing his attention to the group of old soldiers. "As you can see, Mr. Murphy and I are now giving the orders. Firstly, where is the black diamond?" he asked.

They all looked at each other with a collective shrug of incomprehension. Hymie frowned. "We can either do this the easy way or the hard way," he said.

"You're out of your depth, Goldman," said the Colonel. "These men are war-hardened veterans who've survived appalling ordeals through sheer cunning and team work. None of them would be daft enough to bring the carbonado here with him tonight, let alone admit it to a dozy little pillock like you."

It was all water off a duck's back to Hymie, who'd been insulted by experts.

"Search them," said Mike. Hymie reflected on the advice and, finding it good, approached Pettiman.

"Hold it," said Colonel Wittering. "Why should we submit to such an indignity? After all, there are five of us and only two of you. In a fair fight we could duff you up any day," he bragged.

Mike pulled back the hammer on his revolver until it clicked.

"Because this isn't a fair fight and you're so slow that even if you got Hymie here, I could have shot three or four of you before having anything to worry about," he said.

Although narked at the suggestion that he was somehow expendable, Hymie held his tongue. It was just Mike's way, he told himself.

The Colonel conceded defeat. "I suppose so," he said, grudgingly.

"There's no *suppose* about it," said Mike.

Hymie began to frisk the members of the Kit Cat Club in turn, suddenly pausing as he pulled a heavy black sack out of Major Daniels' coat pocket.

"What's this?" he asked, suspiciously. Hymie put his right hand cautiously into the sack and when he withdrew it, found he was holding the biggest, blackest lump of coal he'd ever seen. Except that it wasn't. On closer inspection it sparkled and glittered in the artificial light of the lamps overhead. There could be no doubt about it, this was the carbonado they'd been searching for, for so long.

Major Daniels looked embarrassed.

"You bloody fool!" cried Wittering.

"How was I to know..." began the major, before remembering that he no longer needed to take orders from the pompous fool.

Hymie stuffed the sack with the outsized gem then pocketed it. "Suppose you tell us the whole story for once, major," he said.

"Well, I have so little time left, I suppose I should set the record straight," agreed Daniels.

"Shut up, you old fool!" cried Colonel Wittering, reaching for his revolver again.

"I don't think so," said Mike, correcting him by the simple expedient of raising his pistol to the Colonel's head.

"You wouldn't shoot a former Colonel of Her Majesty's Armed Forces," bluffed Wittering.

"Try me," said Mike. Wittering fell silent at last.

"As I told you before," began Major Daniels, "the carbonado was stolen long ago from the M'Bongo tribe in the Congo. When we got back to Blighty, the Colonel told us he'd traded it with the Uzbegs for services rendered. Only later did I realise he'd kept it himself. I was incensed and took the only course available to me; I stole it back from him," explained the major, "intending to repatriate it. Then I tipped off the chief of the M'Bongo and the other Club members in case the Colonel got to me first. Somehow the Uzbegs found out about it too."

"You bastard!" cried Colonel Wittering.

"Fortunately for me, the Colonel didn't know who'd taken the diamond but presumably he must have thought it was Travers," said Major Daniels, "because recently I learnt that poor old Travers had been found dead. As for the rest of us, Pettiman seems to have gone walkabout and Cholmondeley checked into the nearest asylum, while I went to ground and waited to see what would happen next."

"And what did happen next?" asked Hymie.

"Wittering faked his own death," said the major, "and invited us all here tonight. I don't know how he tracked down Captain Bonser though.

"I only got back to London from Santiago two weeks ago, man, and thought it was just luck when I ran into the Colonel in the Army & Navy Stores in Cricklewood. He told me about the orange in the lion's mouth in Trafalgar Square so I arranged to join the meeting. And all the while he was planning to kill the lot of us, man," said Bonser, disappointed at man's inhumanity to man. "Bummer!" he added.

The Colonel stared at his highly polished boots.

"You see, Wittering, you can't run from the truth," said Daniels.

"Or Usain Bolt," quipped Hymie.

There was a faint rustling sound in the flora behind them and Pettiman seemed suddenly agitated. "Uzbegs!" he cried, unsheathing a vicious looking knife from its scabbard on his hip. Mike turned to face the impending onslaught and for once had the drop on the men in the furry hats as a bunch of them appeared from the bushes, armed to the teeth and ready to unleash hell.

"Hewo, Hansi," said their leader, the man with the implausible moustache.

"Hewo," replied Hymie, resigned to another bout of incomprehensible conversation, punctuated with moments of terror.

"Wher dimon?" asked the Uzbeg.

"It's funny you should ask," said Hymie. "I was just wondering the same thing myself."

"Don't fraternise with the enemy!" cried Wittering, finally managing to remove his revolver from its holster.

"I think they call this a Mexican standoff," said Mike, swinging his pistol from one target to the next without reaching a conclusion as to which one to shoot.

The leader of the Uzbegs began looking all around him, presumably for the Mexicans.

"No, sunshine," came a familiar voice over a loud hailer, "what they call this is a promotion, my promotion. You're all under arrest for breach of the peace, carrying dangerous weapons in a public place and, in Goldman's case, being on Hampstead Heath in the first place. Book them, sergeant!" cried Inspector Decca, emerging from the fog with a small army of policemen.

"Drop your weapons! It's over!" shouted Terse.

But he wasn't able to enjoy the moment for long. Even before the policemen had dispersed to apprehend the miscreants another voice, a woman's voice, rose above the throng.

"Stay where you are, everyone. I'll take it from here, Inspector," said the young woman in question; Charlie Finch, waving her ID card in front of him. She looked particularly alluring in the black figure-hugging combat gear.

"Charlotte Finch, MI 16½. We've had these men under surveillance for some time as part of an extremely confidential undercover operation."

"What operation's that then, Miss?" asked Decca, reluctantly.

"If I told you, I'd have to kill you, Inspector," said Charlie, brightly.

"MI 16½?" queried Terse, giving utterance to what everyone else was thinking. "You're having a laugh. I've never heard of you."

"That doesn't surprise me," said Charlie. "Even the Spooks don't know we exist, we're the most secret of the secret."

A group of men in full combat gear emerged from every direction, trailing red dots from their laser sights on the assembled crowd.

"I see," said Decca. "Looks like we've been crapped on from above again, Terse. Time to head out, guys!" he told his men, who reassembled and withdrew down the path to their vehicles.

"Hansi, yu batard!" cried the Uzbeg leader. "Yu get me in heep big shit!" he yelled, lunging forward, knife in hand, towards the great dicktecktiv. At impact minus one the little red dot on his chest spread to the size of a vermillion football and the Uzbeg chief collapsed dead at Goldman's feet. Hymie quivered with fear at how close he'd come to a violent death.

Wittering meanwhile seized his meagre chance of escape by setting off a brace of old smoke canisters he'd brought along in case of emergency. Chaos ensued on the

Heath, by the boathouse, where ignorant armies clashed by night. Gunshots rang out through the foggy, smoke-filled air. Men ran this way and that; that way and this, trying to kill, maim, capture or escape. Visibility was virtually non-existent.

Hymie, who'd lost his bearings completely, fell to the ground and crawled off in search of cover. The Colonel, however, had other plans and, still painfully aware that Goldman had *his* diamond, somehow managed to track the slippery sleuth through the bushes and confront him in a nearby clearing.

"Move and you're dead," said Colonel Wittering, pointing his revolver at Hymie.

Goldman raised his hands in surrender. "It's over, Colonel," he said. "Any fool can see you're not getting out of this one. Just accept it."

"I never accept anything I don't have to," said Wittering. "Give it back to me."

"What?" asked Hymie.

"The carbonado, of course. You bloody fool!" snapped the Colonel.

"I don't have it," said Hymie.

"Just give it to me," cried the Colonel, pressing the cold steel barrel of his revolver to Hymie's temple. "I've killed so many men already that one more won't matter a damn."

Scared and weary as he was, a kind of dull, irrational defiance gripped Hymie.

"To hell with you, old man! Is that all you've got? A crappy old service revolver and a set of values that died out fifty years ago? I pity you."

Somewhere in the undergrowth a wild creature stirred. Scared by the noise of gunfire and hungry after a long sleep, Kitty the tigress, Queen of Hampstead Heath, was in a heightened state of alert. At the sound of voices nearby she left her lair to explore and ran slap bang into Goldman and Wittering, talking in a clearing on her territory.

Colonel Wittering had now reached the end of his tether with Hymie Goldman. He raised his revolver above his head and fired the final warning shot he hoped would make him see sense.

"Give me the diamond or I'll blow your bloody head off!" he cried.

Hymie fell to his knees and as he did so the shock of the gunfire so close at hand unsettled Kitty. She bounded across the clearing in a few graceful leaps and struck the Colonel at full tilt with her claws.

"Aaargh!" he cried, as he crumpled to the ground.

With a swift bite to his neck, the tigress completed the kill and dragged her prey off into the bushes. Hymie struggled to his feet and ran as fast as he could away from the place. When he reached the path again he was dimly aware of voices shouting in the darkness. Ignoring them, he ran blindly on, not knowing where he was going or why until his sides heaved and his heart sounded like it would explode out of his chest. As he neared the lake a searing pain shot through his shoulder and down his back. Everything around him started spinning, his legs buckled under him and he surrendered to oblivion.

Part Twenty

Curtain Call

Mike sat next to a bed in the intensive care ward of the Royal Free Hospital in London and watched the lifeless form in the bed for the faintest signs of movement. There weren't any. Only the regular beeping from the heart monitor confirmed that the patient was still alive. Patient 61952, Goldman, H., was connected to a battery of tubes regulating his fluid levels like some clapped-out old car.

"They let me go, anyway," said Mike. "Charlie told them we were a couple of right idiots, completely out of our depth," he added. "By the way, you remember our PA, Charlie Finch? Well, it turns out she was working for the secret service. It makes a change from the usual crooks we employ eh?" Mike stared into space. This couldn't be happening. He'd always thought of Goldman as being indestructible; useless, of course, but indestructible.

"I expect you're wondering what happened to the rest of them eh, H? Of course you are. Well, as far as I can tell, most of the Uzbegs and the members of the Kit Cat Club bought it and the ones that didn't are looking at long jail terms. Colonel Wittering got eaten by an escaped tiger. Couldn't have happened to a nicer guy, I suppose. As for the case, it's over, I'm afraid. I rang Lady Wittering to tell her that the diamond had been impounded. I expect it will be shipped back to the M'Bongo in due course. Well, with all the oil and precious minerals out there I dare say the British government is busy trying to keep the Congolese happy. One more thing, mate, the M'Bongo sent their witch doctor to see you yesterday. He spent ages doing a funny dance around your bed and mumbling some gibberish, then left this doll for you." Mike picked up a hideous carved wooden doll with straw for hair and brightly coloured feathers attached to it, then placed it back on the bedside table.

"I don't suppose it'll do you much good, but when you get out of here I'll buy you the biggest pizza we can find in North London," said Mike.

There was the merest flicker on the heart monitor and then the line returned to its normal pattern.

"Take it easy, H.," said Mike, slumping back into the visitor's chair. He'd been there at Hymie's side for days and when the sun went down and came back up he would still be there.

GOLDMAN'S GETAWAY

FEATURING HYMIE GOLDMAN,
THE DEFECTIVE DETECTIVE.

Part One

The Comedians

Blackpool: party capital of the world or grot hole at the end of the earth? No-one can ever decide. It seems to depend on the season, the time of day and whether you were born there. Dancing with a sexy partner on a balmy summer's evening at the Tower Ballroom can be heaven, but out of season in the cold it can be hell; nowhere seems to divide opinion so strongly.

A one-legged seagull was blown along the promenade by a force ten gale and alighted uncertainly on the awning outside a cheap hotel. The tatty poster on the window pane below his foot said it all; "Live at the Sun Lounge, Blackpool, for one night only, Mr Smith and Charlie. Gollocks!"

Mr Smith, a German, had arrived in that Mecca of northern entertainment to ply his trade as a hotel waiter, but had been seduced by the showbiz glamour of the place into developing his own ventriloquist act. How hard could it be to pronounce your "b"s like "g"s and take the piss out of a couple of drunken tourists? "Gollocks!" was the one word review the act had received from a local arts critic in the Sixties, which he'd been using as a catchphrase ever since. It didn't seem to matter to local hoteliers and club owners that he wasn't getting any laughs, just as long as he was cheap and the punters didn't actually walk out.

Slight and unimposing with thinning hair and bulging eyes, Smith had worked the local club scene for years without ever threatening to hit the big time. His dummy, Charlie; two feet six of distressed boxwood and widely regarded as the brains of the act, seemed to be falling apart at the seams and often lost his head completely at moments of high excitement. Not that there were many of those.

"Come on, Smiffy," said the hotel's relief manager, Ray Ames. "Your public awaits."

Smith pushed past him and through a faded velvety curtain onto the low stage at the back of the lounge bar and wondered for the umpteenth time why he'd ever left Dusseldorf. The beer was warm and the English simply had no sense of humour. A solitary spotlight fell on the old stager.

"Ladies and gentlemen, it's lovely to see you, isn't it, Charlie?" He looked optimistically at his partner in crime. Charlie's head was twisted all the way around so that he appeared to be examining the curtain behind them.

"Gollocks!" said Charlie.

A drunk at the back of the lounge sat up and cleared his throat. "Come on then, gottle 'o geer, gottle 'o geer! How do we know his lips aren't moving if he's got his back turned to us?"

"The *short one's* the dummy, you big dummy!" snapped Ray Ames.

"No need to get snotty, mate," said the drunk, "it was an easy mistake to make."

"Yes, he's quite realistic after all," agreed Smith.

"More than can be said for you, sunshine," said Charlie. A couple of people laughed.

"So, let's get on with the show, shall we?"

"Hang on, hang on!" said Charlie.

"Stick to the script!"

"Gollocks!"

Smith looked exasperated while the dummy rolled his eyes.

"I didn't know there *was* a script," explained Charlie, "and I can't read anyway so gog off!"

"Didn't you go to school?" asked Smith.

"We were too poor. We had to gurn all the gooks just to keep warm."

"Ahhh," said someone in the audience.

"Yesh and all the other goys used to play footgall with me."

"What, in the playground?"

"No, they used me as the *gall*."

Smith looked forlornly at the dummy. "How sad," he said. "Were you an only child?"

"Well, we had a dog called Rudolph," said Charlie. "He had no nose."

"How did he smell?" asked Smith.

"Terrigle!"

"I see," said Smith. "Did you have any other pets?"

"No, but that reminds me," said Charlie, "did you put the cat out?"

"We haven't got a cat."

"That's as maybe but the poor gugger's still on fire!" he added, as his head fell off.

There was a commotion at the bar. A group of twenty-something women in party hats and dresses, carrying what looked like balloons, were trying to get served at the same time.

"Please, ladies, keep the noise down, the act's in progress," said Ray Ames. "Show a little respect for the artiste."

"What, that old fart?" queried one of the group. "I've seen better comedy shows on the BBC, and that's sayin' sumat these days. It's been a comedy free zone since Only Fools 'n 'Arses in 1996."

The other women laughed.

"Come on, Denise, you're a round behind," said a girl with an inflated condom on her hat. "It's not every day I get married."

"She certainly does have a round behind," said Charlie, who seemed to have recovered his head during the disturbance.

"Cheek!"

The other women laughed raucously while Denise grabbed a bread roll from a nearby table and threw it in the general direction of the stage. It ricocheted harmlessly off the back of Ray Ames' head and Smith carried on regardless. He'd had far worse things thrown at him.

"I went to the doctors yesterday," said Smith. "It only

took me three weeks to get an appointment. I said 'doctor, I've broken my arm in three places.'"

"Well, don't go to those places!" said Charlie.

"I said, doctor, I feel like a pair of curtains…"

"Well, pull yourself together!" said Charlie.

The hen party seemed to have settled down to the serious business of developing a hangover when another young woman appeared at the bar. She was dressed entirely in black; black top, black leggings and a black balaclava. She might almost have been a man, but for her seductive curves. As she slunk towards the stage, Ray Ames stepped forward to intercept her.

"Madam, would you sit down please, you're spoiling the act."

Several people smirked.

The woman looked around the half empty room in scorn then threw a silver metal projectile at Smith. It embedded itself in Charlie's head.

"Gollocks!" spluttered the dummy, while Smith looked shocked. Who could she be? Surely the act wasn't *that* bad? He began to feel he was pushing his luck and needed to be somewhere else, anywhere else.

"Laugh that off, you old stiff!" cried the woman.

"Well, thank you ladies and gentlemen. You've been a great audience…" said Smith, "but I really must be going!" he blurted, dropping Charlie on the floor and making a beeline for the exit through the stage curtains.

Silently, like a black panther, the woman removed a gun from the black leather holster under her armpit and took aim at his retreating figure.

"Oh no you don't, these babies have got your name on, *Mr Smith*!"

BLAM! BLAM! BLAM!!

There was a thudding sound from the far side of the stage curtain and several audience members started screaming. In the chaos which ensued, Ray Ames scuttled off to call the police, while the slinky assassin fled outside into the night.

Part Two

Dead or alive?

Mike Murphy sat expressionless at the hospital bedside of his erstwhile business partner and tried not to jump to conclusions.

"So, is he dead?" he asked finally.

"Not as such," said the doctor.

"I mean, he's been lying there for weeks without any sign of activity and while that's not unusual for Goldman he can't normally keep quiet for five minutes."

"He's in a coma, Mr Murphy."

"I know, I can see that, but is there anything going on in that thick head of his or is this as good as it gets? Can he even hear me?"

"We don't know for sure. Sometimes they snap out of it and sometimes they don't. It's a difficult case. You're detectives aren't you; you and he, I mean?" asked the doctor.

"No case too large or small," said Murphy, distantly.

"Don't you ever get a case you can't solve?"

"Not really." He looked thoughtful for a moment. "Well, there was one…"

"Precisely; some things are destined to remain a mystery," said the doctor. "There's simply no way of knowing whether your friend is still capable of thinking, whether rational or otherwise."

Mike grimaced. Goldman had never been much of a thinker at the best of times but this was unbearable.

"He could be like this for weeks, months or even years."

"Years!"

"Well, we'd probably have to take a view on his prognosis before it got that far," explained the doctor, reflecting on the acute shortage of beds.

"But he *will* pull round?"

"With luck; we're doing all we can. The best *you* can do is keep trying to stimulate his subconscious mind. Sometimes a familiar piece of music or voice can trigger a recovery. Talk to him. He's still in there somewhere, looking for a way back." The doctor left the room.

Mike shuffled up close to his friend's bedside on the hard plastic visitor's chair and stared into Goldman's lifeless eyes. What could he say that would bring him back? Why, he'd already said it…the case they couldn't solve, the one they'd vowed never to mention again.

"Remember Blackpool?" whispered Mike.

Something stirred in the cold lumpy porridge of Goldman's mind. Nothing was visible on the outside, but in the deepest darkest recesses of his consciousness disco lights began to flash and the sound of Elvis singing "Return to Sender" started playing on the jukebox.

"Thank you very much!" cried Hymie, in his best Elvis voice.

At least, his subconscious mind uttered the words, but to the world outside he was still just a lifeless blob in a bed.

In Hymieworld the comatose detective looked around him and liked what he saw. He was sitting in shorts and a tee-shirt on a sun-kissed beach with palm trees wafting in the breeze and surrounded by beautiful girls in scanty swimming costumes playing beach volleyball. If this was a dream, he had no intention of waking up, ever. So why was he starting to think about Blackpool? After all, he'd promised Mike never to talk of it again. Incidentally, where was Mike?

A pretty girl in a pink bikini walked up to him.

"Can I get you anything, Hymie?"

"This is heaven, isn't it?"

"Well, actually, no."

He looked disappointed.

"It's actually a state of semi-consciousness," explained the girl, "and I'm just trying to get your attention."

"I'm not dead then?"

"No, you're on your way back to the land of the living."

Hymie eyed up the girls as they bounced around provocatively.

"If you'll just concentrate that is!"

"Sorry," said Hymie.

"You had a bad accident, but you need to wake up now," said the girl.

He thought for a while. Nothing. He tried again.

"Give me a clue?"

"There was a tiger, some old soldiers and a black diamond. Ring any bells?"

The fog seemed to lift somewhat. He tried to ignore it and studied the tall blonde girl with the butterfly tattoo on her left buttock who was serving for the match.

"Can't it wait? I've been waiting to see this for so long."

"No. If you don't come with me now then you're going to die," she said, walking away up the beach.

Hymie stood up and started to follow her.

"Oh, alright, if I have to," he said reluctantly. "Have we got far to go?"

"Not far, but it will be tough."

She sat down at a table outside the beach bar and waved to the waitress, who brought over a tray of ice-cold drinks. Hymie joined her.

"Tough? Are you sure you've got the right guy?"

"Yes, of course. It will only be tough because it will take a moment of profound self-realisation and I know that's not one of your strengths."

"Oh, I don't know," began Hymie. "I'm as self-aware as the next man."

"As long as he's an overweight, middle-aged slob of a detective with a pizza fetish and a boob fixation," said the girl, helpfully.

"What are you doing in my dream?"

"I'm from NHS Direct. Now tell me about Blackpool."

"I can't, I promised a friend never to speak of it."

"Would that be Mike Murphy?"

"How did you know?"

"He sent me. He said it was good to talk."

"He did?" said Hymie, sceptically. "Doesn't sound much like Murphy."

"He said it was essential."

He cast a final wistful glance at the beach volleyball players, just to make sure he hadn't been imagining them, then focused on the girl in the pink bikini.

"Where would you like me to begin?"

"At the beginning, where else?" she said.

"Well, it was like this…"

Part Three

In the beginning

Hymie had been about to launch into another of his tall stories when he paused. Where *had* it all begun; the Blackpool saga he'd been trying to forget? He supposed it had started at 792A Finchley Road, like every other case, but there was really nothing memorable about it.

"It was a few years ago…" he said.

"Is that the best you can do?" asked the imaginary girl in the pink bikini.

"It was Wednesday."

"I see."

"Mike and I were sitting around the office trying to decide which case to work on next."

"How about this one?" he said, reading from a letter, "my neighbours have been kidnapped by aliens, can you help?"

"Who's that from?" I asked.

"Mrs Betty Fruitcake from Battersea."

"I smiled. Not her again; she'd been writing to us for years with increasingly ludicrous stories. She was probably just lonely; perhaps it was time she bought a budgie. It sometimes seemed that half of our mail was from escaped mental patients and the other half was special offers for things we'd never use in a million years."

"Such as?"

"Oh, you know, cut price gym membership, left-handed sprocket sets, holidays to the Caribbean…that sort of thing."

"You're not the gym type?" asked the girl.

"If I want pain I can just bang my head on the desk, I don't need to strip off and pay good money for the privilege."

"You're getting off the point, Hymie."

"Which was?"

"Blackpool, the case you couldn't solve."

"Well, I remember it started with a letter from a vicar who lived near Blackpool. He said his sister had been missing for twenty years and he'd promised their mother on her deathbed that he'd give it one last try to find her."

"And you were his last chance?"

"Yes, it's amazing how often we turn out to be someone's last chance."

"You mean your clients have to be desperate to call you?" asked the girl.

"I didn't say that, but people are more likely to pay a private detective when they're in a fix. Anyway, this guy, the Reverend Brown, invited us up to Blackpool on an all expenses paid trip to see if we could help him find his sister."

"What was she called?"

"Something beginning with 'E' …Elaine, I think."

"And you decided to take the case?"

"Obviously, or I wouldn't be going over all this again, would I? Mike was all for going, he said he needed a holiday, but I wasn't so sure we should leave London. I'm not big on travel. In the end there weren't any other options on the table so I phoned the guy and made the necessary arrangements."

"Now we're getting somewhere," said the girl.

"That's what we thought," said Hymie, "but we were wrong."

She looked at him thoughtfully for a moment. "You know what your trouble is; you don't know what you *do* know. It's all in there somewhere," she explained, tapping him gently on the side of the head, "but we need to solve the case quickly if you're ever going to snap out of this coma." The girl clicked her fingers and Hymie seemed to go into a trance.

"I think you'll find it was like this..." said the girl.

Part Four

Something rotten in Lancashire

Everyone has a limit to the crap they can tolerate in life; a line in the sand which, once crossed, leads to total meltdown. If you've ever found yourself turning up for work in your striped-pink pyjamas, or singing the hits of Rodgers and Hammerstein in your underwear on the tube then you'll know exactly what I mean.

In the case of Inspector Ray Decca of London's Metropolitan Constabulary it happened when he realised that Hymie Goldman, the investigating buffoon and general blot on the landscape was actually a greater success in life than he was. He started coming into the office with a large cushion stuffed up his shirt front and pizza stains all over his jacket and when questioned simply said "Oh, I'm Hymie Goldman, you can't tell me what to do, mate!"

Inevitably questions were asked, psychiatrists consulted and the upshot of it all was that Decca was shipped off to a funny farm for distressed police officers, "Crackpots," just outside Lytham St. Anne's, near Blackpool.

Decca's life had been reduced to a series of pointless and trivial rituals. He got up, had his breakfast, read the Blackpool Gazette swathed in blankets on the garden terrace, eat his lunch, went for a walk around the grounds, eat his dinner, went to the lavatory, and watched a few repeats of TV shows before bed. It was a blameless, if institutionalised existence.

One morning as he sat scratching his head over three across in the crossword he was distracted by another resident, a former traffic cop, Dave from Deptford who seemed to be trying to dead-head all the roses with a croquet mallet.

"Nurse! Please get this nutter out of here, I'm trying to concentrate."

"Getting to know you, getting to feel free and easy," sang Dave from the flower bed.

"I never could stand The King and I," said Decca, testily.

An attractive young woman in a nurse's uniform appeared from the house behind him, carrying a tea tray, while a gang of mental health nurses closed in on the Rodgers and Hammerstein fan with grim determination.

"Anything in the paper, Ray?" she asked, placing the tea tray on the table beside him.

"Nothing much. Someone's been nicking figures from the Waxworks again."

"What, again? It's becoming a regular crime wave."

"I know," said Decca, perking up. "First it was Tom Cruise's left leg, then Henry Kissinger and now Bruce Willis has gone missing."

"What, the actor?" asked Rachel.

"No, the waxwork of him, obviously. Otherwise it would have made News at Ten."

"But who would steal a waxwork of Bruce Willis?" she asked.

"I don't know but there are some very sick people out there."

"Perhaps it's a case for Inspector Decca of the Yard," said the nurse, brightly.

They weren't supposed to encourage patients to think about their former lives, but he really did seem to be well on the road to recovery, surely it couldn't hurt. It's probably just kids, having a laugh," she added.

"I don't think so, Rachel. They looked at the CCTV on each occasion and it seemed to be a gang of men. They smuggled Tom Cruise's leg out in a plastic bag but Kissinger and Willis seemed to literally walk out of the place unaided. No-one recognised Henry Kissinger but Bruce Willis caused quite a stir apparently, three people asked for his autograph."

"And did he give it them?" she asked.

"How could he? He was a waxwork."

"Yes, sorry, of course he was."

"Do you think I might go into town today, Rachel?" asked Decca.

"Well, I think so," she said. "I'll mention it to the doctor when he does his rounds, but he did say you needed to start getting out and about a bit more. It's all part of your return to normality."

"I haven't been to a waxworks in ages," said Decca.

"They always give me the creeps but if that's what floats your boat. Just don't do anything I wouldn't do."

"I won't and thanks," said the Inspector, getting up from his chair.

Part Five

Ain't gonna play Sun City

The Sun Lounge, Blackpool was buzzing in a way it had never done before; not with bees nor the frenzied crowds of tourists it had enjoyed in the dim and distant past, but with the heavy tread of Mr. Plod in the persons of the local Homicide Squad.

The cordons had been drawn, the forensic photographs taken and, once the police circus had moved on, all that remained of the cast of dozens were a fat Detective Sergeant with facial hair, called O'Malley and his smart as paint assistant, WPC Arkwright. They were interviewing the Lounge's decrepit owner; local celebrity and bon viveur, Victor Knight. He looked about eighty in the shade in a beige safari suit and brown suede boots.

"Can you think of anyone who'd want to kill the old ventriloquist?" asked O'Malley, with a trace of an Irish accent.

"No, inspector," said Vic Knight.

"Detective Sergeant, sir," explained the policeman.

"I mean, he's been dying on stage in Blackpool every night for the past twenty or thirty years, but no-one would want to *kill* him, Smithy was a local landmark. There was no harm in him; he was just a lovely guy."

"Were you and he *close* then?" queried O'Malley.

"Not in a gay way, you understand. We were just good friends."

"So he wasn't a homosexual?"

"Good heavens, no. Whatever made you think that...not that there's anything wrong with that, of course, some of my best friends..." said Victor, trailing off into silence.

"It's perfectly alright to be gay," said Arkwright, "we're not living in Russia after all."

"Thank you, Arkwright," said the Detective Sergeant, irritably, "but I'll ask the questions if you don't mind. So you weren't his gay lover, Mr. Knight?" asked O'Malley. "You didn't kill him in a jealous rage over his relationship with little Charlie?"

"Charlie was his dummy!" snapped Vic Knight. "Besides, you didn't *know* him," he added, "he was no friend of Dorothy's, in fact he loathed the Wizard of Oz. He was German."

"A German, eh? How long had he been living in Blackpool?" asked O'Malley.

"Oh, for many years, I think he came over in the Fifties."

"You mean he's been doing that act since the Fifties?" queried O'Malley, incredulously.

A lorry pulled up on the pavement outside the hotel, blocking the view of the Church of the Sacred Heart on the opposite side of the road, and Victor Knight paced over to the window in agitation. He opened it and poked his head out.

"I'm sorry, you can't park there!"

"Delivery for Mr. Knight," said the driver, reversing his lorry onto the drive.

"Quick, stop him!" cried Victor, racing out of the room.

O'Malley and Arkwright followed, bemused. They arrived outside the entrance hall just in time to see a heap of horse manure being deposited all over the driveway.

"I'll get you, you bastards!" cried Vic Knight, shaking his fist at the driver as the lorry shot off at high speed down the road.

"What was all that about?" asked O'Malley.

"Just a little practical joke," said Knight in exasperation.

"Yeah, hilarious," said O'Malley, "but why the Sun Lounge, why you?"

"Just a little misunderstanding with the local garden centre," explained Knight, cryptically.

"You were telling us about Mr. Smith," said Arkwright.

"I was," said Knight, leading them back into the lounge bar. "I met him in the Eighties. He was a bit of a lady-killer in those days, a different bird every time you saw him. It was me who encouraged him with the vent act. He'd got tired of waiting table and none of the other dead-end jobs he'd tried paid a living wage so he started talking about getting into showbiz as a ventriloquist. I knew my way around the local club scene so I offered to get him a few bookings and gave him a few gags to get started."

Up in the bell tower of the Church of the Sacred Heart

a flock of pigeons took flight. Inside the tower a man with a briefcase snapped open the locks and assembled the black metal machined parts within with the consummate skill of a professional. He slid the barrel through the broken shutter and took aim at a target in the Sun Lounge across the road.

"Gags?" queried O'Malley.

"Yeah, my wife's just been to the West Indies. Jamaica? No she went of her own accord…don't clap too loud, it's an old building…that sort of rubbish."

O'Malley grimaced. Those jokes were as dead as Mr. Smith.

A red spot appeared on Vic Knight's shirt front and he collapsed in a crumpled heap on the floor of the bar, spraying blood across O'Malley's jacket as he fell.

I think we'd better get forensics back," said Arkwright.

O'Malley dabbed at his sleeve with a tissue and nodded. "What's the bloody matter with this town, Arkwright? It used to be fun, now it's more like Dodge City.

Part Six

Riding the rails

All through the night the train clattered its way North, past the suburban sprawl of housing estates and sheds, industrial parks and pubs, all interspersed with an occasional church spire and low-rise cityscape. This was England; complex and ancient, dark yet beautiful, watched over by a howling moon.

Hymie and Mike sat in silence, trying not to stare at each other. It had been years since either of them had had anything remotely resembling a holiday and although they'd dressed especially for the occasion, they were out of touch.

Hymie wore a black woollen suit, a frilly shirt and a green bow tie; the best he could get at the local charity shop, "Save Old Goats" for under a fiver, while Mike sported a Hawaiian beach look with a flowery shirt, Bermuda shorts and the biggest, blackest sunglasses you ever saw. He looked like a Polynesian hit-man on the run.

"What in god's name are you wearing?" asked Hymie, finally breaking the silence.

"Holiday clothes!" snapped Mike, with a hint of menace. "What did you think?"

"You look like you just lost a fight with a sun-lounger."

"Well, at least I wasn't kitted out by Save Old Scroats!"

"These clothes may be dated, but they're like me..." began Hymie.

"Faded and smelling of old moth balls?"

"...a classic; they'll never go out of style," he added, picking a few balls of fluff from his sleeve.

"They were never in style in the first place," spluttered Mike in disbelief.

"Never mind," said Hymie, "you can always change back into your army surplus gear when we get there. I mean there's no need to freeze your nuts off in the North of England in your beachwear."

Mike glared at him.

"You'll never pull any birds dressed like *that*," said Hymie.

"I've got more chance than you, mate. Everyone knows only gay men wear bow ties. Especially *green* ones."

"That's where you're wrong, dopey. Bow ties are the height of sophistication. That guy on the telly wears one... Dick someone or other."

"Yeah, you look like a dick alright."

"Anyway, it was all they had for a fiver. Besides, I'm off women. They're all certifiable. Getting involved with one is like playing cards with the devil; you know the game's fixed but you just can't help yourself."

"You're really starting to piss me off," said Mike, "let's just go back to the silence."

"Fine by me."

Moments later the train slowed as they pulled into a halt. Hymie rubbed a viewing hole in the condensation on the window.

"Lefgage? Who ever heard of a place called Lefgage?"

Mike peered out. "It's left luggage, you Wally."

"Someone in uniform's getting on," said Hymie.

"What, the police?"

"No, just the ticket inspector," added Hymie, quietly.

"You do have the tickets, I take it?" asked Mike.

"Well, I was just about to buy them when I was distracted…" began Hymie, rising from his seat. "Excuse me a minute, Mike," he added, starting to walk off, "only I need the loo badly."

The ticket inspector was a distinguished looking man with grey whiskers and a pointy face.

"Tickets, please," he said, looking startled at Mike's outlandish clobber.

"Here you go," said Mike, retrieving two tickets to Blackpool from his trouser pocket.

He'd learnt long ago that Goldman couldn't be relied upon for anything sensible. In fact it was difficult to think of anything his business partner *was* useful for, he was just one of those guys.

The inspector punched the tickets.

"Is that guy in the green bow-tie with you?"

Mike nodded.

"Only he was moving at quite a lick when he got to the toilet."

"Oh, it's just Gandhi's revenge," said Mike.

"Well, enjoy your stay in Blackpool," said the ticket inspector, as he moved along the empty carriage.

Mike opened his rucksack and fished out a can of cider and a newspaper. He pulled the ring-pull, took a swig and opened his paper. This was more like it, he thought, stretching back in his seat. Goldman had dropped him in it once too often, but this time he could stew in the loo for the rest of the journey.

Eventually, Hymie returned, just as the train was pulling into their station.

"You OK, Mike?"

"Never better, mate," said Mike.

"The old tricks are the best," said Hymie, "but it didn't half pong in there."

Mike smiled. "Come on, H., we've got a job to do."

Part Seven

A Haunting Melody

As they walked out onto the platform at Blackpool Central Station in the early hours of the morning Hymie caught sight of a beautiful brunette holding a piece of cardboard with an illegible scrawl on it. She seemed to be waiting for someone. They couldn't be so lucky, surely?

"Harry Oldman?" asked the brunette. She didn't say it with much conviction, but they were practically the only passengers getting off the train.

"The name's Goldman, Hymie Goldman, will I do?" he replied, as suavely as he could manage.

"Only if you're a private investigator from London."

"I am," he assured her, "and this is my business partner, Mike Murphy," he added, indicating Mike, who was labouring under the weight of Goldman's suitcase as well as his own overloaded rucksack.

"Pleased to meet you," said Mike, dropping the case.

"You haven't come in fancy dress by any chance?" asked the woman, trying not to laugh.

"No, just casual," said Hymie.

"Well, I'm Melody. Dad asked me to pick you up from the station."

"Dad?" asked Mike.

"The Reverend Robert Brown…but everyone calls him Bob."

"He's our client," explained Hymie.

"He asked me to pick you up, take you to the chalet, give you the keys to the motorbike and sidecar and…"

"Motorbike?" queried Mike.

"And *sidecar*?" Hymie looked confused. "He never said anything about a sidecar on the phone, just that we'd have our own accommodation and transport."

"Well, there you are then," said Melody, "surely you've driven a motorbike before? You haven't lived until you've driven along the beach on a bike with the wind in your hair."

Hymie winced. When you didn't have much hair left the last thing you needed was to get the wind stirring it up.

"Of course," said Mike. "I got my bike licence in the army and as for Hymie, he's never happier than when he's sitting around, so the sidecar should be fine."

Hymie shot him an irritated glance, but said nothing.

"Right, I suppose we'd better crack on," said Melody.

She led them outside to the car park, where they shoe-horned themselves and their luggage into her tiny Nissan Micra, before driving off at a crawl through the outlying countryside.

"Is it far?" asked Mike.

"Not really," she replied, "in fact we're almost there."

"Thank God for that," said Hymie from the back of the car, "I can't feel anything in my legs."

"Where exactly are we?" asked Mike.

"A little place called Weeton. You'll love it," said Melody, driving off the road and down a pot-holed dirt track.

"And this…" she added, pulling up a few moments later, "is where you'll be staying. Dad calls it his retreat."

Hymie gaped at the derelict wooden hut in dismay. "Looks more like a surrender to me," he muttered.

"Well, I'd better leave you two gents to settle in," she said, once they'd finally extricated themselves from the Micra.

"You said something about a motorbike," said Mike.

"Oh yes," she said, walking over to a tarpaulin covered lump at the side of the hut. "Tadaaaahh!" she exclaimed, removing the tarp to reveal a mud splattered relic of a bygone age. "It's a Norton, a genuine British classic, so mind how you drive her," she added, passing Mike the keys.

"What's that great plastic bubble thing on the side?" asked Hymie.

"The sidecar, of course."

"I was afraid you were going to say that," he said. "Are you sure *you* wouldn't like to drive it and leave us the Micra?"

"What, and deny two guests from the Smoke the chance to experience vintage motoring," she said, brightly.

"It'll be fine," said Mike.

"The hut doesn't look much from the outside but it's comfortable enough," said Melody, "and I've stocked up the fridge for you. Dad'll be in touch soon, I expect."

She got into her car and drove off, bumping along the track into the distance until she was a speck on the horizon.

"Well, what do you make of that?" asked Hymie.

"Nice girl," said Mike, "pretty as a picture… but you've done it again, haven't you."

"Done what?"

"Signed us up for some doss house in the middle of nowhere without checking your facts. I only hope the case isn't as bad as the accommodation."

"Look, beggars can't be choosers, we needed a change and it'll probably turn out fine," said Hymie, unconvinced. "You'll see the bluebird of happiness is hovering over the next hilltop."

"Yeah, to crap all over you." Mike picked up their luggage and barged past Goldman into the scruffy shack. "Baggsy first choice of the bedrooms!" he added.

Part Eight

In Xanadu

In the weather-beaten shell of Blackpool Central Police station, Detective Sergeant O'Malley rocked precariously on the back legs of his chair. He was a fat man in his forties with side-whiskers and a moustache. His plain clothes revealed nothing more than a chronic lack of dress sense.

On the opposite side of the desk, WPC Alice Arkwright continued to stare at the open file in front of her, searching for inspiration in the wilderness of procedure and routine. After five years of walking the beat she'd begun to think that police work was mostly about dealing with drunks and idiots and after transferring departments to work for DS O'Malley she'd become convinced of it.

Every day was the same; a morass of endless, pointless paperwork, even in the so-called paperless office. How she craved something different, anything at all.

"It doesn't make any sense, Arkwright, that's the thing d' ye see. I've looked at it every which way, but I'll be jiggered if I know who's behind these waxwork thefts and why," said O'Malley, with a hint of a Dublin accent.

"No, sir," replied Alice, staring out of the window. "It's a puzzle, isn't it?"

"It is that. Still, that's we're here for; to keep the forces of darkness at bay."

"Perhaps we need to establish who stands to gain from the thefts?"

"Well, it isn't the waxworks now, is it?" replied O'Malley, laughing.

"On the other hand, why not?" queried Alice. "I mean, you wouldn't think a bunch of wax figures would be worth a lot, but maybe they were insured for millions."

"I see what you mean. Get onto the insurance company at once."

"It was only a suggestion, sir."

"Worth a try, anyway; better than your last idea of rounding up all the local candle-makers and craft shop owners," said O'Malley.

She wasn't about to rise to the bait. It had been *his* dumb idea, but he had a selective memory when it suited him.

"I reckon it'll be kids from the local college, having a laugh."

"You don't say," said Alice, "and what do you base that on?"

"Instinct, sheer bloody instinct," he replied.

"But we've seen the CCTV recording, sir. There were three of them; short stocky blokes with beards, hardly the student type."

"Beards my foot! They were probably fake ones from the local joke shop. Mark my words, Arkwright, there are students behind this. They'll do anything for a laugh these days."

"So you don't think it could be the work of the notorious Beach Buoys?"

"Of course not! Surely you don't believe that old tosh about a Blackpool street gang running all the crime in the greater Lancashire area?"

Resistance was futile. "I'm learning *so* much, working with you," said Alice.

He smiled, entirely missing her sarcasm. "You stick with me, Arkwright, I'm definitely going places," he said, looking at his watch.

Round about now he was generally itching for a chance to pop along to Scruffy Murphy's for a pint or two, but she wasn't going to give him one.

"Just call the waxworks, find out who their insurers are and pay them a visit. Check out their claims history and if that doesn't look like a goer then try talking to the candle-makers. I'll be making enquiries of me own around the town…"

"I've already interviewed the local pub landlords, sir."

"I don't quite get your drift."

"In case the waxworks were stolen by drunken revellers, sir."

"I see…did you speak to the manager at Scruffy Murphy's?"

"Oh, yes, sir."

"Good work. Well. I've got a private appointment to keep so I'll see you back here at three."

"Right you are, sir," said Alice, writing "Wanker!" on her notepad.

The shadow of a tall figure fell across the frosted glass door to their office, followed closely by a peremptory knock.

"Come in!" called Alice.

The grizzled form of Inspector Decca of the Yard appeared in their midst.

"Who the heck are you?" cried O'Malley irritably.

"Inspector Rey Decca of the Metropolitan Police. Have I come at a bad time?"

"No," said Alice, smiling. "Take a seat, I'm WPC Arkwright and this is…"

"DS O'Malley," said Decca. "They said I'd find you here," he added, holding out his hand.

"Who exactly are *they*?" queried O'Malley, shaking his hand sullenly.

"Your commanding officers," said Decca. "I told them I'd been staying in town on annual leave and had been reading about the epidemic of waxwork thefts."

"Well, I'd hardly be calling it an epidemic," said O'Malley.

"So, I offered my services free of charge and they said I should speak to you," said Decca.

Great! Thought O'Malley, if that wasn't the last thing you needed when you had a tricky case to solve; some smartarse from London poking his big nose in where it wasn't wanted.

"Well, it's very kind of you, I'm sure," said O'Malley, "but we have our own ways of doing things in these parts, Inspector."

"Such as?" asked Decca.

"Look, this is a busy station. We don't just have one case you know. Every week it's something different. Last week a bunch of hooligans threw a giant rubber shark through the front window of Mrs O'Higgins' guest house and that's the third time this month, I've been telling them for years to shut the bar in the bloody aquarium, but will they listen? Of course not."

"I wasn't trying to create extra work for you," explained Decca, "just to see if I could help. I'm actually quite a good detective."

"Well…err, we've been investigating links to a criminal gang in the area," blustered O'Malley, going a little pink.

"The Beach Buoys," explained Alice, "a gang of serious villains, involved in drugs, prostitution, murder…"

"And waxworks?" queried Decca. This was certainly a bloody funny place for a holiday.

"And why not?" asked O'Malley.

"Why indeed?"

"So you see, Inspector, we have it all covered. We don't need any help from the big boys from the big city but if you'd like to leave us your contact details, we'll be in touch if something *big* turns up," said O'Malley.

"Yes, I'm staying at a guest house up the road…" said Decca, cagily.

"Which one?" asked Alice.

"Craa…ckets," said Decca, indistinctly.

"Sorry?"

"Crackpots."

"What the police nut-house at Lytham?" queried O'Malley.

"Yes, but only as a visitor, not a guest."

"Never mind," said Alice.

"Perhaps I'll pursue my own enquiries," said Decca.

"Yes, good idea, Inspector," said O'Malley. "Just be sure to stay on the right side of the fence, eh? It may seem like a backwater up here, but we have some world class villains."

"Don't worry," said Decca, "I'm good at working undercover."

"That's fine, but don't forget to keep me informed and don't get in too deep."

"I'll be in touch," said Decca, closing the door behind him and leaving them to their thoughts.

"Well, that was different," said Alice.

"Nope, happens all the time," said O'Malley, searching through his desk drawer for his hip flask.

Part Nine

Meeting Bob

Maybe it was the fresh air, maybe the distant sound of waves crashing on the shore or maybe they were just dog tired, but Hymie and Mike slept like babes on their first night in "The Shed," as they called it. Eventually, however, all good comas had to come to an end so they got up, dressed and pored over some old tourist maps of the area until they located their client's hideout; a shack next to a church. They ate a hearty breakfast of cornflakes, toast and coffee and headed for the great outdoors.

Outside, Mike pulled on a massive black helmet and a pair of black leather biker's gloves and straddled the Norton, while Hymie bundled himself into the plastic coffin-like sidecar. He looked at Mike resentfully; as senior partner shouldn't he be driving the bike? Being completely useless denied him the option.

Mike kick-started the bike and its powerful engine burst into life, shooting smoke and flames from the twin chrome-plated exhausts. In the junior partner's box-room Hymie had begun looking for the seat-belt, the crash-helmet and the passenger airbag. There weren't any, only what looked like a bottle of smelling salts. He tapped on the plexi-glass screen and screamed at the top of his voice, but Mike couldn't hear him above the cacophony of engine noise. He was going to be squashed like a bug in there! Even the human cannonball at Billy Smart's circus had a better chance of arriving at his destination in one piece. He sat down and closed his eyes.

The old motorbike and sidecar shot off down the track, belching out a trail of dust and smoke in its wake which was probably visible from space. In the thirty minutes it took Mike to find the Reverend Bob's place, Hymie's facial expression ran the gamut of emotions from panic to sheer bloody terror. When they stopped he cried for joy.

"That journey's aged me," he said, when he could finally speak again.

"Yeah, but let's face it, you were always older than your years," said Mike.

"What's that supposed to mean?"

"Well, you're a bit of an old woman," said Mike, "you have to make a drama out of everything."

"Okay, I'll drive back," said Hymie.

"You don't know how."

"I'll learn!" he snapped.

They walked up to the shack, which turned out on closer inspection to be a quaint little cottage, and looked for some name or number to confirm they were in the right place.

"This is it," said Mike, "The Vicary...or it might be Vicarage, the painting on the sign's very faded."

"That doesn't surprise me," said Hymie, ringing the doorbell.

There was a creaking sound as the door opened and then Melody appeared, smiling.

"You found us then," she said.

"Yes," admitted Hymie, tongue-tied, as ever, in the presence of beauty.

"Well, you are detectives."

"And we had a map," said Mike.

She led them into the cottage and took their coats. The entrance hall was small and dark with a yellow tinge to the wallpaper as if from years of nicotine abuse. Pictures of hunting scenes hung here and there on the walls, conveying the atmosphere of a country pub rather than a vicarage.

"Daddy's in the Orangery," she said, "I'll take you to meet him once I've hung up your coats."

Mike and Hymie exchanged puzzled looks. 'What the hell's an Orangery?' just about summed it up.

"It's like a Conservatory with oranges," explained Melody.

She led them through several dimly lit rooms into what looked like an old conservatory at the back of the cottage.

"I see what you mean about the oranges," said Hymie. They were everywhere.

"Hello, gentlemen would you like one?" asked the Reverend Brown, a wrinkled specimen in a v-necked sweater with a dog collar underneath.

"What, a drink?" asked Mike, optimistically.

"No, an orange," said the Rev., pointing at a nearby orange tree.

"Obviously!" added Hymie, looking at Mike like some prize idiot. "No, thanks, we're trying to give them up for Lent," he added, sinking into a nearby armchair like a blancmange sliding off a serving tray.

"Yeah, fresh fruit and veg. brings him out in hives," said Mike.

"Well, I'm pleased to meet you both, anyway," said the Rev., from his white wicker chair.

"I'm Hymie Goldman and this is my business partner, Mike Murphy."

"I never doubted it," said the vicar. "Well, I suppose you'll be wanting to know about the case?"

Yes, please," said Hymie.

The Rev. Brown passed him a blue cardboard file full of papers and waited for him to open it.

"As I said on the phone, my sister Elaine disappeared twenty years ago last Tuesday and I promised mother I'd find her, or at least, what had happened to her. That file was prepared by the last private investigator I hired to look for her, about five years ago; Henry Pie, private eye. He was a fat bloke with glasses…ever heard of him?"

"No," said Hymie.

"You're lucky," said the Rev. "He was a blithering idiot. I'd have been better off flushing my money down the loo. It would certainly have been quicker. Nevertheless, I give it you for what it's worth. It will tell you everything you need to know about my sister, Elaine, except where on earth she is; which was the only thing I actually wanted to know."

"Interesting," said Mike.

"Decidedly," said the Rev. "Well, I wish you boys the very best of British luck in solving the case...for all our sakes. It drove mother half round the bend not knowing what had happened to Elaine. I know the trail is cold, so to speak, but read the file and let me know if you need anything else...introductions, explanations, background information...anything. Don't be strangers, now you know where we live," he added.

"We won't," said Hymie, smiling at Melody. "I've a feeling we'll be back before you know it."

Incredibly she smiled back.

Part Ten

A walk in the Students' Union

It was only a matter of time before DS O'Malley, adding two and two to make five as usual, concluded that there were students behind the thefts from the waxworks and that, as the guardian of the law in the greater Blackpool area, he'd better ask a few questions. So, one Wednesday afternoon, after his customary trip to Scruffy Murphy's for a pint or two he bundled up WPC Arkwright into a police car and got her to drive them to the local Further Education College.

"Students? What are they good for?" said O'Malley, "absolutely nothing, that's what! Just a bunch of feckless wasters who go around causing trouble for honest law-abiding citizens; when they're not sponging off the state, that is."

"You're talking rubbish, sir," said WPC Arkwright. "Where would we be without education? Nowhere, that's for sure."

"Tell that to Mrs O'Higgins and her guests; one minute they were sitting down to dinner, the next a bloody great rubber shark appeared in their midst causing havoc!

Tourism's the life blood of this town, Arkwright, not education. You mark my words."

Arkwright simply rolled her eyes. He was such a dipstick there wasn't much point in trying to reason with him. "Do you really think there's any point in asking questions in the Students' Union, sir? Last time they just took the piss out of you."

O'Malley closed his eyes. He didn't want to be reminded of it, but she was right. He'd only gone to interview the Vice Chancellor about a minor motoring offence, but he'd run the gauntlet of verbal abuse in the Union bar.

They parked in the public car park then made their way across campus to the Students' Union building. It was a 1960s low-rise hovel, full of dodgy insurance agents, students' society notice boards and a stall selling handmade crap from the M'Bongo tribe. O'Malley pushed through the entrance doors and headed towards the Union bar. Inside the building four students stood around with collecting tins, dressed as woodland animals.

"Spare a quid for rabid badgers," said a youth in fancy dress.

"Why are you dressed like a fox?" asked O'Malley.

"Durrr…what's it to you, porky?" said the student, who could recognise a police officer at fifty metres.

"Well, stuff your badgers then," said O'Malley. He walked over to the bar, with Arkwright in tow, and started up a conversation with the barman, who seemed to be cleaning his didgeridoo behind the bar.

"G'day mate, 'n Sheila," said the barman.

"What's an Australian doing behind a bar in Blackpool?" asked O'Malley.

"I came over here on a cultural exchange," explained the Aussie. He was tall and tanned and looked completely at ease between the beer pumps and optics.

"To Blackpool?" queried Arkwright.

"I was misinformed," said Dave, the barman, beaming. "Can I get you a drink?" he asked, "or are you on duty?"

"Oh, we're not policemen," said O'Malley. "We're a couple of mature students. I'm Kev, and Arkwright here is working part-time as a strip-o-gram to pay her college fees.

"Right you are, dudes," said Dave, not believing a word. "So, what's it to be?"

"A couple of beers please," said O'Malley. Arkwright frowned. If she had to drink on duty, she was damn sure she was going to enjoy it. "Make mine a white wine and lemonade," she said.

"So, what are you studying?" asked Dave, as he poured their drinks.

They looked blankly at each other like a couple of rabbits caught in the approaching headlights of a car.

"Are you freshers?" continued Dave.

"That's it," concurred O'Malley, "we're studying vegetable refrigeration."

"Wow, I never knew they taught that here, I thought you must be a couple of marine biologists," said Dave,

"Funny you should say that. In fact, Arkwright is a marine biologist, I'm the vegetable guy…that's what they call me," said O'Malley.

Arkwright smiled. He'd never said a truer word.

"What kind of name is Arkwright?" asked Dave, "it's a surname, right? I thought only the Fuzz called each other by their surnames."

"Oh, he's just old fashioned. My first name's Alice."

"Like the Springs," said Dave.

"That's right." O'Malley just looked confused.

"So, what's new around here?" asked O'Malley. "I heard one of the woodland animals say some of the students had been nicking waxworks for a laugh. They didn't bring them in here, I suppose?"

Dave looked at O'Malley as though he'd completely lost his marbles. "Yeah, mate, Tufty was in here the other day as high as a kite. If I were you I'd ask his friends, Willy the Weasel and Arnie the Aardvark over there," he said, pointing at the students.

"Sure," said O'Malley, walking over to where the four students in fancy dress were playing bar football.

"Hi, guys," said O'Malley, "you haven't seen anyone carrying around some wax figures for a laugh, I suppose?"

"No, sorry copper," said the youth in the fox costume. "If I were you I'd ask someone who gives a shit."

O'Malley clenched his fists. If only there weren't so many witnesses, the guy would be toast by now.

Arkwright tapped him on the shoulder. "Don't let it get to you, Kev," she said calmly, leading her irate colleague outside to their transport. "I told you, you were barking up the wrong tree," she added, once they got outside. O'Malley just glowered.

Part Eleven

A hell of a place

The cult of celebrity is a dark and dangerous thing. It draws you in, sucks out your brain and leaves you exposed to the specious allure of some bozo you imagine can walk on water. You hang on their lightest word as though it were something profound when all they're really saying is blah, err...blah.

Or perhaps you're entranced by a pretty face, a sexy butt or a cheeky smile. So you buy the fanzines, the photo signed by someone else, and a life-sized 3D poster to cover the stain on your wallpaper...or visit a waxworks.

In the waxworks on the promenade at Blackpool, a tall, pale figure stood awkwardly in the midst of a group of rock legends, trying to look inconspicuous. He wasn't one himself, but he was about the right age for a contemporary of Jagger, Bowie or Elton John. Occasionally a visitor would stop and stare intently at him before passing on; none the wiser. The guesses had ranged from Geoff Bowie, David's less successful cousin, to the third McCartney brother, Leppo, a deaf mute who could only play the A-flat mouthorgan. No-one had guessed that it was really Inspector Ray Decca of the Metropolitan Police working undercover while on sick leave.

After days of staring into David Bowie's left ear he'd begun to regret his insane plan to catch the waxworks thieves by pretending to be a waxwork. He'd been arriving at opening time, changing into his rocker clobber in the loo then jumping over the security rope when the guard went outside for a crafty fag.

It was all getting too much. Once he'd sneezed, scaring a party of schoolchildren so badly that they ran screaming from the room and he'd had to hide behind Elton's piano. On another occasion he'd farted loudly as an elderly couple were passing. The old lady had turned to look at her husband in disgust and said "you can't blame the dog for that one, Henry!"

It was Friday afternoon and no-one had been through "Rock of Ages" for eons. Decca had been on the verge of chucking it all in for a fish and chip supper at Harry Ramsden's when three strange men appeared. They were short and thick-set with large bushy beards. Decca tried not to stare.

"Who's it gonna be this time, Joe?" said the shortest one, Tony.

"I think she said Rod Stewart, didn't she Ralph?" said Joe.

The third man looked blank. "I dunno. Don't go

dragging me into this. You know what she's like if you get the wrong one."

"We never get the wrong one," said Tony.

Joe stared at Decca. "Who the hell's he then? He's had a hard life whoever he is, but I don't recognise him."

"It doesn't matter, some one-hit wonder I expect," said Tony. "Now where's Rod?"

"Over here," said Ralph, pointing at a waxwork of Sting.

"No wonder she doesn't send you out alone any more, Ralph. Can't you tell your Rod from your Sting, man?"

"It's in the nose," said Tony.

"Sting's the one with the receding hairline and the ferrety little eyes and Rod's the one with the conk like a lump of squashed sausage," explained Joe.

Tony removed a large black-handled machete from the inside of his coat pocket and swung it forcefully at Rod Stewart's neck.

Schtum!

Rod's head fell to the floor and rolled across the display area, coming to rest at Decca's feet. Any plans he may have had of intercepting the thieves rapidly disappeared. There were three of them and despite their diminutive stature they were armed and dangerous.

Tony bent down, picked up Rod's severed head and popped it into a plastic carrier bag. "Come on, let's go!" he snapped and the three of them filed out of the room in quick succession.

Decca breathed a heavy sigh of relief and looked down at the floor, where Rod's head had been. He'd never been a great fan of Rod Stewart but where was their respect for a true rock legend? There were traces of a white powder on his shoes, which must have come from the three men as they made their getaway. He bent down and rubbed a trace of it on his gums. It was cocaine…or possibly ground chalk; he couldn't be quite sure as he'd been seeing bizarre things for days.

There was no time to change back into his normal clothes so Decca just stepped over the security rope and raced after the three men, waving at the cashier on the front desk, who was a little startled to see one of the exhibits making a break for it.

Decca ran out of the waxworks and along the windswept Promenade. Ahead if him he could just make out three ill-shaped men with beards and a carrier bag as they waited for the tram. He followed at a discreet distance, holding a discarded newspaper in front of him, which was frequently blown into his face by the wind. He arrived at the stop just in time to jump onto the tram, signed for Fleetwood Ferry, as it set off down the tracks.

The tram rattled its way along the front, past the grim grey horizon, blighted as it was by a flotilla of container ships and dinghies, while the few remaining passengers hopped off.

There were only the four of them left by now and Decca was beginning to worry he'd have to follow the bearded delinquents onto the Fleetwood Ferry, when one of them stood up and rang the bell. The tram pulled up and the three men disembarked, walking along the footpath to a dark and dingy pub, set back from the road. As Decca looked on they disappeared inside the pub, "The Last Lights," and were followed shortly afterwards by two other strange men; a large man wearing a Hawaiian beach shirt and a shorter one in a scruffy black suit.

He'd come here for a rest but it was all starting to get a bit heavy now. He badly needed back-up but there was no-one in these parts he could rely on. Oh, how he missed London!

Part Twelve

What's in a file?

Hymie and Mike sat in a café on Blackpool sea-front and read through the file the Reverend Brown had given them.

"Well, it's nothing like any file we've ever produced," said Hymie.

"You mean, it's comprehensive, well organised and he's actually recorded how he reached his conclusions?" said Mike.

"No, of course not," said Hymie, miffed. "Besides, what's it matter if your paperwork wins a Pulitzer Prize if you don't actually solve the case?"

"That's what's worrying me," said Mike. "This is the work of a proper detective and he couldn't solve it. What chance do we stand? We don't even fit in around here."

"So what? We don't need to fit in, just find the Reverend Brown's sister."

"True, I mean this blue-folder guy couldn't find his sister," agreed Mike, "for all his fancy paperwork. And don't forget the vicar called him a *blithering idiot*, so he couldn't have been much cop. Maybe his sister just didn't want to be found. Maybe she died or moved away. Maybe the last detective got scared off? We just don't know."

"That's an awful lot of maybes for this time in the morning. What was the last detective called anyway?" wondered Hymie, flicking through the file. "Henry Pie, Private Eye… what sort of a dick would call himself that? He may still be in the phone book," said Hymie. "Why don't we ask him?"

"Whether he's a dick or whether he was scared off?" queried Mike.

"Either," said Hymie. "Maybe we *should* contact him. There's no reason to think he was scared off, but if he was then we need to know about it."

"Pass the sugar, will you?" said Mike.

Hymie passed the sugar and Mike poured a generous serving of it into his cup. He swigged it and winced.

"That's the salt, you daft sod!"

"Anyone can make a mistake," said Hymie.

"Not like you. You've got a gift for it."

"Come on, let's take a walk along the front," said Hymie. "It'll clear our heads."

They walked for a few blocks along the Promenade, occasionally stopping to admire the tacky souvenir shops disgorging their brightly coloured Kiss-Me-Quick Hats, sticks of Blackpool rock and saucy postcards all over the pavement like some giant day-glo vomit.

"I wonder if those Kiss-Me-Quick hats ever work?" said Hymie.

"What, with a face like yours!"

Hymie shrugged. "Look who's talking."

"Anyway, what good would a bird in Blackpool be to a man from North London?"

"There is that," agreed Hymie. "I was toying with the idea of a torrid holiday romance, but let's get some chips instead."

It was a suggestion guaranteed a warm welcome and they soon found themselves leaning against the railings on the sea front, stuffing their faces with hot chips as the local seagulls wheeled menacingly overhead, crying like lost souls, waiting for a chance to pounce.

"Maybe we should consult a psychic," suggested Hymie. "You can't move for them around here."

"There's one over there," said Mike, pointing at a board outside a wooden booth on the opposite side of the road. "Madam Zaza, Prophet to the Stars."

"How do we know if she's any good?" wondered Hymie.

"Well, she claims to have cured insomnia, predicted the stock market crash of 2008 and foretold the TV comeback of Randy Scott."

"Never heard of him," said Hymie.

"I thought he was dead."

"She's a charlatan" said Hymie. "Besides, we don't need a psychic who can only foretell the past we need some fresh leads. Don't forget, we've got one thing the other detective didn't have."

"What's that?"

"This file," explained Hymie holding the blue cardboard folder above his head for dramatic effect. "More facts than you can shake a stick at; employment history, national insurance records, names and addresses of contacts, last known address…"

A large grey seagull descended from a lamppost nearby and carried off the blue cardboard folder, squawking triumphantly. It flew out over the grey sea and, realising its treasure wasn't edible after all, dropped it into the water.

"Oi!" cried Hymie, "You stupid bloody bird!"

Mike stared gloomily after it. "What were you saying?"

"Nothing," said Hymie.

"It's a good job you've got a photographic memory, eh?"

"Yes."

"And that recreating that file will cause you no trouble at all," added Mike, sarcastically.

"In fact, I do remember *one* thing," said Hymie. "Elaine Brown's last job was as a barmaid at *The Last Lights* pub at the end of the coast road."

"Well, it'll do to be going on with," said Mike. Mine's a pint."

They trudged back in silence to their motorbike and sidecar. Any seagull wanting to get the better of Goldman and Murphy would have to get up very early in the morning, very early indeed.

Part Thirteen

The Last Lights

It was approaching dusk. As Hymie and Mike looked up at the battered sign, swinging on industrial strength chains outside "The Last Lights" pub they both felt strangely as though they were coming home. In the distance, a golden sun slipped silently into the grey Irish Sea like a scene from the death of King Arthur and, apart from the distant cry of gulls clocking off for the day, all was quiet. Eerily quiet.

Three stout, bearded men barged past them, disappearing into the pub's dark interior with a heavy plastic carrier bag.

Inside the pub everything was swathed in a Stygian gloom. The low wattage lamps were turned down lower that a cockroach's kneecaps, as though the landlord were still in shock from a particularly heavy electric bill and the optics behind the bar seemed to be illuminated by left over Christmas lights.

"No wonder they call it the last lights," said Hymie, "I can barely see my hand in front of my face. I think it's actually brighter outside."

"Shhhhh," said Mike, "We don't wanna get chucked out before we've found anything out."

"Watch out they don't short change you at the bar," said Hymie.

"It's your round, you cheeky sod."

Hymie patted all of his pockets in turn and looked expectantly at Mike.

"I seem to have come out without any money, you couldn't sub me, I suppose, old buddy?"

"Give it a rest, Goldman, you tight git." Mike caught sight of a barmaid approaching them. "There are some tables over there," he added, pointing. "Go make some enquiries, there's a good lad."

As Hymie walked through the pub his eyes gradually became accustomed to the dark. He passed a table with two men sat behind it in tweed jackets and wellies. He assumed they were farmers. They were talking about the price of animal fodder and looked like they would have gone on to bore him with anecdotes about strangely shaped root vegetables so he moved quickly on.

A short distance behind them in a private alcove sat a white haired old man with a flat cap and a whippet, who seemed to be playing solitaire. He chuntered to himself and sipped on a pint of beer as he laid the cards on the table.

"Mind if I join you?" said Hymie.

"As long as you don't go nicking me pint," said the old man.

"Please!" exclaimed Hymie. "I'm waiting for my friend to bring me a drink from the bar."

"Tight, eh?"

"I haven't touched a drop," said Hymie.

"Well, I expect your friend has taken a shine to Sarah," said the old man, "so he could be some time."

"Sarah?"

"The barmaid, nice girl, big knockers," said the old man, a little incongruously. "Which is fine as it happens, because I've been waiting to see you for some considerable time," he added.

"You have?" asked Hymie, beginning to wonder if the old guy was off his rocker.

"I have, Mr. Goldman...or would you prefer Shaw, or any of the other names you've been masquerading under?"

Goldman's jaw fell open. He could feel the hairs on the back of his neck standing on end and he desperately started trawling through the various old men with white hair he may have encountered in the past. He drew a blank.

"Do I know you?" he said at last.

"Obviously not," said the old man, "but you can call me Joe, blind Joe." He lifted his head to reveal his sunken eyes.

Hymie looked startled, having failed to notice; presumably due to the all-pervading darkness.

"We're looking for Elaine Brown," said Hymie, "Ring any bells?"

"I know you are," said blind Joe. "She was a wonderful woman, used to work here once. She was full of life, a real joy."

"So what happened to her? Where did she go?"

Blind Joe started shuffling his deck of cards as though he'd suddenly lost interest.

"Never you mind," he said, "I'm not here to answer questions, just to warn you."

"What about?" said Hymie, "The bar food? If it's about the seagulls, you're too late."

"You're not going to like it in Blackpool, Mr. Goldman, I can tell. I should catch the next train out of here if I were you. There's a gang in these parts that doesn't like your sort. Why, they killed two fellers at the Sun Lounge in the last couple o' weeks, just for talking too much."

"Do I look frightened?" said Hymie, bluffing. "I come from north London, mate."

"But you don't have a lucky face, I'm afraid," said blind Joe, "and I'd hate anything bad to happen to a tourist like yourself, like it happened to Elaine."

"Such as?"

"Lead poisoning, if you get my drift."

Hymie looked uneasily around the bar for Mike, but he was nowhere to be seen.

"Are you going to deal those cards, or what?"

"Humour me, Mr. Goldman, and take three cards from the deck."

He did as he was asked, placing them face down on the table in front of the old man.

Blind Joe reached out instinctively for the first card, turning it face up on the table and feeling the card's surface to identify it. It bore a picture of a man in a red cape with the words "The Magician" printed underneath. "The Past," he said. He proceeded to turn over the second card.

Hymie gulped. "The Devil…is that bad?" he asked.

Blind Joe whistled through his teeth. "It ain't good, son." Then he smiled. "Only kidding, it represents the present. It's not necessarily bad, it all depends…"

Hymie was about to ask "on what?" when Joe turned over the third and final card.

It bore a picture of a large man wrestling a lion in his boxer shorts with the single word "Strength" beneath the image.

"The future," said Joe.

"So, what does it all mean?" asked Hymie.

Blind Joe stared into space for a while before focusing on what he presumed was Hymie's face.

"You know, you might just be the man for the job after all," he said, cryptically, packing up his cards and putting his cap on. "C'mon, Ginger." His whippet yawned, stretched out its bony legs and peed all down Goldman's right trouser leg. Hymie lifted his leg and let the urine collect in a puddle on the floor.

"Oi, mush! What about my cleaning bill?" he snapped.

"Good luck to you," said blind Joe, shuffling off towards the pub's entrance, with his whippet, Ginger following behind.

"Next time, leave your stinking dog at home!"

No sooner had the old man left than Mike returned from the bar with two pints.

"What did you do, brew them yourself?" asked Hymie.

"I think I'm in love," said Mike.

"Gawd help us! What are the symptoms?"

"There's a dull ache in the centre of my chest that doesn't seem to want to go."

"My money's on indigestion. If it was a heart attack you'd be falling over the furniture by now," said Hymie, sympathetically.

"Her name's Sarah with an "h" and she's got lovely big..."

"No kidding."

"...blue eyes," explained Mike. "Anyway, you're a fine one to talk, the way you've been mooning after that Melody."

"I've never flashed my backside at anyone...well, not recently anyway," said Hymie, trying to change the subject. "Besides, while you've been chatting up the barmaid, I've been interviewing the locals...at least, I think he was local; some blind bloke with a whippet, called Joe."

"Did you find anything out?"

"Well, err...not exactly. He told my fortune with a pack of braille Tarot cards then pushed off with his dog, Ginger."

"I thought you said the dog was called Joe."

"No, the man was Joe, the dog was Ginger."

"You've been sniffing the Domestos again, haven't you Goldman?"

"Straight up, there was this old blind guy with white hair, sitting where you're sitting now, drinking his pint while his dog sat on the floor by his feet. Look, I've still got the dog pee on my trousers," said Hymie, pointing at them as though that explained everything.

"Had he ever heard of Elaine Brown?" asked Mike.

"Yeah, he said she was a lovely girl."

"And did he know where she'd gone?"

"Err…no, when I asked him that he warned me that I wouldn't like it in Blackpool then starting telling my fortune."

"So we're none the wiser then?"

"No," admitted Hymie, taking a swig of his pint. "Still, all this background information helps to build a picture."

"We've got all the bleedin' background we need, you nurk! Or at least we did have until you gave away the file to a passing seagull."

"I was robbed. Anyway, never mind, tomorrow's another day."

They finished their drinks then walked outside to the motorbike and sidecar, parked at the kerb.

Some distance off on the opposite side of the road, Inspector Decca of the Yard stared at them in disbelief. He took a small notebook from his left coat pocket and wrote something into it. He might have known; even while he was recuperating at a northern seaside resort, the twin spectres of Goldman and Murphy would never be very far away.

If he'd seen them a few weeks earlier he would have put it down to a figment of his fevered imagination and taken a couple of happy pills but as he was now largely medication-free, they had to be real. He removed his mobile phone from his right coat pocket and dialled a London number. There was only one man he could rely on in a crisis like this.

Part Fourteen

Back at the shack

O n the following morning Hymie and Mike sat in the open plan kitchen taking stock of their situation.

"Well, there's bugger all left to eat," said Mike, opening a cupboard door. "One scotch egg, half a jar of pickled onions and a tin of reformed ham."

"What's that then?" said Hymie. Ham that mixed with the wrong crowd, got rehabilitated and is now a better class of ham?"

"Very probably," said Mike, ignoring him, "but I don't fancy it for breakfast, do you?"

"Breakfast? Is that all you can think about at a time like this; food? Look, my massive chum, we've lost the case file, I've been threatened to leave town by a blind man with a whippet and any day now we're gonna get a call from an irate vicar asking where the hell his sister is...but never mind, what's for breakfast?"

"Oh shut it, Goldman. You lost the case file, you got threatened and you ate most of the food. Why don't you just bugger off back to London and leave me to it. I'll even give you a lift."

"What, in that death trap? I'd rather take a taxi."

"So go on then."

"Wait a minute, wait a minute…there's something going on here that you haven't told me about, isn't there?"

"I've got a date," said Mike.

"Oh, yes…the cross-eyed woman with the hump, Sarah with an 'r,' wasn't it|?"

"With an 'h,'" said Mike, "and if you know what's good for you, you won't talk about her like that again," he added.

"I see," said Hymie, "have it your way."

"Besides, while you were farting around with blind Pew I was busy pumping Sarah for all the local news and she was a mine of useful information."

"Really? In what way?"

"She told me all about the recent murders of a local comedian and his hotelier friend at a local dive called the Sun Lounge."

"Fascinating," said Hymie, "but what's that got to do with our case?"

"The police are working on a theory that a local gang is behind it all."

"Yes, but Elaine Brown disappeared years ago. How could it be the same people?"

"I dunno," said Mike, "but anything's possible."

"Come to think of it, blind Joe did mention a local gang in connection with her disappearance."

"What did I tell you? Anyway, I'm off to see Sarah, now," said Mike, "I've had enough of your ugly mug."

"And what am I supposed to do for transport?"

"There's a very good tram service."

"Yeah, if you like old bone-shakers and you live in Blackpool, not out here in the sticks," said Hymie, aggrieved.

"You'll find out much more without me coming along," said Mike. "I may be brilliant, handsome and handy with my fists, but I'm hardly unobtrusive."

Hymie looked at his partner's Hawaiian beach shirt again and nodded. He could hardly skive off with Mike hanging around so it made some kind of sense to let him go off with Esmeralda, or Quasimodo, or whatever her name was.

"Just give me a few minutes for a shower and a shave and I'll drop you off in town," said Mike.

Half an hour later, the Norton and sidecar blasted off down the lane in the direction of the gaudy metropolis that was Blackpool.

Part Fifteen

Sunshine, lollipops and rainbows

Hymie hadn't arrived at the Sun Lounge, Blackpool with any preconceived ideas of what it might look like; which was just as well, as it looked like nothing on earth.

Apart from the boards over the windows and the taped outline of a body on the driveway there was an all-pervading smell of horse shit, which even the most ardent rhubarb grower might have found distracting. He walked through the entrance doors, holding his nose and approached the desk hesitantly.

"Are you still open to the public?" he asked.

"Last time I looked," said the receptionist, "although we're not as busy as we were, what with the murders and the manure."

"Murders!" queried Hymie. The manure was self-evident.

"Yes, didn't you know?" asked the girl. "Two of them, in the last few weeks; the owner of the hotel. Vic Knight, and a ventriloquist called Smith. Where have you been?"

"Oh, I'm from London," said Hymie.

"I see. You'll be used to it then."

"You've kept the place open all the same," he said.

"Well, business is business. Besides, people book months in advance so we can hardly let them down, can we?"

Hymie looked sceptical. If he'd booked this dump months in advance he'd have made an excuse on arrival and gone somewhere else.

"Are you staying or have you come for the cabaret?" asked the girl.

"Oh, there's a cabaret, is there?" he said. "That's brave of them, still performing after what happened to the ventriloquist. Come to think of it, what did happen to him?"

"Oh, he got shot," said the girl.

"Was he *that* bad?" said Hymie, trying to lighten the mood.

"Just in the wrong place at the wrong time, I guess."

"So, what is the cabaret?" he asked.

"A singer," said the girl. "She's called Dusty Roads and she sings Country and Western."

"I see. Well, why not?" said Hymie. It had to be better than staying in the hotel.

"She writes her own music and plays guitar. She plays the standards too."

"Really? Which way is it?" he asked.

"Through where the glass door used to be," she said, pointing, "then second on the left, past the bullet-holes in the wall."

"Thanks," he said, walking off.

He sat at the back of the room with his collar turned up like a comic-book detective and gestured to the waitress.

"Yes, bud?" she asked.

"A Mojito with lots of ice."

"Oh, you've got no chance of anything fancy with our barman, he's Nicaraguan. How about a beer?"

"Right you are," said Hymie, desperate for some alcohol.

On stage a plump blonde girl with artificially whitened teeth was struggling to tune her guitar while she adjusted her microphone. After a few bum notes she seemed to hit her stride and started to strum her instrument in earnest.

"OK, folks, this is a little song I wrote about my car, Peggy; Peggy the VW," said Dusty, strumming a few bars before launching into it.

"She comes in three colours,

Rust, green and blue,

Her aerial broke so I fixed it…

With glue.

She flies like the wind,

When she's rolling downhill,

But her gearbox is knackered,

So she won't go uphill.

Peggy, my darlin' oh, Peggy it's true,

You're no Maserati but you're my V …double you."

"Oh, god, this is awful," muttered Hymie.

BANG!

A pint glass clattered down on the table in front of him, spilling a generous measure of the beer across its polished surface.

"That'll be £6.50, chump, just pay at the bar before you leave!"

"What did I do?" asked Hymie, looking at the waitress in concern.

"I'll tell you, shall I?" she began, a rising inflexion in her voice. "That girl up there is the sweetest, kindest girl you could ever wish to meet. She's only doing this as a favour to help raise money for my granddad's hip operation, so if you want to make something of it then I'll see you outside in the car park later."

"OK, OK, I get it, I'm sorry," he spluttered. "I'll buy her CD. What's the matter with this town?"

The waitress turned smartly on her heels and headed back to the bar, while Dusty droned on endlessly about the appalling mediocrity of German engineering.

As Hymie started to down what was left of his pint, three short, stout, heavily bearded men in overcoats sat down at his table and stared ominously at him. On closer inspection they all appeared to be spray-tanned.

"Do I know you?" he asked, not unreasonably. He wondered if someone had put something in his drink as everything was beginning to seem very strange, even by the standards of a man who existed on the fringes of normal society.

"You don't know us, but we know you, Haimy," said one of the beardy men.

Hymie's mind raced as he tried to figure out who they could be. How had they found him, in Blackpool of all places? What did they want? And were those beards genuine or worn for effect? Surely they couldn't be the Finklestein brothers?

Years earlier he'd had three clients, Clem, Bart and

Roy Finklestein. He'd never actually met any of them, but succeeded in fleecing them for services rendered in trying to find their lost hamster, Stan. Clearly they'd really loved little Stan, because they'd paid him a hundred quid a month for five years before realising that hamsters didn't live that long.

"Is it about Stan?" he asked, quietly.

The three men looked puzzled.

"Look, he was old, it was just his time," added Hymie. "I'm sure we'll all laugh about this one day," he said, slowly rising from his chair.

"Who the hell is Stan?" asked Clem.

"Sit down, Goldman," said Bart. "It's nothing to do with Stan, whoever he is."

Hymie sat back down and tried to relax. At least these nutters weren't the Finklesteins.

"We're only going to tell you once," said Mr. X.

"Well, maybe twice," said his bearded chum, Mr. Y.

"But definitely not three times," said Mr. Z.

"Get out of our town, Goldman!" cried Mr. X.

"Or we won't be responsible for the consequences," said Mr. Y.

Mr. Z was too busy picking his nose to join in the chorus of disapproval.

"Look, I don't mean to be rude or anything, but you're not exactly frightening me. I mean, you're just three short, fat, beardy blokes. My business partner, Mr. Murphy could wipe the floor with you with one arm tied behind his back," said Hymie, wishing Mike was actually there to back him up.

"A man with no respect could come to serious grief in this town," said Mr. Z, once the three of them had stopped frothing at the mouth. "He might find himself waking up with his nadgers superglued to his forehead. Do you get me, Goldie?"

Hymie nodded. He'd been about to make his excuses and leave when a familiar voice called out from behind him.

"Hello, Hymie, how nice to bump into you. I see you've been making some new friends." It was Melody.

The three men froze in their seats. It was as though they'd been dipped in liquid nitrogen.

"More like acquaintances, really," said Hymie.

"Play nicely, boys," said Melody to the three stooges. They smiled nervously at her.

"I'm sure you have somewhere else to be, don't you?" she added.

"Yes, ma'am," they agreed in unison, nodding like three dogs in a car's rear window.

"Have a good evening, ma'am," said Mr. X, leading his associates out of the room.

"Do you know those men?" asked Hymie.

"Not really," said Melody, sitting down in the seat opposite him. She waved a waitress over to their table.

"I'll have a Mojito," said Melody, "and whatever he's having."

"Make that two," said Hymie, smirking at the waitress. She slunk off.

"So, how are you getting on?" she asked.

"Well, we have a few leads, some different angles to explore…lots of angles."

"I see."

"Mike's out following up a lead from *The Last Lights.*"

"Oh, you've been there, have you? What did you think of the place?"

"It was an awful dump."

"Yes, I know. People only go there when they don't want to be found. No-one said the case would be easy," said Melody. "But while you're in town, perhaps you'd like to take me out sometime."

Hymie smiled at her. "I'd love to," he said. "Where would you like to go?"

"Meet me at the Tower Ballroom tomorrow at four o'clock. There's a tea dance on. Behave yourself and I might even dance with you."

She sipped her drink, then placed it on the table and stood up.

"It's been fun, Hymie but I must dash. Daddy doesn't like it if I stay out late."

She finished her drink then disappeared like a mirage in the desert.

Hymie stared after her. He couldn't quite believe he had a date with the hottest babe he'd ever met. He walked over to the bar to settle his tab. Behind the bar stood an old man in a waistcoat.

"I haven't seen you before," said Hymie. "You're not new here are you?"

"I'm not new anywhere, sir. I used to work behind the bar until I retired, but I still help out every now and then."

"I don't suppose you remember a girl called Elaine Brown?"

"I do indeed. She used to work here as a barmaid years ago. She used to put it about quite a bit too, she was a real looker. They all fancied her, you know."

"Did she have any *special* friends?" asked Hymie, proffering a twenty pound note.

"I can't say as I remember too clearly, sir."

Hymie proffered another.

"Now I come to think of it, there was a rumour she was involved with that ventriloquist feller."

"Mr. Smith?"

"That's him, the chap that got shot just over there," he said, pointing at the stage where Dusty Roads was murdering another Country and Western standard.

"Thanks," said Hymie.

"That'll be £24.95, said the barman."

"Take it out of what I just gave you," said Hymie, heading off to find a taxi.

"Cheapskate," muttered the barman.

Part Sixteen

The Man from the Smoke

A granite-faced, clean-shaven man in his late thirties sat on a crowded coach as it pulled into Blackpool Central bus depot. His name was Sergeant Barry Terse and he was there to visit his boss, mentor and yes, damn it, his friend; Inspector Ray Decca of the Yard. So what if the guy had completely gone off his rocker and was looping the loop at ten thousand feet? He clearly needed his help.

When the Inspector had called him up in the middle of the night raving on about some waxworks thefts in Blackpool he'd tried to pretend he was the Chinese takeaway, but it hadn't worked so he'd had to promise to come and visit him in cloud cuckoo-land. As he'd tried to explain to Decca on the phone, no-one in their right mind would be nicking waxworks, but then as his erstwhile boss was in a psychiatric hospital and this was *The North*, perhaps normal logic ceased to apply.

He put the dog-eared copy of *The Oxford Book of Quotations* he'd been reading into his rucksack and prepared to get off the coach. It was a 1950s edition he'd bought cheap in a charity shop to impress his bosses at work with a quote for every occasion. It was hopeless. He took the book out again and flicked through it one last time. Who the fuck was G.W. Hunt anyway? If he started quoting people no-one had ever heard of he was just going to look like some schmuck. He knew he should have bought *Zen and the Art of Motorcycle Maintenance* instead. Ah well, he could kiss goodbye to that twenty pence. He placed the book down on his seat as a gift for the next passenger and stood up to get off.

Sometimes it was better to travel than to arrive. As the coach finally pulled to a halt there was a surge of bodies, all desperately trying to be first off. A large group of immaculately coiffured ladies from the Manchester Women's Institute gravitated effortlessly to the front.

"Mind out, mind out!" said Terse, pushing the other passengers forcefully out of the way. "I have an errand of mercy to perform," he added, bludgeoning one of their number; a lady with a purple rinse, with his rucksack. By the time he reached the front passenger door there was a trail of mown down passengers in his wake like a strike in a bowling alley.

"Driver!" cried one of the passengers, holding her head, "that man's a menace, call the police."

"Madam, I am the police!" barked Terse, flashing his Metropolitan Police ID card.

There was a momentary pause in the carnage as the crowd digested this shocking revelation and Terse exploited it to the full by jumping off the coach.

Decca had texted to say he would meet him at the bus station, but there was nobody there except a Sikh gentleman with a long beard and turban, studying the timetable on the wall with exaggerated concentration. As Terse stared at the man he sidled up to him suspiciously.

"Psst! It's me," said the Sikh.

Terse stared at the man in disbelief.

"Decca!" explained the Sikh.

"Good lord, sir! What have they done to you?" said Terse.

"It's a disguise, you fool!" snapped Decca.

The sound of a gang of Women's Institute members re-grouping on the bus filtered through Terse's confused mind.

"Let's get out of here," said Terse.

"Follow me!" cried Decca, running out of the bus station and along the pavement in the direction of the nearest pub.

Inside "The Castle" the two policemen sat nursing their pints in a quiet corner.

"Why the disguise, Chief?"

"I think they're on to me, Barry."

"Who?"

"The Beach Buoys."

The sergeant stared pitifully at his former boss. This man had been a shining beacon of law enforcement in Greater London for years. Now he was sitting in the snug of a Blackpool pub with boot polish on his face under the delusion that an American pop group from the Sixties were after him. How sad and pointless it all seemed.

"Why, sir? Why would a Sixties surf band have it in for you?"

Decca removed his turban and placed it on the table in front of him.

"Don't be ridiculous, Terse. Not the Beach Boys, the Beach *Buoys*. They're a local mob of thugs and gangsters, generally up to no good and seemingly beyond the law. Which reminds me, did I mention I saw Goldman and Murphy the other night? They were standing outside a pub called *The Last Lights*. Admittedly it was dark, but they're not hard to recognise."

"Ah, right, I see, sir," said Terse. The jury was clearly still out on his former boss's mental health. "But why would the Beach Buoys be following *you* around and what would those two idiots be doing this far from London?"

"I must admit, even *I* thought I was seeing things when Goldman and Murphy showed up, but it looks like they're on some sort of case."

"What, more missing hamsters?"

"I know; it's unbelievable! As for the local crime gang, they have informants everywhere and they're sure to know I'm after them by now," said Decca. "I saw them with my own eyes nicking body parts from the Waxworks."

"What, *wax* body parts?" queried Terse.

"Obviously," said Decca.

"Well, so what? Who cares? Leave it to the local police. You're meant to be here for a rest and some sea air."

"Sea air my arse," said Decca. "I've a feeling they're moving more than waxwork body parts around this town, Barry…" he said, lowering his voice to a whisper. "I mean cocaine."

"I'm sure you're right, Chief, but the fact remains, it's not your problem."

"Technically you may be right but I've met the local police. A bigger bunch of numpties you couldn't wish to meet. There was an Irish DS called O'Malley who constantly took the piss out of me for coming from London, as if that somehow meant I couldn't solve a case in Blackpool, and his assistant; a nice girl called Arkwright, who lost interest when I told her where I was staying."

"Where was that then, sir?"

"A local rest home for policemen called *Crackpots*! I ask you, what kind of an idiot would call it that?"

Terse suppressed a snigger. 'Someone with a sense of humour' he thought. "Well, who's to say she wasn't right, sir?" he said. "There are plenty of us stuck fighting crime at the sharp end who'd give their eye teeth for a few days rest and recuperation in Blackpool and here's you throwing it all away to get back to the madhouse."

"You can take the man out of the job, but not the other way around, Barry."

Terse yawned. It wasn't so much that his former boss was talking bullshit as the fact that he'd had a long day and needed some sleep.

"You know me, sir, always happy to bash a few bad guys, but I could do with a kip. Can you recommend a place to stay?"

"I can do better than that, Barry; I've booked you into the Premier Inn down the road under the name of Brian Wilson. Well, you can't be too careful," said Decca.

Part Seventeen

Muffins and mayhem

The Tower Ballroom, Blackpool is a grand and stylish place, widely regarded as the jewel in the crown of venues in the north-west of England, if not further afield. Every week it hosts a myriad of dances, shows, talks and exhibitions for visitors from all corners of the globe; flocking to its sophisticated and glamourous charms like moths to a flame. They rarely get burned, of course, except on that curious occasion a few years ago which came to be known as the *Victoria Sponge Massacre*.

It began innocently enough. Hymie Goldman had told his business partner, Mike Murphy that he was meeting his new love-interest, Melody at the afternoon tea dance. Mike, seizing the opportunity to impress *his* new amour, Sarah, with an "h," began badgering him to make it a double date. Finally, Goldman's resistance had crumbled. He needed a lift anyway.

H, M and S arrived shortly before 4pm and, after expressing an interest in afternoon tea, were directed to a table among the throng in the elegant hall by an immaculately attired young lady in a black dress with a white embroidered apron and cap. The room itself was an elaborate Victorian ballroom with a spectacular wooden dance-floor in the centre, surrounded by dozens of tables and chairs for those who either preferred tea and cake to dancing or needed to catch their breath after overdoing it in the tango.

Once seated, they placed an order for tea with plenty of cake, scones, clotted cream and strawberry jam, and sat gawping at the elegance and splendour of their surroundings. At the far end of the room lay a magnificent antique stage, above it a stylish hand-carved and painted façade bearing the words "Bid me discourse, I will enchant thine ear," while the walls on either side were festooned with ornately decorated balconies. It was clearly the destination of choice for the discerning geriatrics of the north-west, who seemed to delight in swaying rhythmically across the dance-floor to the sensual sounds of a bygone era. To Mike and Hymie it was the most ostentatious café they'd ever been in.

"I don't think she's coming," said Hymie sadly.

Mike looked at his watch and scanned the horizon for cake while Sarah tried to sound reassuring. "Oh, she'll be here. There's a woman for every man. If you look hard enough."

Hymie cast a last despairing look at the dance-floor and then stopped in his tracks.

"Mike, she's here!"

Mike turned around to follow Hymie's gaze. "Well, that's a surprise. It looks like she really does want to dance with you after all, mate. I'd get out there sharpish if I were you."

"But I can't dance."

"I don't think it matters," said Mike, "just get out there, hold her in your arms and try not to tread on her toes."

"You don't think it will compromise my professionalism, dancing with the client's daughter?"

"What professionalism?"

Carried away in the moment, Hymie leapt from his chair as though he'd just sat on a hedgehog, attempted in vain to straighten his tie and strode boldly out onto the dance-floor. Melody put her arms around him and smiled as they drifted off into the land of dreams.

It was just as Hymie surrendered to the sensual pleasures of dancing with a beautiful woman that Decca and Terse clapped eyes on him.

"Goldman at four o'clock, Terse."

"I've already got 'im in me sights, Chief," said Terse, narrowly resisting the urge to look at his watch. "I was just wondering how we were gonna get 'im out of here without causing a disturbance," he added. "Shall I just lob this scone at his head?"

A smile flitted briefly across the Inspector's face at the thought of it.

Out on the dance-floor, Hymie didn't need the night or the music, he was floating on air; his feet buoyed up by the nearness of Melody and her silky smooth touch. Still, it came as something of a surprise when a scone, liberally plastered with jam and cream ricocheted off his shoulder and hit a lady with a purple rinse, Barbara Willoughby-Smythe in the side of the head. Clearly with Terse to think was to act. To say the lady took this broadside in good spirits would be something of an exaggeration. She wiped away as much of the squashed scone, jam and cream as she could and glowered, gimlet-eyed around the room until her searchlights locked on to the culprit. Sergeant Terse had made the mistake of clenching his fist in triumph as his projectile first made contact with Goldman's shoulder. She snorted with rage as she recognised her assailant as that rude policeman from the coach station and rallied reinforcements from the Manchester Women's Institute who were sitting posting cakes into their faces at a table nearby.

Hymie remained blissfully unaware. The only thing troubling him was why a gorgeous bird seemed to be enjoying dancing with him. Had he come into a fortune overnight or was this all just a dream? He simply decided to go with the flow. After all, it was what he did best in life.

Mike meanwhile had clocked the men from the Smoke and was trying to catch Hymie's eye. It wasn't proving easy. Goldman seemed to be off with the fairies; floating around the room in a world of his own.

All across the ballroom, things were getting ugly; far uglier than Goldman's dancing.

The crowd seemed to be coalescing into four distinct groups or gangs; the Manchester Women's Institute under the nominal leadership of Mrs Willoughby-Smythe, a group of antediluvian sailors from an amateur Gilbert and Sullivan society, recognizable by their peaked caps bearing the name "HMS Pilchard," a group of short, heavily bearded men with fake tans and dark glasses; Hymie's friends, the non-Finkelsteins, and two policemen from the Met., a long way off their beat; Decca and Terse.

The Londoners looked out of place and were clearly not popular with anyone. Rightly regarded as being the cause of the trouble, they were also massively outnumbered.

In a surge of righteous indignation, the ladies of the Manchester Women's Institute collected armfuls of cakes from their own table and others and bore down on the policemen with grim determination. Decca gulped while Terse finally checked his watch and realised he needed to be somewhere else...anywhere else. But it was too late! Armed to the teeth with scones, fairy cakes and a devastating array of crème-patisserie the purple-rinsed harpies unleashed their armoury of confectionery.

"Run, sir!" cried Terse. They were the last words he was able to utter before being obliterated in a tidal wave of cake-borne destruction. Decca turned to look for the door but had no chance to escape as he was mown down seconds later by a barrage of flying carbohydrates. They fell where they had stood, like the last victims of the devastating volcano at Pompeii; two human forms modelled in cake.

Barbara Willoughby-Smythe looked on in triumph. She may still be having a bad hair day, courtesy of Terse, but her face said it all; no-one messed with the ladies of the Women's Institute and got away with it.

Meanwhile in the chaos, hostilities seemed to be breaking out in all directions. Many of the ballroom's regulars had legged it at the first sign of bother, leaving a hard core of trouble makers behind. The sailors of HMS Pilchard, not wishing to be left out of this once in a lifetime cake-fest began picking a fight with the non-Finkelsteins, but they were so short and agile it was quite difficult to actually hit them.

Cakes were flying in all directions. To assistant duty manager, Bobby Battenberg it seemed to be raining cake. Nothing they'd ever taught him in training had prepared him for this sort of thing, but he did his best. He stepped out into the melee on the dance-floor and, blowing his emergency whistle, started waving his arms about wildly.

"Ladies! Gentlemen! This has to stop!"

For a few seconds it looked like he was about to turn the tide, but then one of the waitresses, who'd never liked him since he'd insulted her favourite boy-band, decided to settle an old score. Removing a slice of black forest gateaux from a nearby cake-stand she flung it enthusiastically at the back of Bobby's head. Unfortunately, he turned around while the cake was in flight and caught the brown gooey mess squarely in the face. The whipped cream, cherries and chocolate slid down his shirtfront and jacket, leaving him a spent force as the voice of authority so he made a strategic withdrawal to his office to call for back-up.

Not even Goldman could remain oblivious to the carnage. At first the notion of flying cake had seemed rather jolly and somehow in keeping with his delirious state of mind, but the close shave with Terse's scone and a subsequent encounter with a flying slice of strawberry cheesecake had brought him to his senses. Mike had reluctantly thrown it at him as the only possible way of attracting his attention. Once Mike had apprised him of the presence of Decca, Terse and the Beach Buoys, not to mention the impending arrival of the local police force, Hymie had rallied sufficiently to appreciate the need for a hasty retreat.

"Melody, I'm sorry but we need to leave," said Hymie, sadly.

"Where are we going?" she asked.

"I mean Mike and I need to leave. There are people after us."

"People?"

"Well, I use the term loosely," he said. "Two policemen from London. They've got it in for us."

"They follow us around asking awkward questions," added Mike.

"So you're both just going to run out on us?" said Sarah, with a dollop of whipped cream sliding down her impressive cleavage.

"Yes," said Hymie. "Reluctantly, of course."

"But we'll be back," said Mike.

"Oh, fantastic!" said Sarah, sarcastically. "You're a right couple of charmers, aren't you, running out when the going gets tough. What about my dry cleaning bill?"

"Any other time we'd move heaven and earth to stay," said Hymie, ignoring the bill.

"But needs must," said Mike.

Melody put her hand on Hymie's shoulder and whispered in his ear.

"Meet me at the entrance to North Pier in an hour's time," she said.

He nodded.

"Well, you'll certainly have a lot of making up to do the next time I see you, Mike Murphy," said Sarah.

"You can count on it," said Murphy, following his cake-covered partner to the nearest exit.

Part Eighteen

A nod's as good as a wink

Four police officers sat staring at each other in a small interview room in Blackpool Central Police station. Two of them; DS O'Malley and WPC Arkwright had the unflappable air of people who belonged there. On the other side of the desk, Inspector Decca and Sergeant Terse of the Met., looking much the worse for their recent run-in with a wall of cake, would clearly have preferred to be elsewhere.

"Do you have any idea how many holding cells we have?" asked O'Malley.

"Twelve?" ventured Terse.

"It was a rhetorical question!" snapped O'Malley. "The point I was trying to make was that *you*," he continued, glaring at Terse, "have managed to fill them all with little old ladies, amateur thespians and tourists in one ill-advised act of infantile stupidity at the premier entertainment venue of the North-West!"

"Well…I…err…" said Terse, not wishing to take all the credit.

"Shut-up, Terse!" cried Decca, who firmly believed

that when you were in a hole it was advisable to stop digging.

"So, Roy," said O'Malley, looking at the Inspector, "I take it you don't mind me calling you Roy?"

"Be my guest, although my name's Ray," said Decca.

WPC Arkwright smirked.

"Roy, Ray...it's all the same really. You're still a Grade A idiot," said O'Malley, shrugging off the suggestion that he should be embarrassed. "Look, Ray, from one copper to another, I'm appealing to you, what are we doing here, eh Ray?"

Decca looked a little surprised. "You know, that's a question I've often asked myself; what's it all about? What are we here for?"

"I only meant, what the hell are you playing at causing a scene on my patch? I wasn't looking for a metaphysical debate on the meaning of life. Are we clear, Ray?"

"Crystal clear," said Decca. He wasn't at the psychiatrists now.

"Good. Now, I've only brought you in here to avoid any unpleasantness," explained DS O'Malley. "Fortunately, no-one was injured. So if you can just assure me that you're both willing to pay for any damage, dry-cleaning bills and hair-do's for the party from the Women's Institute then I suggest you just leave quietly via the rear exit and never darken my door again. We don't need the paperwork. Do you agree?"

"Do I understand you, correctly?" began Terse, "you're running us out of town?"

Decca was about to tell Terse to put a sock in it when

he reflected and found himself in the unusual position of agreeing with the Sergeant.

"But this is Blackpool, not Dodge City!" snapped Decca. "I think you'll find you can't do that, even this far off the beaten track."

"Fine, have it your way," said DS O'Malley. "Stay, by all means. We only have the inconvenience and a little loss of face…if you really want me to file the reports WPC Arkwright has written about you then you can say goodbye to your future career in the police force. You'd be lucky to get a job handing out traffic tickets in the Outer Hebrides."

"But I can help, damn it! I'm a good policeman. Even Terse here is a good policeman," said Decca. "Since I last saw you I've been staking out the waxworks on the front and I've made a breakthrough. There's this gang of short, heavily bearded umpah-lumpah types."

"The Beach Buoys?" said Arkwright, "I knew it!"

"So you do know about them," said Decca. "Anyway, these characters seem to have been using the waxworks to store and transport Class A drugs around the area. I caught them decapitating Rod Stewart."

"Your testimony may carry more weight if you weren't an escaped mental patient covered in cake," said O'Malley dismissively.

"But what he said makes sense," admitted Arkwright, quietly.

"Look, O'Malley, I'm not making this up. Doesn't the eyewitness account of an Inspector of the Metropolitan Police count for anything in these parts? I know you want us off your patch, but if we can help you round up a major drugs cartel before we leave then that has to be worth a punt, surely?"

"What do you suggest?" asked O'Malley.

"Get a warrant to search the waxworks and let Terse and I take a look at the mug shots for some of the likeliest local criminals," said Decca.

"Especially any short ones with beards," added Terse.

O'Malley looked at his watch, "Scruffy Murphy's" would be opening soon and he had some unfinished business with a pint and a short.

"I expect we could make a few enquiries," he said, grudgingly. "Arkwright, see to this would you, I have a call of nature to attend to. And get rid of those trouble makers from the Women's Institute while I'm out too."

"Yes, sir," said Arkwright. She was still doing all the donkey work, but at least there was a glimmer of a hope of arresting some real criminals for once. A change was as good as a rest.

Part Nineteen

Beating a hasty retreat

I t was all in a day's work for Hymie and Mike; go out on the town, cause trouble, leg it before the police get there. It didn't even matter if someone else caused the disturbance, just as long as you got out before the rozzers arrived, everything would be fine and dandy. So it proved to be. Yes, there was that worrying moment when they thought they'd have to climb out of the toilet window, but at the eleventh hour Hymie had bribed a security guard to let them out of the fire escape. It had been costly, but it was better than being apprehended while your arse was hanging out of a window-frame or, worse still, stuck in one.

They'd surfaced in a side alley beside the entrance to the Tower Ballroom, just in time to see Decca and Terse being stretchered away in cake overcoats. It couldn't have happened to a nicer pair of idiots.

They started to walk away from the carnage, heading downtown, before ducking into a café for a long overdue case discussion. Once the coffee and biscuits arrived the feast of reason began.

"What was it my old dad used to say?" said Hymie.

"I can't wait," said Mike. "To hear you, the old sod never shut up. I swear you make it all up as you go along."

"I see," said Hymie, narked. "Well, one of his favourite expressions was 'finding the truth is easy, you just eliminate all the stuff that makes no sense.'"

"No wonder we're not getting anywhere," said Mike, "by the time we've discounted all the stuff that makes no sense there's nothing left."

"At least we're getting somewhere on the romance front," said Hymie. "We've both been blessed with more luck with women than we've ever had in our lives before. We should have come to Blackpool years ago!"

"I don't deny it," agreed Mike. "Which is why we're in no hurry to solve the case, but it would be nice if we had something to report to the Reverend Brown when he finally catches up with us. I mean, 'we don't know what happened to your sister, Elaine and by the way, a seagull ate the file' just makes us look stupid."

"Well, obviously we'll put some positive spin on it," said Hymie.

"Go on then."

"Err…well, err…Elaine Brown had a relationship with the ventriloquist who got shot."

"Mr. Smith," said Mike.

"That's him. He used to work at that crappy hotel where the owner got shot."

"The Sun Lounge," said Mike.

"Yeah," said Hymie. "She used to work there too, as a barmaid."

"So far, so good," said Mike, "there's definitely something dodgy going on at the Sun Lounge."

"Exactly, people linked to the place seem to be dropping like flies."

"So, do you think she's dead?" asked Mike.

"I dunno. But if she is we're gonna need some proof."

"Right," said Mike. "But if we assume she's dead for now, who killed her and what was the motive?"

"What did she know?" asked Hymie.

"Or what did someone think she knew?"

"Well, it's usually either sex or money," said Hymie, "sometimes both. Was she killed by a jealous lover or did she know too much about some illegal activity?"

"Like drug dealing or racketeering," said Mike.

"You may be onto something," said Hymie. "Now I come to think of it, Elaine Brown used to work as a barmaid at *The Last Lights* too. Now that place really is a dive. What did Melody say about it? 'People only go there when they don't want to be found.' That's it, Mike! She was hiding out there. We have to go back."

"I thought Blind Pew warned you to get out of Blackpool," said Mike.

"All the more reason for *you* to go," agreed Hymie. "Just watch out for the whippet, my trousers have never been the same since."

"You're pathetic. You should be ashamed of being afraid of a little dog. As it happens, I don't mind at all. Apart from the obvious attractions of Sarah..."

"I know," said Hymie.

"I happen to think there's more to that place than

meets the eye," said Mike. "Remember that bunch of bearded midgets we followed in there? Well, don't you think it was funny how they just disappeared once we got inside? On top of which, we still haven't figured out what Decca and Terse are doing here. They don't strike me as the Blackpool type."

"Nor did we until we got here," said Hymie, "and now look at us; the place is like a home from home."

"Anyway, I've got plenty of avenues to explore, so what are you gonna be doing while I'm bustin' a gut?"

"I've arranged to meet Melody on the pier," admitted Hymie.

"What, so I'll be working flat out while you're chatting up your bird?" said Mike.

"Mike, please, she's the client's daughter and an integral part of the case. Besides, you'll be conducting investigations with a certain barmaid, won't you? So don't pretend you're getting a raw deal."

"Yeah, but they say you shouldn't mix business with pleasure."

"Chance would be a fine thing," agreed Hymie.

"If you're planning a night on the tiles, how do you plan to get home? We've only got one motorbike and sidecar."

"I know, and it's my turn to drive it," said Hymie. "Keys!" he added, holding out his hand.

Mike passed him the keys. "It'll be worth it, just to watch you making an even bigger ass of yourself than usual. Incidentally, do you have any idea how to drive it?"

"Oh, I'll be fine," blagged Hymie. "I've seen you drive it often enough. How hard can it be?" He picked up the helmet and gloves Mike had left on the table beside him and headed outside.

"Be lucky, mate," said Mike.

"You too," said Hymie. "I'll see you back at the Shed later."

Part Twenty

Shipwrecked

The pleasure pier is a peculiarly British institution; no seaside resort should be without one as they draw the crowds like some giant people-magnet. Holidaymakers never tire of walking the planks above or alongside the waves, particularly when combined with the delights of the amusement arcade, the ice-cream parlour and the end of the pier show. Blackpool is blessed with three of them, the oldest being North Pier, designed by the late, great Eugenius Birch in the 1860s and a modern wonder of the world ever since. Till now it had survived fires, vandalism, two world wars and the ravages of the Irish Sea but as Goldman was on his way there its chances of continuing this run of luck seemed remote.

Fortunately for him, the Pier was only a short walk along the Promenade from the Tower Ballroom so he pocketed the keys to the Norton and made his way to what he hoped would be an illicit rendezvous with Melody on shank's pony. It was a beautiful evening, cold but bright, with a battery of gaily coloured electric bulbs along the sea front lit up like a million stars against the purple sky.

The entrance to North Pier looked like a Mexican Luchador's leotard; brash, colourful and in your face. Hymie poked his head inside the amusement arcade beneath the "North Pier" sign just in case Melody was there, but all he saw was a bunch of louts whacking a mole with a rubber mallet. They'd probably never seen a real mole before, but obviously enjoyed senseless violence so he turned around and walked out again. He walked further along the promenade and leant against the handrail looking out to sea. God it was grim. Spectacular, in a garish, Las Vegas kind of way, but also somehow bleak and remote from civilisation. He wondered if this was what the end of the world would look like; a perfect sunset over a grotty heap of man-made squalor. Would she turn up? Admittedly she'd turned up at the Tower Ballroom, but twice in one day?

"Hello, Hymie," said a voice behind him. "What kept you?"

He turned to find Melody sitting on a bench inside a green wooden rain shelter, smiling at him. She was truly beautiful; shining blue eyes, a mass of brown curls and an hourglass figure. Why on earth was she interested in him?

"Well, I had to wait for a taxi and then I realised I hadn't got any cash so I started to walk," he said, just for something to say.

"Come and sit beside me then," she said, patting the bench. He did as he was told.

"Since I've met you, Hymie, I've been feeling very differently about the world in general."

"Oh, sorry," he said.

She laughed. "Don't be. I don't know how or why exactly, but you make me feel so happy."

"Don't let me stop you," he said, smiling.

"Nothing seems to faze you. You take everything in your stride. Kiss me, and promise that you'll stay, whether you solve the case or not."

He certainly wanted to, but he didn't quite believe she could be for real. It didn't even matter that she seemed to have written him off as a private detective. Sitting this close to her, even the prospect of a life sentence in Blackpool failed to revolt him.

"You won't disappear if I kiss you, will you?" he asked, edging closer still. "I've met your sort before, figments of the imagination. Aren't I a bit old for you?" he asked, giving her every last chance to let him down gently before he committed himself.

"Don't be silly, life's too short to worry about things like that, believe me, I know."

It seemed a bit unfair to lumber such a sweet girl with him as a romantic lead, but his resistance continued to crumble like a landslide in a nutty slack factory.

"I understand, you've lost people you loved, haven't you?" asked Hymie, "like your Aunt Elaine. Do you have any memories of her?"

"No, not really...I was only little when she die...I mean, disappeared. My father told me stories about her as I was growing up; about how wonderful she was and how she adored me. You know what parents are like."

Hymie thought about the sad and disapproving looks his parents had given him and fell silent.

705

"Did you know I'm adopted?" asked Melody.

"No," said Hymie. "So the Reverend Brown isn't your real father?"

"No," she said. "That's what adopted means,..but I've always looked on him as my dad. He was always there for me."

"I'm sorry, but you're lucky in a way; parents can be so judgemental, like they own you or something."

"I just wish he could put Aunt Elaine behind him and move on. But then, of course, if he had I'd never have met you."

'Poor girl, she really did have problems!' thought Hymie.

He turned to face her and their lips met in a passionate kiss. It almost took his breath away. She tasted like ripe cherries and smelt like wild flowers and he was lost in her embrace.

"Et in arcadia ego," she whispered, as their lips parted.

"Sorry?" said Hymie. "Was that Latin?" asked the man who could barely speak English.

"Yes," she said, smiling. "Growing up I had the best of everything; my own horse, skiing-holidays, a private education. It was only later I realised that everything comes at a price." She stood up, walked over to lean on the handrail on the sea front and gazed out to sea. Hymie followed her.

"Years ago the wreckers used to lure ships onto the mudflats along this coast. When the ships were grounded and couldn't get off the mud the gangs used to run out, steal their cargoes and murder their crews. Well, who needs witnesses?"

"How quaint!" said Hymie, "nowadays they just wait till you come ashore and rip you off instead."

"Oh, Hymie," said Melody, "how I wish we'd met under different circumstances; better circumstances. There's so much you don't know about me."

"Well, I am a detective, you know…perhaps I could find out?"

She giggled. "So you're going to figure me out?"

"Precisely, or at least, Murphy and I are. We may look like visitors from another planet and we're certainly a long way from home, but we know what we're doing. Liberty, egality and fraternity are our watchwords."

"I didn't know you were French," said Melody. Hymie looked confused.

They walked hand in hand down the Promenade to where Mike had parked the Norton and shared one final dazzling kiss in the moonlight before heading off in opposite directions.

Part Twenty-One

Burned

Hymie stood alone at the kerbside and eyed the Norton warily. Now that Melody had gone he could at least *try* to ride it, instead of posturing beside it. He knew he'd look a right idiot if he fell off the bike, but at least there were no witnesses. He retrieved the helmet and gloves he'd stashed in the sidecar and, wrestling them on with difficulty, mounted the bike with a confidence borne of ignorance. If Mike could ride it, how hard could it be?

It had been a long day and he craved the peace and quiet of the Shed, not to mention getting on the outside of whatever was left inside the larder.

Hymie turned the key in the motorbike's ignition, kicked down on the starter as he'd seen Mike do and was met by a reassuring roar as the engine burst into life. He knew where the accelerator was and by a process of elimination worked out where the front brakes were but other than that he was still clueless. He looked down at the bewildering array of pegs and posts and began to have serious doubts he could actually drive the thing. Still, there was no point in feeling lost and out of his depth; it was a long walk home so he simply had to work out how to ride it. With another lucky kick the Norton lurched off down the road in first gear and Hymie decided to settle for that. Sod the embarrassment; no-one was going to recognise him anyway.

It's amazing how slowly the scenery passes by at ten miles per hour, when you're used to travelling faster. Still, as it was now dark and Hymie was rather preoccupied with not falling off the bike, there was precious little scenery to focus on. Neon lights winked, chip wrappers fluttered by and the occasional curtain twitched at the passing of the slow-motion joy-rider from North Finchley. The Norton contented itself with a low growl of disapproval.

Out on the open road, as he headed through the outlying district of Weeton with a million stars twinkling overhead, Hymie began to relax. There was something strangely reassuring, even soothing about travelling at ten miles per hour and he found himself reflecting on Melody and what a wonderful place Blackpool was. There was a distant ringing like fairy bells and an attractive orange glow in the sky over the place he was heading to and for once it seemed that God was in his heaven and all was right with the world.

It was only as he drew closer to the Shed that he realised all was not well, not by a million miles. The orange glow in the sky had been transformed into a flaming inferno with grey smoke billowing up into the clouds and two fire engines were dousing what was left of their accommodation with jets of water.

Hymie released the accelerator and applied the brakes with such force that he was nearly thrown off the bike. He narrowly managed to hold on, dismounted and pulled off his helmet. All that was left of the Shed was a charred ruin; they wouldn't be kipping there any longer. More importantly, where on earth was Mike? Hymie looked around at the animated figures weaving in and out of the disaster zone and wondered who to ask. A fireman with an axe, wearing a respirator, was busy breaking down the front door, then Hymie got his answer.

"There's someone in there!" cried the man with the axe.

Hymie felt sick and his heart began to race. The heat and noise were overwhelming and a dozen terrible thoughts flooded his mind; had someone started the fire on purpose? Was someone trying to kill them? Had Mike been asleep when the fire started? Was Mike still alive? He seemed paralysed with fear; of the known and worse still, the unknown. How could he ever cope without Mike? As he dithered, three of the bravest men he'd ever seen charged into the collapsing building as though they were going on a picnic. After the longest sixty seconds he could remember they charged out again, dragging a fire-blackened body behind them.

"How is he?"

"Dead," said one of the firemen, surprised by the question. "No-one could have survived in there."

Hymie froze. It couldn't be happening. A few short moments ago he'd been the happiest man alive and now the bottom was falling out of his world.

"Mike!" screamed Hymie. "It isn't possible! He can't be dead, he was indestructible." He tried to fight his way to the charred corpse to prove his point as if the firemen were trying to keep something from him. They dragged him away, kicking and screaming.

"Let go of me, you bastards, he can't be dead, I won't hear of it!"

"It's alright, sir, we understand. We've already called for an ambulance. If there's anything that can be done for your friend they'll take care of it," said one of the firemen kindly, wrapping a blanket around Hymie's shoulders. He slumped to the ground, his eyes fixed on the giant, black, twisted form that had once been Mike Murphy. Nobody was doing anything about it because there was nothing to be done.

An ambulance came and took the body away and then the local police arrived and took Hymie's statement. Later he couldn't even remember what he'd told them. What was there to say? How could you sum up the life force that was Mike in mere words? His epitaph was that he'd left his friend feeling numb; empty and bereft of hope without him. Mike's death had certainly left a bloody big hole in his life.

Part Twenty-Two

Sinking the Beach Buoys

Once DS O'Malley had left Blackpool Central police station en route to his local pub, WPC Arkwright had taken Inspector Decca and Sergeant Terse into the smaller of their interview rooms to examine some mugshots of local crooks and ne'er do wells for the purpose of suspect identification. Decca had promptly identified three prominent members of the Beach Buoys gang and Terse had nodded in agreement, despite not having been there at the time. Not that the identification of the suspects was difficult; with their diminutive stature, large bushy beards and fake perma-tans even Blind Joe from *The Last Lights* could have had a stab at it.

"It's a sad story," said Arkwright. "They were a world famous troupe of acrobats, clowns and jugglers at one time; *The Tumbling Zabagliones* they were called. They toured the world with Jimbo's Travelling Circus. They had it all; fame, money, nice shoes. They played all the big venues too; anywhere you care to name..."

"Highgate Public Lavatory?" suggested Terse.

"Yes they played there," said Arkwright.

"So, what went wrong?" asked Decca.

"It was the old, old story; television killed Variety, and you don't get much more Variety than *The Tumbling Zabagliones*," said WPC Arkwright.

"Tragic," said Terse, picking the wax out of his ear with a pen top.

"Of course, they tried to find other employment. They worked nights at the garden centre, started their own restaurant business and did the occasional cabaret spot at *The Sun Lounge* but it was no good. They became addicted to fake tan to make up for the fact that they couldn't get the overseas tours any more, grew beards to try and change their appearance and finally turned to crime. It's all here in my report," said Arkwright, placing a brown cardboard file on the desk in front of Decca.

He flicked through the file, tutting to himself as he did so.

"Everything from lewd and drunken behaviour to shoplifting manure from the garden centre," said Decca.

"Hardly world class villains," said Terse.

"Ah, that was just for starters," replied Arkwright, with growing enthusiasm. "If you flick on a few pages you'll see they graduated to drug dealing, protection rackets... and *murder*."

"Well, for serious criminals they don't seem to have many convictions," said Decca. "I can't see any mention of murder anywhere."

"Nothing was ever proven," said Arkwright "but there have been too many coincidences over the years, if you know what I mean. Personally I believe they killed Elaine Brown, Mr Smith and Vic Knight."

Decca and Terse exchanged meaningful glances. Clearly WPC Arkwright had been overdosing on Agatha Christie.

"Well, I can certainly confirm that these were the men I saw removing body parts from the waxworks," said Decca, "and that there was white powder concealed in some of the waxworks. Does that give you enough to get a search warrant?"

"I believe so, Inspector, in fact I'm sure of it," said Arkwright, making a note on her pad. "Would you care to join us, in the interests of inter-force co-operation?"

"Thank you, WPC Arkwright," said Decca.

"Call me Alice," said Arkwright.

By the following evening DS O'Malley had his search warrant and had assembled a crack team of likely lads for what he referred to as a "search and apprehend" mission, but which was known locally as an "S and D" or "seek and destroy" job.

As dusk fell on the mean streets of Blackpool, about an hour after the waxworks had closed for the day, a black unmarked Transit van pulled up on the kerb outside and a dozen coppers in mufti leapt out, racing around the building's perimeters to cut off all available exits.

An outsize officer in riot gear, Big Ron, walked up to the entrance doors and tapped twice on the glass very quietly. Unsurprisingly there was no response. At a signal from O'Malley, Ron smashed the door down and led the forward party through the reception area and on into the waxworks.

"In London we usually ring the doorbell first," said Terse, helpfully.

"We ain't in London," said Ron.

DS O'Malley texted the rest of his search party to let them know they were inside the building then, leaving one of his men on guard at the front entrance, they spread out through the showrooms and offices with instructions to call for support if they needed it. Decca and Terse stayed in the main group, Team Alpha, with O'Malley, Arkwright and Big Ron.

While the other officers dispersed through the upper floors of the building, Team Alpha headed down three flights of stairs to the basement in search of the storage and despatch areas. If the waxworks was being used as a distribution centre for controlled substances then the goods receiving and despatch areas would be central to the operation. After walking long interminable dark corridors and walls plastered with "Keep Out" signs, the five police officers finally arrived at a set of PVC door flaps and peered cautiously through. Ron and O'Malley pushed forward through the flaps and found themselves in a large storage area full of waxworks. This seemed to be where they examined the new exhibits before either unleashing them on the public or putting them back into storage. Decca noted there was a large group of American presidents, probably heading for deep storage; Ford, Reagan, Carter and Nixon, all of whom seemed to be getting along better in wax than they ever had in the flesh.

'So far, so good,' thought Arkwright, but then she noticed a strip-light flickering in the despatch office at the far end of the warehouse. "I think there's someone here, sir," she whispered to O'Malley. He gestured to them all to be quiet and they tiptoed along the side of the room until they could see inside the office itself. Inside were a group of orange-coloured men with beards, standing arguing with guns in their hands, around what looked like a bathtub full of baked beans. A man's head protruded from the top of the beans as though he were the star attraction in some ill-judged supermarket charity event. Decca recognised him as Mike Murphy and pointed him out to Terse, who smiled.

"OK, Team, this is it," said O'Malley. "We've got them cornered. Arkwright, go and get back up, the rest of you, follow me." He removed a miniature loud-hailer from his pocket and switched the power on, while Arkwright slouched off, annoyed at missing another showdown.

"This is the police! We have you surrounded. Put down your weapons and come out with your hands on your heads."

The Beach Buoys inside the despatch office panicked.

"Shit! The Fuzz! What shall we do?" said Joe.

"Shoot our way out," said Ralph.

"Wait, wait," said a third member of the gang, Tony, who was noted for having a cool head in a crisis. "We got a hostage, don't we?"

The other gang members nodded with relief. You could always rely on Tony to get you out of a fix.

"We got a hostage, coppers!" cried Tony, "so back off or the guy gets it."

"Shoot him!" shouted Terse.

O'Malley gave him a disapproving look.

"Look, this is my case, just button it, right?" said O'Malley. "Who's that guy in the bath anyway?"

"Mike Murphy, a private detective," said Decca. "Usually seen in the company of a little guy with a big gob; Hymie Goldman."

"Where's he from?" asked O'Malley.

"London," said Decca.

"Shoot him!" cried O'Malley.

The Beach Buoys looked at each other in dismay while Mike closed his eyes and slowly disappeared below the surface of the bean bath. As he was completely naked beneath the tomato sauce and wearing handcuffs he didn't have a lot of options. He wondered what Houdini would have done in his shoes and how long he could hold his breath beneath the sea of beans.

"I always thought Tony was a bit of a half-wit," said Joe.

"Yeah, hostage my arse, let's get outta here now!" said Ralph. "They don't give a crap about this great lummox." He opened the door of the despatch office and ran out into the warehouse, shooting wildly at the police with two handguns as he went. A couple of his comrades in arms followed suit, dodging behind packing crates as they took pot-shots at the police. A pitched battle ensued, with bullets ricocheting off the concrete walls, floor and ceiling.

"Eat lead, coppers!" cried Tony, as a volley of shots echoed around the room.

Fortunately for the police, the Beach Buoys seemed to be rotten shots. Occasionally they would hit one of the wax figures and then a cloud of white powder billowed out, filling the air. Ronald Reagan's nose was shot off, Gerald Ford lost his head completely and Richard Nixon was left giving the victory salute as he had a couple of fingers shot off. All the while the air became cloudier and cloudier with the white narcotics until it started to have a noticeable effect on those present.

"I'm feeling strangely anxious, sir," said Terse, "aren't you?" He swayed from side to side with his arms wrapped around himself like some kind of bizarre spinning top.

"I feel fucking amazing, Barry!" replied Decca. "I know I'm often tough on you but I fucking love you, Barry."

"I know, sir. It's just this stinking job. We spend all day every day doing tasks no-one else could stick for a minute so we have to be hard, sir."

"Watch that guy behind the mushroom cloud, Ron," said O'Malley, "he's pointing a black banana at you."

"I'm afraid I'll have to hand myself in, sir," said Big Ron, offering O'Malley his pistol, "I just shot Jimmy Carter."

"Don't worry, Ron, it wasn't the real Jimmy Carter," said O'Malley. "It was probably just a fig-leaf of your imagination."

"It was definitely him, sir, he was wearing a peanut in his hair."

Inside the despatch office Mike surfaced like an enormous red whale from a sea of baked beans and sprayed tomato ketchup out of his nose and mouth. When the beans trickled off his eyes he was pleased to see that the room had emptied and he was alone. Well, no-one wanted an audience when they were in the bath. As the

Beach Buoys had realised, if you put an ex-bouncer in chains he'd try to escape, but if you stripped him naked, handcuffed him and covered him in baked beans he'd be too embarrassed to go anywhere.

The shoot-out seemed to be gradually losing momentum when the police reinforcements arrived from the other parts of the building. Arkwright emerged from the long corridor at the head of a band of six officers and they stood surveying the scene of confusion in wide-eyed amazement.

As they did so, one or the Beach Buoys sprang from behind a nearby packing crate and took aim at the WPC with his handgun. Before he could pull the trigger, one of the police marksmen gunned him down where he stood. The diminutive figure collapsed to the floor, clutching his chest.

"Fuggerbubber…," he spluttered, before expiring on the hard concrete floor.

"What did he say?" asked Decca.

"Fuck knows!" said Terse.

"Thank you, Terse, clear as mud," said Decca.

After the shooting the Beach Buoys seemed to lose the will to fight on. They put down their weapons and surrendered. Gradually everyone came down from their collective high and normality returned to the waxworks. The Beach Buoys were arrested and taken into custody. The police officers reflected on all the paperwork that lay ahead of them and even Mike was liberated from his baked bean hell and given a large rug to hide behind.

Part Twenty-Three

Through a glass darkly

After Mike Murphy had been cremated in their makeshift holiday cottage, Hymie drank a bottle of rum and slept the sleep of the doomed in the Norton's sidecar. He dreamt a deep dark dream, haunted by crowds of people he'd hoped never to hear from again; old friends and creditors, dead clients and relatives and even his landlord at 792A Finchley Road. They all taunted him for being a failure, and told him to crawl back to wherever he came from and hide. Even the ghostly figure of Mike passed by, on its way to the afterlife, to berate him for not doing more to save his life; "think of all the times I saved your worthless hide, Goldman…and where were you when I needed you?"

Hymie awoke to a sudden downpour of rain. His mouth was dry and there were cold beads of sweat on his brow so he threw back his head and let the raindrops roll down his face. He studied what was left of the Shed and remembered why he'd felt so bereft the night before. There was nothing left to do, but tell the Reverend Brown to stick the case where the sun didn't shine and get the hell out of there. He couldn't even face seeing Melody again, he just felt totally defeated.

He climbed onto the rider's seat, kick-started the Norton and crawled away at ten miles per hour with his tail between his legs. As he rode through Blackpool the wind blew up a gale and nearly flung him off the bike so he parked at the roadside and retreated into the nearest safe haven, the glass-fronted Sea Life Centre.

Inside it was dark and quiet, with the exception of a small school party in the distance, so he bought a coffee and sat in a corner with his thoughts. Inevitably, they were so depressing that he soon decided to take a walk around the place and commune with the fish instead.

He walked past tank after tank of outlandish, brightly coloured fish then pushed through some double doors and entered a large gallery with public seating. The room formed a huge glass tank above and around the central seating area and he was soon distracted by the wide variety of sea creatures swimming and floating by. He squinted at the squid, gaped at the guppies and shuddered as a shiver of sharks passed by, but they couldn't distract him from his dark thoughts for long.

When he set out to make a fool of himself there were few people who could manage it as comprehensively as Hymie, but if he'd known where it would end, he'd have never set out in the first place. Of course, he wasn't in his right mind any longer and hadn't been since he'd first set eyes on Melody, but you only had to look at the mess he was in to realise the folly of love. It was a kind of madness. Mike was dead, the gang that killed him would be after him next and he was further from solving the case than when he'd started.

A small schoolboy walked past him and started tapping on the glass.

"That's probably not a good idea," said Hymie.

The boy hit the glass harder. "They can't get you, mister, they're behind glass."

"Yes, but they're *sharks*," said Hymie. "They can smell fear. All you have to do is make the smallest crack in the glass and they'll break out and have you for lunch."

"What, at half past ten in the morning? Don't be ridiculous!" said the boy and walked off.

It had all seemed so promising at first; a decent fee with free accommodation and transport and when they'd stepped off the train, Miss World had been there to meet and greet them. Then, like every other case, it had all turned to crap. The accommodation and transport had turned out to be death traps, a seagull had stolen the case file and a whippet had urinated down his leg. He'd been threatened by every low life and weirdo in the north of England and to add insult to injury even Decca and Terse had turned up to mock him.

There was something rotten in the state of Blackpool, reflected Hymie. He should have smelt the stench of corruption much earlier. The whole town was full of sharks and he didn't mean the ones with fins either. Even that old fraud, the Reverend Brown was probably in on it. Why else would he invite two little known detectives from North London to take on a seriously cold case in Blackpool if he wasn't looking for a couple of patsies to take the rap for something? But for what?

Surely if you wanted to find someone from Blackpool, you hired a detective from Blackpool. They should have tried harder to find the previous detective, if only to prove he was still alive. If only he could get to the bottom of it, Mike may not have died in vain. Hymie stared into the cold blue depths of the marine aquarium and sighed. It was no good, he would never solve it. He was out of his depth in the North West and they all knew it. All he could really do was to make sure Mike got a decent burial back home in Finchley and have it out with that guy, Brown one last time. Perhaps if he backed the old scroat into a corner he'd let something slip.

Part Twenty-Four

Tea at the vicarage

When he arrived at the vicarage it looked more dilapidated than Hymie had remembered. Perhaps in some sad way the loss of his friend and business partner, Mike had made the whole world seem more run down and dirty. Hymie hammered on the door, no longer caring who he offended, let alone the Reverend Brown, who he held responsible for Mike's death.

"Who is it?" enquired the aged clergyman.

"Hymie Freakin' Goldman!" cried Hymie, vehemently. "I want a word with you, you old fart!"

The vicar fell silent. Although he'd hired Finchley's second worst private detective in a moment of madness he didn't seem in any hurry to renew their acquaintance. "I see," he said at last. "I'd be happy to receive a report in the post," said Brown.

"Well, forget it!" said Hymie. "Open the door."

"So be it," said the vicar, releasing all of the door locks before opening it very slightly. "I take it you have an update on my sister's disappearance?"

"Yeah, something like that," said Hymie, pushing his way into the cottage.

"You'd better come into the lounge," said the Reverend Brown, nattily dressed in a crimson silk dressing-gown and Turkish slippers. He closed the door behind his visitor and led the way. He poured out two glasses of scotch from a glass decanter and passed one to the aggrieved detective.

"It's a pity you weren't here earlier," said the vicar, once they were both seated. "Melody was here and she was telling me all about you. I think she has a crush on you, Mr Goldman."

"Really?" said Hymie.

"Well, there's no accounting for taste, I suppose. Women are a law unto themselves."

"Yes," agreed Hymie, "but I didn't come here to exchange pleasantries. You'll have heard that my business partner, Mike Murphy is dead."

"No, that's terrible news, how did it happen?"

"You mean you don't know?"

"No, I assure you, I don't," said the vicar, shocked.

"He was killed when that crummy wooden shack you stuck us in burned to the ground!" snapped Hymie.

"That's awful. It's been in the family for years. Sorry, I didn't mean to sound unsympathetic, you must be very upset."

"Yes," said Hymie. "It got me thinking…"

"Thinking what?"

"That you knew more about your sister's disappearance than you were letting on. You hired Mike and I, as strangers to the area, to blunder around asking awkward questions so that someone would try to shut us up. Well they did and Mike's dead, so who the hell was it and why couldn't you have levelled with us in the first place?" said Hymie. He downed his scotch in one and threw his glass at the fireplace. It was an electric fireplace and the glass bounced off, shattering on the stone wall.

"I'm sorry, Mr Goldman. I didn't expect this to happen," said the vicar. "I genuinely did want to find out what had happened to Elaine, partly to keep my promise to our dear mother, but also because she was my sister. I know she was involved with some unsavoury characters, like that ventriloquist chap, Smith, but she wasn't a bad person. I knew you'd face some hostility, the last detective I hired left town for that very reason, but I thought you and your friend could handle it."

Hymie glared at him with contempt.

"Well, you were wrong, you stupid old git! Mike's dead and my business is well and truly shagged."

"Like I said, I'm sorry," said the vicar.

"Right, fine. Well, that's all hunky dory then!" snapped Hymie. "As this is probably the last time we'll meet, Reverend Brown, if that's even your real name, I'd better give you your stinking report." He stood up and started pacing the room, as he'd seen many a detective do in old movies. He picked up a framed photograph from the mantelpiece and gazed intently at it. "Who's this?" he asked.

"My sister, Elaine, in her twenties. She was a very attractive woman, wasn't she?"

"Yes," said Hymie, thoughtfully, replacing the photograph. "Where was I? I know. We didn't find your sister, but I'm pretty sure she's dead. She mixed with a dangerous local criminal gang and most people who mix with them disappear sooner or later. You'll recognise them by the beards and the fake tan, but I'd give them a wide berth if I were you. Now, I really need to get out of here before I end up swimming with the fishes, so I'd like my fee please. It will be two thousand pounds…or else."

"Or else what, Mr Goldman?"

"Oh, I'll leave you to fill in the blanks…I'll trash your cottage, tip off the police that you're involved in criminal activity…whatever it takes. I'm a desperate man," concluded Hymie, wildly.

"I see. Well, I was saving up for the church roof fund, but if it sends you back to where you came from, it will be money well spent," said the vicar. He walked over to a small writing desk, removed a chequebook and wrote one out. "I trust that will be the last I hear of you, Mr Goldman," said the Reverend Brown, with a hint of menace.

"You can count on it," said Hymie.

He walked out of the room, heading for the front door, but when he got there the door seemed to be shaking in its frame to the accompaniment of a loud banging sound. A mountainous silhouette was framed against the sky through the door's opaque glass panel. As hacked off as he was, Hymie still opened the door with some trepidation.

There on the mat, in an outsize orange boiler suit and black boots, stood Mike Murphy.

"Good God, man, I thought you were dead!" said Hymie.

"No, just resting," said Mike. "Whatever made you think that?"

"When I saw them pull your dead body out of a burning building, that's what," said Hymie. "I got back to the Shack and the place had been burnt to a crisp."

"It wasn't me," said Mike. "It was a waxwork of John Candy which the Beach Buoys lifted from the waxworks."

"The Beach Buoys?" queried Hymie.

"Keep up, Goldman. That's the name of the local criminal gang you've heard about. They needed a diversion for some big drugs deal they were pulling off and took me hostage as they thought I knew more about the whole business than I did. Fortunately, the police raided their HQ before they finished me off."

"Well, it really is good to see you, Mike…but you need to get changed; you look like an umpa-lumpa on steroids."

"As my entire wardrobe went up in flames at the Shack I'm afraid I can't oblige mate. Besides, what are you doing here?"

"I came to get our money," said Hymie.

"I didn't realise we'd solved the case," said Mike.

"It didn't seem to matter," said Hymie. "I just made him an offer he couldn't refuse."

Mike laughed. "I don't suppose you got paid then," he said.

"You'd be wrong," said Hymie, waving the cheque at him. "So, if you'll just drive us back to the station," he added, throwing Mike the keys to the Norton, "then we can get back to civilisation in a couple of hours. I'll even post back the keys when we get there." Hymie closed the door of the vicarage behind him and followed Mike down the drive to where he'd parked the Norton.

It hadn't been a great case, but there were definite signs that they might get out of it in one piece after all and that hadn't seemed at all likely even a few minutes earlier.

Part Twenty-Five

The girl in the pink bikini

"**S**o that's where it all ended," said Hymie. "We got away with it, but we never did find out what had happened to Elaine Brown." He suddenly felt as though he was alone, that he'd been repeating the whole sorry Blackpool saga over in his mind for nothing and then he seemed to come to with a jolt. He was back on the beach, sitting at the table outside the café with the gorgeous blonde in the pink bikini sitting opposite him. It hadn't occurred to him that she was just a manifestation of a part of his own psyche. He smiled at her and she smiled back. In the distance some scantily clad girls were playing beach volleyball as the cerulean waves lapped at the golden shore. Yes, he was still living in his fantasy world alright.

"I thought you said this would work," said Hymie.

"It nearly has," said the girl. "You're nearly there. You're doing very well."

"I wish I could believe you," said Hymie.

"Try it," said the girl. "You've remembered so much already, you only need to keep trying a little longer and you'll remember something you should have noticed at the time."

"What? Like the fact that by leaving, Mike and I turned our backs on the best chance of happiness we ever had. Melody and Sarah, with an 'h,' could have been made for us."

"So could lots of other women," said the girl.

"Can I get back to the beach volleyball now?" asked Hymie, losing interest.

"No," said the girl, firmly. "Think! You need to remember what you noticed at the time, but didn't quite see for what it was. You need to find that moment of self-realisation I was talking about if you're ever to escape the past."

"Give me a clue," said Hymie.

"You were just telling me about it; when you went back to the vicarage you noticed something."

"I did?" said Hymie, surprised.

"Yes. Are you a detective or just some hopeless loser who's lost in his own mind? Was there ever a moment when something struck you as a little odd?"

"What, in one of *our* investigations? The whole thing was odd, bloody odd. Now you come to mention it though, when I picked up that photo off the mantelpiece and looked at the picture of Elaine Brown twenty years earlier it was like looking at a picture of Melody."

"So?"

"Melody must have been Elaine's daughter! So that's why the Reverend Brown brought her up as his own... he was her uncle, not her father. He must have known who Melody's father was and had some idea about why Elaine disappeared. So why did he hire us when he knew all these things already?"

"Brilliant," said the girl. "You may be green but you're not a complete vegetable."

"But what really happened all those years ago?" asked Hymie.

"Well, as you've done so well and remembered what it was you hadn't noticed in the first place, I'll tell you," said the girl. "Elaine was killed years ago by her lover; the useless ventriloquist, Mr Smith. He'd become disillusioned with the entertainment business, when he realised it wouldn't pay him the kind of money he thought he deserved, and turned to crime, which paid better, by joining the Beach Buoys gang.

Elaine found out and threatened to expose him to the police so he killed her and enlisted the gang in disposing of the body. Her daughter, Melody was left in the care of the Reverend Brown, who adopted her. As time went by and Melody grew up she went off the rails and became involved in the Beach Buoys gang herself. Eventually she learned what had happened to her mother and who her real father was…and then she took her revenge on him."

Hymie's eyes opened wide. "She killed her own father. Poor Melody! No wonder she was so badly mixed up."

Mike, who'd been dozing in the visitor's chair next to Hymie's bed, stood up and walked over to the window. He looked out at the enormous car park and wondered whether Hymie would ever come out of his coma.

"Well, she'll have a long time to think it over, now she's behind bars," said the girl in Hymie's head.

Hymie stared at her and she seemed to flicker before his eyes. He turned to look at the beach volleyball match, but they'd all walked off into the sunset. Even the sea seemed to be floating away into space. There was a loud blaring sound like some enormous brass band tuning up and an army of orange men holding placards marched out of the sea before disappearing into a large pink sand-dune.

"Who are you, and what are you doing here anyway?" asked a girl's voice. It was the voice of the girl in the pink bikini.

"I'm Hymie Goldman, and I'm a private detective."

Mike could scarcely believe his ears. He leant across Hymie's bed and pulled the alarm cord. "Nurse! He just spoke to me. He told me his name and that he was a detective. Can you open your eyes, Hymie?" he asked.

Hymie slowly opened his eyes and murmured "yes, of course," before closing them again against the brightness of the lights.

"Well, that is good news, Mr Murphy," said the nurse. She checked Hymie's vital signs and nodded. "He's made a definite breakthrough. I'm pleased to say he's back in the land of the living at last."

Hymie opened his eyes again and looked around the room. He felt like he'd been on a long journey in economy class and was in dire need of a rest.

"I worked it all out, Mike."

"Worked out what?"

"Blackpool."

"It's really good to have you back."

Part Twenty-Six

Curtain Call

No one just wakes up from a coma and carries on with life as though they'd taken some kind of power nap. Maybe they do in tacky TV shows and Penny Brothers' novels but not in real life. So Hymie spent some time recovering from his ordeal. He had to learn to walk again, to speak coherently for the first time ever and even to feed himself properly, although if the food stains down his shirt were any indicator then he'd never been much good at that.

People are transformed by trauma and Hymie was no exception. Some days a great wave of emotion would hit him and he would find himself crying at daytime television. On other days he would swear he could see the girl in the pink bikini in the distance at his local park. While it was a great relief to him to have finally solved the Blackpool case it didn't make him any better off. It had all happened so long ago that there was no point in going back to see if he could make a go of it with Melody.

To Mike it soon felt like Hymie had never been away, let alone undergone a profound metamorphosis of the soul. From the outside he still seemed to be the same blabber-mouthed nutcase he'd always been, although his new perspective on the Blackpool case seemed uncharacteristically incisive. Perhaps the old fool had consulted a real detective on the quiet. Over the years, Mike had occasionally thought about Sarah with an 'h' and wondered what she was up to but, ever the realist he had seen it for what it was; a holiday romance, the high spot in a failed investigation.

Within a few short weeks the pressing demand for NHS beds and the chronic state of the hospital's cuisine had convinced Hymie that he would be better off at home so Mike had brought him some new clothes and a soft black hat and driven him back to 792A Finchley Road in the Fleetwood. Everything was as Hymie remembered it: out of date, clapped-out and broken; a warm and familiar environment for him to recuperate in.

The only change seemed to be the new secretary, Lucy. She was small and mousey and although Hymie viewed her with suspicion when they first met, having been burned once too often by the hired help, he soon grew used to her. She brewed a mean cup of tea and could queue up for a bacon roll in the Black Kat café with the best of them.

One afternoon, after he'd been staring at the pattern on the wallpaper for several hours, something seemed to occur to Hymie and he started pulling all of his desk drawers out at the same time. Mike heard the commotion and rushed into his partner's office.

"What is it? What are you looking for?"

"Oh, nothing of any consequence," said Hymie.

"If it's that half-eaten bowl of cornflakes you left in there, we threw it out when it started to smell."

"No, it wasn't that," said Hymie. "If you must know, it's an old letter. I received it a few weeks after we got back from Blackpool and I couldn't bear to open it at the time."

"Is it from her?" asked Mike.

"I think so," said Hymie, stooping down. He rummaged around in the space behind the drawers in his battered old desk and finally retrieved an envelope with a Blackpool postmark. He opened it and read the letter inside. His eyes welled up as he finished reading it and dropped the letter on his desk. Mike picked it up and read it to himself. It said:

"Dear Hymie, I was sorry to hear of your abrupt departure. I can't blame you as I was dishonest with you, but I've had cause to regret it since. You always said you would find me out, but I never quite believed you. Please don't judge me too harshly in the years ahead. If you still think of me, remember that I loved you once and always will. Melody xxx."

Mike folded up the letter and replaced it on Hymie's desk before sitting in the visitor's chair opposite. There was absolutely nothing he could say to make his old friend feel better so he skipped trying. "I hear the weather's good in Rio at this time of year," he said.

"Well, you know, I've always had a yearning to visit Copacabana beach and maybe now's the time," said Hymie.

"We're certainly due a holiday," agreed Mike, "preferably

somewhere warm and sunny, where the women are cheap and the beer's cold."

Hymie stretched out in his office chair and sighed. It didn't pay to dwell on the past. All good things came to those who waited and they'd already waited long enough. This time he felt certain everything would work out fine.

"So, what are we waiting for?" he said, throwing the letter in the waste-bin.